"Careful what you wish for, Will. You might find you don't like what you find, at all."

Hadn't he already said she'd changed?

He pushed to his feet, into shadows, so that she couldn't quite find his gaze, but his earnest expression stole every bit of breath she'd managed to suck in as he stepped forward into the fire's circle of light.

"I doubt that," he murmured.

She wanted to answer—some terrifically witty response—but, nope, there wasn't enough air left in her cells, let alone her lungs. All she could do was stare into the sparkling depths of his eyes and wonder what it would be like to swim strokes in the icy blue there.

As she watched, they flicked down to her parted lips and back again. "You're an enigma to me, Kitty Callaghan. And I've always enjoyed puzzles."

She wanted to warn him that she was more puzzle than he knew. She was one of those boxes with hidden mechanisms, cryptic clues and booby traps if you pressed the wrong place. She wanted to but she didn't, because the moment he stared at her lips, all she could think about was what it would be like to kiss him. To taste him and breath

After all this time.

And in that moment

that since the very

than just about anything else in her life.

STRANDED WITH HER RESCUER

BY
NIKKI LOGAN

First Published in Great Britain 2016
By Mills & Boon, an imprint of HarperCollins*Publishers*
1 London Bridge Street, London, SE1 9GF

© 2016 Nikki Logan

ISBN: 978-0-263-91993-6

23-0616

Our policy is to use papers that are natural, renewable and recyclable products and made from wood grown in sustainable forests. The logging and manufacturing processes conform to the legal environmental regulations of the country of origin.

Printed and bound in Spain
by CPI, Barcelona

Nikki Logan lives on the edge of a string of wetlands in Western Australia with her partner and a menagerie of animals. She writes captivating nature-based stories full of romance in descriptive natural environments. She believes the danger and richness of wild places perfectly mirror the passion and risk of falling in love.

Nikki loves to hear from readers via www.nikkilogan. com.au or through social media. Find her on Twitter, @readnikkilogan and Facebook, nikkiloganauthor.

For my beautiful boy, Gus.
The sonorous metronome
to which I wrote my books.
How you would have loved all this snow.

"Dogs are wise. They crawl into a quiet corner
and lick their wounds and do not rejoin the
world until they are whole once more."
—Agatha Christie

PROLOGUE

Five years ago, Pokhara, Nepal.

WILL MARGRAVE LEANED a shoulder against the rounded earthen interior wall of his villa overlooking Pokhara and peered through the window down to the terrace flats below. The topmost flat was furred with the gentle, swaying grasses native to this part of Nepal, peppered with small clusters of shrubs and fully fenced all the way around to the kennels out back of the house. The yard had to be large, to do its job housing his sixteen rescue dogs.

Maybe it was the richness of the light, or the majesty of the mountains or the mirrored reflection of Phewa Lake but everything in this environment just sat so...comfortably in it.

Including him.

Will leaned forward into the window's curve to watch the solitary woman below mingling with his dogs. Kitty Callaghan liked to start her day early and she liked to start it outside. On her second day here, he'd spotted her halfway down the terraces, meditating under the watchful protection of the Annapurnas as the sun rose behind the mountain range, doing her best impersonation of a normal, still person. Usually she was anything but, and today she was clearly in a more active mood, jogging back and forth in the fenced-in yard, tapping the noses of one dog then the next and darting back out of reach as they joined the game, drawing a canine cluster back and forth with her as she ran, not minding how silly she might look or how much dirt they kicked up.

Dogs and dirt didn't bother Kitty any more than the

looming mountains and composting toilets did. It was one of the things he liked about her best.

Not everybody loved the silent granite sentinels that marked Nepal's border. Mountains were dominant, powerful forces—for better or worse. Some people found them oppressive and ominous, almost claustrophobic. People like his wife. Though how Marcella could stand anywhere on this hillside under these vast, wild skies and feel closed in was a mystery to him.

Like so much about her.

That mystery had once intrigued him—back when he'd assumed her secrets would unfurl like a lotus as the months and years passed—but intrigue had a way of losing its appeal when your marriage eroded as steadily as the rock beneath your feet.

Down below, Kitty laughed as one dog got the better of her. She arched back when Quest reared up and placed his paws on her slight shoulders, her face turned up to the gentle morning light—twisted away from Quest's errant tongue—and the magic of her laughter cascaded like water down the terraced hillside.

And like warm breath down his spine.

Ugh… Moments like this one didn't help his resolve. Looking at those wide grey eyes in perfect pale skin and not wanting to just…dive right in to see what curiosities lay behind them. Sitting up late at night by the fire, hovering on the precipice of the kind of conversations he missed so desperately, lying to himself that he could get a handle on the feelings that had been escalating ever since she arrived ten short days ago to film her series of freelance pieces in Nepal.

Ten *long* days knowing that Marcella was the kind of woman he'd always wanted—glamorous, talented, creative—but beginning to fear that Kitty was the kind he actually *needed*.

And he didn't want to need anything from anyone who wasn't his wife.

Eleven months ago he'd given Marcella his promise along with his heart, and he was not about to betray either of those. If he had to break his word to a woman, it wasn't going to be the one he had pledged himself to in front of God.

They could make this marriage work—*he* could make it work.

Will shoved the ache down deep inside as he withdrew from the window. Kitty Callaghan needed to go. She didn't have to leave Nepal—she could finish up her work—she just had to get out of this house. This town.

This marriage.

And she needed to do it soon, before the questions her presence raised began to eat away at the foundations of his already shaky relationship.

Will balled his fingers into fists and headed for the stairs.

He wasn't even halfway down before his heart started hardening against her.

The slow rise of her head, the easy, surprised-to-see-you smile she offered him... It was all fake. Kitty knew the precise moment Will stepped out of his house, even as she had her back to him and the massive Annapurnas towering up behind him. She didn't need Quest's excited stare to tell her he was approaching, either.

She could feel him.

She could always feel him; in the tickle of her neck hairs and the tightening of her belly. Some kind of primitive intuition doing its thing. Still, she gave him her brightest, most welcoming smile. Because it was something she could do. A gesture that celebrated the bond she'd formed with him, in a perfectly appropriate way. One that said she knew exactly how lucky she was to be here.

'Morning, Will.'

'Got a moment, Kitty?'

There was something in the hard shadow in his eyes, the stiff way he was holding himself. The same way he did when one of his dogs indicated positive on a shard of clothing during a missing-hiker search. His tension infected her, too, and Quest fell away from their game, disappointed but accepting.

'Sure.'

Will held a courteous hand low to her back as he guided her out of the dog yard, then seemed to think better of it and tucked it down behind his own body. As if she were tainted.

'Something wrong? Is Marcella okay?'

Because some mornings his wife really wasn't. Those mornings she looked as if she hadn't slept more than an hour. If at all. And not in a good, first-year-of-marriage, up-all-night kind of way.

'Marcella's fine. I just need to speak to you.'

Instinct told her to get ahead of this conversation, to get some control over it. She spun to face him and he nearly barrelled into her. He caught himself just before impact, then stepped back as though—again—she were infected with something nasty. He backed up a little further for good measure.

That extra step particularly hurt.

'Something you didn't want the dogs to hear?' she joked, though it cost her.

'Kitty, I...' He glanced out at the mountains all around them for inspiration. This wasn't like him. The two of them had had nothing but easy conversations in the ten days she'd been in Nepal. Easy, deep, fabulous talks that felt as if they were continuing old exchanges from years ago.

'You're making me nervous, Will. What's going on?'

'I need to ask you to leave,' he blurted.

How embarrassing that her first response was to misunderstand him. She frowned and glanced back at the dogs. 'The yard? I thought it would be okay to—'

'Pokhara, Kitty. It's time for you to go.'

She blinked at him. 'No, it's not. I have nearly three weeks before it's time.'

And, boy, she was not looking forward to that day.

'Marcella shouldn't have invited you to stay the whole month. It's...' He gazed back at the mountains. 'It's too much, Kitty. Too long.'

An awful kind of humiliation washed through her. That she had presumed he would be okay with it just because his wife was. Or seemed to be.

'You said I was welcome,' she breathed.

In his own words, with no one twisting his arm.

'That's what you do say, in this situation, isn't it?'

When someone makes a horrendous presumption, did he mean?

'So...' Her head spun, and not just from the altitude. 'Was I never welcome or am I no longer welcome?'

She didn't really want to know the answer, either way, but she *absolutely* wanted to hear it from his lips.

'You've finished filming our rescue operation...'

Part of the heat that rushed up her throat was because, to an extent, Will was right. She'd finished the main filming for the dogs, she'd been enjoying Pokhara and getting a feel for the country since then. Imagining what a fantastic piece it was going to make, visually.

And spinning out her time with him.

'And we've got too much going on—'

'No, you don't.'

Marcella barely painted, never went out if she could avoid it; she lurked around their property alternating between long bouts of flat melancholy and excited bursts of energy. Meanwhile, Will trained every day but he had a comfortable routine that didn't wear the dogs out. And only two emergency calls in the ten days she'd been here.

His lips thinned as he stared at her. The first time he'd made actual eye contact.

'Kitty—'

'I pick up after myself. I went to the market on Monday to save Marcella the trouble.' And—PS—paid for a carload of supplies. 'So what's the real issue?'

Of course, a dignified person wouldn't ask. A dignified person would just accept that things had changed and head off to start packing. Smiling, thanking them and giving her hosts a modest gift when she went. But there was nothing dignified about the panic that Kitty was starting to feel at Will's decree, and not just because of the humiliation. Sometime between arriving and now, she'd realised that she was the happiest she'd ever been in Pokhara. Having that taken away was terrifying.

And the thought of never seeing Will again only compounded it.

'You can't really want to stay,' he urged. 'Knowing we don't want you here.'

Something told her that 'we' was actually 'I', because his wife had clung to her since the day she'd arrived, and Marcella was too Southern and too well brought up to renege on a promise.

'No,' she snorted. 'I don't. But I'm not leaving without knowing what I did to get myself banished.'

She had a sneaking suspicion, actually, and a whole new flood of shame went on standby, ready for his answer.

For the first time, he softened, and it was so much worse than the hardened exterior he'd presented up until now. Because it was *Will*, not this icy doppelgänger.

'You must know, Kit. You're doing it right now.'

She lost her grip on the humiliation and it flooded her face. For ten days she'd worked so hard to keep a lid on her inappropriate feelings. To pretend the emotions didn't exist. But they had a habit of leaking out when she was with him. Any time she wasn't totally vigilant. Talking, laughing.

Or just standing very close, like this... Peering up at him.

'I...'

Really, what could she say? She knew she was feeling it, and she knew what she was feeling. She would be naïve to imagine she wasn't showing that at all, but Will hadn't let on before, or objected to the conversations, the shared space, the accidental body contact passing on the stairs.

She'd even begun to think he might have enjoyed it. Just a little bit.

Obviously not.

'It's okay, Kitty, I get it. We've been spending a lot of time together—'

Her heart hammered.

She wasn't about to be condescended to like a teenager. If he'd picked up on her feelings, why had he indulged them? Why not just shut them right down?

Shame ached through her whole body.

This *was* him shutting them down.

'I just think it would be better for everyone if you headed off to do your own thing,' he said.

Get the heck off his mountain, he meant.

'We were friends,' she said, numb and flat. Too hurt and too confused to even put any energy behind the accusation.

His eyes darkened and swung away from her. 'You must want to see the rest of Nepal.'

No, not really. She'd been happy here, happier than any other time in her life. It was *this* mountain she loved, not just any Nepalese mountain. *This* town. *This* man.

That was why she had to go.

She could not love Will Margrave, and he certainly couldn't love her, even if he wanted to, which—judging by the enormous tension in his body—he did not.

'I'm married, Kitty.'

Yes, to the woman who'd invited her into their home. Was this how she'd repaid Marcella's kindness? By making her husband uncomfortable enough to ask her to leave?

She dropped her eyes to the dark, rich earth. She'd caused this. She had to be the one to fix it.

'Okay,' she murmured. 'I'll go.'

She stumbled away from Will without raising her eyes again. And she didn't look at him as she wrestled her stuffed backpack down the stairs, or as she hugged a weeping Marcella, or as she closed the door of the aging taxi behind her.

In fact, she didn't raise her gaze until she was safely away from that Pokhara hillside, just in case he saw something there she would never recover from. Something worse than love.

Shame.

Which made that pitying gaze out by the dogs' yard the last of Will Margrave she would ever see. And pity the last thing he would ever feel for her.

And she promised herself, in that moment, never to drop her eyes again.

CHAPTER ONE

Present day, Churchill, Canada.

'YOU MUST BE KIDDING!'

Kitty Callaghan bundled herself tighter in her complimentary blanket and swapped her hand luggage into her right hand to give her left a break.

'Sorry, ma'am,' the polite woman said, widening her arms to usher her towards the exit. 'Canadian federal law. No one can stay inside the airport after shutdown.'

'But I have nowhere to go,' she pointed out, though it was hardly necessary since this was the same official who'd been working for hours to find beds—or even sofas—for the one hundred and sixty-four passengers who'd found themselves stranded in their remote dot-on-a-map after smoke started billowing from their aircraft's cargo hold thirty-five thousand feet over Greenland.

'We've done everything we can to find accommodation for the final six of you. Three will be bunking down in the medical centre and two will be guests of the Mounties tonight in their holding cells. That's every bed we have in town.'

Which left her sitting up all night in some waiting room.

This was the price she paid for being good at her job. Or maybe for simply doing it. Airlines had a way of not appreciating it when you captured their stuff-ups for posterity. She'd been way too busy filming the whole emergency response that had followed the pilot's spectacular touchdown of the massive airliner on the remote, ice-patched runway to get herself higher up the queue for overnight accommodation. By the time she'd started paying attention to where she was going to spend the rest of the night, there had been no more room at the inn.

'You don't have a hotel here? Or even a B & B?'

The woman's compassion wasn't making her feel any better. 'Actually we have nearly as many hotel rooms as residents but they're all booked up because of bear season. And we're out of volunteers with sofas.'

'*Bear* season?' Kitty blinked her confusion, glancing around. 'Where are we exactly?'

Other than someplace snowy somewhere on a high arc between Zurich and Los Angeles up over the top of the planet. She'd been sleeping comfortably when the captain had made his emergency announcement and the chaos that had followed really hadn't been the time to be pumping the flight crew with questions.

'Churchill, Manitoba, ma'am,' the woman said proudly. 'Polar bear capital of the world.'

Churchill...

All the ice the A340 had come sliding in on suddenly seemed to relocate to her chest.

She'd heard of Churchill...

'And what is bear season exactly?' she said, tightly, to buy herself the time she needed to get her fibrillating heart under control.

The woman smiled, oblivious to the sudden extra tension in the near-empty terminal. 'Oh, hundreds of bears migrate here to wait for Hudson Bay to freeze over, to go hunt on the ice for the winter. Numbers are at their peak right now. They're everywhere.'

'Maybe I could snuggle in between two of *them* for the night.'

The woman had a right to be disappointed at Kitty's tone, but *she* had a right to be snitchy. Her plane had caught fire in mid-air. She'd endured an emergency landing then been bounced out into the bitter cold via the emergency slides with nothing but the light dress on her back, the complimentary blanket she'd been snuggled in, and her cabin bag, which she'd packed with the minimalist precision of a pro. Just her camera gear, some basic toiletries and an e-reader; none of which were going to help her out here. She had nowhere to go for the night except the heated police station waiting room because apparently this one was off-limits. And to top it all off, she'd landed in the only place on Earth she'd never planned on visiting—not because of its resident bears, but because of one *human* resident in particular.

Desperation set in like a low-hanging cloud. 'What about your house?'

The woman had no reason to continue to be kind to her, but she did. God love Canada. 'I've already sent two people home to my husband. Both on the sofas. Someone is on their way to get you and drive you into town, ma'am.'

'Can't they just keep on driving me to the nearest city? Something with beds?'

Apparently that thought was *just hilarious*.

The woman laughed. 'The only way in or out of Churchill is by plane or train. And Winnipeg is a thousand miles to the south.'

Right. Which part of *polar* bear did she miss? Their trusty pilot must really have been desperate to get them out of the air to have landed them in the sub-arctic.

'When will they send another plane, do you think?' she asked weakly.

The woman glanced at her watch and frowned. 'Let's just get you sorted for tonight.'

This wasn't the tightest spot she'd ever been in, though it was the first involving live predators, and the thought of sitting uncomfortably in some waiting room for hours scarcely appealed. Especially when there was no guarantee that she'd get on a flight tomorrow. Or the day after, or the day after.

Her lashes drifted shut.

Desperate times...

'Does Will Margrave still live up here?' she breathed.

He'd moved to Churchill right after the quakes in Nepal. Right after he'd lost Marcella. She'd exploited a working relationship with a clerk at the Department of Foreign Affairs to find out that he'd come home to Canada—come *here*—and then she'd pretended to delete the knowledge from her brain.

'You know Will?'

She'd thought she had. Once. 'It's been a while.'

The airport officer moved immediately towards the phone. 'We don't usually ask Will because his cabin is so far out of town. Kind of isolated—'

Of course it was. Because this day wasn't perfect enough.

'Just try him, please,' she urged. 'Make sure you tell him it's Kitty Callaghan. My full name.'

Kitty glanced out at the airport car park as the woman made her call. The sideways sleet was illuminated against the darkness of the night by floodlighting and she wondered whether the lights might serve as a beacon for any rogue bears wandering past looking for a late-night snack.

'Any airport in a storm...' she muttered.

The airline officer's surprise drew Kitty's focus back across the terminal.

'Okay! John can take you straight there,' she called, hurrying across the shiny floor. 'The taxi ride is on us.'

Suddenly, the police waiting room didn't look quite so bad. Compared to facing Will again. 'Right now?'

The woman glanced at the clock on the wall. 'As soon as your taxi gets here. Looks like it's your lucky day!'

Lucky.

Right.

It wasn't as far as the airport official had implied, as the crow flew, but no self-respecting crow would be out in this weather. The roads gouged through the hardening Boreal sog were slow going, impossible to see more than ten feet ahead of the old SUV that served as one of Churchill's two taxis. It crept along deeper into the forest until they finally pulled up in front of a shadowy cabin with dim firelight glowing inside.

Proper Snow White territory.

'Here we are,' the driver chirped as a hooded figure appeared in the cabin's entrance. He reached across Kitty to open her door and she clambered out into the bitter cold in pumps already soggy from the dash across the airport car park. Immediately her lungs started hurting with the cold.

'Enjoy your stay,' the driver grunted, more to himself than to her, before crunching his vehicle in every ice-topped puddle back up the long drive.

She turned and stared at the shadowy forest cabin.

'Heat's escaping,' a gruff voice called from the open doorway. Then the figure turned and went back inside and only the puffs of mist where his words had been remained, backlit by the light pouring out of the cabin.

Lord…

Time had done nothing to diminish the effect of his voice on the hairs on her neck even as they gathered frost straight out of the sub-arctic air. The gruff rumble turned her insides to jelly just as much now as it had in Nepal. Fortunately, jelly couldn't stand up to the frost in her chest any more than the frost outside it.

Ice was good like that.

The timber protested underfoot as she eased herself up the frosty steps and squelched into the cabin's boot room where she kicked her sodden purple pumps off amongst the rugged footwear already lined up there. The blanket was doing almost nothing to keep her warm, now. But the cabin beyond the boot-room door glowed with warmth and it was enough to lure her over the threshold and back into Will Margrave's world for the first time in five years.

'Help yourself to coffee,' he rumbled from the shadowy back of the cabin, somehow managing to make the friendly offer about as unfriendly as it could possibly be.

'Right,' she said, glancing at the large coffee pot simmering on the old stove. 'Thanks.'

She turned the steaming mug in her numb hands as Will came back into the room, his face still shielded by the fleeced hood of his coat, only adding to her tension. He passed her, wordlessly, and moved into the boot room to shrug the coat off and onto a hook.

Sense memory kicked her square in the belly.

A stranger hearing him for the first time would expect some kind of old salt of the woods. But the man who returned, bootless and coatless, seemed scarcely older than the thirty he had been in Nepal five years ago. His brown hair was messy thanks to his hood and it hung down over his eyebrows. Stubble followed the angles of his jaw up to his cheekbones. He looked as if he should be in a cologne advertisement on a billboard.

Kitty cleared her throat to clear her mind. 'Thank you for—'

'You still okay with dogs?'

The question finally drew his eyes to hers and she found herself as breathless as the very first time she'd ever gazed into them. *Iceberg,* she remembered. The ethereal, aquamariney, underwater part. An old ache spread below her skin. She had never expected to look into those eyes again.

Will tired of waiting for her answer and broke the spell by moving to the door and opening it wide. Two thick-coated dogs burst in and, behind them, a third. Before Kitty could do more than twist away from them, three more bounded into the room and immediately pounced on her. A seventh held back, lurking by the door.

'Oh…!'

Will barked their names but Kitty was far too busy protecting herself from the onslaught of their wet noses and tongues to pay attention to who was who.

'You keep your dogs in the house?' she cried out of surprise as their assault finally eased off.

Those ice-blue eyes weren't exactly defrosting as the snow on her blanket had. 'You think that they should be out in the weather while you enjoy the comfort in here?'

Well, things were getting off to a *great* start!

'No, I…it's just that you kept them outdoors in Nepal.'

And winters there could be brutal, she was sure. She flinched as doggie claws scraped on her bare arms.

'Churchill isn't Nepal,' Will grunted, then made a squeaking noise with his lips and six of the seven dogs happily mauling her immediately turned and grouped around his legs. The seventh needed some manual assistance from Will.

As he reached around the dog to pull it back, his hand brushed her thigh where her summery skirt stopped. Her skin was too cold and numb even to feel it, let alone to blush at the unexpected contact, but her imagination was in no way impeded by the cold. If anything it was doing double duty standing here in this cabin with Will.

'You're freezing,' Will observed, unhelpfully. 'Not exactly dressed for the conditions.'

A sense of injustice burbled up immediately, as strong as it had once before. Only this time she defended herself. 'Actually, I was perfectly dressed for Zurich where I departed, and for Los Angeles where I should be stopping over by now.'

Two tiny lines appeared between his brows. 'You don't have anything else to put on?'

She shuffled her blanket more firmly around her and wished the fire would do its job more quickly.

'Our luggage won't be released until tomorrow.' Assuming it hadn't been damaged in the fire. As if to make his point, her body unhelpfully chose that moment to shudder from the chill.

Those glacial eyes stared needles into her but then he broke the gaze by sweeping his thick sweater up over his head and tossing it gently to her. 'Put this on, my body heat will help warm you faster. Tuck the blanket around your legs while I get you some socks. And stay by the fire.'

The sweater he removed smelled exactly like the cologne she'd imagined him advertising before. With a healthy dose of man for good measure. Because he'd left the room again in search of emergency socks and because she could disguise it in tugging the thick sweater over her head, Kitty stole a moment to breathe his scent deeply in.

Her eyelids fluttered shut against the gorgeous pain.

All the progress she'd imagined she'd made in the years since Nepal evaporated into nothing as Will's scent filled the spaces between her cells. She'd come to believe she'd fabricated her memory of that smell, but here it was—live and warm and heady—exactly as she remembered.

Except better for the passage of five years.

Like a good wine.

'Folk at the airport must be in quite a spin,' he grunted, returning to the room.

She abandoned the blanket for as long as it took her to tug the large socks on and pull them almost to her knees. Between their heat from below, Will's body heat soaking into her torso and the fire at her back, she finally started to feel the frigidity abating.

From her skin, anyway.

'Not a sight they've probably had before, I guess. The plane was bigger than the entire terminal.'

'Oh, it's happened before,' Will said, easing himself down onto the edge of his dining table, across the small space. About as far back from her as he could be without leaving the room again. 'Courtesy of being the best piece of concrete for a thousand miles.'

Talking about airfields was a close second to talking about the weather. Awkwardness clunked between them like a bit of wood broken loose in the stove.

'I'm grateful you can give me a bed,' she finally said. 'And that you remembered me.'

Those eyes came up. 'You thought I wouldn't?'

She swallowed against their blazing focus. 'Wouldn't remember me? Or wouldn't help me out?'

'Either.'

Thought. Feared. Potato/potahto. 'I wasn't sure whether you'd say yes.'

His grunt sounded much like one of the six dogs that had settled down into every available corner of the room. 'And leave you to the bears?'

She glanced back at him, though he seemed as far away now as Nepal was from this place. The only sounds in the cabin were the crackling of the wood stove and the wide yawn of one of his canine brood. Neither did much to head off her sleepiness.

'So, where should I...?'

That seemed to snap him back to the present from whatever faraway place he'd gone. Remembering Marcella, she imagined.

Sudden sympathy diluted her own tension.

Will had lost so much.

'Second door on the right,' he said, standing aside to unblock her way. 'Bathroom is across the hall. Go easy on the water use—I truck it in.'

The irony of that in a region practically mired in water most of the time—

She picked her way carefully through supine dogs but stopped just as her hand found the doorknob. 'Seriously, Will. Thank you. I wasn't looking forward to sleeping in a waiting room.'

'I'm better than that, at least,' he murmured, holding her gaze.

No *'you're welcome'*. Because she probably wasn't—again. No *'it's lovely to see you again, Kit'*, because it almost certainly wasn't.

Had she really expected open arms after the last conversation they'd ever had?

Will sagged against the door the moment his unexpected guest closed it quietly behind her. How far did you have to go to outrun the past? Clearly, the top of the world still wasn't far enough.

Five years...

Five long years and that time had compressed into nothing the moment Kitty Callaghan had stepped through his front door. The moment he'd answered his phone. His heart hadn't stopped hammering since then. Maybe he should have just let it ring, but he'd recognised the number and he knew that the airport wouldn't have called him at this time of night without very good reason.

It had never occurred to him that the reason would be her.

'Shove up, Dexter,' he murmured nudging the big brown male blocking access to his favourite chair. The dog grumbled but shifted, only to *whomp* down with exaggerated drama a few feet away, and Will sank down into his pre-loved rocker.

Old man's chair, the woman who'd sold it to him had joked.

Yup. And if he had his way he'd still be rocking gently in it by a roasting fire when he'd been in the north long enough to earn that title.

Just him and his dogs... As it was supposed to be.

Last time he'd seen Kitty, she'd been hurriedly tossing her belongings into the back of a dodgy Nepalese taxi and scrambling in after them. Couldn't get off their hillside fast enough. Marcella had wept as her favourite new distraction had departed only ten days into her month-long stay, but he'd kept a careful distance—his heart beating, then, at least as hard as it was now—relieved to see the last of her, certain that Kitty's departure was going to make things with Marcella right again.

He'd worked on their relationship for three more years and it had never been right again.

Which made having Kitty here an extra problem. A man didn't move halfway around the world to escape his past only to invite it right back into his front room. Especially not given how they'd left things.

But... Polar bears.

'It's bigger than it looks back there,' a soft voice suddenly said behind him.

He lurched upright in his chair.

For so long the only voices other than his in this place had been canine. But, somehow, the walls of his cabin absorbed the soft, feminine tones. As if her words were cedar oil and his timber walls were parched.

He struggled for something resembling conversation.

'Plenty of prefabs in town, but I wanted something a little more personal.'

'And private,' she remarked, glancing out of the window. 'It's very isolated.'

Yep, it was. Just how he liked it.

'A mile's a long way in the Boreal. But I have neighbours up the creek and Churchill's only ten minutes away if you know the roads.'

Twenty-five if you didn't.

Did he imagine it, or did her eyes get a shade more anxious at the seclusion? Maybe she, too, was remembering the electricity they'd whipped up between them back in Nepal.

He didn't whip up much of anything these days. No matter who was asking.

It just wasn't worth the risk.

'So...I think I'll head to bed,' she said and, again, it

somehow had the same tone as the crackling fire behind him. 'In case they get the plane back in the air early.'

That wasn't going to happen. Churchill was set up for small aircraft—twenty-to-thirty-seaters coming and going across the vast Canadian North like winged buses—and its apron was barely big enough to turn a colossal jet around, let alone get it airborne without a support team. Someone was going to have to fly engineers and safety inspectors up here to help prep the plane for its return flight. And no way were they going to pack a wounded jet full of passengers. Not after they'd taken such risks to get everyone down safely.

But it was two in the morning and Kitty was almost grey with fatigue, so he wasn't about to put that thought in her head.

Time enough for her to find out tomorrow.

'I'll be up at dawn,' he said, instead. 'I'll check on the status for you and wake you in plenty of time.'

'Okay, see you in the morning.'

He turned back to the fire.

'And, Will...?'

Seriously...what was it about a female voice here? His skin was puckering up as if he'd never heard one before.

'Thank you. Truly. I really appreciate the sanctuary.'

Sanctuary. That was exactly what this place had been when he'd bought it. Still was.

Though not so much since his past had stepped foot so confidently in it.

CHAPTER TWO

WILL SQUATTED IN his navy parka and clipped a final boisterous canine to its long chain in the expansive yard, their happy breathing and his murmured words taking form as puffs of mist in the frigid mid-morning air. It hadn't taken Kitty long to track him back there—she just had to follow the excited barks and yips.

Where Will went there were always excited yips. And there were always dogs.

She'd woken pretty late after the adventures of the night before and found two pairs of thermal leggings, a vest, new socks, a scarf, gloves and a pair of military patterned snow boots sitting on the chair just inside the guest-room door. With no idea what she'd find outside, she'd put on all the thermals under her Zurich sundress, the socks and boots, and Will's sweater over the top of the lot. But she'd only had to open the door to the cabin before realising that wasn't going to be quite enough. A spare coat pilfered from Will's boot room helped seal all the heat inside.

Kitty tugged the scarf more tightly around her throat and curled her gloved fingers into the ample sleeves of Will's coat.

Outside the toasty cedar cabin, the air cut into her lungs like glass—even worse than the night before. The temperature had dropped overnight until it was too cold even to sleet, and her throat and lungs burned with her first breaths outside the warm cabin.

Despite the ache, every breath she took seemed to invigorate her. She felt awake and alert and...attuned, though that made no sense. Standing out on Will's front steps cleared her mind in a way that only yoga had before. Except here, she was getting it without the sweating.

The creak of the bottom step last night was more an icy crack this morning, twitching every ear in the place in her direction, before seven sets of pale eyes turned towards her.

'No run for them today?' she called across the open yard.

Will took a while to turn to glance at her. 'Later, maybe.'

He straightened from his crouch and plunged one hand into the big coat pocket in front of him and rummaged there for a moment. Then he withdrew it, and set about scooping out a generous serving of mixed kibble into each of seven identical bowls recessed into the top of seven identical kennels. As soon as he gave the visual signal, six of the seven dogs leapt nimbly up onto their roof and got stuck into their breakfast.

His left hand found its way back into its pocket and stayed there.

'How did you sleep?' he asked without looking at her.

'Great actually. The darkness out here is very...'

Enveloping. Subsuming. Reassuring.

'Dark?'

She laughed. 'It's very sleep-promoting.'

'That's the forest breathing out,' he replied. 'And low pollution because we're so remote. You'll get used to the extra O2.'

In Nepal, everything had been just a smidge harder because of the reduced oxygen levels in the high-altitude Kathmandu Valley. Did that mean everything would be a bit easier here in the low, flat, sub-arctic forest?

When would 'easy' start, then?

'Shouldn't that make me sleep less, not more?'

'You sleepy now?'

Now? With him crouching there, looking all...good morning? Nope, not one bit.

But she wasn't about to admit that. 'Thank you for the clothes. Just happen to have them lying around?'

Or was she wearing the clothes of some...special friend?

'The supply store opened up early on account of the emergency landing. I headed in there at dawn before it got picked clean by your fellow passengers and got you a few basics. I'll take you in again later if you like, so you can pick out your own gear.'

This kindness from Will...given how they'd left things... She didn't know quite what to do with it.

'I don't really plan on being here long enough to need more.'

The look he gave her then was far too close to the last one he'd ever looked at her with. An amalgam of pity and disappointment.

'They're not going to put you back on a faulty plane,' he warned. 'They'll have to send a replacement, or squeeze you onto the regional services we usually get.'

He returned the kibble tub to the ramshackle shed that held all his tools and equipment, but as soon as his hands were free again back they went...into his pockets. Only, this time, he caught the direction of her gaze.

'Curious?' he asked, a half-smile on his lips.

Yes... But she was no more entitled to be curious about what was below Will Margrave's pockets now than she was five years ago.

He reached in and drew out a tiny, dark handful of fuzz.

'Oh, my gosh!'

'Starsky's,' he murmured. 'One of three.'

'How old is it?' she asked, staring at the tiny pup. Two slits in its squished little face peered around. Beneath, she got a momentary flash of electric-blue eyes.

Sled-dog eyes.

'Born day before yesterday.'

Two days! 'Should it be away from its mother this soon?'

'Won't be for long,' he murmured. 'Helps to forge a bond with the pup from the get-go. Reinforces dominance and trust with the mother.'

Trust. Yes—that he could just take a newborn pup from its mother even for a few minutes… That she would let him…

'It can't see or hear yet but it has all its other senses,' he said, stroking it gently with his work-roughened thumb. It curled towards him in response. 'And emotional awareness. It will come to know my smell, my voice. The beat of my heart. Knows it's safe with me from its earliest days.'

He did have that kind of voice. All rumbly and reassuring. And that kind of smell. She took a step back against the urge to take in another lungful like last night.

Will returned the pup to its mother's kennel and buried it in under her alongside its two littermates—another black one, and one that was white as the snow all around them with subtle grey mottling.

'So no departing flight this morning, I take it?' she asked as he straightened.

He turned and faced her. 'Let me explain something about bear season…'

'I know, I know… They come for the ice—'

'Not just them,' he interrupted. 'Tourists. Hundreds of them arriving and leaving every day. For eight weeks we're overrun and then we go back to being the sleepy little outpost we usually are. You should be prepared for this to go on for days. Maybe longer.'

Days? Days of this careful eggshells? Of not talking about Marcella or the quakes? Of not mentioning what happened between them five years ago?

'I'll look for somewhere else to stay, then.'

He slashed her that look of his. The one she remembered, the one that used to give her pulse a kick. The *aware* one. As if he saw right through her. And suddenly she regretted the extra layer of thermals. Heat billowed up from nowhere.

'If there was nothing available last night there'll be nothing today. No one else can leave either.'

'Unless someone got eaten by a bear,' she joked.

He didn't dignify that with a comment. But his glare spoke volumes.

Kitty scanned the dog yard carved in amongst the thick Boreal forest and the chains tethering each animal to their cosy little doghouse. That would stop the dogs running wild but it would also stop them running for their lives if a bear happened along.

'How often are dogs attacked by bears?'

The glare redoubled.

'Bears don't kill dogs,' he said irritably. 'Dogs kill dogs.'

She glanced at his pack, so carefully tethered out of reach of each other. But then she remembered how they'd all piled in together last night quite happily.

'The Boreal wolves are much more likely to attack for territorial reasons. We have a few around here.'

And wolves were mostly nocturnal.

Understanding flooded in. 'That's why you brought them all into the house last night.'

'Most dogs up here live, grow old and die tethered up outside unless they're working. But I lost a young male to a wolf a few weeks back.' He dropped his eyes away from hers. 'He did a good job defending the pack—'

Better than me, she thought she heard him say under his breath as he turned partly away to coil up a length of rope.

'—but his injuries were too severe.'

'The wolf killed him?'

'I killed him,' Will said, his movements sharp. 'The wolf just started it.'

Kitty blinked. He'd had to put his dog down by his own hand?

'I'm sorry, Will. That's rough.'

He shrugged, but it wasn't anywhere near as careless as he probably wanted her to believe. 'The vet flies up from Winnipeg once a month. In between, we have to DIY.'

'Still. You're more about saving lives than taking them.' He'd been rescuing people in need since he was a boy. It was in his blood. He'd been raised by a second-generation search-and-rescue man.

She thought she saw him wince, but he masked it in the turn of his body back towards the cabin.

'Breakfast?' he said, as brightly as his gruff manner allowed.

'You haven't eaten?'

'I don't generally eat before noon,' he said. 'But the fridge is stocked up. Help yourself.'

'Really? You were all about the big breakfast in Nepal,' she murmured, turning to follow him. Then it hit her... Could he not bring himself to have that without his wife?

'Breakfast was Marcella's thing,' he said. 'It meant something to her. Family starting the day together.'

And he'd loved her enough to indulge it.

Sorrow soaked through her. And something else, something closer to...envy. Which pretty much made her the worst person alive. Still hankering for another woman's man, even though that woman was dead.

'Will, I'm so sorry about—'

'Stay as long as you need to,' he said brusquely, gathering up his tools. His words couldn't have been colder if she'd found them lying scattered in the snow. 'You have a fire and food and the best Internet in town.'

'I don't want to be an inconvenience.'

'I'm not planning on being your entertainment,' Will said, gruffly. 'I have work to get on with. There's no inconvenience.'

'No,' she muttered as he turned to wander off. She felt about as welcome as that time in Nepal. 'Of course.'

But as she went to follow him inside, her foot hit a patch of ice and she scrabbled out for the most stable thing she could find.

Will.

He twisted and caught her under one elbow and one armpit—all terribly graceful—and steadied her back onto her feet. The last time he'd been this close she'd stumbled, too. Down some steps in Nepal. That time when Will had caught her hard up against his body, she'd clung to him just as she clung now, and her pulse had rioted in exactly the same way. He'd set her back on her feet, turned and simply walked away, but not before his jaw had clamped in a way that had made her think he'd felt the zing too.

Now, he dropped his hands away from her the moment she was back in charge of her legs, but his eyes fell to her lips and were the last part of him to turn away.

Five years had changed nothing, it seemed.

She still wasn't welcome in Will Callaghan's life.

And his body still said otherwise.

'Take Dexter,' Will called as she headed outside that afternoon all rugged-up. 'If he growls, head back in immediately.'

She paused on the second step and looked down at him working on the motor of a quad bike. 'Why? What will it be?'

'Something bigger than you.'

She'd spent all day indoors—too afraid to go further than dash distance from the phone in case her flight was suddenly scheduled—but by late that afternoon she'd gone a little stir-crazy. Will, good to his word, had busied himself all day and left her to her own devices. She'd poked around the cabin and browsed through his books but there was only so much reading a girl could do. Especially one who usually filled her days to overflowing with to-do-list. It didn't take long for the tiny cabin surrounded by all these trees to start closing in on her. Enough that she'd temporarily forgotten how wild this place really was despite its modern comforts.

Dexter was stoked to be released from his tether and tasked with being her bodyguard. He galumphed alongside her into the trees, breaking out in wider and wider arcs, sniffing everything he found. Kitty trod carelessly at first but then Dexter's obsession with the Boreal floor drew her eyes downward, too, and she realised what it was she was walking on with her spanking new boots.

Living creatures.

The ground was blanketed with lichens, waterlogged plantlets and mosses, all of it jewelled with icicles. Leaves the colour of bruises poked up from between a mossy groundcover so green it was almost yellow. Something white that looked as if it belonged on a reef rather than a forest floor. Some kind of pale parasitic plant, growing happily on anything that didn't fight back, alongside earth-toned fungi piggybacking on a tree's circulatory system. Such a perfect natural system working in balance; crowded and chaotic and tangled, but everything was getting exactly what it needed to survive. And all of them poking above last night's snowfall. Now and again, a rare patch of actual ground, something hard underfoot. Not the ground that was made of dirt and went down and down until it hit bedrock—this ground sat on permafrost; a layer of ice, far below, that never managed to thaw, even in summer.

Which would explain the bone-numbing cold rising up through the forest floor into her boots.

She stepped out of the thicker copse of trees to the edge of a clearing and stared into the distance. Orangey brown as far as the eye could see, everything frosted with ice, punctuated by the one-sided Tamarack trees that reached for the sky, and dotted with little swamps of frigid surface water. Really this was just one big, thriving wetland. All of it in soft focus, courtesy of the gentle fog.

She filled her lungs with the cleanest air she'd ever tasted and eased it back out again just as slowly.

It took her a moment to realise that Dexter was growling.

It started low in his long throat and then burbled up and out of his barely parted lips, his tail stiffening and vibrating minutely. He'd turned his stare straight back into the forest, the direction she would have to go to get the short distance back to the house.

Thoughts of all the things out here that could be bigger than her flashed through her mind. Bears, wolves, even caribou could do some damage if they were in the right mood. Or the wrong one. Her eyes darted around for anything with which to defend herself, then she gave up and peered deep into the empty stand of trees she'd just left, breath suspended.

Out of nowhere, a massive flash of grey bounded towards her out of the darkness. She hadn't even seen it lurking! But before she could do more than suck in enough breath for a scream, Dexter's tail lifted from its low, stiff position to a higher wave. Less like an accusing finger and more like a parade flag.

'Jango!' Will stepped out of the shadows behind his dog.

A sawn-off log made for a convenient place to slowly sink down in lieu of collapse. Jango sneezed and bounded off with Dexter to explore, leaving Kitty with only Will to defend her. Even without the firearm he'd slung over his shoulder, she trusted he could do just that. Probably with his bare hands.

He was just that kind of man.

Maybe that was why she'd fallen so hard for him back in Nepal.

'Did I wander too far?' she asked, immediately contrite.

'I needed to give Jango a run to see how her leg is doing, thought I might as well come this way.'

Pfff... 'Worried about the tourist getting lost in your forest?'

'Just worried for my dog,' he corrected carefully.

That brought her eyes around to the hound snuffling around a distant tree. 'What happened to her?'

'She lost a pad to frostbite,' he said. 'Standing guard over an injured hiker last winter.'

Concern stained her voice. 'And she's still healing?'

'She wore a mediboot all summer. It's just come off.'

Kitty couldn't shake the feeling that it was an excuse. Maybe he didn't trust her outside alone. Once a rescuer, always a rescuer.

'It's stunning out here,' she breathed, turning back to the open stretch where Boreal eased out into more open wetlands. 'Is it all like this?'

'Where it's not tundra,' he grunted. 'Or Hudson Bay.'

He extended his hand to help her to her feet. It took two deep breaths before she could bring herself to slide her fingers into his. But two layers of arctic gloves muted the old zing and she only had to contend with the gentle pressure of his strong hand around hers until he released her.

'Listen, Will…'

His back tightened immediately and he turned away from what was coming. She caught his elbow before he could spin away fully.

'I wanted to…' Lord, how did you start a conversation like this one? *Thank you for telling me your wife died.* 'When Marcella—'

'Sorry it was such a group announcement,' he interrupted.

It was part of what had first drawn her to him, Will's ability to just know what she was thinking. 'Don't apologise. I was so grateful to have heard after everything we'd seen on the news feeds. The quakes... I messaged you. Twice.'

She'd tried to convince her network to let her go to Nepal, to report on the recovery—desperate to see Will still breathing with her own eyes—but in the end the vast numbers of media streaming into the city had only been putting more pressure on Kathmandu's limited resources. Instead, she'd kept herself glued to the feeds coming into her network, looking for the slightest glimpse of Will working with his rescue dogs in the capital. Even as she'd reminded herself why she shouldn't even care. It hadn't occurred to her that either of them faced such risk staying to help out after the first quake.

He winced, but then his gaze lifted and locked onto hers. 'I wasn't really in a position to chat.'

No. He'd just buried his wife.

Metaphorically.

He tugged his arm free and turned to stride away from her along the squishy Boreal floor.

Will's eventual message had shattered her and, as she'd quietly wept, she'd known a deep kind of shame that she was crying not just out of sadness that her friend had died, but also for relief that Will had not.

'How are you doing now?' she risked, catching up with him.

He shrugged, and she supposed it was meant to appear easy. 'That was two years ago.'

'You don't set a watch on losing someone you love. Or on a traumatic event like that.'

He stomped on in silence but finally had no real choice but to answer. 'I'm doing okay.'

'Long way from Nepal,' she prompted, stumbling over a particularly thick thatch of sod grass.

He slowed a little so that she didn't have to scamper after him like an arctic hare. 'I was a bit over mountains.

So I looked for the widest, flattest, most open space I could find where I could also work rescue.'

She could well imagine his desire to come home to Canada, too. Back to what he knew. To regroup.

Kitty scanned the distant horizon and the miles and miles of squat flat Boreal stretching all the way to it. 'You sure found flat.'

Dexter and Jango continued to frolic, dashing around and sticking their noses into any space big enough to accommodate one. Given they spent much of their day tethered to their kennels or to a sled, working, this kind of freedom was probably a rare luxury. And sneezing seemed to be Jango's way of celebrating.

'What happened to your dogs in Nepal?' she risked.

His silence was almost answer enough, but then he finally spoke. 'I had four dogs with me in Kathmandu when the second quake hit, so they survived. I left them behind with Roshan when I left. There was still a lot of recovery work for them to do there without me.'

Only four survivors…

She'd had the privilege of filming most of Will's sixteen dogs out hunting for lost climbers on the Annapurna Mountains, or a pair of hikers caught down in the valleys, or just training out in the field. He'd probably never imagined the horrific circumstances they'd be working in just a few years later. Or that he would lose so many of them in a single event.

'Hard, leaving the four behind…' she probed.

In the silent forest, his voice had no trouble drifting back to her. And when it did it was raw and thick and honest—the Will she remembered from Nepal.

'Harder staying.'

He had suffered immeasurably. Losing his wife, the place he called home, the dogs he trained and loved. Facing death and despair every single day for weeks.

And she was asking him to relive it now.

Heat rushed up from under the collar of her parka. 'Sorry, Will. Blame my enquiring mind…'

It took her a moment to notice that he'd fallen behind her as she picked her way through the moss. She turned. Regret stained his ice-blue eyes, then changed into something more like dark grief.

'No. I'm sorry, Kitty. Your questions are perfectly reasonable. Under the circumstances.'

For the first time since she'd arrived in Churchill he was normal with her. Human. The old Will. The man who had made her breathless with just one look. Faint with the accidental touch of his callused fingers. It was absolutely the right time to go deeper, to wiggle her way in under his protective barriers and hunt for more of the old Will.

Except that Old Will had as little place in New Kitty's life as he did in his own.

The past belonged in the past.

'So, how are you settling in in Churchill?' she asked, to give him a break.

He sighed. 'I keep to myself for the most part. That is reason enough to get noticed up here.'

'I would have thought the north was full of people keeping to themselves.'

'Turns out there are rules to being an outcast. Some social niceties that even hermits are expected to deliver on.' He glanced at her expression. 'I may not have made quite the effort that they were expecting.'

Kitty slid him a sideways glance. 'You shock me.'

On anyone else, that slight twisting of his lips might have been a smile. On Will, it never paid to assume. But her heart flip-flopped regardless. 'Still, the airport lady seemed to think well enough of you.'

'I'm working on it. So what was in Zurich?' he asked, artfully moving the conversation on. 'A story or a man?'

There was nothing in the impassive question to give her pause, yet it did. Maybe it was the irony of *this* man asking her about *other* men. Will Margrave was precisely the reason she'd had no meaningful relationships since the last time she'd seen him. She'd thrown herself into her work for the twelve months after being so rudely ejected from Pokhara, and soon she'd been way too busy escalating her career to entertain more than the most casual of relationships. Too caught up globetrotting and network-hopping and hunting down the big stories.

She'd gone to Nepal in search of a powerful story, not a powerful attraction. Regardless, afterwards she'd struggled to find a man who could reach the very high bar Will had set.

Perhaps she should thank him for her successful career. He'd given her the shove she needed to be great. Greater.

'I was in Zurich shooting a story about Switzerland's textile industry. Tax haven meets innovation.'

'Industry?' He frowned. 'Doesn't seem like your kind of thing.'

He would say that. The woman he'd met five years ago was into human-interest stories and spectacular natural places, not commercial ventures and tax law.

She pressed her lips together. 'We all change.'

Especially when you were as highly motivated as she had been. Focusing on your career to the exclusion of anything else. 'I'm a foreign correspondent for a Chinese TV network now, CNTV. Their business programmes. Based in LA.'

If by 'based' you meant a postage stamp of an apartment that she rarely ever returned to because she was on the road so much. The world's most expensive storage facility.

'Foreign correspondent makes a little more sense, I guess.'

Was that a compliment or a criticism? It was impossible to tell from Will.

'Nothing wrong with ambition,' she huffed. 'And I go where the stories are.'

Certainly, her career had gone where the promotions were. Hopping from network to network as opportunities presented themselves. The closest she came, these days, to the hobo-like habits of her past.

Lord how she missed the hobo days, sometimes. When her boss's boss was hammering them for a particular angle or cutting a deadline by days it was hard not to long for the freedom she used to enjoy creating her own stories, following her nose, rolling with her instincts.

But she'd traded all that for a steady income and a bigger font on her credit.

'Plenty of stories to be found up here,' Will murmured. 'Maybe you can knock off a few while you wait for your airlift out. Though you might struggle to find something to interest the business set.'

'You don't think cashed-up people want to see polar bears?'

'I know they do. I've escorted some of them around the district. Though I am curious why you don't seem to want to. Most people would have started nagging hours ago.'

Didn't *want* to? Was that what he thought? The truth was so much more complicated. If she saw a polar bear, how would she stop wanting to see polar bears? Or eagles. Or manatees. Or deserts.

She'd gone for a clean break—and for corporate stories—for a reason.

'I'd like to see a bear,' she breathed on a puff of mist before hurriedly adding, 'Though not out here.'

Again that tiny mouth twist. 'So take a few days to look around.'

Easy for him to say. It wasn't Will's heart aching at the potential of this place. It wasn't his soul trilling to be standing here, knee-deep in lichens and moss. It wasn't his lungs aching with so much more than the coldness of the air around them.

Will wasn't the one who had to leave Churchill the moment her number came up.

She'd already felt what it was like to be banished from somewhere that had rapidly started feeling like her soul home. Why would she set herself up for that again?

'I'm on deadline for the Zurich piece. If I'm not back in the studio within a few days, this story is going to get cut and aired without me.'

And then who knew what angle it would take? There was no shortage of producers who would love to steal the feature slot she'd fought for. A slot that was scheduled just eight days from now.

Will frowned. 'There's every chance you won't be, Kitty. You need to be prepared for that.'

She chewed her lip. 'Maybe I can cut a rough from here on my laptop, and file that as a starter…'

'I have the best comms outside of the Port because of my rescue work,' Will went on. 'There's a satellite set up out back of the cabin. If you need to be talking to your network in China or sending them rough cuts this is the place to do it from. *Mi data es su data.*'

The man certainly knew how to appeal to a woman's sense of duty… But it didn't stop her chewing her lip.

'Or shoot something entirely else.'

'I'm not sure the business types at CNTV will be queuing up for an exposé on the hidden delights of the fifty-eighth parallel.'

'So don't do it for them, do it for *you*. Call it research if you truly can't bring yourself to just relax and enjoy a few days of downtime.'

Relax? No, not while Will was around. She wouldn't be making that mistake again.

Old Kitty would have chased whatever story excited her and would have told it in whatever way she wanted and then sold it to whoever had the most sympathetic vision. And if no one wanted to buy it she would have whacked it online, free, for the world to enjoy. Because the story was king back then. Money came much further down the list. Back in her idealistic, self-determined, passionate free-lance days. Back before she was employed by particular networks to tell particular kinds of stories with particular kinds of agendas for particular kinds of audiences...

Back before New Kitty was born.

But wasn't there some saying about making hay while the sun shone? Or the snow fell, in Churchill's case. She was in the sub-arctic, cut off from the rest of the world, forced to take some time off from her competitive, all-consuming career. If there was a better opportunity to take a few days out of being *Action Kitty* to just remember how it felt to be *Hobo Kitty* she really couldn't imagine it.

And keeping busy...now that definitely held a heap of appeal. But she made a last-ditch effort to say no.

'Your plane practically fell from the sky, Kit. As ex-cuses go that one is both solid and on public record. You're stuck here for days, and insurance is picking up the tab...'

Kit.

Time had done nothing to dispel the fluttering of her heart when he used the diminutive form of her name. A presumption he'd made five years ago and she'd never been inclined to correct. She'd come to like it. Wait for it, even.

The reality was she was stuck here until tomorrow, if not later. Given how much work she yet had to do on the footage still on her hard drive, she'd be spending most of it in her room, tinkering on her laptop. If she stayed an-other day—or, God forbid, *days*—she could fill the time with research for a future story. That would keep her busy and out of Will's way.

'I guess that does open up a certain opportunity.'

'And accommodation is free,' he added.

'Not if I find somewhere else to stay.' Which she would,

because he wouldn't want her here any more than he had in Nepal. Will was just doing what was expected when a jet liner fell out of the sky in your back yard.

He turned in front of her and stopped her progress. 'You won't find anywhere, not for a few days. Besides you don't need to relocate. You're welcome to stay in my spare room as long as you need it.'

She stiffened her spine and locked gazes. 'I was "welcome" in your home once before, remember?'

And there it was—streaking up his jaw out from under his scrappy beard—a subtle flash of red. The first real evidence that he remembered how they'd parted all those years ago.

Which meant he'd probably be on the lookout for repeats. Which meant she'd be on eggshells for ever, trying to give him nothing.

Everything in her screamed caution not to set herself up for more hurt. A single night was one thing…

'I really don't want to be a bother.'

His lips twisted. 'I'm sure we can give each other plenty of room in a forest this big.'

No, Kitty. You're no bother.

It's fine, Kitty. No trouble.

Relax, Kitty, it's out of your control.

On the scale of denials, Will's effort was non-existent. Still…maybe picking up after herself and keeping out of his way would be adequate repayment for his dubious hospitality. And her story would get filed. And she'd have some fun reliving the old hobo days.

Win-win.

'Okay. I guess it wouldn't hurt for me to see a few things while I'm here.' She watched him, carefully. 'You know…research.'

The look he gave her then was uncomfortable in the way only Will could make it. As if he saw right through her flimsy excuses. As if he knew exactly how he made her feel and how she *would* feel until she collapsed, emotionally wrung out, into a plane seat and flew far from here.

As if he knew her better than she knew herself.

Pfff. This was Nepal all over again.

CHAPTER THREE

A DAY LATER, Kitty clung desperately to the back of Will's jacket as his quad bike flew them out to the local weir that dammed Churchill River. Will was the closest resident to it, which, apparently, made checking on activity at the weir his responsibility.

'I go out dawn and dusk,' he'd told her as he'd whipped the cover off the quad and hauled it out of the little shelter that kept it frost-free. 'Put the flag up and then lower it again. Check on conditions. I take a different dog each time.'

This morning it was Bose's turn. He'd seemed to know exactly what was happening and his excitement levels were off the chart waiting for them to get moving. Once they got under way, the golden retriever ran full tilt alongside the quad, breaking away to thunder through not quite frozen pools before veering back in to run hard up against Will's left foot.

The quad bounced and slid along the snow-dusted track, crunching through the surface ice formed on puddles and practically flying over every dip and mound. Before long, gripping the back of Will's jacket wasn't enough to keep her firmly in her seat and the wind chill made her gloved fingers ache. So she slid her arms around his waist and dipped her head against the whipping snow and hoped to heaven that he didn't mind the intimacy. Or wouldn't read into it.

Warmer and more secure. And totally necessary.

Yeah, you keep telling yourself that.

The lie got harder to buy every time she breathed a lungful of him in.

As they came up over the final bend, Bose took off

ahead of them and bolted down the long strait as fast as
his legs could carry him, towards a watchtower overlooking the river.

'Churchill Weir,' Will called back. 'Two hundred
thousand cubic metres of rock piled up across the river
to control water flow and create a reservoir for boating
and fishing.'

Though obviously not so much in the frigid weeks leading up to winter. It was an impressive—but utterly vacant—facility about a mile up from where the Churchill
River opened out into Hudson Bay. A mini-marina with
boathouse, pontoon berths, first-aid facilities, fire pits,
and the three-storey watchtower that served double duty
as a lookout for tourists. The steel tower was fully caged
in, in the event of a bear-related emergency, presumably.
The massive structure could hold fifty people at a pinch.

Just two people and one dog was a pure luxury.

Kitty climbed to the top of the tower while Will checked
over the marina and raised a wind-shredded Canadian flag
for the day. Bose dived right into the icy river, splashing
around like a kid in summer. He found a stick and chased
it, tossing it up and letting it drift away on the current before crunching through the ice on the edge of the shore
and diving back in after it.

Eventually, man and dog joined her at the bottom of
the watchtower.

Around them, the river water churned and surged in the
gusty, cold air. Icicles clung to the exposed leaves where
it whipped up into a froth amongst the water sedge and
polar grass. All around were banks of the rich red stick
willow that grew so abundantly up here. Kitty pulled her
woollen beanie down more firmly against the icy wind that
buffeted her face with invisible needles. Even the gentle
snowflakes felt like blades when they were tossed against
her wind-whipped skin.

'Bear!'

She gasped and crouched, pointing to the far side of the weir where a polar bear was in the process of hauling itself out of the river and up onto the bank. It did a full body shake that rippled its massive loose skin, then sauntered out into the middle of the parking area before pausing to think about the world.

It took barely a moment to find them with its beady black eyes once it had turned its nose to the air.

'Inside,' Will ordered, tugging her back into the towering metal lookout. The door closed behind the three of them with a reassuringly heavy clang. They were safe, as long as the bear didn't decide to curl up out there for a nap. People had frozen in less time. Even with two layers of thermals and borrowed down jackets. And even in late autumn.

'Can it smell us?' she whispered.

'No question,' Will said. 'But we won't smell lardy enough to seriously interest it.'

She looked at him quizzically.

'Bears hunt seals for their blubber, not their flesh,' he explained.

'And they can smell it?'

'Two kilometres away, yep.'

'And they don't eat anything but seals?'

'They *can*, but protein is not what they're hungry for. People are way too stringy for them, as a rule.'

Kitty looked at the rangy bear. Its legs were like tree trunks, but its pristine coat hung loose around its frame where body mass was supposed to be.

'He does look hungry,' she said, softly. 'How long since he's eaten?'

'Hard to know. The fact he's swum upriver might be a sign he's got energy from a recent feed, or it might be a sign he's getting desperate. Ranging more widely.'

And every week the ice didn't come was a week longer this bear had to go hungry.

'He looks pretty relaxed.'

'Polar bears love their alone time,' Will murmured. 'They can be social but they like nothing better than striking out alone on the ice and hunting.'

Kitty stole a glance at him.

'What?' he said when he caught the direction of her stare.

'I was thinking that it takes one to know one.'

'Nothing wrong with keeping to yourself,' he said, somewhat defensively.

She went back to staring at the bear from their high position. As her first polar bear went, it wasn't quite what she'd been expecting.

'Why isn't it white?'

'Blubber again,' he said.

She turned from the bear to him.

'High oil content of their winter diet,' he expanded. 'The seal fat stains their coat from the inside out.'

She huffed out her disappointment. '*Seal-fat-yellow*. Wouldn't *that* be a good name for a paint swatch?'

'Give him time.' Will chuckled. 'This fella looks scrappy now but when his moult is finished and he starts feeding up he'll be absolutely breathtaking. You expecting him to tap dance?'

'Skinny and lipid yellow was not what I imagined my first bear would be like.'

'A wild polar bear just hauled himself out of the river right in front of you. Have you really changed that much?'

The criticism bit as sharply as the wind still whipping around them. The implication that nature wasn't good enough for her now.

'It's hard to buy into the *wild* part when he's stretched out in the middle of a marina car park,' she improvised to shift his focus. 'Maybe I should try and see one somewhere a bit less manmade.'

There was a time she'd have gone crazy for a first sight-ing like that. Back when life was still an adventure. Before everything got so very...structured.

Will snorted. 'I'll take you out there if we get a chance.'

Kitty hopped from foot to foot to stay warm and turned to look at Bose, who had finally ceased his busy laps up and down the stairs and lingered on the metal platform, whimpering piteously.

'Is he upset by the bear?' Kitty frowned.

'His feet hurt on the frozen metal,' Will murmured, bending down to the agitated dog. A moment later he cursed. 'I need your lip balm, Kitty. His feet were wet from his swim. His pads are freezing to the structure.'

The cold must have been affecting her brain; she wasn't usually this slow to connect the dots.

'Your lip balm,' he repeated, more urgently. 'Come on, city girl, you had it out earlier. I know you have it on you somewhere.'

She rifled in the pocket of Will's jacket and produced the little squeeze tube of mint lip jelly. The one arctic-useful thing she'd had on the plane with her.

Will folded himself right down and squeezed a slimy trail of jelly around each of Bose's bonded paws.

He massaged the balm into each pad, loosening the ice's hold on the dog's feet and preventing them from re-bonding. Without waiting, Will hoisted him up onto his shoulders. Bose didn't look thrilled to be so awkwardly positioned but it was clearly preferable to being stuck to the watchtower, suffering.

Across the clearing, the bear took offence at all the commotion and hauled itself onto massive feet before wandering off into the distant trees.

'Sorry, big fella,' Will murmured as it departed.

He took his time clanking noisily down the three levels of steel watchtower, balancing the dog precariously over his shoulders and giving the bear enough time and motivation to get well clear, before standing aside so Kitty could unlatch the heavy steel safety gate. As soon as they were out, Will relinquished Bose to the snow-protected ground, and he immediately sprinted over to where the bear had been lying to discover its scent. None the worse for his misadventure.

The surreality of the whole morning caught up with her as they got back to the quad bike and she took a moment to just stare at Will.

'Two days ago I was in one of the most cosmopolitan cities in Europe at a posh product launch,' she said, over the wind. 'It was all suits, caviar, and networking. Now I'm stranded a thousand miles from anywhere with Grizzly bloody Adams, a pack of domesticated wolves and a bear.' She lifted her eyes to him. 'And there's *dog hair* in my lip balm.'

'Welcome to the north.'

Will's easy grin warmed her even as the wind cut bitterly across her face. She stared at the mangled, near-empty little tube of lip balm.

'Maybe you can claim it on insurance,' he chuckled.

But when she continued to blink at him silently he laughed outright, the first time she'd heard that particular aphrodisiac in five long years.

'Could be worse, Kit. Be grateful I didn't ask you to pee on his paws.'

Had half a decade changed him as much as it had changed her?

Will tethered the last of his dogs after their early afternoon run. Around him their tongues lolled like happy tentacles. All but Starsky, who was still on puppy-guarding duty.

The Kitty Callaghan who'd stepped off that crippled aircraft was highly strung, driven, and more concerned with what her employers wanted than what she did. Half falling out of the sky didn't seem to bother her anywhere near as much as possibly missing a deadline.

Who *was* she?

The woman he remembered was a free spirit, endlessly passionate, full of creativity and curiosity. Nothing had deterred her from pursuing her dream—right up until that last morning, anyway.

She'd blown into Nepal chasing a story about the world's oldest woman and come across his canine rescue unit on her way through. Like the rest of the world, she'd assumed that all alpine rescue in the Himalayas was done by helicopter or by Sherpas with yaks, and she'd assumed that Everest was the only mountain worth falling off. The beautiful Annapurna range—and the team of dogs he ran on them recovering hikers in trouble—were a revelation to her. Just like that, her plans flipped from a week-long visit to a full-month stay.

And his wife had volunteered *them* as hosts. In the too eager way desperate people often grasped at displacement activities. Not that he'd recognised that at the time.

Kitty's spirit—and the way Marcella had responded to it—only highlighted how much vigour his wife had lost since arriving in Nepal eleven months before. Impossible, you'd think, in one of the most spiritual places on the planet. Kitty's enthusiasm for her work had only reminded him how many months it had been since Marcella had picked up her paintbrushes to capture Nepal's gorgeous light. And the way Kitty had interacted with his dogs with zero self-consciousness had reminded him how effortless some things could be. How easy he and Marcella had been with each other in the beginning. Which had only reminded him of how *not* easy things were in Nepal. The place where their young marriage was stripped back in the mountain wind and their flaws and imperfections so brutally exposed.

But having Kitty in their house had been like having

one of his wife's sisters there, and for ten happy days he'd had *his* Marcella back: delightful, happy, engaged Marcella. Pre-Nepal Marcella. More or less.

As a result, he'd spent the first week swinging between gratitude that Kitty's presence had given him his wife back for a bit, and deep shame that it had taken a stranger to accomplish it. In between, he'd struggled not to notice Kitty's many virtues.

He should have known Marcella would decline the moment Kitty left. Hell, he *had* known, and he'd still made the decision to ask her to go. Because having Kitty there day after day had seemed a much greater risk to his marriage than Marcella's wildly fluctuating moods.

As it had turned out, the real risk had been lurking deep below the earth.

'Step up, Bruiser,' he commanded, and the biggest and blackest of his team moved up to stand patiently in front of his squatted thighs.

He checked his wheel dog over quickly, paying particular attention to the place between his pads where chunks of rock ice sometimes got caught after a snow run, and then tethered him to his kennel, and gave Bruiser a full body rub, mussing his thick coat and getting into all his favourite places. He let himself out of the yard and scuffed his boots as he came up the stairs to shake them free of slush.

He felt the heat the moment he entered the cabin. When he went out on long training runs, his fire generally burned right down to ash coals making the house cool on his return, but Kitty had clearly kept it stoked while she'd passed the morning, and—his nose informed him as he shrugged out of his coat—she'd made soup. In his kitchen. Not from scratch, but she'd hunted and gathered a couple of tins for her lunch and left the rest simmering awaiting his return.

His muscles softened. It had been a long time since someone had looked out for him like that. Thoughtful, but not over the top. If he'd walked in here and found her in the kitchen waiting for him in an apron with a hot bowl of stew, a slab of freshly buttered bread and a smile, he might have had to walk right out again. But this—just the casual kindness of a stoked fire and simmering canned soup left—*this* he could handle. And almost get used to.

Which was reason enough to not let it happen again. She would be back on her way any day now and he would be back to his solo existence. The one he'd worked so hard for. And she would get on with her life unimpeded by him.

'Kitty?'

He stood by the fire and listened out for her reply from the back of the cabin. Nothing. He took a moment to look out of the kitchen window to the forest yard behind them. Also nothing.

Surely, she wouldn't have gone exploring again alone? Not after all his warnings about taking a dog for security. His heart began to thump. The fear was as instinctive as the presumption of stupidity. He'd lost enough in his life for the former, and rescued enough stranded tourists for the latter.

A quick glance confirmed her military-patterned boots were still sitting in the boot room so wherever she'd gone, she'd gone there inadequately dressed for the conditions.

He opened the front door and stuck his uncovered head out into the silent Boreal. 'Kitty?'

Nada.

Okay, now his heart started hammering in earnest. He jogged back past her boots. Maybe she'd had a call from the airline and forgotten them in her rush to depart for the airport. He scanned the living room; maybe she'd left a note he was yet to find. Or maybe she'd just gone and would send him a thank-you card later.

Or not at all… It wasn't as if they were friends or anything.

He nudged the door to his spare room open, feeling guilty for intruding on her space. When did it start to feel like *her* space? It only took a nanosecond to confirm that her belongings were all still there.

Okay, that only left the frigid outdoors…bootless.

Immediately, old memories surged up and chilled his blood. She wouldn't last an hour.

Why the hell hadn't he taken her with him on the dogs' training run? He wouldn't make that mistake again. He wouldn't leave her for a moment. She would have to beg him for some privacy.

Maybe if he'd been that insistent with Marcella—

But as he rushed back through the cabin, a noise from the shadowy far end got his attention. He skidded to a halt and frowned up into the darkness. There was nothing at the far end of the hall but a coat closet, where he kept a mountain of winter wear packed in tight. He did a fair impersonation of a wolf, tilting its head. *All the better to hear you with…*

Then he moved.

'Will!'

Kitty's outrage as he flung open the coat closet door smacked headlong into the rising panic he'd been so woefully managing.

'What the hell are you doing?' he cried.

'Working!' she shouted back as she stumbled out of the closet.

'What?'

She pulled one earphone out from under her dark curls and held up the compact, professional microphone. A cable ran from them both down to the laptop perched on the floor of the closet.

'I spent the morning scripting the Zurich story,' she said. 'Now I'm laying down a narration track to edit the story to.'

Her phone glowed bright in the darkness, illuminating a bunch of text.

'In the closet?'

Okay, he hadn't been quite this hysterical for a long time. He fought to get his emotions under control.

'You have a lot of coats,' she defended weakly. 'It's perfect.'

He stared at her a moment longer before turning and walking away—and the adrenaline left his body as swiftly as it had come.

'It's an old field trick,' she called, ditching the mic and earphones and scurrying after him. 'In the absence of a recording booth you make an igloo out of bedcovers or use a closet full of clothes to absorb the stray sound. Yours was perfect. Why do you have so many coats?' she puffed.

The image of Kitty smothered beneath a mountain of quilts recording her damned audio threatened to morph into an image of her trapped beneath a mountain of mud and rubble. Which he knew was both illogical and impossible, but it wasn't his logical brain pumping anxiety hormones through his body. It was his most basic lizard brain.

The place where all his fears had set up camp.

Kitty was not Marcella. Nor any of the hundreds of Nepalese he'd helped recover from their rocky tombs.

'Will...?'

She trailed him at a careful distance, reminding him of Tanner when he'd first come into his team. The rangy dog had been so poorly kept by his previous owner he'd looked for betrayal and violence in every shadow. Will hated that he was making Kitty look like that, but he would deal with self-loathing later. Right now he was all about breathing.

He sagged down onto his rocker. Its familiar feel and motion helped him to calm down.

'I'm sorry if I worried you,' she began. But it was clear that she thought his reaction disproportionate to her crime. And inconsistent with a lifetime of courage under fire hauling other people out of danger.

Which meant she knew what this was *really* all about.

He hated her seeing him like this.

'Sorry,' he choked, shaking the awful images free. Trying to. 'Another time, another place.'

'Does this happen often?' she asked gently, knowing better than to touch him. Or to offer him her pity.

His breathing seemed to be getting harder, not easier. He tried to relax his grip on the timber arms of his chair.

'Nope.' Because he didn't let it. 'Special one-time performance.'

'It's okay, Will. After what you went through—'

'You have no idea what I went through,' he snapped.

How could she, when he'd told no one? But she wasn't about to be snarled off the topic. That was something else he remembered about her. Tenacious as hell. And endlessly patient. It was what made her so good at her job.

'I'd be happy to listen. If you want to talk.'

Talk? Why would he do that? He'd worked so hard to put it all away from him. So he could function.

Why would he want to relive the urgent drive back to Pokhara when he'd heard about their village? Back to the temporary field camp he'd convinced Marcella to join their neighbours in rather than go back into their big house up the hill while the aftershocks were still coming so frequently. Finding half a mountain piled up in that field instead, wet and dense. House gone. Neighbours gone. Dogs gone.

Marcella gone.

The loyal woman who'd followed him to Nepal and been so very miserable there.

All he'd had, then, were the clothes he'd stood in, the single team of exhausted dogs he'd been out working with when the landslide had hit, and his work.

There was always work.

'It's okay to miss her,' Kitty tried again.

What could he say to that? Better that she believe this was just a simple case of grief. Or post-traumatic stress. Better that she not know what was really going on. That maybe if he'd protected his own family in Nepal rather than other people's, then a beautiful woman would still be alive today. Or that if he'd just manned up and accepted reality, Marcella never would have been standing in that field that day. Or even been in Nepal. She would have been back home in the US, with her family.

Safe.

Alive.

'I just need a minute,' he gritted, still struggling against his own lungs.

She stepped back and considered him. Then spoke carefully. 'I've been cooped up in that closet for too long. Think I'll take a quick walk.'

But before she could do more than step towards the boot room he found the air he needed to remind her, 'Take a dog!'

CHAPTER FOUR

Take a dog…

Even in the midst of an obvious personal crisis, Will had enough sense to keep her safe. Kitty stomped her boot more fully on as she stepped outside, his coat clenched in her fist. Giving him the space he needed. Giving him some privacy.

And some dignity.

She wouldn't need a dog because she wasn't going to go further from the cabin than she could dash back to in thirty seconds. Just because she didn't want to humiliate Will by watching his meltdown didn't mean she was going to leave him to do it completely alone. If he needed her, she was going to be close by. She owed him that much.

Despite everything.

She'd been patient and understanding, and respectful of his loss—his failure to reply to her shocked messages—until, eventually, she'd just accepted his need for privacy. And accepted that it was going to have to be enough just to know that he had survived.

She didn't get to know if he was okay.

She shrugged more fully into her parka and then let herself into the dog yard where all seven of Will's dogs guarded the entrances to their kennels, snuggled inside or kept watch from the flat roofs.

'Hey, Jango,' she said, approaching the closest. The female snow dog did what she always did when she got over-excited—she sneezed. Full-body sneezes. It was kind of her thing. As if all that excited emotion had to get out somehow. She stood on the roof of her kennel and wiggled and sneezed as Kitty ran her forked fingers through her thick, pale fur. Her light eyes closed blissfully at the contact. The patch of pink pigment on her otherwise black nose was the only distinctive marking Jango had but it made her easier to identify amongst the three almost identical huskies in Will's pack.

Jango's closest neighbour reached to the furthest lengths of his tether and strained forward for his own pat, dodging and weaving like the clown he was to get attention.

'Yeah, I see you, Ernie.'

She visited every dog in the yard. Buying Will some time. Filling hers. Every dog had its own personality, even tethered as they were. Dexter was the serious one, Bruiser was the surly one. Bose was just as happy tied up as he had been running alongside the quad yesterday. Tanner kept a wary distance and Starsky... Well, she was a new mum, exhausted from raising her pups. So Starsky perpetually looked half asleep.

But every dog had one thing in common, and that was the focused excitement when Will walked into their yard.

Starsky blinked wary eyes up at her, so Kitty squatted to reduce the threat to her pups and murmured in her most comforting voice, 'Hey, girl...'

The side of her kennel thudded, rhythmically.

'How are your babies doing, huh?'

There was no way she was going to reach in there with her hand as she'd seen Will do, but Starsky was obliging enough to roll onto her side submissively, which made the three balls of fluff tucked in tight around her belly easier to see. Two black and one a stark white explosion of fur. The white one opened its tiny mouth wide in a massive, red yawn.

She'd never been particularly clucky—you had to spend time with people in order to spend time around their babies and she was always way too 'busy' to make friends—but something soft and squishy rushed through her at Starsky's beautiful nurturing as the dog nudged each pup with her nose to reassure them they were safe.

And it softened further that Starsky understood she was safe with *her*.

'Want to hold one?'

Will's voice behind her was at once full of awkwardness and apology. Kitty spun to face him, scrutinising him closely for signs of distress.

'Am I limited to one?' She smiled. As gently as she could, yearning to see the same expression in Will's eyes that she'd seen in Starsky's. The knowledge that he was safe with her.

'Thank you, Kitty,' he said, though it obviously cost him. 'For giving me the space. That kind of took me by surprise.'

Old Kitty would have pressed him, then; to force her help on him. But she didn't, she just smiled and nodded.

So maybe she had changed, some.

Will squatted next to her and reached carefully in, murmuring words of security and strength to Starsky and drawing out a pup in each hand. He kept a black one and passed her little yawning friend to Kitty.

'Open your jacket,' he said. 'Tuck it in close so it can feel your heartbeat.'

Surely that wouldn't fool even an inexperienced newborn? Not while smell and texture and pulses were such a massive part of its existence. Though, her heart was practically tap dancing simply for being near Will so maybe the pup would not notice much difference after all.

She unzipped her jacket low enough to tuck the white pup snugly between her breasts where it was close and warm against her thermals.

'Who is his father?' she murmured low enough to reassure the pup and its mother, who was keeping the closest of eyes on her babies.

'Diego, the dog I lost to the wolves.'

'Oh,' she said sadly. 'What an awful shame.' She peered down. 'You'll never know your daddy, little one.'

'He'll know me,' Will murmured. 'I'll sub for Diego.'

Will would make a good substitute father. Or the real thing. He just had that kind of temperament—patient, reliable, confident. Once, she'd entertained thoughts of what it would be like to have children, but she never could quite picture who the father might be. And when finally she did meet someone she *could* picture, he was only free to be daddy to someone else's kids. She'd put that thought away from her and focused on raising a career instead. As a result, she didn't really do soft and squishy any more. But as it thrummed through her, it was nice to know it was still in there.

Somewhere.

'Want to name him?' Will asked, not quite meeting her eyes.

'Really?'

'Go for it.'

She studied the little white fluff-ball down her front. Coat as white as snow, eyes as dark as night, tongue as red as blood.

The old folktale came leaping to mind.

'Grimm.'

Will turned his curiosity to her.

'I can't really call a boy dog Snow White, can I?'

Will smiled. 'Well, you could. We're a gender neutral team, but I like Grimm. It suits.'

'What about yours?'

Will drew the dark pup out of his pocket and looked at its underside then back at its face. Deep into its eyes. 'She's "Zurich".'

Kitty snapped her gaze up to his. She fought against the warm little glow and reminded herself that it was just as likely that he'd run out of names in the easier part of the alphabet.

'Did you just name a dog after me?' As if it weren't an honour. As if it weren't the greatest, *Will*est gesture.

'Dark hair, big grey eyes.' He shrugged as her heart thrummed. She did everything she could not to let him see the effect his gesture had on her. Maybe he misread that as offence because he retreated almost immediately from the intimacy.

'Kind of bitey,' he said, deadpan. 'Plus I don't have a "Z" in the team yet.'

The humour was the lifeline she needed to haul herself out of the dangerous swill of feelings. She wrapped both hands around it and held on.

'What about that one?'

He named the other black one Midnight.

She gave Grimm a final caress, leaned in and tucked him securely back under his mum. Then she pushed onto her feet. 'What will you do with them when they're bigger?'

Keep them, she hoped.

'Depends on their super powers.'

'Their what?'

'Every dog here has something it's particularly good at. Something fitted to a specific role in the team.' He returned Zurich to Starsky's care, too. 'Three of the four huskies are just runners—that's their super power—but Jango and the other dogs do double duty with other jobs.'

'What other jobs?'

'Bose and Jango are live trackers. Starsky and Tanner are cadaver dogs.'

Will's reality came home to her. This was his job—death and loss were everyday to him whether or not he encountered them every day.

'That's why they're different breeds,' she realised. Like the mixed team he'd had in Nepal. 'You train them every day?'

'Partly for harness fitness; partly to reinforce their individual places in the team and mine at the head of it.'

Jango leapt up and pressed muddy paws onto Will's clean coat. Kitty braced herself for his reaction, but he didn't even flinch. He just stepped away. For a man who'd been such a wreck fifteen minutes earlier, his composure now was impressive. That was how she knew Will Margrave best—in control.

'These are northern working dogs—not city dogs who have to live with kids and walk in busy streets and play well with others. Their strong personalities are part of what make them good at their jobs, so I want them to be able to express them, not water them down.'

She ran her eyes over the yard. 'I wish workplaces operated like that.'

Her senior producer obviously did not subscribe to the Will Margrave school of management. Mei-Xiu had no idea how to harness individual talent the way Will did with his dogs. For Mei, team achievements were significant only in as much as they reflected on her. Every day, she looked to see who might be growing better or brighter than she was so that she could quietly temper their success.

That was how Kitty had first become *foreign* correspondent. Mei-Xiu had seen her potential and taken pains to banish her from the CNTV kingdom entirely. All the way to Los Angeles where she was officially out of sight and out of mind. How disappointed Mei must have been when the wider access had only resulted in better content—and more of it—from her professional rival. Though Mei was nothing if not adaptable and always managed to find a way to claim partial credit for Kitty's work.

'Is that your way of saying you wish everyone would just toe your line?' he said.

She turned to him and lifted her chin, taking extra care to keep the thump out of her voice. 'You admire unleashed personality in a dog but not in a person?'

His eyes darkened. 'I didn't say I didn't admire it. Confidence and capability are always appealing.'

A warm glow kindled to life. Finding her traits appealing was just a pained heartbeat away from finding her appealing.

'I just think it's obvious where Kitty Callaghan would fit in a team,' he went on, and the glow sputtered out. 'At the front.'

'Says the man who gets the free ride while his team do all the hard work.'

His smile, when it came, was like an unexpected burst of sunshine through the ever-present Churchill cloud and the words dried up between them, replaced by something that defied language. Something that busied around them like a hundred arctic bumblebees—soft and caressing—and had to be felt, not heard.

Until Will shook them away.

'So, listen, I have this thing on this afternoon…in town. I was going to leave you home for it but after—' He caught himself, glanced at the cabin, and changed tack. 'But I've changed my mind. How about you come in with me?'

Thing? That could mean anything from a supply run to a date. Something told her Will wouldn't find it hard to find female company even in a Y-chromosome-dominated town, in which case she absolutely was not about to hang around like a third wheel.

Not again.

She didn't need to be looking around town, she needed to be finishing her rough cut. But that shadow behind Will's gaze said that he wasn't about to let her out of his sight and, truth be told, she wasn't in a hurry to spend any more hours alone in a room.

'I guess there is only so much time a girl can spend in the coat closet,' she joked. 'I'll have a look around for the afternoon while you do your…*thing*. Get my own coat, maybe.'

Her luggage had been delivered but it still didn't have much of sub-arctic use in it.

Will frowned. Actual, genuine disappointment.

'I've kind of grown used to you getting about in mine.' Blue ice seemed to swill behind the fringe of his lashes. 'It suits you.'

'In an alternate universe where people wear sacks, maybe. I wouldn't mind something a little more...tailored.'

'Tailored?' He blinked at her. 'Seriously... What happened to you this past five years?'

'I grew up, Will. Had to happen sooner or later.'

His regard grew uncomfortably long before he finally spoke again. 'Not really sure what will be left on the shelves after one hundred and sixty freezing passengers have stripped the place of emergency gear, but no harm in looking, I guess. I'll take you somewhere less known. Then you can come with me on my thing when you're done.'

On his date? No, thank you.

'I'll make my own way back—'

'I'll bring you home,' he cut in.

There it was again. The idea that he was responsible for her. Or that she was answerable to him.

Still, who knew how long she would have to wait for one of Churchill's two taxis...?

'I'd like to see more of the town,' she stated for the record. 'As long as I'm not in your way.'

'No more than here,' he grunted.

CHAPTER FIVE

WILL MIGHT AS well have rolled himself in seal blubber and gone to hang out with the polar bears in the conservation area. He was handsome, mysterious and half soaked in *eau de unattainable* and, unsurprisingly, everywhere they went in town, thick-lashed eyes followed him.

The local ones just slid sideways as he passed, as if Churchill's women knew from experience not to stare outright. But the out-of-towners didn't know him, so those gazes—and there were many of them—sat on a spectrum anywhere from *appreciation* to outright *invitation*.

Will seemed oblivious to it all—or uncaring—but Kitty saw and felt every glance.

As he'd warned, the Trading Post had been thoroughly picked over by the rest of her flight and the tourists in town, running their stock disappointingly low. But Will had bundled her back into his truck and driven her to the fringes of town before pulling in at a supply company that seemed to specialise in water pumps, fishing gear and woollen balaclavas.

Kitty glared back at him as she entered.

'Don't judge a book by its cover,' he said.

Clearly, while the Trading Post was busy with visitors to Churchill, *this* was the store of choice for locals. It was packed to bulging with every comfort for northern life—everything from organic eggs to snowmobiles.

'Coats are down the back,' Will said.

At first she was blind to anything but the swathes of green-grey and bark-brown. But if drab was the look she was going for then she'd keep on wearing Will's enormous, thick parka. It didn't take her long to find her way to the back of the building. Stores were run by people, and people were the same wherever you went—they put the things they wanted you to see up front and kept the other things—the special things—tucked away somewhere safe. Like gems just waiting to be discovered.

Bingo.

Kitty stepped beyond the rack of functional coats into what was probably a 'staff only' area, drawn by the flash of a colour she didn't really have a name for. It was half-way between orange and cherry, kind of metallic in look with a big fluffy grey hood. Quilted yet svelte, the goose-down coat drew in at the front and waist courtesy of a series of black straps that ran the length of the extra-long coat like rungs of a ladder. Kitty shrugged out of Will's big, drab parka and into the candy confection, taking care not to miss a single strap.

It was patently ridiculous. But it was completely perfect. And it fitted her like the matching gloves she would sell a kidney to find back there.

Sometimes, a girl just wanted to stand out.

'Got that in on special order for someone,' a smoker's voice behind her said, 'then she didn't like the colour.'

Kitty turned to face the shop's owner. He had a woollen, knitted bear mask on around his weathered face. Complete with adorable little curved ears. She ignored it entirely. In polar bear central a Grizzly just didn't seem that out of place.

'I *love* the colour.'

'I guess you'd need to.' He chuckled past his bear nose. 'Fits you real well, though.'

She ran her hand down the shimmery surface.

Yes, it did. Plus it was the most feminine she'd felt since stepping foot on the A340 in Zurich. It took her a moment to come to terms with the very simple reality: She wanted to look pretty. *For Will.* And she wasn't the slightest bit sorry about that. She was tired of looking like a reject from the military Goodwill around him.

'You back there, Kitty?'

In the mirror, he appeared behind her as if she'd conjured him. She spun to face him, sliding the big hood up to half subsume her face.

He stumbled to a halt and stared at her.

She plunged her hands into the coat's deep pockets and struck a pose. 'How do I look?'

Will took a moment to clear his throat. 'Like a tourist.'

Clearly an insult coming from a local but, given he wasn't taking his eyes off her, she wasn't going to lose much sleep over that.

Something deep within her cheered. 'It feels fantastic.'

Blue eyes followed her hands as they traced up and over every metallic curve. The soft fur lining of the hood brushed her cheeks like a caress.

'I'll take it,' she called to the storeman. 'Can I wear it out of here?'

Given the price tag, and given he'd been stuck with it for who knew how long, she could probably walk out of here naked but for the coat and the man wouldn't raise an eyebrow. Will fell in behind her as she paid for it, some batteries and a simple pair of woollen black gloves to replace the thick, feel-nothing mitts he'd loaned her on the first morning.

When the transaction was complete she turned back to a still-silent Will and gave him her biggest grin. 'Yay!'

Maybe if she was excited enough for both of them she could counter his apparent sudden gloom.

Or was he just thinking of having to step out in public with a human hotdog?

'I guess I don't have to worry about losing you in the forest again,' he quipped as he opened the store's door for her.

See? Feminine. He hadn't opened it for her on the way in.

Kitty tamped down a triumphant smile. 'Technically you don't have to worry about me in the forest *at all*. I'm a big girl, I can look after myself.'

'If this is what happens when you shop for yourself, I'm not so sure.'

Yeah, yeah... She'd be offended if not for the fact that he was still sneaking sideways looks at her.

He stopped them next at a busy café in the heart of town. It was filled to overflowing with tourists but seemed equally popular with the locals.

'Best coffee in town,' Will had said as he pulled into the car park crowded with buses and pulled his collar up higher before shoving open the driver's side door.

Inside, the place was festooned in cobwebs, as were some of the staff. Ghouls, zombies and witches everywhere, with a carved pumpkin candle on every table. A portly man served at the coffee counter clad in a black onesie with a white skeleton painted on it and a pretty young girl with a bloodied hatchet through her blue hair worked the register. It was hard to know if the hair was part of the costume or not, but its vibrant colour lent her tan skin a luminescence that only made her lovelier.

'It's Halloween.' Kitty spoke aloud, though she hadn't meant to.

Will slid her a sideways glance. 'You think?'

What was it about this man that he could make her feel as callow as a teenager with a few short syllables...?

'Halloween's not really a thing in Australia,' she explained as they joined the back of a longish coffee queue. 'I didn't make the connection.'

But now the grizzly bear in the supply store made so much more sense.

'I'm wondering if you can still call yourself Australian

if you haven't been to the place in years,' Will said, catching the skeleton's eye and tossing his chin in greeting.

'If that were true I'd be stateless, the way I move about.'

They shuffled forward in the line by one. She glanced around and realised how easy it was to tell the locals from the visitors. Like her, the tourists had bright, clean, brand-new snow gear. And they outnumbered the locals ten to one.

'Gathering no moss?' he said.

'Building a career.'

'And what about a life?'

'Churchill. Nepal. Montana. Newfoundland...' She counted them off on her de-gloved fingers. 'You want me to go all the way back to your childhood?'

In other words: *Pot. Kettle. Black.*

He turned a baleful expression on her as they approached the front of the queue. 'I had a life.'

His use of the past tense dug in right under her ribs. 'And I've got one. It's just different from yours. What's wrong with rolling stones, anyway?'

He turned those icy blues onto her. 'What's wrong with moss?'

The skeleton greeted him by name and slid a freshly prepared coffee and a folded piece of paper straight to him before taking Kitty's order. Like some poorly executed intelligence drop. The business of the following minutes forced a pause in the conversation but it also took some of the heat out of it.

'I think we can both say that we've done and seen things that most people never would,' she said when at last they were free of the noisy crowd. 'That's common ground, right?'

His eyes grew bleak. 'True enough.'

The silence was almost less bearable than the conversation.

'So what is it you're doing in town today?' She rushed rather than endure it.

'Bear sweep,' he said, simply.

She blinked at him. 'A what?'

'It's Halloween.' *As she'd so astutely reminded him.* 'We sweep the town and then set up a perimeter around it with our trucks so that the kids can safely go trick-or-treating.'

Kitty paused with her coffee halfway to her lips. The thought of grumpy Will Margrave involved in something quite so…civic…managed to nudge out the mental image of children in costumes finding themselves nose to nose with a hungry polar bear. Churchill kids grew up into Churchill adults and so the healthy respect the locals had for the bears had to start somewhere. But it had simply not occurred to her that candy-toting kids and hungry carnivores could not possibly share the same streets.

What a story this would make…

'Like circling the wagons,' she realised.

'Pretty much. With patrols armed with tranq guns and a chopper keeping watch overhead.'

'All for one night of candy and costumes?'

'For one night of community bonding. And of freedom. These kids see little enough of it.'

She considered him for only a moment, then made her decision. Shopping could wait.

'Okay if I tag along?' She reached into the back seat and snaffled up her video camera.

He'd driven her past Churchill's packed and multifaceted community centre—school, leisure centre, health centre, playground, library, swimming pool, ice rink, theatre and gym—but she'd assumed the indoor *everything* complex was like so many towns with sub-zero climates… All about the weather.

Here, it had the primary purpose of keeping Churchill's kids safe from bears, and a town where the children perpetually moved from their homes to virtual enclosures for their own safety made for a really interesting angle.

He glanced at her equipment then back up to her eyes. 'Is your interest professional or personal?'

'Professional. Of course.'

Although, if there was anything sexier than rescuing people from mountains it had to be protecting little children from bears, right? She wasn't going to miss out on the chance to watch Will help do that.

'Or I could just strike out on my own?' she suggested, smiling.

Will glared and she started filming.

'These are our streets,' he said, waving the hand-drawn sketch he'd received in the café in the vague direction of her camera. 'Between now and dusk we just move through town along with dozens of others, checking every nook and cranny. In about two hours, we'll move to a spot on the edge of town to form the perimeter barrier and the armed patrols will take over down here.'

And, so, she trotted along a few metres behind Will dressed in her fine new coat with her camera as he moved up and down four of Churchill's streets while the sun sank lower on the horizon. The town was a curious mix of traditional Canadian architecture and bright timber cabins all mixed in amongst the prefabricated industrial-style buildings you'd expect in a port town. Trucks, SUVs, quad bikes and tourist buses parked wherever they could get a spot. More than one yard had used discarded rubber tyres from the massive vehicles that moved around out on the tundra to create a raised garden bed for things that just couldn't grow in permafrost. They painted them brightly, adding to the colourful mosaic of street art.

It reminded her of the ubiquitous, bright prayer flags in Nepal.

She glanced at Will and wondered if he'd ever made the connection.

'So if we find a bear,' she interrupted her own thoughts and pointed the camera at him, 'what do we do?'

He shrugged. 'Shut yourself in the nearest vehicle and call the Bear Patrol.'

She hit the brakes. 'I'm serious, Will.'

He stopped and turned back to her. 'Standard procedure. Everyone up here leaves their vehicles unlocked for exactly that purpose. But don't worry, with this many people swarming around I don't think any self-respecting bear will stick around. The issue is that a bear caught short at sunup may have crawled under a house to sleep until dusk and not be aware.'

So, that was why he kept giving the undersides of houses a burst with his torch. She took extra care to capture him doing that.

'Bears and people co-exist well most of the time,' he went on, after straightening from another one. 'It's only when something unexpected happens that things get sticky. They aren't out looking to pick a fight, they're just scavenging.'

Dirt-covered scavengers hiding under houses...

Kitty sighed. 'I'm seriously going to have to reassess my mental image of polar bears.'

'Wait until you see them in their own habitat instead of ours. I'm not sending you home until you have the full picture.'

She peered up at him as they turned up a particularly shadowy street. 'The airline is already keeping me captive. You planning on adding to that?'

'Got something better to be doing?'

She blinked back at him. The truth was she had nothing lined up for after the Zurich story. She'd been looking, but nothing had captured her interest or her imagination. Which pretty much summed up her life these past weeks.

Months, maybe.

Will folded himself down to peer under a porch. Instinct

told her that there was nothing that he couldn't handle, but they weren't really prepared for a skirmish with a three-hundred-kilo wild animal.

'So what do the professionals do with a *hangry* bear?'

'Trap it. Airlift it back to the conservation zone and leave it with some food as an incentive to stay put.'

Kitty's heart squeezed. Another story danced seductively in her mind. Oh, the stories she might film, here, rather than talking about tax evasion and textiles…

Sigh.

'And if it comes back for another go at the flight-with-food upgrade option?'

'Repeat offenders spend a dull few weeks in the holding facility before they're relocated one hundred miles from here. So they associate town with the negative experience and the wild habitat with the positive one.'

'Are they that easily persuaded?'

'Bears are like people,' he murmured, this time straight down the lens. 'They just want food and shelter for their families. To keep them safe. To survive.'

The street's shadows seemed to infect Will's gaze. Kitty tugged her furry new hood more firmly around her face against the stinging, frozen wind.

'Come on,' Will said, noticing. 'Time to circle those wagons.'

Halloween was what had pulled him out of the deep morass that he'd been trapped in when he'd first arrived in the north. Little children—vulnerable, distracted—wandering the streets of this remote, hostile place, trusting that the grown-ups would have their backs. He'd almost pulled out when he'd discovered what he'd signed up for, that he was expected to keep *kids* safe against *bears*—the man who couldn't keep his own wife safe against dirt—but he was Churchill's new Search and Rescue man, refusing to protect their young just wasn't an option.

And so he'd come. And he'd driven home again with the first real hope he'd felt in months. Seeing their optimistic little ghoul-painted faces, seeing those smiles and knowing that all he had to do to keep them safe was *be there*...with his lights on... It had reminded him of how many lives he had saved by being there with a dog or two in tow.

Even if he hadn't managed to *be there* when it had counted for his wife.

He pulled up in his assigned spot on a rise above town, thirty feet left of Mark Quelot in his shiny new SUV and right of Dom Brennan's battered old delivery truck, his headlights shining away from town to create a bright barrier no lurking bear would be foolish enough to walk towards. Kitty clambered into the truck's back seat and locked her camera off to film on full zoom down into town where little scarecrows and mini-vampires and superheroes started wandering from house to house ahead of the early sunset. Witches and dragons and werewolves. But no ghosts. No zombie brides. And definitely no polar bears.

Kitty freed the camera and turned it on him on the realisation. 'No one wears white.'

In the warmth of the truck's cab, she had dropped the grey fur hood that had matched her eyes so perfectly. But losing the hood only meant the coat's rich sheen could spill up onto her pale skin, giving her a warm glow even in the gloaming light of dusk. Fortunately, the camera relieved him of the burden of not staring.

'No white,' he murmured, doing his best to pretend the camera wasn't there. He shuffled more comfortably behind the steering wheel and kept his eyes nailed to the vast space around them for a bear-shaped shadow that almost certainly wasn't coming. 'If someone calls a false alarm, that's Halloween over for everyone.'

Last time, he'd done this alone—just him and his still

dark thoughts. This year, it was kind of nice to have company.

Even if it was thoroughly distracting company.

Her shimmery coat rustled as she turned more fully to him. Even in seats as soft as these ones, sitting still for over an hour was clearly excruciating for a woman who never really *did* still. Kitty reminded him of a shark—as if she stopped swimming, she stopped breathing. Her body, her mind... Just something needed to be busy. Maybe she'd just forgotten how to be still.

'How many jobs do you have up here?' she asked, killing the camera and dropping it to her lap.

'Jobs?'

'Roles,' she clarified. 'How many functions do you fulfil in Churchill?'

'I run land-based search and rescue. That's a twenty-four-seven kind of gig.' Perpetually ready, seldom called on.

'And what else? Apart from helping out at Halloween?'

'I check on the weir daily.' Which she knew. 'And I help out with forest patrols. Sometimes drive special groups around.'

'And you help with bear stuff,' she guessed.

'What makes you say that?'

'Because you know so much for someone who's only been here two years. And because the locals seem to hold you in some regard.' She narrowed her eyes. 'Even while keeping a careful distance.'

Huh. She made him sound just like one of their bears. And kind of antisocial.

'Are you paid for any of those jobs?' she asked outright.

There was the woman he remembered. Tone deaf. No sense of propriety at all. Just have a thought and act on it. He never did mind that about her. After months of Marcella's careful communication, he'd forgotten how it was to be direct about something.

So he couldn't really complain about it now.

'Manitoba pays me part-time to run the S and R team. That's enough to live on.'

'Pfff. Not at northern prices. I just paid nineteen dollars for four camera batteries.'

Now she wanted to know his expenses? What was she doing? But he'd never been one to shy away from a challenge. So he gave her something without really giving her anything—because he knew that would drive her nuts.

'Don't buy them in tourist season,' was his sage advice. Not surprisingly she didn't appreciate it. 'Why all the interest in my financial status, Kitty?'

Her gaze grew cautious. 'Just wanting to understand how it's all working.'

He thought about letting her off with that. But then he remembered one of his favourite sports five years ago. Baiting the savvy journalist. Testing her mind. Making her do laps.

'That was *what*. Not *why*.'

'I just want…' No one did consternation like Kitty Callaghan. Those little folds right below the dark curls of her fringe only made her more attractive. 'I think I'm trying to make sure you're okay. That you're not struggling.'

Something twisted deep in his gut and the fun sucked right out of this conversation.

'I'm fine. I keep telling you.'

'Well, you would say that, right?'

'You want a doctor's note?'

She puffed a breath into all the tense silence. 'I just want to see it. For myself.'

'Why?'

'Because…' The frown again. She couldn't tell him why she cared—or wouldn't—but when Kitty Callaghan was backed into a corner she just made her own exit. He remembered that about her, too. 'What happened…earlier today…'

Here it came. He should be grateful she'd let it slide this long.

'Was that about Nepal?' she asked.

Lucky he'd had a couple of hours to formulate some kind of easy answer in his head. And he was mostly happy with how casually it came out.

'*That* was about me being frustrated you might have gone and got yourself eaten by wolves. And wondering how I was going to explain that to your employer.'

'My employer wouldn't care as long as my story was filed first,' she snorted, then sobered. 'But what I saw in your eyes wasn't frustration.'

He turned his attention back out to the light field ahead of them and scanned for bears.

His throat felt as if it were full of rubble dust again. 'Can't I just be irritated at how much of my time is being wasted running around after you?'

Kitty's wince made him feel lousier. But she was only here for a few more days. She would go back to her world and he would stay here in his.

And that would be that.

'You've seen a lot of death,' she pushed, bravely.

'You forget what I do for a living?'

'I know that the people you find are usually snap-frozen on some ice face. Or alive. The earthquakes were very different. That must have been rough.'

It was too exhausting…keeping up hostilities. Besides, while they were talking about strangers under buildings, they weren't talking about Marcella under a tonne of mud. So he relented a little.

'I just brought the dogs to the site,' he played down. 'We did our thing, and as soon as they indicated positive, another team swept in to do the digging and we moved on to a different site.'

Indication after indication after indication.

'Must have been exhausting for them.'

Memories flooded back. *Not just them.*

'Exhaustion is less of a risk than becoming disheart-ened. The cadaver dogs were indicating every twenty seconds. But the rescue dogs—' the ones trained to find people *alive* '—I had to recruit civilians to go lay in the rubble for them to find. To keep them motivated.'

Her big eyes grew impossibly bigger. 'Will, that's awful.'

He shrugged. 'Too many finds and a cadaver dog be-comes traumatised. Too few and a rescue dog stops work-ing. You need to manage them carefully. Give them lots of relief.'

'Is that why you went home to Pokhara? To swap your teams out?'

He sagged back into his leather seats. 'You want de-tails, Kitty? Is that it? Your journalistic mind can't rest until I've painted you a graphic picture of what happened to Marcella?'

'I think *want* is too strong a word,' she said softly. 'But I'd like to understand, yes.'

'The landslide?' he gritted. 'Or me?'

'Both, perhaps. Have you talked about it with anyone?'

He gave her his steeliest glare, the one that he only re-served for really bad behaviour in his dogs. They usually quailed at it. But she didn't, and any moment Kitty's gen-tle probing was going to poke straight into a nerve cluster.

'*Stop press! Wife buried alive under half a mountain. Man flees from ruins of life.* What's hard to understand about that?'

Most of the blood drained from her face, except two pink splashes where her courage clung stubbornly on.

'Your anger is your grief—'

He raked his fingers through his hair. 'No, Kitty, my anger is *anger.* I had things all ordered, here. Workable. I had a quiet existence where I could put the past behind me and focus on my work. And now you're determined to drag it all back out into daylight for dissection.'

'I just want to know that you're okay,' she repeated, throwing everything she had left into not allowing the tears he could see brewing behind her eyes to tumble down her pale face.

But he was not about to let himself be moved. 'I'm good.'

'You have no real friends here, Will,' she pointed out. 'No close relationships. That's not okay.'

He chopped the air with an impatient hand. 'You have zero friends and it's a career move. I do it and it's a dysfunction. What's with the double standard?'

'I have friends,' she mumbled.

'None so close that you'd let them know you were okay up here. The only calls you've made were to your office and your parents. Even then you only left a message. Do you truly have no one else who cares for you?'

This time even the pink splashes blanched out. He always had struck back hard.

'Okay,' she relented. 'New subject…'

He splayed a hand and pressed as hard as he could on either side of his skull to dislodge the ache. 'I don't think there are any subjects perky enough to rescue this conversation…'

'Then how about nothing at all? Let's just get through this watch and call it a night. With any luck the airline will have called while we were out…'

Why did that only make him feel more dismal?

He lasted about twenty seconds before the thick silence just about killed him. That same silence that he loved when it swilled around him in his cosy, secure forest cabin. He reached for the door handle.

'You stay put,' he said sternly. 'I'm just going to check in with the perimeter leader.'

And other patently obvious untruths…

The frigid air assaulted his lungs as he left the warmth of the truck cab, but he figured if some little kid could be out in it bound up in origami bed linen then he would survive. Downhill from their position, Churchill was practically aglow with every light in the town illuminated to add to the security and spectacle of this special night. He found himself a convenient patch of shadow between the spill of his own bright headlights and Dom Brennan's, and he tried to dissolve into its darkness, kicking himself for letting Kitty get under his skin.

What did he expect? She was trained to sniff out stories and she had an IQ to rival Einstein's. The two in combination made her well equipped to see through his poorly constructed lies. How long would it be before she started piecing the truth together? She probably had half the story already—Marcella had grabbed onto her like a lifeline when she'd visited, so Kitty probably knew more about his failing relationship with his wife than he did which meant it wouldn't be long before she arrived at the fact that he was responsible for his wife's death.

If he'd been more of a man, he would have packed Marcella up—no matter how she'd protested—and sent her back to the family and life that she'd been trying so very hard not to pine for. If he'd had more courage, he would have pulled the pin on the marriage that had already been flailing eleven months in, and Marcella never would have been in Nepal when the quakes had struck. The hillside house overlooking Pokhara would have been vacant when the earth beneath it had sluiced away.

If he'd had the courage.

He glanced back at the darkened truck. Kitty probably judged him, already, for the thing that had built up between them five years ago—he had been the married one, she hadn't—but did she know just how much of a failure he was as a husband? As a protector? As a basic human being?

Maybe, maybe not. But he certainly wasn't going to start drawing her a roadmap no matter how much she pried.

Not if he could help it.

CHAPTER SIX

THERE WAS NOTHING about the silence of the drive back to the cabin that was worse than the silence of the long wait in Will's truck while the trick-or-treating wound up, but somehow it seemed closer to Kitty—thicker—without the company of a dozen other Churchill residents and their trucks spread out along the ridge overlooking the town. Or maybe it was just that there was no distraction to hide behind now.

Kitty turned to him as he drove. 'Listen, Will...'

'What happened to you after Nepal?' he interrupted before she could get her thoughts in a row. Offence being the best kind of defence and all. 'You were so soaked in passion last time we met. So in love with life.'

Yes, she had been—with life, with Nepal... And halfway to falling in love with Will. The first time she'd ever been totally and utterly at the mercy of her heart. She'd wandered around the alpine town, perpetually giddy, half from the oxygen-depleted air and half from just being around Will. It had been all she could do to channel that emotional energy into other things, more appropriate things.

As if that were going to help.

'Life happened to me,' she hedged, not about to expose herself. 'I grew up.'

'You were twenty-three. And you'd seen more of the world than most people your age.'

I was hardly an adult, either. If she were, wouldn't she have had more sense than to develop feelings for someone else's husband?

She shrugged and hoped it looked more careless than

she felt. 'I realised I couldn't waft about for ever, telling any story I liked, living on the hospitality of strangers in every corner of the world. I had to get serious about my career. Build some reserves. Build some prospects.'

'See, that's what I mean.' He threw a frown her way. 'The Kitty Callaghan I knew wouldn't have cared about reserves and prospects.'

Maybe she should have. Then she could have saved herself a tonne of grief.

'You told me you barely knew me,' she reminded him. Back when he'd booted her off his mountainside. 'How would you know what I was then? Or what I am now?'

He must have remembered that conversation, too, because he winced. Did he not like being reminded of the whole sordid *not* affair? Was it just another thing he'd filed away firmly in the past?

'I came home after Nepal, spruced up my résumé and started hunting for stable work.' She counted slowly to three as she eased a breath out. 'The end.'

'Neat coincidence—that your great new life started right after Nepal.'

Air backed up high in her throat and pressed on her heart. There was no way she could answer him with the truth on this one. How hard his comments had hit her. How shamed she'd felt as she'd fled Nepal. For falling for a married man in the first place, for failing to disguise it. For bumbling along like some infatuated teen until he'd had no choice but to send her away. He wasn't responsible for her actions, now or then. But she didn't want to give him that, either. She still had some pride, no matter how dented.

'I'm saying it was my doing. Not yours.'

But the doubt all over his face said otherwise.

She fidgeted with her seat-belt edges. 'Is that what this is about, Will? You're trying to decide how guilty you should feel?'

'I made you feel unwelcome. Like a freeloader.'

Yeah, he had; and a whole bunch of things besides. Some of them terrifyingly new.

Her head filled with the many sideways glances in Nepal as he had worked with his dogs. With the way she'd struggled to keep the feminine tinkle out of her laughter at his tales or the admiration out of her glance as he'd come back in tired and cranky from a long day of training. With the careful distance she'd tried to put between them whenever they had been alone.

With the many times she failed.

Was she doing a better job of hiding it five years on or was he already starting to get twitchy at the signs?

'I'm a big girl, Will. I make my own decisions. I thought it was time to get a bit more serious about my future.'

He dragged his eyes off the road and onto her, long enough, this time, that she began to tighten up inside. But his truck didn't waver. And neither did his gaze. 'I don't like thinking that I…damaged you.'

Her chest ratcheted in another notch. She was not about to give him that. 'I'm hardly broken, Will. I'm just older. As changed as you are.'

He frowned. 'You think I'm changed? How?'

She stared at him. 'You're…flat. Inside.'

She wanted to say 'dead' but it seemed too confronting for him to hear. And despite the hurt Will had caused her in the past, she wasn't interested in returning the favour. Not intentionally.

But how much could she say without saying too much?

'What you do for a living is amazing. In Nepal, I watched you working that mountain and was blown away by your courage and focus. Your natural intelligence. Your gift with the dogs. None of that has changed on the surface but there was something…deeper…underlying all of that and it's gone now. It's like your faith in the world has vanished. Like you're just going through the motions.

And I understand why that might be, but it used to light you up from the inside and make all those other aspects more pronounced. That's what's changed.'

His eyes slashed sideways, but the lurch of his Adam's apple took the sting out of the graze.

'You're strong for everyone all the time. I just wanted to be there for you now so that you could let that go for a few minutes. So I could carry all the weight for you. I wasn't quizzing you for the sake of it or to snoop. I'd like to think that I could put a friend's well-being above my professional curiosity.'

'We're friends, are we?' he gritted.

Thump, thump, thump... 'You tell me.'

He glowered at her in the shadows of the darkened cab and she thought he was going to let the silence answer for him. But then he spoke, to make it perfectly clear.

'I honestly don't think we can be, Kitty.'

Her guts flipped back on themselves and twisted into a knot that choked. 'Why not?'

He pulled to the side of the empty road and the inertia swayed her in her seat. The truck's headlights slashed out into the dark, dark forest ahead. He turned to her and gave her his full attention.

If she weren't so angry she'd have thought about how alone they were. How close...

'Because it hasn't gone away. That thing between us. If we're being honest.'

Shock stole her breath—and then shock pawned it in some dingy back-alley store never to be recovered—but somehow she managed to squeeze a few words out without a break in her voice.

'What *thing*?'

But far more notably: *Between* us?

He just stared at her, daring her to continue denying it. But she wasn't about to expose herself like that. Not to him. If he wasn't interested in being friends, fine, but she wasn't going to do his dirty work for him. She sat up straighter and met his eyes head-on. 'What thing, Will?'

Because he'd made it clear five years ago that *her* feelings were the reason she couldn't stay.

But the longer he sat there in silence, staring, the clearer it all became. And the clearer it became, the more heat burbled up around her until it just had to come spurting out of the only available opening.

'Are you serious?' she hissed like the pressure cooker she was.

'You're angry?'

'Five years, Will! You've let me think that throwing me off your mountain was all about me developing a thing for you. That it was my own fault.'

Five years!

He frowned. 'I never said it was just you—'

'You never said it wasn't!'

And then, a heartbeat behind that, a tiny voice whispered in her heart and did a joyous little backflip.

It wasn't?

'Why would I send you away if it was just *your* feelings at stake?' he defended weakly. 'I would have just distanced myself.'

No… No! He didn't get to make this her fault, too. 'You said you loved Marcella—'

'I did love her.'

'—and then you sent me away.'

Oh, wasn't this fun? Reliving it together. But it felt so much better doing it angry. There was no room for sorrow while she was this worked up.

He dropped his eyes. 'I know.'

'And at no time anywhere in there did you happen to mention that the attraction was mutual!'

Confusion twisted his features. 'I assumed it was obvious.'

'No,' she gritted. 'It was not obvious.'

Because if she had known, she would have left long before being asked.

He stared at her in the half-glassy way that told her he was replaying the whole miserable incident from her point of view. And that meant she was witnessing the exact moment he realised what she'd believed all this time. What he'd sent her off that mountain believing.

'Damn, Kitty—'

'I cannot believe you!'

'That was a hard conversation for me, too,' he defended. 'I didn't exactly rehearse it.'

'Five years, Will!'

He took a deep breath, studied his white knuckles on the steering wheel for a bit and then came back to her. 'Okay. I get it. I might not have been fully explicit—'

She choked on the umbrage.

'—but the fact remains that was why you couldn't stay. Because I loved my wife and we were having a tough time. I couldn't develop feelings for you, let alone trust them.'

Her outrage started to wane as empathy took hold. But she didn't let it go without a fight.

'Having a tough time, how?' Though what her heart was screaming was, *'What kind of feelings?'*

To buy himself some time, Will pushed the truck into gear and moved off slowly. It was the vehicular equivalent of nervously clearing his throat. Kitty sagged back into her seat, waited. She would wait another five years if it meant putting Nepal behind her once and for all.

It took him nearly that long to reply.

'What did Marcella tell you about her background?' he asked as he negotiated the turn-off to his cabin.

The change of tack threw her momentarily but she dragged her focus along on the tangent. 'I know she was from Louisiana. Big family. I know her family wanted her to teach but she wanted to paint. That's about it.'

'Did you know they didn't want us to marry?'

It was surreal, talking about this so dispassionately. As though she weren't still harbouring her feelings for Will—or a facsimile of them.

'No. I didn't.'

'They wanted Marcella to go to a theological college. Really, I think they would have been happiest if she'd just got on with the job of having a family. Like her sisters. They rode her pretty hard.'

'Shouldn't they have been excited about you two marrying, then?'

'Not when they discovered I was going to Nepal. But that only made me more attractive to Marcella. She redoubled her efforts, then.'

Her efforts?

Kitty blinked. 'You think she married you to get away from her family's influence?'

He glanced at her after he took the corner. 'I know she did.'

'The woman I met adored you.'

'I believe she wanted to. But mostly I think I was just a convenient ticket out of Louisiana to a life she could forge for herself. A way to be free and just paint.'

Deep sadness washed past his eyes. Her freedom wasn't that long-lived, in the end.

'Turns out Marcella didn't know herself as well as her family did, and I sure didn't. At first, she loved the light and the scenery and the excitement of the bohemian lifestyle, but it wasn't long before she stopped painting. Stopped going down into Pokhara city to explore. She struggled in Nepal, almost from the start. Found the culture confusing, the diet too different, the mountains oppressive.'

The majestic Annapurnas? She'd found them so inspiring, herself. So incredibly wild.

'About the only thing she related to was the faith; the Nepalese were about as gentle as she was. But I was just getting established and so my work called me away from home a lot, kept me busy. Took me from her when she needed me.'

The woman she'd met started to reframe in her mind. All that midnight roaming, all those fragile smiles. All the wine... Will was assuming responsibility for that. Or maybe he'd always assumed it.

'Deep down I knew why she married me. But I went ahead with it because I saw so much potential for the person she was going to blossom into away from her family. I thought one of us would be enough to start with.'

'It wasn't?'

He pulled into his drive and killed the engine, then sat staring out into the darkness around his property.

'Five years ago Marcella was at her lowest ebb. I'd retreated into my work and she was grasping at any displacement activity to distract her from the reality of the life she'd chosen.'

'And then I arrived,' Kitty realised.

'You saw her at her best,' he acknowledged. 'Having you there was like having one of her sisters there and she perked right up. She was infected by your light and sunshine and even, a little bit, by your love of the place. She saw Nepal differently through your eyes. But when you left she slid right back again.'

He turned in his seat. 'That's why I asked you to go, Kitty. Because it was the lowest moment in our marriage and because having you there reminding me of what was possible was just too dangerous.'

Dangerous. Not difficult, not hard.

Dangerous.

Something twisted around her lungs, slowly constricting.

'I should have found a way to tell you that I was sending you away because of my feelings, not yours. I'm sorry.'

Five years was still five years, but somehow she

couldn't find it in herself to be angry in the face of his sorrow. Still, the thumping in her chest threatened to swell up and block her airway.

'What feelings?'

Blue ice glanced up. 'Do you remember our conversations? Do you remember the laughter, Kitty? The connection?'

Half of her was frustrated that he was avoiding the question. The other half of her was still thrilling that they were having this discussion at all.

'Yes,' she breathed.

'Did you miss it, ever?'

Every day.

'Yes.'

He just nodded. As if to say 'me too'.

'That's why I think we can't be friends. Because that's there. Still there.'

If anything was going to stop her being Will's friend it was the memory of that last day. Turned out she wanted to be that friend more than she feared it.

'Guess I'm just more of an optimist,' she said, simply.

The mood in the truck thawed. It wasn't charged, it was just…clear. He tipped his bent head up to her.

'How much of that Zurich story do you still have to cut?' he asked.

She sank back into the passenger seat as if it were a sofa. 'All of it. Someone interrupted my audio recording.'

How could a smile change so essentially from one moment to the next? Somehow, this one was full of olive branch and acceptance. 'Can you do a bunch of editing tonight, make some headway?'

'Probably.' Definitely. She was going to need a good clear space from Will to process everything he'd just said. 'Why?'

'Because I'm doing a favour for someone tomorrow morning, bussing a bunch of science teachers out to the research centre. Will probably take most of the morning but I can show you the conservation zone while we're out there. Maybe see some wild bears doing their thing, more to your satisfaction.'

She grinned at him from her comfortable nook in the darkness. 'If their *thing* isn't tap dancing, I'm going to be very disappointed.'

'Up to you. You're welcome to tag along. Properly welcome,' he added when she lifted a questioning brow.

'If I get a call from the airport...?'

The ticking clock intruded as surely as if she'd wound down her window; it sucked all the warmth from inside the vehicle. Had they both forgotten that the moment her flight came up she was off, back to her busy, busy life far from here?

'Leave it in the hands of fate,' he murmured, levering his door handle. 'I leave here at seven-thirty. With or without you.'

CHAPTER SEVEN

'GOOD NEWS!' THE WOMAN from the airline said down the phone early the following morning when Kitty called to check on the status of her repatriation. 'Your airline has made the necessary arrangements with the local airline to start getting you all home.'

The emotion Kitty felt at that news wasn't quite the rush of relief she expected. Instead it was a slow, seeping disappointment. But she wasn't entirely sure what she was so disenchanted about. Missing out on some sightseeing?

Or missing out on something more?

'But...we have quite a backlog of passengers to clear,' the woman went on. 'I don't have you on either of today's flights, I'm sorry. Tomorrow perhaps.'

Perhaps? 'Are you serious?'

'It's bear season, ma'am, and we have one hundred and sixty people to re-seat on flights that are already full with paying customers. We're re-seating by original seat number.'

Which meant the passengers in First and Business Class would be shipped out first and then they'd start chewing their way through good old cattle class. Kitty's sense of social justice reared up and bellowed over the disappointment of just moments before.

'I *am* a paying customer,' she reminded the airport official, even though she was handing her a legitimate opportunity to stay longer in Churchill. Which meant staying longer with Will.

'We're doing our best, ma'am.'

If she said *ma'am* one more time... She was twenty-eight, not seventy-eight.

'Okay,' Kitty sighed into the phone. 'Just keep me informed. Thank you.'

She lowered the handset on Will's portable phone then went hunting for its charging station just for something to do. To walk off a little of the irritation. Of course they had to have a system; it would be chaos if they were just randomly issuing whatever seats they had available. And of course they had to get the people who'd paid a year's wage for their seats out first even if they weren't the kind of people who were even on wages.

Unlike her.

Her income was directly linked to her ability to file stories. Her programme director had tersely accepted that her being stranded was outside her control. He'd ordered Kitty to stream her raw vision to their Shanghai headquarters so someone else could cut it. But she'd be damned if she'd let someone else cut her story. Or submit it. Or steal it.

Especially if that someone was Mei.

Features on CNTV's Sunday morning business programme were way too hard to secure.

So she would quietly ignore her director's request as long as she could and cut the story herself, here, then stream the finished piece to Shanghai. Less data cost for Will. More control for her.

But all of that could wait. She had places to be and bears to see…

'Looks like you've got company,' she called down the hall as she gathered up her things.

There was a longish pause before Will answered and she briefly wondered if he'd changed his mind. Just because things between them had thawed a little last night…

Thawed a lot. Somewhere in her five-year history with Will she had assigned him Superman status—maybe because of what he did for a living, maybe because of some intrinsically capable quality of his own—but every Superman had a mortal side and, last night, Will had shown her his Clark Kent.

For a moment.

'All right. Bring your camera,' he called.

She glanced at her open suitcase where she had a digital SLR, a pocket camera, a high-def video camera. And of course her phone. 'Which one?' she yelled.

In the end, she brought all of them, causing Will to roll his eyes as she bundled towards his truck.

'Lucky we're not hiking,' he muttered.

She glanced at him as he moved around to the other side of the vehicle. The scrappy beard was gone. 'Did you shave?'

'Nope.'

That's what you get for asking a dumb question.

They stopped in at the weir to do the morning check and raise the flag, after which it took just fifteen minutes to get into town and pick up the bus and keys from Will's associate, Travis.

'My eldest is getting his wisdom teeth yanked, today,' Travis explained. 'Otherwise I'd be doing this run myself. I'll go back for the group this afternoon.'

She glanced at Will. 'We're leaving tourists alone out in the tundra?'

Pfff. Two days in town and she was declassifying herself as a tourist?

'Sure,' Will said. 'They wanted a true northern experience.'

He went about loading her gear onto the front seat of the bus, right behind the driver's seat. The first thing she saw as she climbed up into the bus behind him was the shotgun subtly tucked in next to it.

'Really?' she asked, distracted by the firearm.

He stopped and turned. 'No, Kit. Not really. They're teachers, not survivalists. We're dropping them at the remote research centre where they have a full, fully supervised day programme waiting for them. On the way back you and I will detour and see if we can spot any bears.'

Heat rushed up her neck.

For a woman so close to thirty, she sure spent a lot of time flushing around Will.

'Having a bus licence one of your many talents?' she asked, to move the focus off her new super power—gullibility.

He paused before answering and she wondered if he was thinking about the best answer. Or the safest. 'It's not far. And these are quiet roads.'

She caught herself just as she was lowering herself into the seat closest to the doors. 'You're unlicensed for large vehicles. Are you kidding?'

'There's a good chance Trav is probably unlicensed and he owns the bus.' He grinned. 'Stuff like that is a bit more…negotiable up here. If you *can* drive a bus safely then you can drive a bus in Churchill.'

Turned out Will *could* drive a bus. He navigated the luxury people mover easily out of town and pulled up at the front of the airport where thirty science types climbed on fresh off their just-landed flight. They came from all over Canada, up to study different aspects of the subarctic biome, and this was just the first of several visits they were planning on making out to the research centre. They'd lost one day of their research trip to the same ice rain holding her hostage but they'd lost none of their enthusiasm. Within minutes, the bus filled with excited science-speak. And *passion*. So much of it. The bus was awash with people who loved what they did for a living and knew they were making a difference. Kitty sat back and just soaked it all in, glancing now and again at Will, who was taking the roads very seriously.

I remember this.

This was her: fresh out of uni with a double major in Journalism and Media when she'd thought she was going to solve the problems of the world—or at least expose them to great fanfare and critical acclaim. Lord, that had been a lifetime ago. Now she worked for a cashed-up corporate network in China and produced stories about rich people for even richer people.

And she couldn't remember the last time she'd got an excited flush going to work. Even flying somewhere new had grown tiresome.

The roads might have been as quiet as Will had promised, but it was still a forty-minute drive out to the research centre, picking their way through the tundra, all those teacher noses pressed to the glass to get their first glimpse of the natural habitat. Up close, tundra wasn't flat at all; it was pocked with lakes and swamps, with causeways of passable sedges only where the permafrost below had pushed the ground up into ridges. And it wasn't solid, either; a sparsely treed, waterlogged moor littered with enormous boulders dumped there by a prehistoric glacier and with a thin crunch of seasonal ice starting to form.

Behind her, the group's leader chatted to the others about 'isostatic rebound' and 'Goldilocks Zones' and they all nodded and took notes and generally grew more and more fascinated as they whizzed by all that view.

'The flora up here only has between fifty and one hundred frost-free days to grow,' the man said, 'which of course informs the diversity.'

Of course it did...

Kitty caught Will's eyebrow lift in the rear-view mirror. 'Learning stuff?'

She faked taking notes onto her hand, and muttered under her breath. 'Informing…the…diversity…'

He chuckled and went back to getting his passengers safely to the research centre. It was a massive building designed to sit naturally in the landscape while also managing to stand out architecturally. She'd expected it to be out in the middle of nowhere—and it was—but it wasn't out there alone. It was sited on an old, ramshackle air-force base.

'Officially, the Canadian military were studying the aurora out here during the fifties,' he told her as the thirty passengers all filed off, offering him their cheery thanks. 'With rockets.'

Officially? 'You don't think so?'

'Check it out on a globe and not a flat map. Straight over the top of the planet, it's a very short distance to Russia as the crow flies.'

Or as the missile does. Her journalist's curiosity was immediately piqued. The image of two superpowers with stockpiles of missiles all pointed at each other—*just in case*.

'There we go.' Will grinned. 'That's what I've been waiting for.'

She brought her focus back to him. 'What?'

His fingers brushed the creases between her brows and her skin leapt at the gentle touch. Was that the first time that he'd ever touched her intentionally? Almost intimately?

Her heartbeat certainly thought so.

'That spark of imagination,' he said. 'The intrigue. I've missed that.'

'You don't think the Zurich story sparks my imagination?'

The look he gave her said *no*. Clearly. 'You don't look like that when you talk about it.'

'CNTV's viewers are hardly going to be excited by a seventy-year-old, speculative *what if*,' she said.

'I don't much care what excites them. I'm more interested in what excites you.'

He didn't mean that. Not the way her deviant mind suddenly went. But the very idea that Will Margrave would give any thought at all to her excitement levels...

Her throat tightened right up.

'Didn't you promise me bears?' she squeezed, sinking back into her seat to put some much-needed distance between them. And to dislodge the delicious tension suddenly stretching between them.

They left the research centre and its decaying military neighbour and headed back towards the shore. The journey was more tranquil without the energetic hubbub of thirty science teachers but it was also less educative. Kitty made herself happy just soaking up the view out of the bus's massive front windows. At least one of those views had Will in it, seated at the wheel of this big vehicle, shotgun by his thigh. Commanding. Masculine. Utterly cowboy-esque. The sort of view she never would have let herself enjoy in the past but now would hold close to her heart for ever.

You're checking out the bus driver, a tiny voice admonished and she had to turn her chuckle away to the passing landscape.

They bumped back on asphalt then travelled parallel with the vast Hudson Bay coast until Will called back to her. 'The conservation zone is right ahead, but we're not licensed to go in there, so we're going to lurk on its fringes.'

'Huh... So there's some licences you *do* care about,' she replied. 'Good to know.'

He gave her a look that was almost as eloquent as flipping her the bird. But when he spoke all he said was, 'You might want to lower a few windows for your photos.'

Open window. Wild animals... 'Is that safe?'

Blue eyes flicked to her in the mirror. Saving people was his life's work; he wasn't about to risk someone carelessly. Even her.

Right.

'Only the small top ones drop. You'll have plenty of time to put them up again. There's not going to be a bear stampede when we get there.'

Minutes later, Will pulled the bus to a halt and checked

the full perimeter before turning back to her. 'Want to open that gate for me?'

She followed his gaze out of the front window to the massive swing gate with the faded 'Private Property' sign dangling on it. Then she brought them back to him. 'You're kidding, right?'

He smiled. 'Then close it right up after I've driven through.'

She thought about protesting that it wasn't his land, or that she'd be eaten by a bear, or that he should get his bus licence before being authorised to order someone to get off one amidst wild animals, but then it occurred to her that this was a test.

Will was testing her. And, in Will, a test was almost as good as flirting. It was how he let you know he was there.

And she never failed tests. Ever.

On principle.

'Fine.'

She slung her legs free of the plush seat and descended the three front steps down onto terra firma when Will opened the folding doors. She wanted to be cool; she wanted to just leap off, open the gate and close it again afterwards without so much as a glance around her. But this was bear country and, while she absolutely trusted Will, she didn't trust the bears. So she couldn't help glancing around her anxiously as she hurried to pull the gate wide and then close it again when he was through.

'Reminds you you're alive, doesn't it?' He laughed as she scampered back on, puffing.

She sagged back into her seat as the pneumatic doors closed them safely in. But, yeah, it really did. Her pulse was up, her blood was flowing and she had just enough adrenaline still whipping through it to heighten her senses. Already the place where the tundra met the deep grey waters of the bay was looking brighter and more magical.

'You're going to tell me there's no bears for miles, aren't you?'

His laugh burst through the empty bus. 'Not *miles*...'

He trundled the bus about that far at a reasonable pace before he slowed and started scanning the horizon. Then he just quietly positioned the bus and killed the engine. Kitty couldn't help craning her neck. Then standing. Then walking the full length of the empty bus, scanning three hundred and sixty degrees all around them. The snow-dusted tundra stretched all the way to the horizon on two sides, and it fell away to Hudson Bay in front. This must have been the limit of that terra-forming glacier because it seemed to have bulldozed a mountain of worn, round boulders here. Most as big as the bus that was keeping them safe. Nothing more than cake sprinkles to the power of glacial ice.

'To your right,' Will said quietly.

No, she'd just looked right, but she followed his finger and sure enough...

Just like the one at the weir, this polar bear was doing a whole lot of nothing. Vast amounts of nothing, in fact. It was stretched out on a couple of flat, low rocks that weren't yet completely buried in snow, sun-baking. Except that there was no sun visible through the clouds. And no heat to bake in. Was ice-baking a thing? Kitty rushed to get her cameras out, but the bear didn't move an inch, making her scrambling unnecessary.

'I was looking for something yellower,' she justified as she lined up her shot. This bear looked as white as the snow around it.

'Transparent hair follicles,' Will said as she fiddled with her exposure settings. 'We just see it as white. It's still the same colour.'

She turned and stared at him while his attention was fully on the bear.

'Bear, Kitty,' he said softly, without taking his eyes off the horizon.

Right...

Her longest lenses got her nice and close. She fired off dozens of urgent shots before realising the bear truly was not moving. Nor planning to, it seemed. Blinking, yes, but not about to come barrelling at them like something from the natural history films she'd studied at university.

'And over in the willow on your left,' Will murmured. Not because the bear might hear him but just because it was the kind of moment that demanded whispering.

The second bear stretched up from its sleeping place in the willow sticks and stuck its nose in the air to breathe them in. They must have smelled vaguely interesting because it hauled itself out and onto all fours before wandering in their general direction. Without the stretch, she never would have seen it in there. A person could walk right past and not know it was there.

The thought was sobering.

The willow bear lumbered ever closer as her camera whizzed, but at the last minute it changed trajectory and lazily wandered over to the rock bear and nudged it with its snout before sitting down hard on its big bottom, sending up a puff of snow.

Kitty wondered if there was smoke coming from her camera at the rate she was taking pictures.

'That's a play entreaty,' Will said from somewhere behind her. She hadn't noticed him move. 'Get ready...'

Rock bear seemed entirely uninterested in any gestures from its friend, turning away to peer out to sea. But—just as Kitty lowered her camera—it reared up into sitting position and then straight up onto its back feet with an openmouthed roar. On four legs, it had to be five feet tall; on two legs, it was a giant. Heart hammering, Kitty thrust her still camera back to Will, who had moved in behind her, and she scrabbled for her video as the bears began to tussle and lunge at each other, twisting and surging in combat and sending snow dust flying. Through the lens of her video camera, their massive canine teeth glinted against the northern sun as they showed them off for each other. But the bears weren't in any hurry and they weren't terribly serious; having woken from their respective naps, they were more interested in playing…and playing…and playing.

'How long could this go for?' Kitty finally asked Will as the bears continued their mock battle, this time back on all fours, advancing and retreating like an ursine tango.

'Until they get tired.'

'Shouldn't they be conserving their energy?'

The loose skin under their thick coats swung as they scrapped with each other. Kitty tried to imagine what they would be like all padded out with a tonne of seal fat.

'I think they know the ice isn't far away, so perfecting their fighting skills is more important than preserving the last remnants of body fat they have left. They have to get ready.'

She turned to look back at him. 'For what?'

'The real deal. The bears out on the tundra are mostly males; they're friendly now but when the ice comes they'll have to fight for feeding grounds and for access to females. The battles won't be so gentle then.'

The thought of those beautiful coats streaked with blood…

'I'm trying to imagine them battling over a female…'

'It's worth it,' he said from behind her. 'For the right woman.'

Her chest squeezed until she reminded it that he was talking about Marcella. His loyalty heartened and hurt to the same degree. That she would never know that kind of love…

Kitty let her camera sag. But the spectacle was too great as the willow bear began to chase the rock bear.

'This will look so good in slow motion,' she mumbled to herself, zooming in to capture more of the run.

With no warning, her lens was blocked by a massive pink palm as Will stretched his hand around her from behind and lowered the camera until all she was filming was the bus floor.

'You're missing all the action,' he admonished, close to her ear.

She twisted her camera free of his hand, but didn't move out from within the warm circle of his body. His breath against her ear caused an avalanche of tingles.

'I am now...' she muttered, irritated at the instant response from her undisciplined flesh.

But he wasn't going to be deterred. 'Just watch, Kit. Record it in your memory instead. This could be the only time you see it.'

Will might as well have asked her to step off the bus and go out to join the game of bear chase; if he did it in that breathy voice, that close to her ear, she would say yes to just about anything. She lowered her camera to the upholstered bus seat and tucked it safely into the crease. Then she lifted her gaze and just watched, half mesmerised by the nature show, half mesmerised by the heat-soak of Will's body so close to hers.

As rapidly as it started, the chase was off, and the willow bear plonked down exactly where it stopped and turned to consider the world. Instantly deep in bear thoughts. The massive rock bear slowed its jog first to a lope and then to a gentle stroll. But its blood—and its curiosity—were up now and it turned its massive head in their direction. Kitty moved to close her window.

'Look at the size of him, Kit...'

He was right. That bear wasn't getting through that small top window any time soon.

She leaned forward as the bear approached the side of the bus and disappeared below the view of the windows. Pressed against the glass, she could just see him sniffing around the bus's wheels.

'He's nibbling the tyre!'

Will stretched over the top of her to monitor the bear, too. 'A nibble's fine as long as he doesn't sink those canines in.'

The thought of having to be rescued from the tundra in an incapacitated bus was almost as unappealing as trying to change its tyre with two bears passing her the tools.

Rock bear wandered the length of the bus, peering up at the windows curiously. Kitty was tempted to follow it along the aisle, but her view pressed against the window was probably better anyway. At the rear of the bus, the bear pressed back up onto two feet and wobbled there, precariously, peering in through the tinted windows of the bus.

'Oh, Will…!'

Immediately after she made the sound, it turned and pinned her with its gaze. It plonked back to Earth and strolled directly to her row in the bus where it paused—for a bear heartbeat—before pushing once again to its back legs and ducking its head to peer through her open window. It found her eyes and locked onto them hard with its small dark ones.

All breath caught in her throat instinctively at the massive size and proximity of the hungry predator.

Vaguely she was aware of Will's hands closing around her shoulders and slowly easing her back from the window as the bear twisted its big head right in through the opening.

'Easy, now…' Will crooned in that sure, velvet tone he had. Whether his words were intended for the bear or for her, it didn't matter. They helped to ease her racing heart, just the same.

The bear stretched its curious head forwards, sniffing the air and gazing around the bus's interior. Up this close it was far more teddy-like than a dangerous animal had a right to be, its small fortune-cookie ears, broad brow and wide-set eyes set in damp, golden fur. By far its most dominant feature was the enormous wet black nose, which it pressed as far forward as its thick neck would allow through the narrow window.

Close enough to touch.

The puff of its hot, stale breath made the loose hairs around her face dance.

It seemed incongruous that such a massive animal should make such a thin, sharp whine, and it took a moment for Kitty to realise that it was coming from deep in her own throat.

'Shh...'

Will eased her back into his body and crossed strong arms across her chest—as if that would keep her safe against the bear should it have a brain snap and surge right through the glass. But it didn't, of course it didn't. One look at the bear and Kitty could tell it was simply curious about this new arrival in its otherwise empty day. Not to say that it wouldn't have shown any interest had they happened to have pockets full of bacon, but this bear wasn't interested in eating either of them. It just wanted to look.

As she had the thought, the bear drew his big head back out of the upper window and stretched up more fully to peer over the roof of the bus, pressing its dinner-plate paws against the glass for balance. Even standing down on the ground, his shoulders were higher than Kitty's standing up high in the bus. Extended like this, he truly dwarfed them.

And then he was gone. Back to the ground, back to his friend from the willow. Back to his ice-baking.

Kitty sagged into Will, struggling to catch breath that had grown choppy and to master the thick clog of tears that seemed to be frozen—just as she was—deep in her chest somewhere.

'What do you think of our savage predators now?' he murmured against her ear.

Her answer was more croak than speech. Will leaned past her, kneeling amongst her camera gear on the seat to slide the small window back up into locked position, and then returned both his feet to the ground, turning her in the circle of his arms.

'Wow,' she croaked, peering up at him wide-eyed.

'Glad you came?'

Glad was way too tame for the emotions she was feeling. Somewhere deep down she wished she were being much cooler in this moment—or at least more loquacious—but single syllables seemed to be her limit while her body was still reacting instinctually to the presence of such an arch predator.

Slowly—so slowly—she became aware of things around her again. The growing warmth of the bus's air now that the window was closed. The shotgun now propped within easy reach on the seat next to them. The closeness of Will's body against hers.

She fluttered her fingers up to touch her bear-blown hair.

'So close...'

Okay, two syllables were better than one. She was getting there.

Will's fingers joined hers to help put her hair to rights. Each one started a riot in her flesh where they brushed. 'He just wanted to say hi.'

Will's smile radiated the heat she needed to unfreeze her speech cortex. She peered up at him as if it were the first time she'd seen him. And—totally of their own accord—the fingers of her right hand reached up to lie against his cheek.

'You did shave.'

Three words. Excellent progress.

His laugh took him a pace away from her and, once achieved, he seemed to remember the sense of that. Which only served to highlight how eager she was for him not to do it. He rubbed her upper arms firmly and restored some sense with the blood flow.

'I feel like I'm drunk,' she wobbled.

'It's the adrenaline,' he said. 'Here, get some of this into you.'

He produced a thermos of coffee from somewhere and poured her a liberal dose into the cupped lid. Then she sagged down amongst her camera gear and sipped it while watching the two bears continue to interact out on the tundra. After an eternity—and a second coffee—the two parted ways and one wandered back to its willow bed.

'I had them all wrong,' she breathed, warmer now inside and out.

'They're dangerous because of their size and because they're unused to being around people, but they're not more of a killer than the foxes they share the tundra with. Or the seals they eat.'

'His paws on the window. Like dinner plates.'

'They're big animals.' She knew when she was being humoured but, right now, humouring was what she needed. In the absence of stroking.

'I just wanted to touch it…' She frowned, remembering.

Will laughed. 'I know. I was there. That wouldn't have been a good idea.'

The image started to come back to her and she chuckled. 'It was like I was hypnotised.'

'You resisted, that's what counts.'

'You had to restrain me,' she pointed out.

That seemed to remind them both of how closely they'd stood, Will's arms crossed across her soft body, pulling her back into his hard one.

She studied the empty cup in her hands, then brought her face back up. 'Thank you, Will. Truly. I will never forget this day.'

He relieved her of the empty thermos lid, his brush lingering on her fingers as he did. 'You're welcome. Maybe we'll get another chance to see them.'

We. Not you.

Old habits—the desire to protect herself—made her shrug. 'If not for the fact that the airline started flying people out today.'

Which meant she could be leaving as soon as tomorrow.

Confusion chased the disappointment across his strong jaw just as the two bears had lumbered across the whitened tundra. And he took a step back. 'Well, then, you'll always have your first bear.'

He returned the shotgun to its place by the driver's seat and Kitty took her cue. It took only moments to return all but one camera to her equipment bag.

'So whose land are we trespassing on?' she asked brightly, to do her bit in putting things back on a safer footing.

He took his time fitting the thermos back into its holder. 'Relax, it's mine.'

She turned and stared. 'What?'

'Marcella's life insurance,' he began, awkwardly. 'It was enough to buy this land. In her name.'

Kitty peered back out at the stunning, bear-littered tundra.

'It was a way to preserve it for the wildlife for ever. Against any future development. The great-great-great-grandcubs of those bears will still be resting there in a hundred years, thanks to her.'

Tears rushed in and made blinking them back impossible. So she swiped at them instead.

'Does that upset you?' he asked.

She tried to reply and found that she could not. Marcella was making a difference even from beyond the grave. That simple truth hurt her in ways that Will could not possibly imagine. She'd never felt more inadequate than at this moment. Because what kind of a difference was she making…?

'I think it's beautiful,' Kitty finally squeezed out, heart

aching. 'The perfect thing. She would have loved paint-ing this.'

'Yeah,' he agreed, his own voice not quite steady.

He keyed the bus up to rumbling, giving the distant rock bear cause to lift his big head and see them off, and effectively ending the conversation. Kitty sank back into her seat and stared out of the window at Marcella's land.

So beautiful and fragile... As she had been.

As if bears weren't exciting enough for one day, she saw through the window something else that she hadn't yet seen in Churchill. It was only a glimpse, but it was there.

'Blue sky!' she called up to Will.

He followed her glance and willingly grabbed the change in conversation. 'Yep. The ceiling is officially lift-ing. If your luck holds you might even get a hint of aurora before you leave.'

She knew the eyes she turned up to him would be as big as bear paws. It would be hard to top today's beauti-ful experience but the Northern Lights—proper lights, in the actual north—would come close.

Bears. The aurora borealis.

And an opportunity to hang out with a thawing Will Margrave...

As disasters went, this unexpected layover in Churchill was working out better than she'd imagined.

CHAPTER EIGHT

CNTV's SHANGHAI OFFICE picked up after three rings and she wondered which of three senior producers was doing the graveyard shift. A woman barked into the receiver, long distance.

Kitty's eyelids squeezed closed. 'Evening, Mei-Xiu...' Her Wicked Step-Colleague.

'Kitty? Where the hell is your story?' her producer said in clipped English.

Hello, Kitty, how are you? I heard you had an emergency landing in the sub-arctic. Hope you're okay...

'Did you get the voiceover track I filed?' Kitty cut in. 'And the script?'

'Wen-Hau was looking at it today,' Mei snipped. 'But it's not much to work with. I need the raw vision.'

Yeah she did—if Mei wanted to file the story herself.

'I was up all night cutting it,' Kitty stressed, down the line. And not sending the vision until it was fully cut was the only way she would keep control of the story. 'I'll get it to you tomorrow.'

'Oh, sure,' Mei-Xiu quipped and Kitty had no trouble imagining her perfectly made-up face turning ugly. 'Tomorrow, the next day. What's the rush? It's just the Sunday feature.'

'I'm still in Churchill,' Kitty said, extra loud to compensate for the long distance. 'I'm wait-listed but—'

Mei's reply could have stripped paint. She had quite the grasp of English colloquialisms when she wanted to. 'Do you know how many correspondents would kill for that feature spot?'

Yes. Intimately. She'd been them for so long.

'Tomorrow,' she promised, though her heart wasn't in it.

Mei scowled. It saturated her voice. 'Arctic tomorrow or Chinese tomorrow?'

Right… Because it was already tomorrow in Shanghai. That invisible clock that constantly ticked in Kitty's ears kicked up a notch. Maybe she should call the airport back… But no, she could edit this story much better from here than she could sitting in a crowded airport with insufficient Wi-Fi to go around.

'I'm on it, Mei. Trust me.'

Yeah. That wasn't going to happen. Nobody trusted anyone else in their game. Right now she was threatening to make Mei-Xiu look bad to the programme director and Mei wasn't going to take that sitting down. She'd climbed about as high as she was ever going to and younger, shinier performers were coming up under her all the time. Mei was desperate enough to bin any story she did send and just say she never received it.

'You file by Thursday or I file something for you.'

The phone went dead.

Goodbye to you, too…

Kitty flopped back onto her bed, exhausted already, and stared sideways out of the massive picture window. Out back, the dark trees were dusted with snow that hadn't quite managed to thaw out from overnight. So pretty… It was tempting just to lose herself in that picturesque vista rather than apply herself to a story she was rapidly losing heart for.

She rolled over and reached for her laptop, which had the first five and a half minutes of her eight-minute feature already cut from last night's editing session. Will had left her to it on getting back from the bus trip—he'd been a little bit too relieved, she'd thought—and busied himself elsewhere. He'd even brought her the thermos so she didn't have to emerge to refresh her coffee.

Kind, if not for her sneaking suspicion that he wanted to force some personal space.

Five years hadn't done anything to diminish the energy between them yesterday morning. The way his voice caressed the hairs on the back of her neck. The way the heat of his skin reached out across all this cold and brushed against her. The way her head rushed simply from standing near him—in a way that had nothing to do with all the extra oxygen in the air. It was as thrilling as it was distracting. But none of it meant that Will was necessarily interested in starting up where they'd never left off. Judging by the way he'd arranged things so she barely needed to poke her head out of the room all day, then conveniently had business last night, maybe he was already in damage-control mode. So the best she could hope for from this unexpected stranding on the sub-arctic isle of Margrave was that they might end up slightly better friends than they'd managed before.

Still, when you had fewer actual friends than you could count on the fingers on one hand, that was no small achievement.

Her laptop beeped at her as it prepared to drop into power-saver mode and she snapped back to the present and refocused on her day's edit and the pull shot from one of Zurich's medieval church spires to the ultra-modern Prime Tower. It might not fill her with the kind of excitement that tussling bears did—not even remotely—but, right now, her relationship with her career was the only one she should be focusing on.

Because success wasn't going to make itself.

Will stood over Kitty as she slept, sprawled out across her bed, a half-eaten apple still in her hand.

'Kitty?' Nothing. She didn't even twitch.

Wow, she really slept like the dead. Just how late had she worked? He swapped his torch to his left hand and placed the right gently on her shoulder, feeling like an intruder all the while.

'Kitty? Come on, wake up.'

He wanted to feel closer to her, the kind of close that meant it was okay to slide his hand across her shoulder and brush her cheek to wake her more gently. But whatever mood had simmered between them on the bus had evaporated on the journey back—back to reality where setting up camp right inside Kitty's personal space wasn't an option without duelling bears to distract her—and the simple stew lunch that had followed had become a much stiffer affair than he would have liked. On his side as well as hers. He'd immediately started feeling self-conscious about how he'd taken advantage of her awe and wonder to get his paws all over her. Worse than the bear prints on the bus window.

Right after lunch she'd fled into her room and thrown herself into cutting her story and so he'd disappeared outside to make himself busy. Real busy.

For hours.

He shook her again. 'Kitty, time to get up.'

His eyes did what his fingers couldn't—traced across her face, her lips, that soft, dark hair that fell slightly across both. He remembered that day in Nepal when she'd run with his dogs, almost in slow motion, back and forth, her hair in her eyes. Hypnotic. He'd ached to do that, then.

'Time to get up, lazy bones.'

He spoke more loudly and gave her a firmer shove. That got her attention somewhere in dreamland. She frowned, then licked those red-flushed lips, and blinked her confusion back at him. The moments before she remembered who and where she was were like an unexpected boot to the ribs.

'Morning,' he squeezed out.

She pushed herself roughly upright with one hand and her hair away from her face with the other. 'God, is it?'

'Not literally. It's just gone four p.m.,' he added when her confusion didn't let up any. It was adorable. 'You fell asleep somewhere between lunch and now.'

Her eyes dropped to her laptop, still sitting open but sleeping as deeply as she just had been. 'Oh, no...'

'You'll get there,' he reassured, though he had no idea if that was true. 'What's your deadline?'

She blinked at him, still drowsy. 'You don't want to know...'

He was holding onto a bit of 'don't want to know' information himself... 'And if you don't get it in on time?'

'Then someone else will file my story,' she murmured, sleepily.

'And that's bad?'

'I've worked on getting that feature all year.'

'But the story still airs, right? It will just be cut by someone else.'

When exactly did a stare officially become a glare? Kitty certainly knew how to hover on the fence line.

She pulled herself up into a sitting position. 'It's my story. I wanted to edit it. The rough cut as a minimum.'

'Why? You've been paid for the trip, your expenses are covered, you've scripted it and sent them the voiceover. Does it really matter who pushes the buttons?'

'The same way it *doesn't really matter* who takes the dogs you trained and uses them to track.' She sighed, stretching and cricking her long neck. 'Editing is not a rough science. It's all about tone.'

'I didn't realise this was going to be an art piece. I thought it was a business story about a burgeoning textile industry.'

Okay, now it was officially a glare.

'It's still my story. With my name on it.' The two forks formed between her brows again. 'At least I hope so. I want it to be right.'

Her wits must have finally coalesced because she stared

at the thing in his hand and finally asked the million-dollar question. 'Why are you carrying a torch?'

'Don't freak out...' As if that was going to make it any better.

She pushed to full alert. And full height. 'Tell me...'

'The power's out.'

Her skin colour lost two shades at that news. 'What? How long for?'

'No idea. It's not us. Must be at the Churchill station. Could be a couple of hours more.'

'More?' Her cry was almost a squeak. 'How long has it been out?'

'About as long as you have.' In other words, half the day.

Her panicked gaze turned to her laptop but her frantic taps on the keys didn't bring it back to life. 'It's been running on battery all this time! You have to fix this!' she cried.

'As much as I would love to gallop in all Prince Charming right now, there's really nothing I can do. Except lend you my fully charged laptop.'

Not his first preference—he would rather see her relax a little—but the panic on her face apparently brought out the chivalrous best in him.

That idea almost reassured her, except that then her face folded again. 'No, I was three-quarters through the edit. I'd have to start over...'

Then she brightened again. 'Oh! But I was backing up on the cloud. Yay!'

He scrunched up his face, hating to burst that happy little bubble again.

'No power...' he reminded her.

'So?'

'So no Internet.'

Bubble officially burst.

'Oh, God.'

'It will probably be back on later tonight,' he said calmly, refusing to indulge her panic. 'Nothing you can do. Except get up.'

He leaned down and took both her hands and hauled her over the bed edge and onto her feet.

'What am I getting up for?' she grumbled.

'A road trip,' he volunteered. Something that wasn't at all affected by a power outage.

'Didn't we do that yesterday?' the grizzling continued.

'Not like this. Dress warm.'

He backed out of her room to the sound of her snort. 'Is there any other way to dress up here?'

'Dress *extra* warm,' he modified. 'You're going to need it.'

CHAPTER NINE

WILL WASN'T JOKING about the cold.

Kitty felt somewhere between an invalid and a princess as Will packed in layers of furs and blankets around her where she sat, awkwardly, at the front of his sled. Clearly the space was designed for something other than a human but he'd gone to the trouble of layering a few cushions down to make her more comfortable. Over in the yard his team were going berserk, barking and vocalising like mad. Once she was all tucked in, he disappeared for a moment and returned in moments, practically being towed by two of his harnessed dogs. He wrangled them over to the sled and they both turned and assumed the position. They clearly welcomed what came next.

'Bruiser and... Ernie?' she guessed, calling over their excited yips.

'The two biggest.' He nodded, wrestling the pair until he had them more or less tethered. 'You need strong dogs closest to the sled to counter its slide and take most of its weight.'

Bruiser sent a surly glare her way as he was tethered and Ernie gave her a simultaneous tail-wag and over-the-shoulder tongue-loll.

'They seem like an unlikely pair,' she commented. 'A goof and a grump.'

Will grunted. 'They're all business when the harnesses are on. Work well together.'

He was gone only moments before returning with two more dogs.

'Bose and Jango go on point,' he said as he fixed them immediately in front of the wheel pair. 'Right behind the leader. Their job is to ease the rest of the team neatly around corners.'

Kitty noted the absence of dogs between the front and back pairs. 'What "rest"?'

'Starsky and Tanner would usually run between everyone else. They and the point pair do the least physical pulling and have the least mental work to do.'

'So…more than half your team is freeloading?' She tucked her furs in more firmly and tried not to look like the biggest freeloader of them all.

He grinned. 'In a real emergency, I need the choice of four fairly fresh search dogs when we get to our destination.'

He disappeared again and returned with Tanner trotting alongside quietly. Dexter stalked confidently on his right.

'A good lead dog is born, not trained,' he said, clipping Dexter's harness in three places to the laid-out rigging and then clipping the point pair to that. 'He has to love to be in charge naturally, to think, to stay focused. And he has to want to succeed, to keep the rest of the team moving by straining on.'

Dexter was earnest and smart. She would happily follow him into the wilderness, because he seemed like the kind of dog who would bring her out again. In fact, she had!

'Do I sense a little gender bias?'

'Nope. Females make great leads, because they aren't as easily distracted as the males.'

Right now, she was pretty darned distracted by the sight of a male bent right over connecting Dexter to his rig.

'He looks very serious about running,' she said, shifting her focus from Will's rear to Dexter's.

The dog leaned into his master's rough affection. 'It's what he lives for.'

Tanner hung close to Will's ankle but he made no move to tether the gentle dog up after he approached the sled.

'Does Tanner stay home when Starsky's busy raising pups?' she asked.

A pair wasn't a pair without two of them…

'Are you kidding? There would be a riot. Sometimes I tether him up front with Dexter. He's had a rough past so he doesn't mind the security of pairing with the alpha. Even if he'll never lead himself.'

She looked into Tanner's soft, shy eyes with a certain amount of affinity.

Neither of us the right stuff, boy…

'Shove over,' Will said, casually.

Tanner was so apoplectic about getting to ride in the sled he completely forgot to be wary of strangers and he leaped into the sled, cold damp paws and all, wiggled himself in next to her and tried hard to maintain his canine personal space. That lasted about fifteen seconds. As soon as Will hiked the dogs on, the jerk and jostle of the sled as they scrambled up to speed meant that it was easier for Tanner to slide down into a lying position than sit perched upright. He sank, and he spread, until he was pressed warmly and bodily up against Kitty.

Knowing his history, she tried not to startle him with any sudden moves but it didn't take long for her fingers to find his coat under all her blankets and she curled them into his cool fur. Underneath it wasn't cool at all.

'Well, look at you,' she cooed, scrunching her fingers. 'Travelling like a rock star.'

Tanner tipped his nose up to her and gave her what could only be described as a smile and her heart melted just a little bit.

Something about wounded animals… Of all sizes—

She turned her head just slightly until she could see Will in her peripheral vision.

And all species…

'Hike!'

The next twenty minutes was a combination of distinct hard sounds, whistles and clicks as Will urged his excited dogs onward. He perched on the sled when the team ran fast, pedalled with one foot when they slowed, and leapt off to run behind when they hit a slight rise. Every one of them had a different mushing style—some leaning left, some leaning right, legs kicking in different directions—and all of them wore little black booties to protect their feet.

Without exception, wildly lolling tongues seemed to be a vital part of their technique.

Their barks and yips finally eased into a far quieter and far steadier percussion of feet on snow, heavy pants and the icy air rushing past her ears. It was impossible to talk to Will standing behind her so Kitty just relaxed, snuggled deeper into her blankets—and her complimentary dog—and watched the forest whizz by. Once they'd been going for some minutes, they hit their rhythm and Will's involvement—and gymnastics—lessened. He stood behind her, braced wide, like some Roman chariot driver. The more the team relaxed into the run, the more Kitty did, and it became impossible not to lean back against the solid strength of Will's legs.

With his heat from behind, Tanner's to her side, all the blankets she was snuggling into, and the sinking twilight around them it wasn't long before the oxygen-saturated air did its thing to her eyelids again. In that moment, nothing else existed in the world except his strong voice, the rhythmic tattoo of twenty paws thudding on snow, the whoosh of wind against her ears and the five sets of lungs heaving in and out. No work politics. No complicated history with Will. No baggage. It was almost hypnotic; a kind of Zen-like relief that she hadn't had since she'd stood on the side of a mountain in Nepal and danced with Will's dogs.

How funny that the last true moment of peace in her life also involved dogs.

And it also involved Will...

'Woah...' he called, pulling back on the leads and drawing her eyes open. 'Woah!'

When they slowed enough, he jumped off and ran behind the sled, using his full body weight to ease the team to a halt.

Tanner sprang off and ran forward excitedly for a reunion with his friends before they'd even fully stopped.

'That was amazing!' Kitty called, her smile practically frozen to her face from the sub-zero air.

'Liked it?'

There was more than just distraction with his dog tasks in the tautness of that question. 'You thought I wouldn't?'

'Not everyone gets off on being peppered with offcast snow and showered with trailing dog saliva.' He grinned.

'Well, when you sell it like that...'

But this was Will's life. And it was almost as if he were seeking her approval.

She tumbled herself off the sled clumsily as Will set about freeing each dog from its rigging and tethering them instead to nearby trees. She carefully folded up every one of her rugs before helping Will to offload various bits of equipment from the rear of the sled.

'What's in this tub?' She groaned at the heaviest.

'They burn thousands of calories on a run,' he said. 'Need to stay hydrated and fuelled.'

The tub contained a high protein kind of mush and he mixed it with warm water from an old foam cooler. He splashed half the resulting slush into the tub's lid and put both down for the dogs to share between them. Steam rose like a thermal spring.

'Tanner's not getting any?'

'He hasn't earned it yet.'

While the five dogs gobbled their refuel, Kitty peered around at the clearing Will had brought them to. She had no way of knowing which direction they'd come but since they hadn't hit either the bay or the river then it could only be south or east. Either way it was deeper into the real Boreal. Caribou country. And wolf. And probably bear. Animals that would see their portable lights a mile off.

But as long as Will wasn't worried, she wouldn't worry. Much.

The five dogs eventually settled but Tanner seemed to know his workday was just beginning.

'Okay,' Will said. 'Time for you to earn your keep.'

Kitty turned her focus to Tanner only to find him looking back at her with a degree of expectation. So was Will.

'Me?' she squeaked.

'I need you to play dead.'

'What?'

'Tanner's a tracking dog,' he reminded her. 'He needs some fresh meat to track.'

She stared her disbelief at him. 'You want me to go out into the forest, alone?'

'What, you never played hide-and-seek as a kid?'

On the very rare occasion that she'd had someone else to play with.

'Not amongst wild animals!'

Although that wasn't strictly true. Australia was full of creatures that could kill you, they were just smaller than the ones here. If she could crawl under the house at home, exploring amongst spiders, then she could surely find a log to hunker down behind, here.

'This is a lichen study area. Fully fenced Crown Reserve,' he added meaningfully.

She narrowed her eyes. 'I'm amazed you were able to open that gate without a support crew.'

'Ha-ha. Stop hedging.'

'No wild animals?' she checked.

'Nothing bigger than your fist.'

'And I just…hide?'

'Jog out as far as you can in three minutes. I'll take

Tanner five minutes the opposite direction and then we'll find you.'

She peered out into the dark trees, her gut tight. 'And if you don't?'

'I'll find you,' he repeated, firmer, and there was something in the sure way he said it... It made her heart race.

She sagged. Hadn't he promised her something amazing? Lying cold and miserable on the forest floor scarcely counted, even if the journey out here had been pretty spectacular. 'Oh, fine. Off you go. I'll go that way.'

She chose a direction completely randomly.

'Here,' Will said, walking over to her and exchanging her scarf for his. There was a moment of biting cold and then she was wrapped in the warmth—and delicious smell—of Will Margrave. 'You'll get yours back when we find you.'

Was that supposed to be some kind of reward? Because right now, with Will's scent gently rising around her nostrils, she didn't really want her own scarf back.

Watching Will jog out of the clearing with Tanner's nose full of her scarf scent was one thing, but leaving the security and familiar comfort of the rest of the dog team armed with nothing but a torch in hand was altogether tougher. That took a few deep breaths and a couple of muttered curses. But leave she did, and she set up a gentle trot herself and wove her way between trees and crazy patches of stringy lichen and fallen logs looking for the perfect hideout.

Please don't let it be a bear den...

She found a place where one spruce had toppled against another and a whole bunch of opportunistic climber vines had twisted their way around both, creating a natural igloo of leaves and snow. She wriggled herself inside the viney cluster, out of view, checked to be sure there were no other occupants and made herself comfortable on the damp earth below.

* * *

Had she imagined that she'd be out there for hours?

It seemed as if she was barely settled before she heard Tanner's distant whiffling. And Will's encouraging calls. No words, just voice. Confident and in charge. He used a whole different set of commands and sounds for the tracking part of Tanner's training and she leaned against one tree trunk within her leafy hide, wrapped Will's scarf around her more firmly against the cold seeping up from the ground, and listened to him approach.

'Come on, boy, that's it… Friends don't let friends get lost in the forest.'

The thought that Will might consider her his friend helped warm her little hideout. So did the fact that he was talking with no idea how close he was standing to her hideout. She held her breath so that neither of them would hear it.

The snuffling grew closer. Doggie breathing combined with a high-pitched kind of whine as Tanner tracked her closer.

'Find Kitty, buddy. Let's bring her home.'

Maybe that was something he always said when hunting for survivors, but there was something in the determined way he said it, something that wiggled in between her ribs and closed a fist around her heart.

Home.

How long had it been since she'd had one of those? She'd had houses—well, apartments, really—first in Sydney, for a while in Manchester, then in Los Angeles where CNTV posted her as their North American correspondent, but she never spent more than a few weeks at a time in any of them. Most of the time her LA apartment looked like something out of a real estate ad: clean, orderly, impersonal. Which pretty much described her life.

When you ran as hard and as far as she did when she was chasing a story, you didn't have time for homey touches. Or relationships. Or any of life's pleasures, really. You only had time for work. And accountability. And focus.

They didn't give Pulitzers out for happiness.

Will's voice grew more eager. 'Close in, buddy, close in…'

The snuffling was practically atop her and it was only a moment before a wolf-like snout intruded suddenly into her hiding place, but, instead of bursting in, Tanner withdrew again, barked, and after just a moment she heard Will's voice praising him. For signalling or marking the place, or whatever else he was trained to do. Will's praise was effusive and enthusiastic and she poked her head out in time to see them playing a raucous, twilight game of tug-of-war with a well-chewed toy. There was romping, there was rolling; whatever else it was, it was clearly the best reward Tanner could ask for.

Kitty cleared her throat. 'Is no one going to check whether I'm alive?'

The moment Will released Tanner he bound over to her and knocked her flat back into the snow, clearly expecting the adoration to continue. She was hardly about to let him down. Eventually they both ran out of steam, and Tanner lay spread half across her in the snow. She was head to toe white flakes. And only a little bit freezing.

'Good boy,' she said, rubbing that place behind his ears she'd seen Will do with Dexter. 'Thanks for finding me.'

Will gave a signal and released him to bound off into the forest.

Kitty took the gloved hand Will extended and he pulled her onto wobbly feet. It was impossible not to fall against him in that moment before she could dig her feet more firmly into the snow but, even when she did, he was slow to release her. He pulled at one of his gloves with his teeth and then slipped his warm fingers up under her hair, resting it against the hammering pulse-point at her jaw.

It only thudded faster at the contact.

'You're alive,' he confirmed.

At least she hadn't fainted from the contact. But she was having a hard time tearing her gaze away.

'You okay?'

'Yeah. I'm good,' she breathed. 'That was fast.'

'He's a good tracker, and we didn't have a lot of distance to cover. Plus you smell really fresh.'

Her hypnotic fascination fizzled like the steam coming off the dogs' gruel. 'Thanks very much! Last time I play dead for you.'

'Fresh as in "recent".' Will laughed. 'It takes longer to track aged scents. You were practically a hot apple pie on a window…'

He meant that as a compliment, she was sure.

'So, that's it?' she asked, turning back in the direction she thought she'd come and then realising she had no idea what direction she'd come from. 'Mission accomplished for Project Amazing?'

Will took her by the shoulders and spun her ninety degrees and then gave her a gentle nudge.

'The sledding was the first part,' he said, falling in behind her and crunching along in the snow. 'Tanner's training was the second.'

She slowed and turned to study him. What else was there to do deep in the forest a zillion miles from anywhere?

His grin hurt her heart as he sized her up.

'How are you at lighting campfires?'

When night fell in the north it really fell. Because of the angle of the sun at this time of year, twilight was slow to form but it was fast to end. People had no idea what dark really was until they'd sat in the deep Boreal halfway to the arctic circle after sunset. Even in the clearing Will had made their camp in, and even with the fire he'd managed to dig into the side of a curved fallen limb behind them, the blackness was all consuming.

But then the clouds cleared somewhat, enough to reveal a phenomenal blanket star field unravelling across the sky above them.

And suddenly she was seeing *everything* in the darkness.

'Okay, you get points for this,' she said, slightly to her side but without taking her eyes off the sky.

Will chuckled across from her, half wrapped in the same rugs and furs she'd folded so neatly earlier. The ones that weren't wrapped around her.

'I haven't seen stars like these since—'

She practically swallowed her tongue in her haste to suck her words back in.

'It's okay, Kit. You can talk about Nepal.'

'I don't mean to. But it keeps coming up. Because it's the only place we have in common.'

Although not now. Now they had Churchill, and when she'd gone from this place she would remember him working here instead of at the foot of some sad, traumatised mountain.

As she had the thought—of leaving here, leaving Will—she was suffused with an almost overwhelming grief.

'I remember the stars there so clearly,' he murmured.

'Do you miss it?'

'Parts of it. The people, the spirituality...'

'Do you think returning will ever be an option?'

He blinked up at the heavens for the longest time. Stars blinked in and out of view as dark clouds high above them powered across the sky. 'No. I don't think so.'

And so the tragedies continued...

'I'm sorry that you've lost that, too.'

He brought his eyes to hers, blinked the shadows away and refocused. 'Got anywhere special like that for you?'

She wracked her brain and was sad to find it absent of any special place. Really absent. 'I haven't really been in one place long enough…'

He turned onto his side, to face her more fully. 'What's with the crazy pace?'

'Been busy.' She shrugged.

'Have you even taken a holiday?'

'Are you kidding? With all the travelling I do the last thing I want to do is do it in my leisure time.'

'I mean just…stop. Lie on the sofa for a week, reading. Go to movie marathons. Blow it playing Candy Crush. Anything but work.'

'I get breaks between stories now and again.' Though not really. Not if she could help it. 'Like this. This is downtime.'

'If not for the fact you're thinking about work constantly, here.'

Well, not constantly. In fact, she'd started to feel guilty about how many times she hadn't thought about work since sliding down that emergency slide. Hence she'd gone really hard on the edit yesterday and last night.

'I was spontaneous in Nepal,' she reminded him. 'I stayed a whole ten days to get the rescue story.'

'Uh-huh. How often have you done it since then?'

Kitty twisted her back under her warm blankets to try and shift the pressure on her chest—as if some kind of forest spirit were sitting on her. Oxygen flowed down into her lungs, relieving the sensation, and she sank back into the blankets gratefully.

'You okay?'

'It's just…breathtaking,' she hedged, glancing up at the star field. It was too early in the night for the aurora, but she would absolutely take the phenomenal star show. Any day.

'So, tell me about work,' Will muttered.

She didn't shift her eyes from the stars. 'What about it?'

'Why you push yourself so hard. What you're doing it for.'

Her ribs shrank into each other. 'Surely, a man like you understands wanting to be the best at what you do.'

'A man like me?'

'Driven, ambitious, determined.'

'Is that how you see me?'

She rushed to undo the offence she could hear in his reply. 'Those are all good things in my book.'

'I guess I am determined. And possibly driven. Never really thought of myself as ambitious though.'

'You say that like it's a disease,' she muttered. 'I see it as a virtue.'

'I guess you would…'

She took a long breath and reminded herself that she'd been wanting to have this kind of conversation with Will Margrave for years. She didn't necessarily get to pick the topic. Or the timing.

'Success makes me happy.'

'Happiness makes you happy,' he corrected. 'Success just makes you too busy to notice that you're not. Trust me.'

'Really, Will? You're going to lecture me about working to the exclusion of everything else? Isn't that exactly what you're doing here in Churchill? Keeping busy enough that you don't notice the loneliness?'

'My work saves lives,' he defended, darkly.

'And mine's trivial by comparison?'

'I didn't say that.' Will puffed into the air.

But he had no problem leading her to admitting it; that compared to the kinds of stories she used to tell, the ones she told now really were pretty inconsequential. But most of the time she did a fine old job of deluding herself.

Occupational necessity.

'We don't all have the vocational calling that you've had, Will.' Trained since he was a boy by the search-and-rescue uncle who raised him. Really, what chance he was going to be anything but a rescuer, too? 'For me, work actually earns the name.'

Blue eyes blazed into hers, really seeking. 'It didn't used to.'

Shame stole any reply—at her thoughtless words and because he was essentially right.

He studied the skies for a while. 'I'm sorry if I hit a sore point.'

'It's not.' *Pfff.* 'I just don't appreciate having to defend myself.'

He easily brushed her defensiveness off. 'Please. You love defending yourself. Those long, late-night discussions we had about just about anything. I sometimes wondered if you took the conflicting view simply to get me worked up.'

Just how transparent had she been five years ago? Will had the sexiest brain she'd ever met; back then, she'd debated with him ardently in lieu of getting to touch him—it was all she'd had.

The fire popped loud enough to startle Ernie, and Will freed himself of blankets and went to tend it.

'If you could go back in time six years, would you still go to Nepal?' she asked.

He poked at the fire for the longest time. 'Yeah. But I wouldn't have taken Marcella.'

'To save her from the quake?'

His poking paused. 'To save her from discovering who she was. And who she wasn't.'

'What do you mean?'

'Marcella had this firm view of who she was, who she wanted to be—the bohemian artist, the loving wife living in this great, spiritual place. She married me, we moved to the Himalayas, had this great traditional Nepalese house on a lake… It should have been perfect. But, the reality was she was more like her parents and sisters than she knew and, in some ways, discovering that killed her long before the quake did.'

Who she was... Who she wanted to be... Kitty curled deeper into her blankets—wasn't that exactly what she'd spent five years doing? Trying to be someone different. Someone manufactured? The kind of someone who had a terrifically successful and glamorous career. Enviable, even?

What if she was no more suited to the lifestyle she'd created than Marcella had turned out to be to hers?

He turned to face her. 'What about you, Kitty? Would *you* still go to Nepal, if you had a do-over?'

'Yes.' Bam. Just like that. Though she'd never given the idea a moment's thought.

His gaze grew thoughtful. 'Even with how it ended up?'

'Yes.' She didn't need to consider. No matter how she felt about leaving it. 'Nepal was...freedom, for me. No obligations, no expectations, total creative freedom. You and Marcella, the people in your village, just accepted me for exactly who I was. Even your dogs welcomed me.'

He grunted. 'Don't read too much into it, Kitty. Dogs are pretty accepting.'

Don't read too much into it... Was that a warning to her now?

She frowned. 'Were you always this much of a killjoy?'

His teeth glowed in the firelight. 'I respect you too much to lie to you.'

A fist gave her heart a quick squeeze. Or was it her lungs? 'Really? I never would have guessed.'

That surprised him. 'My questions are designed to know you better, not to find fault.'

The same breathlessness that she'd endured in Nepal hit her now, even in this oxygen-rich forest. 'Why would you want to know me better?'

He hung his head as he agitated the fire then turned it

sideways to peer back at her across the clearing. 'Because I feel like I missed out on something, back in Nepal.'

Thump, thump, thump.

That was exactly what she felt. But hearing him say it left her almost faint. 'Careful what you wish for, Will. You might find you don't like what you find, at all.'

Hadn't he already said she'd changed?

He pushed to his feet, into shadow, so that she couldn't quite find his gaze, but his earnest gaze stole every bit of breath she'd managed to suck in as he stepped forward into the fire's circle of light.

'I doubt that,' he murmured.

She wanted to answer—some terrifically witty response—but, nope, there wasn't enough air left in her cells let alone her lungs. All she could do was stare into the sparkling depths of his eyes and wonder what it would be like to swim strokes in the icy blue there.

As she watched they flicked down to her parted lips and back again. 'You're an enigma to me, Kitty Callaghan. And I've always enjoyed puzzles.'

She wanted to warn him that she was more puzzle than he knew. She was one of those boxes with hidden mechanisms and cryptic clues and booby traps if you pressed the wrong place. She wanted to but she didn't, because the moment he stared at her lips all she could think about was what it would be like to kiss him. To taste him and breathe him in.

After all this time.

And in that moment she knew that she'd been wanting that since the very first moment she'd met him. More than just about anything else in her life.

'Did you see those science teachers this morning?' she asked, desperate for something neutral to break the energy stretching from him to her. 'How passionate they were about their work?'

'I didn't need to see them. I could breathe it.'

'Is that how you feel about running your dogs? Does it give you that kind of buzz? Or is it just…routine, now?'

'When we discover someone,' he started, 'it's the most natural of highs. Adrenaline. Excitement. Elation. Pride. Grief if they haven't made it. Sorrow that we weren't quicker.'

His voice carried a hundred memories. Good and bad.

'But recovery moments are few and far between in search and rescue. Ninety per cent of my job is mundane stuff like training, preparation, equipment checks. But even the mundane bits still interest me, or I wouldn't do it. Life is too short.'

It had been a long while since the mundane parts of her job had interested her. Even some of the cool parts— the international travel, the public profile—no longer excited her.

'Do you remember why you started doing it?' she pushed, without really understanding why. She just needed to know if she was the only one feeling this way.

'Yes. Because of my parents.'

The ones who'd gone out sailing off Newfoundland and never come back. Marcella had told her. No wonder he handled death so bravely with that kind of formative training.

'And do you still feel the same about it?'

Will's face creased with curiosity. 'Yes.'

There we go… She fell to silence. What else was there to say?

'Are you having doubts?' Will nudged. 'About your job?'

'No.' Producing stories was all she knew. She'd been doing it since she graduated. Who was she if she wasn't Super-Correspondent? Right down to the cape and lettered chest. 'Maybe.'

'Is there anything else you want to do?'

She tipped her face to the sky where the clouds were

closing back in, backlit by the rising moon. 'I couldn't start over, after everything I've given up...'

Although the opportunity was getting further away with every year she sank into her career. Just like Mei.

'What things?'

'Friendships. Those close relationships that need nurturing to keep them alive.' She shuffled in her blankets.

'What about romantic relationships?' he asked softly.

She turned to him. Forty-eight hours ago she never would have had this conversation with Will, risked it. But forty-eight hours ago they were still virtual strangers.

'At first I avoided getting to know anyone beyond one date just in case I found myself—' repeating the mistakes of the past '—getting too involved. And then there was no point even going on that first date because it only led to disappointment.'

Not to mention the lurking shadow of a man none of them could hope to match.

'A home,' she went on. 'Who knew I'd start hankering for that? I return to an entryway full of mail, no car because it would sit on the street more than drive on it. I don't even have potted plants in my apartment because I'm not there often enough to keep them alive.'

And if she couldn't care for a potted plant what hope for the children she'd probably never have? Marriages took time. Children took time. And energy. And total focus. How could she ever achieve that with her punishing schedule?

'So walk away. It's just a job, Kitty. You'll find something else.'

'I can't walk away. I'm not done.'

'When will you be?'

She stared at him.

'Senior correspondent? Producer of the show? Network head? President? When will you wake up and think "I'm done. I've made it."'? And what will you have missed on the way?'

It was only the deep compassion she saw in his face that kept her from getting up and walking off. That and the fact she had no idea where they even were.

'People don't walk away from fruitful careers.' She sighed, curling her fingers firmly in her fists. Certainly not without something better to go to.

'People do. All the time. This town is full of them. Tell me—' he leaned in '—what would you do with your life if *you* could go back six years? If you never started working for CNTV. If you weren't answerable to anyone but yourself.'

How could she answer that? Who was she, even, six years ago? It was almost impossible to remember. She wasn't about to tell Will her most secret fantasies of pottering in a home studio making films *she* cared about, mothering a clutch of kids by a man who looked dangerously like him—someone exceptional, someone bright and capable and not afraid to sit up all night talking when the passion took them. Someone with their own priorities who wasn't afraid to give her a high place amongst them.

'It's a moot point, Will. No one gets to press "reset" in the real world.'

'I did,' he reminded her. 'I got rather a big shove, if you recall. I don't want to see the universe shaking you quite that hard to get yours, Kitty.'

She dropped her gaze. 'I appreciate your concern. But I'm fine.'

Her career—such as it was—had served her well all this time. It was hardly perfect but it put food on the table and gave her a focus. What exactly did he imagine she would do with all that time if not work?

Hopes of anything more were just that—dangerous hopes.

Will's eyes had become dark shadows in the fire's dim

glow and she realised it was little more than coals now despite his prodding. How late it was getting and how cold she was.

And not all of it was from outside.

She'd woken up in a lot of new places in her time but at least she knew what she had, and she knew what she was doing no matter where she was. She might not have been setting the world on fire as she'd once dreamed, but a monthly pay-cheque had a lot to recommend it.

She tucked her blankets more firmly around her and assured him.

'Truly. I'm fine.'

CHAPTER TEN

IT WAS A LONG, silent journey back to the cabin under the thick cover of cloud. Will put his trust in the dogs' night vision and they ran steadily along, though not as fast as they'd made the outbound journey. His heart just wasn't in it. He glanced down at Kitty, and the headlamp fixed to his forehead did the whole searchlight thing where she and Tanner squirrelled under the rugs, her hand gently stroking the dog's nose where he'd laid it across her lap.

That was a first. For both of them.

Ahead, Dexter wavered and began to show interest in things off to the side. The rest of the team followed him and the sled moved dangerously towards the snow-buried foliage lining the track. Will shook himself out of the hypnotic stupor caused by the dogs' steady *one-two, one-two* pace and focused on communicating with his lead.

'Haw, Dexter!' he called into the night, half as loud as he usually would.

The rig straightened up and all five dogs hit their regular rhythm again.

It had been two years since his mind had been this addled. The last time had been the shock of the landslide— it had just robbed him of the ability to do any mental processing for weeks. Fortunately, there had been no shortage of work to keep him busy. He'd driven his remaining dogs near into the ground with the endless recovery work and it had only been when the demolition had started that he'd eased back. He hadn't been able to fully check out but he'd at least been able to function.

He was every bit as vacant right now, but for very different reasons. That time it was losing his whole world.

This time it was finding it—finding Kitty. Something he'd not ever let himself want. Yet here she was, in his sled. In his cabin. In his life, albeit temporarily. And there was no good reason that she couldn't be there this time.

Except for his fear.

There weren't many moments quite as compelling as catching yourself responding to the impassioned glitter in the eyes of the woman sitting across the table from your wife. Awkward! As soon as he'd caught himself, he'd vowed he would never let it happen again.

Yet here it was…happening again. Just because Marcella was gone now didn't make indulging his simmering hormones any less risky a proposition. Kitty had an international career to be getting on with—she could hardly pull up stakes and replant them here, a thousand miles from the nearest big city. Not without regretting it later. The last thing he needed in this world was another woman looking to escape her own life.

Look how the last time had turned out.

The glowing cabin approached and Will leapt off the back of the sled to haul it to a stop. 'Woah…'

Kitty disentangled herself from all the rugs. 'Looks like the power is back on.'

Which meant she'd be working all evening. Which meant she'd hide out in her room again.

Which was probably a good thing.

He grunted. 'Looks like.'

It took him twenty minutes after she'd gone in to de-harness the dogs and give them another small feed to replenish their energy before he let them out for a fast forage break, then into the safety of the cabin for the night. They immediately separated to lie in their favourite corners of the house. Somehow the little cabin just absorbed them all, like shadows. He stripped out of all his layers, boosted

NIKKI LOGAN 141

up the fire and got it roaring again and then restarted all the appliances that needed resetting after a power outage.

Immediately his landline started blinking.

He headed to his kitchen and pressed the message re-call button on the way past.

'This is a message for Ms Kitty Callaghan,' the voice said before identifying itself as being from Kitty's airline. Will froze in the middle of pouring himself a glass of water. 'Ma'am, we're happy to advise that you have been re-seated on a Winnipeg-bound flight departing Churchill at noon tomorrow. If you can please check in one hour before, that will give us time to screen your luggage and get you validated. Thank you very much, see you tomorrow no later than eleven.'

Beep.

A chill worse than the one he endured standing on the back of the sled in winter soaked right through him and he let the water jug sag to the benchtop.

Kitty was leaving—he glanced at his watch—fourteen hours from now.

Fourteen hours and he would be waving her off as he had five years ago, with a polite smile and a carefully blank expression. Just as he was getting to know her again. No, not 'again', just as he was getting to know her for the first time, properly.

He pressed down with both sets of palms on his bench-top.

Then again it was also fourteen hours and he could go back to his regular life; his predictable, ordered existence with his dogs. Back to being accountable to no one but himself. Back to a warm, silent cabin in a deep, peaceful woods where no one conjured the past every five minutes. Where no one challenged him to be different. Or better. So maybe it was for the best.

Quit while they were ahead.

'Kitty?' he called, abandoning his water in favour of letting her know she needed to start packing. 'Kit?'

The silence drew him up the hallway towards her room. As he passed the bathroom, the door sprung open and she stepped out and ran square into him, all clean and damp from her shower. All warm and pink and cosy in her cute pyjamas.

His gut tightened at the soapy freshness.

'Oh! Sorry,' she laughed before remembering that she was annoyed at him for his insensitive probing, and he tried to imagine ever getting bored of that sound. Her voice cooled a little. 'Did you want something?'

'Your airline called.' He coughed his throat clear. 'You're scheduled for noon tomorrow.'

That look on her face... Those moments before she managed to mask it—that was exactly what he imagined his expression had been on hearing the airline's message.

Shock. Denial. Resignation. Acceptance.

Like the stages of grief played out over seconds.

'Oh. Great.' But she didn't move, and those lines between her brows didn't lessen any. Whatever she'd used on her hair, or her skin, it wafted up to tease his senses. 'Um, okay...I guess I should pack then.'

Did she mean to make it that much of a question? Her grey eyes lifted and found his. Almost as if she was giving him an opportunity to disagree.

'Guess so,' he said carefully, taking another step back.

She gathered her bathroom things more closely to her chest and turned for her room. Before she disappeared into it, he spoke up.

'Hey, Kitty...?'

She turned much quicker than his gentle query required, her eyes lit by something he couldn't define. 'Yes?'

Was she still waiting for him to disagree?

'Give me your towel. I'll lay it out by the fire. So you don't pack it damp.'

'Oh.' The indefinable something extinguished. 'Thank you.'

Had gratitude ever sounded so insincere? What exactly had she been hoping he was going to say?

Her hand brushed his as she passed the towel to him and the softness of her fingertips against his own struck him. They were so different. She moved in high places, travelled the world and had interview appointments with CEOs of the biggest corporations. She had the hands of a musician or a writer...or a news correspondent.

He had calluses as rough as the pads on his dogs' feet and his only appointments for the foreseeable future were a twice-daily obligation at a remote flagpole.

No matter what kind of professional rut she was in, staying in Churchill was no more realistic an option than Marcella living in Nepal had turned out to be. Great in principle, exciting and novel in planning, but hard work and isolated in practice. And it wouldn't be long before she was regretting giving up that fine career. Or resenting him for being part of it.

Just like Kitty's philosophy on dating... So much easier to just not even start.

Not that this was easy.

He dragged a chair nearer to the fire and draped her damp towel across its back, and that same smell that had teased his nostrils in the hallway set up a full assault now. It filled the room with some flowery scent and managed to subjugate the usual smell of spruce wood, leather and dog.

Who knew how much time he lost immersing himself in that smell? But somewhere in there he sank into his own leather rocker.

'Will?' Kitty asked quietly from the doorway.

He shot from his chair, as his uncle had raised him, and

turned to face her. She'd thrown a thin sweater on over the pyjamas, which went some way to reducing the cling against her skin, but the soft fabric did nothing to lessen the cosy, relaxed feel he got just looking at her and the pale blue did amazing things to her eyes.

'I was wondering if you were planning on eating?' she said. 'I know it's late…'

Shame kneed him in the guts. It was ten p.m. and he'd only taken food for the dogs with them on their evening sled ride. She must be starving.

He really had been living with wolves too long.

'I could eat,' he said casually, forcing the shame down. Though he really wasn't that interested. The last supper of a condemned man and all that. 'What do you feel like?'

They did the whole, awkward whatever-you-like/no-whatever-*you*-like dance and, in the end, he pulled together some whipped eggs and Parmesan before gently sizzling it into a fluffy omelette. At the final stage, he drizzled butter over the lot before searing it on both sides and sliding half each onto two plates. It was all very French.

'Marcella teach you that?' Kitty asked from right behind him, making him fumble the pan at a crucial moment.

But he recovered. 'Her grandmother, actually. It was a family favourite.'

She perched on a stool at the end of his kitchen bench, her long legs crossed casually, forking mouthfuls of the impromptu dinner in at a pretty steady rate. Either she really was starving or she was trying to avoid conversation. Finally, she carefully laid her fork onto her empty plate and looked up.

'I'll be sorry to leave, tomorrow, Will.'

Nope. No, you won't. You need to get back to your world before one of us does something stupid…

'I hope I've met my obligations regarding northern hospitality,' he said.

Her smile didn't reach her eyes. 'Thoroughly. Rogue

polar bears, Halloween, dog-sledding. What more could a girl from Down Under ask for?'

The gentle tease was almost as good as the waft of soapy scent. It tingled wherever her words fell. The way snowflakes felt on bare skin.

In fact, his senses were almost fully engaged by Kitty: her distinctive scent, the sight of her all soft and just show-ered, the tinkle of her teasing laugh, the brush of her soft skin against his. Pretty much all he was missing now was taste.

And that little question mark would never be answered.

No matter how it plagued him.

'I'm glad I got to see you,' she said quietly, eyes seri-ous. 'To set things right between us.'

That smacked just a little bit too much of closure, which, in turn, smacked just a little bit too much of good-bye. Knowing something had to happen and wanting it to happen weren't necessarily the same thing. Sometimes you did the hard thing for the right reason—even though it felt all kinds of wrong.

How long had it taken him to learn that? Maybe if he'd manned up and sent Marcella home she would still be breathing and laughing and painting today.

'To undo what I did?' he tested, wanting to keep her out here with him as long as possible.

Her eyebrows dropped, then her lashes followed suit.

'I didn't like leaving Nepal,' she said. 'And I didn't like not knowing what was happening with you. That you were okay. Stay in touch, going forward, huh?'

She sounded very resigned, which only served to make him more depressed.

But he fought it. This was what he wanted. 'You know where I am. Email will always be open.'

But she wouldn't use it. The moment her wheels left the runway she'd start retreating back into the real world. And, in the real world, Kitty Callaghan and Will Margrave didn't stay in touch. He knew them both well enough to be sure of that.

It was just too fraught.

Awareness zinged back and forth between them, almost tangible enough to feel. They'd never been short of chemistry and it was making itself known now. It only served to validate the distance he'd kept five years ago. And was forcing now.

Look what happened when he let his guard down.

'Well…' he hinted, glancing up the hall. Putting himself out of his misery.

Something behind her gaze flattened and it killed him to be responsible for that. Once again.

The hard thing for the right reason…

Kitty needed to be heading south again. Back to her world. Back to the life she'd been steadily working on. That life didn't include a remote little bear town and it didn't include a search-and-rescue hermit or his dogs.

'Yes. I should get packing.'

Packing meant leaving. Which he wanted, but you wouldn't know that by the thud of his heart.

'No editing tonight?'

She looked startled enough that he wondered if she'd even remembered her story waiting to be cut. 'Looks like I'll be back in the hotel tomorrow afternoon. I should be able to get it finished then.'

Without him and his endless outdoor distractions. 'In time for your deadline?'

Something flickered across the back of her gaze. 'Close enough.'

She didn't exactly look enthused by that, but she slipped down off the stool and hovered in the opening to the kitchen.

'Thanks for the eggs.' That simple sentence seemed to hold so much more meaning.

'You're welcome,' he said, trying hard to invest just as much in his. 'See you in the morning.'

She hesitated, lips parted, but then her hips turned, her shoulders followed and finally her face turned for her bedroom.

Her eyes were the last thing to leave him.

Kitty sagged against her closed bedroom door, forcing her breath in and out. Mastering it. It had threatened to overwhelm her out in the kitchen where every minute that passed was a minute closer to her departure in the morning. Thank goodness for the training that had taught her how to regulate her breathing so that she could present to camera, live, even after dashing across a war zone. That was all that had kept her conversation flowing while her mind had been so busy crying out for Will.

If her career had taught her anything, it was how to fake it until she could make it.

She wasn't ready to leave. She wasn't even sure she *could* be ready. Four days ago fate had bounced her down an emergency slide in Churchill and she'd thought it was simply safe harbour. She'd had no inkling that she would find a thing here in this isolated, insular place that she'd thought she'd never have. Ever.

A second chance. With Will.

And she'd just left that second chance standing, all handsome and rugged, in the kitchen. Waving her off with a relieved smile. Much like the one he'd worn in Nepal.

Panic welled up around her ankles. Had she done it again? Outstayed her welcome… Misread the signals… Had she assumed that Will was as happy to have her stay as she had started to feel here? He'd joked about northern hospitality but was that what all this had been?

Obligation?

He certainly wasn't making any grand efforts to stay in touch.

You know where I am. Email will always be open...

Yeah, not exactly compelling evidence.

She paced her tiny room, shaking out the anxiety through flapping hands. As much as she didn't want to pack, she needed to be moving, otherwise she was going to sprint back down that hallway and say something that she really shouldn't. She and Will had only just become friends. After five years. She wasn't about to blow that by blurting out her feelings just because she lacked self-discipline. She'd survived the humiliation once before—just—but only by throwing her life totally off orbit and into a new direction. If he rejected her again she really wasn't sure what was left to do to help her get past it.

What she *was* going to do was pack, head back to some comfortable, anonymous hotel in Manitoba's capital, cut her story and file it with CNTV, get on a connecting flight for Los Angeles, and get on with the rest of her life. A new story. A new country. A new focus.

The sort of life that was just so noisy it drowned out the weeping of her lovesick heart.

She froze, a stone settling deep in her gut as she sank down onto her mattress.

Love?

Please, no, not again.

Hadn't she learned a thing from past experience? She couldn't love Will Margrave any more now than she had in Nepal. There might no longer be a marriage standing between them but nothing else had changed about their relationship. She honestly didn't think she could survive another dose of his pity.

Kitty started tossing things into her suitcase carelessly, abandoning her finely developed packing system—everything rolled, everything in its place—and scouring the room for anything she'd left behind. Normally she would take her equipment on as hand luggage but, nope, she threw that in as well, forcing her belongings—like her feelings—behind the very sturdy, very final suitcase zipper.

Ziiiiip.

That sound was a symbol for her life. It meant a new start. A new adventure. It meant flights and planning and research and interviews, and all the things she did that kept her so busy three hundred and sixty-five days a year. That zipper had become a marker for the passing years of her life. One after the next after the next…

She sagged back onto the end of her bed.

So many years. And what did she have to show for it? No home. Precious few friends. Zero romantic relationships.

But one hell of a résumé.

Only one of those things was going to take her to the top.

She stared at her trembling hands with a curious detachment. As if they weren't even hers. Then, finger by finger, she curled them, then flexed them, then wrapped them around the nearest loose item and tossed it into her suitcase.

These cases weren't going to pack themselves.

CHAPTER ELEVEN

'WAKE UP, SLEEPYHEAD.'

Kitty twitched and roused and let herself be dragged—reluctantly—out of slumber to the sound of Will's voice. There were certainly worse ways to start a day. But that cosy pleasure only lasted moments before the cold reality intruded.

Today was the day she would leave Churchill. And leave Will.

'Kitty?'

She rolled onto her side and opened her eyes. Didn't they just do this? 'Why is it so dark?'

'It's night time,' he whispered. 'Well, morning, really. Very early.'

'Why am I awake?' she grumbled.

Mornings really weren't her forte. Especially not when she'd lain awake so long angsting about her future.

'I have a surprise for you,' Will said, a little louder. Every word brought her closer to consciousness.

'In the middle of the night?'

'Look out your window.'

If there wasn't a wolf standing there…with a bear…riding a moose…she was going to be mightily cranky. She'd never in her life slept as much or as well as here in Will's cabin and a rude midnight awakening was not high on her list of must-dos before leaving today.

She peered through her lashes at the Boreal beyond the picture window. It was its usual mass of darkness. But there was something else, a kind of glow hovering over all of it.

She pushed herself higher and craned her neck. 'Is there a fire?'

But no, that made no sense. Fires were orange. She squinted to get a better look.

The glow started on the horizon, like the urban glow of a city—a far bigger city than Churchill would ever be—and far greener.

'I thought the port was in the other direction?'

It spread like a gas, unevenly and fast changing, wiping out all but the brightest stars and backlighting the clumps of cloud still lingering in the sky until they, too, glowed a sick kind of emerald.

She shot up into a seated position, eyes still firmly on the sky. 'Wait… Is that the aurora?'

'The corona has been maxing all week,' Will murmured. 'But it's been happening behind the veil of thick cloud we've had since you arrived. I let the dogs out for a nature break just now and saw that they'd lifted.'

Maxing and coronas and veils made no sense but the colours swilling across the sky made perfect, painful sense. Because making the decision to go hadn't been hard enough. The treacherous fates had thrown in a curve ball at the eleventh hour.

She shot to the window and pressed her hands onto the freezing glass. It startled her into full awareness.

'I was hoping it would still be pulsing,' he said from the darkness behind her. 'That you'd get to see it. I thought you wouldn't mind being woken…'

By the moment, the green gas thickened and gathered until it formed twisted ropes of colour that warped and wove across the sky.

'Will…' The warm whisper of his name on the glass formed a pool of mist. Then she spun. 'Can we go outside?'

'It's freezing,' he warned. 'Properly freezing. That's why visibility is so good tonight.'

'I'll put on everything I haven't packed,' she vowed.

She grabbed her sweater from dinner, the jeans she'd laid out for the morning, her insulated parka, her beanie and her warmest socks and gloves and pulled the lot on over her thick pyjamas. Then she turned back out to the Boreal to reconsider just how cold it might be before hauling her thick eiderdown off Will's spare bed and throwing that around her shoulders as well.

'Come on, Michelin Man,' he joked.

She practically waddled down the hallway behind him.

She'd sat on the outdoor sofa on Will's timber deck just once in five days, and only long enough to re-lace her boots. It would have been startlingly cold to sit on it if not for the fact that she didn't, walking instead to the middle of the deck and peering upwards.

'Oh, good Lord…'

The colour and intensity of auroras diminished with every degree of latitude you got away from it. Further south, human eyes saw the lights totally differently from how the cameras, there, captured it. She'd only ever seen *these* lights—proper Northern Lights—in magazine shoots. Yet here they were in all their multicoloured glory.

Even for puny primate eyes.

'Take a seat, Kitty,' Will rumbled. 'You've got plenty of time. The sky scanner shows the clouds are still lifting.'

She sank down onto the sofa and tucked herself in more firmly against the cold from below.

Overhead, the strands of colour danced and flowed between Earth and the endless spreading star field. The few remaining clouds looked like sea ice floating on the surface of a dark ocean of night. And the aurora were schools of luminous plankton swarming below the ice. The longer Kitty stared, the harder it became to distinguish sky from ocean; as if she were looking down on it, rather than up.

'It's so beautiful…'

And so bright it was making her eyes water, because surely she was too old and too seasoned to get choked up by the sight of the Northern Lights.

'I'm glad the sky cleared enough while you're still here,' he said, hopping from foot to foot.

She might have put on half her wardrobe but Will was only wearing what he'd come and woken her in and his parka hastily thrown over the top.

'Here,' she ordered. 'Come and get under the quilt.'

He hesitated and she wondered for a pained heartbeat whether he would rather freeze to death than sit that close to her and maybe have her get the wrong impression, but then he moved and joined her. She lowered the blanket and laid it across their legs.

His agitation slowly eased just as Bose's had on the tower all those days ago.

And then, as the aurora swirled and churned, threads of the prettiest pink began to form, merging with the green in a way that just looked so…right…in the sky. Yet at the same time so incredibly alien. A tortured, twisted night rainbow. Against the stark shape of the Tamarack and spruce trees, it was like a fairy-tale world reflected perfectly in the mounds of white snow piled up everywhere.

'Now you're shivering,' Will muttered, throwing the quilt off himself.

'I'm sure we can get both of us under…'

He glanced at her, then seemed to decide something. 'Stand up. Come on… Up.'

She stumbled to her feet as Will did. He took the thick quilt off her and wrapped it around himself like a giant towel before sinking back into the sofa corner and stretching one long leg down its length. The other fell to the deck. Kitty glanced at the bare sofa between his denim thighs.

'Once in a lifetime, Kit,' he said, a green glow ebbing and flowing on his face. 'I'm sure you'll survive.'

He was talking about the lights, she knew, but the other life experience he was offering her…

She wasn't about to pass that up.

Besides, without the quilt she was as cold as he must have been just now.

She took a deep breath and sat in the vacant space in front of Will. Immediately he folded the fluffy thing around both of them, his arms crossing across her chest the way they had in the bus out on the tundra. With his body heat behind and the thick downy quilt in front she was in a warm little cocoon of heaven.

'God, that's better,' he groaned.

Uh, yeah, it really was. For reasons that had nothing to do with the temperature. As warmth soaked into her, it was hard to fight the sensation that this was how she should have been living life all along—with someone's arms around her.

Will's arms.

His heart beat steadily against her shoulder and she was glad their positions weren't reversed so that he couldn't feel the puppy-like peppering of her own excited one. He might not buy that it was just the lights getting her pulse up.

The aurora began to dance in earnest as if to their combined rhythm.

It didn't take long for her neck to start aching from the constant head-tilt and so she settled back against Will's chest and rested the back of her head on his shoulder. He adjusted his position slightly to make space for her there. It occurred to her, vaguely, to be embarrassed by the picture they presented but she would deal with humiliation later. Right now she was just going to enjoy the light show while she had the chance. And the touching. She fitted perfectly into the curves and dips of his torso. And his padded shoulder was like a comfy, masculine pillow.

A forest gust sprang up and battered against their warm little igloo, blowing a few of her curls loose across her face.

'I got it,' Will murmured against her ear.

He liberated one strong hand from the quilt and brushed

the curls away with the bared knuckle of his little finger, tucking them more securely under the thick fold of her beanie. When he was done, she wiggled back up against him, until his jaw rested against the wool he'd just patted flat.

If the gods sent out a bolt of lightning through all that swilling green and struck her down right now, she'd be pretty darned happy to go.

Like this; surrounded, protected.

Loved.

Or at least a plausible facsimile of it. It wasn't real, she knew that, but she could enjoy that fantasy for just a few moments, couldn't she?

The sky warped and wove as she watched, though even that failed to upstage the sensations beginning to form under the quilt insulating them like a layer of snow. Behind her, Will's chest rose and fell more quickly and he brushed his jaw absently along her beanie, first in subtle strokes timed with the swirls of green and then more purposeful, more bold. As if testing to see what she'd do.

About all she *could* do was lean into every stroke and sigh softly as the electrical energy high above them suddenly seemed to swill all around them, in and between their limbs. Will's fingers tightened their hold on the quilt, pressing his arms more firmly around her and bringing her closer to the hot breath she'd been quietly enjoying against her ear.

And then he stopped—froze, really—poised on a gaping precipice. As if he was too afraid to take the next step. Or as if he was fighting some great internal battle.

Every cell in her body refocused on what was happening on this sofa rather than in the heavens above.

'Will...'

Even that single syllable couldn't do much more than form as a tiny sigh in her throat.

But a sigh was all he needed...

One moment, the place below her beanie—the place he'd tucked her curls—was icy cold from exposure to the frosty air and the next it was alive with wet heat as his lips pressed there, firm and determined. Just once, but roaming. Her chest heaved at the contact and she leaned into his kiss, her eyes fluttering shut.

'Kitty...'

She must have met him halfway because as she breathed in he was there, mouthing her throat experimentally and, by the time she breathed out, his lips sought their way across her jaw and she was twisting her neck to make it happen. The gentle rasp of his scrappy beard growing back in tantalised the cold-nipped skin of her face right before his lips made proper contact.

Kissing Will was like a homecoming. The correction of a years-old error. It felt *meant* that it was witnessed by these cosmic bands of mystery.

Kissing Will was right.

It joined them in a way she'd never let herself imagine, but had always, always wanted. It warmed her from within. And it said one thing...

Home.

She breathed him in, filled her lungs with him; with the microscopic traces that made Will who he was. They sent her own chemicals into a frenzy. He pressed in closer, shoring up the kiss, and twisted further to bring her into the warmth and safety of his body. One hand abandoned its quilt duties to curl beneath her head, holding her steady for his lips, and the other one forked in under her beanie to tangle in the curls there. As if he'd been wanting to do that for ever. Their covers fell partly away but their friction generated such an inferno it didn't matter.

She was never leaving these arms.

Not now that she'd finally found her way into them.

But a girl had to breathe...

She sighed against his lips. Against his smile. She'd

been functioning on extra oxygen for so many days now, it bought her precious extra moments without before she had to tear her mouth from Will's.

'I knew it would be like this.'

'Knew it? Or hoped it?' He nuzzled against her ear, not entirely steady.

Feared it.

She trembled as the frigid air met the wet trail from his lips, and his arms tightened. 'You weren't mine to want back in Nepal.'

Some secret part of her worried that he still wasn't. That this was just a moment conjured by the other-worldly lights still swirling overhead and by his long years of isolation. That it would end when the lights did.

He pulled back on a lazy grin. 'You can want me tonight. Knock yourself out.'

Something about his words rattled in her brain—zinged, really, as if they were trying to get her attention—but her head was way too foggy for actual conversation.

In lieu of speech, he leaned into her again—over her—and reclaimed her mouth with his. Slow and teasing. Smiling and deadly. Hot when everything around them was so very cold. It drove all sense clear out of her tiny mind.

They kissed—and they kissed—until the enormous moon was three-quarters of the way across the night sky.

'I could do this for hours.' He sighed, pulling back and sagging next to her. Close enough for her to see two tiny mirrors of the Northern Lights reflected in his smoky gaze.

'I think we already have.' She chuckled.

'I meant the hours we have left,' he said, still clouded by their heady kissing.

She lifted her face and stared at him.

'Before your flight,' he clarified, as though all the kissing had sucked the sense out of her.

In those few words, everything that had happened in Nepal came crashing back into focus—all the feelings she'd tried to suppress, struggled to ignore, when Will had sent her away the first time—and she realised what a monumental mistake she had made.

He was letting her go? Again?

She struggled against his warm body to sit up, which left Will with no option but to release her. He pushed up to sitting, too. 'Kitty—?'

'I just need…a moment.' To sort this out in her head. Why it should matter. Why it *did* matter.

She'd just talked herself into reaffirming her commitment to her career. So, getting on the plane and heading south shouldn't have been such a terrible concept. But some part of her—a part that had been frozen, asleep for a really long time—secretly wanted it to matter very much to Will. For him to rail and protest and mourn the coming dawn. For him to want her *not* to go.

Rather than accepting it quite so…readily.

She scrambled to set her feet back on the frost-crunched deck.

'Kitty—'

'What are we doing?' she cried, wrapping her arms around her torso. Her heart hammered against her arm, even faster now than when she'd been coiled in Will's embrace.

'What we've wanted to do for five years?'

She spun on him. 'But why? Just hours before I fly away from you. What was this for you, just a nice way to pass the time?'

She should ask herself the same question.

'You leave in the morning,' he urged. 'What other chance will we have? And then there you were all warm and sleepy literally in my arms under this gorgeous sky…'

'So you thought you'd just lob a grenade into the beautiful moment by kissing me?'

He took a wounded step back from her rising anger. 'I thought I was making it more beautiful.'

She struggled against the need to sag. Because—God help her—he *had* made it more beautiful.

'Kitty, what's wrong?'

Screw it. Acquiescing graciously might have saved her dignity five years ago but it hadn't done anything to help her heart. She wasn't going so quietly this time.

'You're just going to watch me get on that plane?'

'You have your job…'

'But you're just going to kiss me half to death then drive me to the airport and wave me off into the sunset?'

He winced. 'I'm not going to enjoy it…'

God, she hoped he was talking about the parting and not the kissing.

'You're not going to ask me to stay. Or even hint?'

'What right do I have to expect that of you? To throw in your career for me?'

Confusion tore at her heart. Because he had *no* such right, but that was exactly what she wanted him to do. Because that meant he wanted her *here*.

When doing nothing meant he didn't.

'So what was this, then?' She flicked a trembling hand in the direction of the sofa. 'A casual bit of sport?'

His eyes skirted across the trees. 'You must have felt the chemistry—'

'Oh, that was you letting off a bit of accumulated steam?'

'*That*,' he barked, and it was mostly mist, 'was me wanting to answer a question that's been five years in the making.'

To be fair, she'd had that exact same question… But she wasn't feeling all that fair right now. Not when the first thing out of his mouth after leaving hers was a reminder of her departure. As if he didn't want her to forget.

Or maybe assume.

'And did you get your answer?' she whispered.

'Yeah,' he breathed, his face perplexed. 'I did. But like all important questions, answering it has only raised more.'

She snatched up the quilt and dragged it around her shoulders. No point both of them suffering from exposure. 'Like what?'

'Like why you kissed me back with such enthusiasm if it was such a bad idea.'

How about because she had zero self-control around him? Or because out here in the forest she'd imagined for a moment that real-world rules didn't apply. The rules that said sensible women didn't kiss men they knew they'd never see again.

'I leave in *hours*, Will. What is the point of starting something we can't finish?'

So much easier to say—to think—now that they'd stopped.

'Something tells me we are well and truly finished now,' he muttered.

The sarcasm did exactly what it was supposed to do—it forced distance between them. She recognised the protective mechanism even as she went with it. She edged towards the front of the deck and away from him as he spoke.

'You have a life to go back to, tomorrow—'

'Not much of one.'

'—a career.'

'That I'm not exactly loving.' She was too angry to be reasonable.

Will threw his hands in the air. 'Your being dissatisfied with your life is no reason to assume you can just move into mine.'

Kitty reared back as if the blow had been physical, and time collapsed around her.

The years since he'd last accused her of insinuating herself into his world dissolved into nothing. She tried to speak but the word came out more of a pained croak.

Will hissed.

'What I mean is...' He grasped around for a better way to say what he obviously wanted to say. But he didn't find it. 'No, I guess that's exactly what I meant. I'm not a ticket out of your imperfect world, Kitty. You're going to have to sort that for yourself.'

Her chest heaved beneath the quilt as much as Will's did beneath his coat. *Her* coat, the one she'd borrowed from him so many times.

That little intimacy nearly broke her.

'I guess there's nothing left to say, then,' she finally said, controlling her speech as tightly as she clutched the quilt.

He took a moment to gather himself, and he stood, back to her, while she was powerless to do anything but stare.

What could you say when you'd just had your heart ripped out?

Again.

'I've got a job on in the morning,' he said, turning back briefly. 'Not sure if I'll be home in time for the airport run. You'd better plan an extra thirty minutes for the taxi.'

The rising grief had finally subsumed her vocal cords, preventing her from answering. She could only nod.

'Good seeing you again, Kitty.'

And then he was gone. Only feet away but somehow already across the world. He would be gone in the morning—he'd be sure to be—which meant the rigid set of Will's back and the judgement bleeding from his eyes like the green from the aurora would be her final memory of him.

Her fingers drifted up to her lips.

When she wasn't dreaming of that kiss.

She sank back down onto the sofa and stared up into the blazing light show. Had she imagined it dancing before? Now, it seemed to shift more like the mourners behind a funeral procession, peering down on her in silent concern and compassion.

And not a small amount of bewilderment.

CHAPTER TWELVE

'I TRUST THE TOWN took good care of you,' the taxi driver checked, setting her wheeled luggage on the airport kerb. 'Next time we see you I hope it will be under less dramatic circumstances.'

He meant the emergency landing, but it applied just as well to the scene out on the deck last night with Will.

But, no, a return visit was definitely not on the cards. 'Thank you.'

Will had been as good as his word, making himself—and his dogs, as she'd sadly discovered—completely absent while she readied herself to leave. She'd had a twenty-minute wait for one of the two taxis in town and she'd passed it at Will's dining table, sitting stiffly, dreading—but breathlessly waiting—for him to walk back in. So that she could apologise. So that she could say goodbye.

So that they could get some closure.

In the end a hastily scribbled note had to suffice for all three. Will probably covered off on his last night.

'Welcome back, Ms Callaghan. We so appreciate your patience...'

The woman at the check-in counter was in full service recovery mode, and readied herself for the barrage of complaints she'd obviously had from other delayed passengers. But Kitty was in no mood to fight for justice.

She was in no mood for anything that took energy.

'No problem,' she muttered, peering out of the massive wall of windows.

Sure enough two small aircraft sat there, modern jet engines, but designed for no more than thirty people. She'd certainly travelled on much worse, but the sight of them sitting out there as slick as the film of ice on the tarmac left her feeling more dismal than usual.

In an hour, she'd be in the air, leaving Churchill behind her. An hour after that she'd be back in her hotel room, juggling room service and her overdue edit. The morning after that, she would be on her way back to Los Angeles and an apartment in dire need of a good airing out.

Boarding pass in hand, she turned and wandered towards one of a dozen empty seats in the small terminal.

'You don't understand…' a tense young woman was saying at the adjacent desk. 'I need to get to Winnipeg as fast as possible. My sister's in early labour. I'm her birth buddy.'

She wanted to tell the stranger that, yeah, they did understand, and empathise, but there was just so little they could do about the numbers they were trying to ship out on such a limited number of seats. She wanted to tell her that— six days ago—she would have been just as frustrated, but that spending time in Churchill had a way of changing how you approached life. She felt no urgency, now, although CNTV were screaming for her edited story and she knew she needed to get far away from Will. Inside her head, it was all very calm.

The hour would pass, the plane would depart, life would return to normal.

Although she wasn't sure she ever would.

'Your flight leaves right after the first one,' the woman assured the panicking passenger.

'The flight I'm on zigzags through every mining, milling and hydro town between here and Winnipeg,' the woman cried as Kitty sank into one of the wide plastic chairs. 'It's going to take hours. There must be something you can do for me?'

One day ago, Kitty would have happily given up her direct plane seat for this woman.

How much difference a day made.

Sorrow blanketed her heart, cold and heavy. She didn't have the energy to pull out her tablet and get stuck into her share of the complimentary Wi-Fi. Or her laptop to continue editing the Zurich story. Or her diary to see what the next few weeks held. She did have enough energy, though, to stare sadly at the massive polar-bear skin hanging in the display case on the wall across the terminal and feel a certain amount of empathy for it.

She felt just as flat.

Laid just as bare.

Fool me once, shame on you. Fool me twice...

Who was she kidding, imagining for a moment that there might be a happy ever after for her and Will in his fairy-tale forest? Or thinking that she'd miraculously earned some kind of second chance. She'd walked squarely into last night and had no one to blame but herself. Five years ago, he'd let her infatuation run until it had got uncomfortable enough to call a halt to. Maybe it had been mutual to start with, maybe it had just flattered him or amused him; regardless, he'd pulled the pin on it on his terms, not hers.

Last night he'd gone one better and kissed her—repeatedly—fully intent on still putting her on her plane today.

That was not cool.

That was not the man she thought she knew.

How was she supposed to put Will out of her head, now? Her heart? Knowing how well he kissed, how good he tasted, how comfortably her body fitted into his on that sofa. Hard enough doing it after Nepal when she hadn't ever touched him, but now...

Ugh.

And how was she supposed to go back to work for CNTV—all its fierce rivalry and treachery—knowing, now, that she would have said yes in half a heartbeat if Will had asked her to stay. As clear as the air in Churchill—

she would have embraced a new and simpler life and she would have done it with wide-thrust arms.

She couldn't just turn off that kind of discovery.

Everything she'd worked for, everything she'd sacrificed at the demanding altar of success meant absolutely nothing against the possibility of a future with Will Margrave, and it was *because* she had such ambition that she wanted more. She wanted it all. The man. The family. The creatively satisfying career.

The life.

That was where her ambition lay now.

Maybe she'd never been cut out for the fast track at all. Just like Marcella, maybe she'd put so much of herself into creating a new persona she couldn't bring herself to walk away from it.

One thing was crystal clear... If she was going to sacrifice all the things she wanted most, it was not going to be for some mid-level correspondent role in the gladiator arena of corporate news. If she had to be alone then she wanted to be creating her stories on her timeline, her way. Like the hobo she was at heart.

Hadn't she earned that?

As the freedom settled like fresh snow on her mind, a weight as colossal as the A340 that had brought her to Churchill lifted off her and fell away, like the lid of a coffin that she hadn't even realised she was imprisoned in. A coffin made of glass—she could see out but nothing could get in. No hope. No happiness.

No air.

Kitty shot to her feet, stumbled to the exit and practically fell on the button for the power doors. They whooshed open and pure, oxygen-saturated, throat-hurting air rushed in and shocked her awake from a sleep half a decade long.

She couldn't go back.

She couldn't stay, either, not here, but she just couldn't—

she *wouldn't*—go back to her job or her stuffy little apartment in Los Angeles or her single-focus life the way it was. Will's latest rejection didn't hurt any less for being awake again—if anything it hurt more—but his rejection had led her to this realisation; his kisses had woken her from her coma. But his rejection had also brought her back full circle, to the place and person she was when he first sent her away and, for that, she would always be grateful to him. And she would always miss him.

And mourn him for ever.

At the counter, the woman kept on arguing.

Out on the tarmac, her flight kept on refuelling.

Standing half in and half out of the terminal door, Kitty kept on breathing.

Will rested his forehead on the timber top of his dining-room table, the note clenched in his fist, refusing to look at the clock over his kitchen. If he didn't know the time, then he didn't know whether or not Kitty was still in his town or whether she was a kilometre over Manitoba. Whether he still had time to catch her or whether her plane was accelerating down the runway even now. Whether she was gone from his life as he'd accepted or whether she might still be in it for just a few minutes longer.

He'd run the dogs hard this morning—too hard judging by their sideways glances and gun-shy expressions on returning—because speed was the only thing that kept him from imploding. The sharp sting of snow on his face. The numb ache of the cold. If he couldn't feel his skin then maybe if he just kept going he'd stop feeling his other organs, too. One by one, until that lump in his chest stopped aching for good.

He couldn't take her to the airport. He knew he didn't have it in him to stand politely waving as Kitty taxied away from him.

Not again.

If that made him a coward, so be it.

He turned his head sideways and loosened his fist on the paper.

Dear Will,
Thank you for the refuge. My unscheduled stay in the north was both enlightening and exhilarating...

Her choice of language plucked at the fibres deep in his chest. Not 'thanks for the bed' or 'appreciate the hospitality' or 'cheers for the accommodation'. Subconscious or not, Kitty went with *refuge*. As if that was the part of it that she'd valued the most—his protection. A refuge was something you sought when times were tough, when you needed to flee from something. When things just got too hard. Exactly what Churchill was for him when he first came here.

He totally understood the instinct.

And he definitely understood exhilaration. He'd been swamped in it out on his deck last night. Too much, in fact. Maybe so much that he had nowhere else to go from there but down.

I wonder how much more of both it would have been if I hadn't spent half my time with you unconscious.

It was impossible not to smile, even through the gut-tightening of the 'with you' part. Of all the things he loved, of all the joys his work brought him, he would gladly trade them all for the chance to rouse Kitty from that cosy slumber every single morning. And right there was the great tragedy between them.

Because he could believe it with his head...but not with his heart.

You have yourself a piece of heaven here in the forest, Will, I hope you know that.

Funny, when he thought about heaven at all it always came furnished with the happy, crazy love his parents had shared. He never imagined he'd be enjoying it alone.

The way things ended between us is the only thing I would change about the past days. I didn't want that to be the last thing we remembered about each other. I'm sorry.

Not nearly as sorry as he was. And it shamed him even more that she was apologising to him. For what—being strong enough to own her feelings?

That wasn't a weakness.

Kitty xx

Those were the letters that killed him, those two little 'x's. Because he knew what they stood for. And he knew, now, what two of Kitty's little kisses tasted like, and two were never going to be enough. It was a shame grown men didn't cry because this was the moment for it. The moment that her kind and gentle nature leaked through all the protective spikes. She couldn't help making good on what *he'd* caused.

'Idiot,' he murmured into the table timber, rubbing his thumb over Kitty's signature on the note. 'Freaking idiot, Margrave.'

He'd had this exact same conversation with himself five years ago as Kitty's taxi had rattled away down the hill. When he'd sent her away rather than manning up and confronting their attraction. Last night, he'd seen Kitty's hurt—practically tasted it on the frozen air—but he'd still walked away from her without explaining why.

And—once again—Kitty had paid the price for *his* lack of courage.

He simply wasn't up to history repeating itself.

He'd worked his guts out trying to save his marriage over the three years after Kitty had left, trying to be there for Marcella when maybe what he'd really needed to be doing was packing her up and sending her the heck home. Back to the conservative life she'd fled. But he hadn't—because he'd known it would kill her, spiritually, to slink home with her tail between her legs. Or worse, to be sent. And he knew she was too Southern to go back on her commitment to him. And so he'd let it slide, tried to bring her joy in other ways. But he'd failed in that just as, ultimately, he'd failed Marcella.

And then the quakes had done, literally, what he'd been afraid he'd do, spiritually.

Seriously… Someone needed to revoke his search and rescue licence with protective instincts like that.

Churchill was no prize despite its northern charms. It was remote, sometimes hostile, dead quiet except when it was bulging at the seams in tourist season, and services had a habit of simply stopping for random hours on end. That kind of life—that kind of solitude—wasn't for everyone, especially a pathologically busy woman more used to international hobnobbing. Yeah, old Kitty had loved Nepal, but she'd only been there ten days and, just like Pokhara, a few days up here was a far cry from a few months. Or years.

Marcella had loved those first weeks, too.

What if Kitty hated the place—and him—after a few months? Sending her away now was hard enough. What hope that he would ever find the courage to do it after he'd had her in his life? In his bed. In his heart.

Will pressed his thumbs to his throbbing temples.

Who was he kidding? She'd already set up a little base camp in there. She'd been there for years, quietly in her own little corner refusing to be completely set aside, resisting his efforts to wedge her back down. In his heart she was still running up and down the slope in Pokhara, playing with his dogs and embracing the Nepalese and their mountain lifestyle. If she could find genuine joy in a run-down village at the base of the Himalayas, couldn't she lean to love a small town in the sub-arctic?

And shouldn't it be her call?

His head came up.

Who was he really protecting by sending her away? He couldn't kid himself it was his marriage, this time. Or Kitty, given how destroyed she'd looked last night. There was only one person he was protecting by banishing her from his world again.

Five years ago he'd let her leave Nepal believing she was the failure. The least he could do—*the best he could do*—was not send her away from Churchill believing that again.

'Screw it,' he said and looked up at the clock.

Afterwards, Will wondered what might have happened if he hadn't sat at his dining table for quite so long contemplating the semiotic subtext of Kitty's farewell letter. Or if he'd cut ahead of the cab leaving the airport rather than courteously waiting for it to pick its way across the pocked and icy entryway. Or if he'd parked in the tow zone to get inside quicker.

Would any of those things have made the slightest difference?

As it was, he'd stood in the little airport terminal, his palms resting impotently on the icy glass, and stared at the lights of her departing flight. It was barely a glimmer now, through the steady snow, almost at the end of the runway. But it was categorically *gone*. And it had taken Kitty with it.

He got no points at all for a fruitless eleventh-hour airport dash.

Much too little, way too late.

'Did she forget something, Mr Margrave?' a friendly voice said from behind him.

He turned his confusion back to the airport staffer. 'Who?'

'Your billet.' Then at his blank expression she clarified, 'I was the one who called you earlier in the week.'

He shook away his irritation. It wasn't this woman's fault that he was such a monumental screw-up. 'No. I was just hoping to catch her before she left. To tell her something I'd…forgotten.'

'You've got about seven minutes, then.'

That brought his gaze up again before it snapped back out to the empty runway. 'What? Didn't the chartered flight just leave?'

'Ms Callaghan swapped tickets with a woman who needed it more. Her new flight has just finished loading up…'

Will followed her finger where she pointed out of a side window. A twenty-four-seater sat there, waiting.

'Scheduled to leave in seven minutes. Oops, six now—'

She didn't get any further, and Churchill just wasn't set up with the right kind of security to stop a steam train from barrelling through the doors out onto open tarmac. Will's sled boots hooked into the icy surface of the asphalt as the door swung shut behind him.

'Mr Margrave…? You can't—'

That was as far as the anxious woman got and the staff on the runway could do little else but look up as a steam train sprinted past them for the fold-down steps. He burst onto the waiting plane in a flurry of displaced snow.

'Will?' Kitty's voice squeaked at him from near the back of the plane. 'What are you doing here?'

A dozen curious eyes stared at him and one very anxious flight attendant telegraphed her alarm in the tense grip on his forearm.

'You haven't left.' The spectacular redundancy of his announcement struck him and he struggled to find a way to make the statement—and the scene he was making—a little less absurd. 'Why not?'

'Someone was desperate to get home fast,' Kitty said, as if that explained everything. 'I gave her my seat on the direct charter.'

The hostess tugged on his arm. 'Sir, I'll have to ask you—'

But he paid her no heed. 'And you're not? Desperate to go, I mean.'

Kitty's eyes rounded. 'I'm…um…'

The flight attendant surrendered her harpy's hold on his arm to turn and alert the captain to his unexpected intrusion in the tiny cabin.

Three minutes. To sum up a lifetime of baggage.

'I got your note,' he said, helplessly, down the aisle, still partly bent over to avoid hitting his head on the low roof. As good a place as any to start.

'Okay…?'

'I wondered if—' Lord, as if this weren't hard enough without an audience '—you might want to talk about it?'

She blinked at him. 'No. I left a note.'

His panic levels rose as the fuel in the jet did. *Right.*

'I just…I wanted to explain myself a bit better. About asking you to leave.'

Kitty's porcelain skin flushed and she glanced around.

It killed him to make a difficult discussion so much harder. Will turned to the flight attendant. 'Look, can we get off for a few minutes…?'

'I wish one of you would.' She glared. 'Security are on their way.'

He knew Airport Security. Justin owed him a few favours, so something told him that he wouldn't be rushing. But this wasn't a quick conversation, either.

Unless he made it one.

'I don't want you to leave, Kitty,' he blurted. 'I want you to stay. With me.'

If her blood thundered any harder it was going to start spurting out of the creases in her skin. Wouldn't that look pretty on this brand-new aircraft?

'You didn't want me to stay. You were very clear.'

He looked as pained as she felt at the memory. 'And now I do.'

'And what if you change your mind again tomorrow?'

'I won't. I've thought it through.'

She took a deep breath. 'So have I. I'm going to make a few changes to my life. And I can't do that here.'

Her words wrapped around her like a shield. She just couldn't take any more hurt today.

'I... Good,' he mumbled. 'If that's what you want. We don't get a second go at life.'

For a few lovely days she'd thought she might have.

'Doesn't it bother you?' he rushed. 'Wondering if you might be walking away from the most amazing thing in your life?'

Yes, it bothered her. But she wasn't about to admit it.

She sat up straighter. 'You have a very robust ego, Will.'

'I'm talking about me, letting you leave.'

The flight attendant glanced at her watch and stepped closer to Will. Any second now Security were going to rip him out of that door like some kind of full-body alien abduction.

'I'm not sure that more time is going to help you answer that.'

'Give me a chance—'

'You've had your chances,' she pressed. 'Two of them. And you blew it both times. I get that you were confused the first time—' *and married* '—but what's your excuse now?'

He wanted to answer; she could see it in the pinch of his face. The fold of his brows.

'You're protecting yourself from something,' she went on. 'But I need someone who will protect *me*, Will. Do you understand?'

The confession came from somewhere dark and cobwebby. Somewhere she'd never really poked around before. She didn't even know that was what she wanted until she heard it in her own voice.

But it was truth.

She wanted someone to put her first. Even if she fought them on it.

Her fellow passengers weren't even trying to be discreet any more. Their faces swivelled between the front and back of the plane like a Wimbledon crowd. Even the attendant forgot her obligations long enough to become engrossed.

'Marcella thought she wanted me but it was the dream she wanted—heroic husband, bohemian lifestyle, exotic country. Really she just wanted out of her family situation. And I was her exit. And then you were so unhappy with your job...'

Last night suddenly made so much more sense.

I'm not a ticket out of your imperfect world...

'You thought I was using you?' she whispered, horrified.

'No, Kitty, I... Not now.'

'But you did? Last night?' The air puffed out of her. 'The second time I gave you my heart wrapped in a big bow and you thought it was...what...some kind of lazy whim?'

'It was a fear, Kitty. It wasn't rational.'

'I'm not Marcella, Will.'

'I know.'

'And I wasn't using you. I just didn't want to lose you again.'

'You don't have to. Stay.'

'No.' Anger made her rash. Tired of being messed around. Even by him. *Especially* by him. 'I'm quitting my job. As soon as I get back. You were right that I need to take control of my own happiness.'

Will's face fell. 'Tell me you haven't had a taster this week. Of what we could be together. *How* we could be.'

Saying it again wasn't going to change anything so she just stayed silent. Her eyes dropped to her lap.

The whole flight looked to her. Wanting an answer to the unanswerable.

She looked back up at him. 'You broke my heart in Nepal, Will. By sending me away. You made me think that my feelings were something dirty. Then you made me feel the same way last night.'

'Kitty, I—'

'And again just now. But they're not, Will. They're the purest and most honest thing you would ever have known.'

She curled her fingers around the clasp of her seat belt. 'I have a story to finish, a job to quit and an apartment to sublet. Then I'm going home to Sydney to start over. I have so much work ahead of me and none of it is getting done sitting on this tarmac.'

Security arrived at the planeside, drawing Will's attention away.

'You leaving won't stop me from loving you,' he gritted as a security guard stepped up behind him in the doorway and clamped an authoritative hand on his shoulder.

Behind Will, the flight attendant gasped more loudly than Kitty did and it drew most of the passengers' focus off her just as she needed the respite. Just as her world dropped clean away from her as the tundra would be from this plane in about thirty seconds.

'You don't love me,' Kitty choked.

Thud, thud, thud...

'I beg to differ,' he said, all confidence despite the audience. As if just saying the words gave him a shot of courage. 'I've loved you for five years. I just didn't let myself.'

'You barely knew me, then, Will. You don't know me any better now.'

'Easily remedied,' he urged. 'Stay. And let me in.'

But, of course, she couldn't. Not if he could ever think she would use him like that.

'I'm sorry, Will,' she whispered.

It was only then that his eyes dropped to her white-knuckled grip on her seat belt. But he didn't go without a parting comment.

'Promise me that wherever you go next, whatever you end up doing, you'll do it for yourself, because it makes you happy,' he said as the single hand on his shoulder was joined by a second one on his arm. 'Not because anyone else has an expectation of you.'

There were too many tears in her throat to have a prayer of answering him. Besides, the insistent hands were now dragging him out of the plane. But Will used the final seconds before the attendant pulled the steps shut to catch her eye and hold it. Long enough that he saw her nod. It was the easiest—and the hardest—agreement she'd ever made.

The plane door and the one between the cockpit and the cabin were secured. Kitty turned her face to the window to avoid the speculative glances of her fellow passengers—or, worse, the compassion—as the aircraft started backing out into the runway apron, battling the flood of tears that she couldn't release. Not here.

Everything Will had said was pinging around her mind. That he'd been burned by Marcella. That he'd been afraid. That she needed to sort herself out.

That he loved her.

The idea of it was as terrifying as it was revolutionary. No one had loved her before, and she hadn't loved anyone either. Anyone but unattainable Will. Because if you ran hard enough and long enough then people only saw how incredibly busy you were and they failed to notice how lonely you were.

And if you did for enough years…then you did too.

A girl could go her entire life that way.

Sudden sorrow soaked into her like the melting permafrost of the Boreal that she could only just see beyond the snow out of her window. Then a breathless tightness slammed into her just as the aircraft began to taxi towards the runway.

'Are you all right?' the flight attendant asked as she did her final pre-flight check up and down the cabin. 'You're very pale.'

'I'm…um…'

Impossible to speak without air in your lungs, and to describe her body's reaction to leaving Will behind for ever. Even though it was what she wanted.

Apparently, not all of her agreed.

'Perhaps you need some air.' The flight attendant reached over her to operate the nozzle above her seat but then examined her critically. She searched right in behind her eyes. Finally, she clucked, her face full of conspiracy. 'No. That's not going to be nearly enough.'

As soon as Will was off the plane and the aircraft door was sealed, the airport's security, Justin, wordlessly dropped his firm hold on him. They'd flown bear rescues together. Justin knew he wasn't going to cause a scene. Not further than the one he'd already caused, anyway. He led Will a safe distance away and then stood officially by as Kitty's plane squared up on the runway. There were a dozen windows on the aircraft but hers was on the other side so Will wasn't even going to get a final glance. Just…nothing.

Grief sat like a stone in his gut.

He'd failed—again. But at least this time he'd taken a risk. Put her first. And if nothing else, then Kitty was leaving Manitoba knowing that he loved her.

What might that be like—being actually and genuinely loved?

Marcella never had loved him. Not truly. And if Kitty did she would have stayed, wouldn't she?

'Sorry, Will,' Justin said quietly. 'I have to escort you off-site.'

Will kept his gaze firmly pinned to the thickening snow and the tail lights fading within it. 'Yeah, okay.'

He started to turn, but as he did Justin frowned and squinted out into the airfield. 'What the—?'

Kitty.

He knew it, without even turning around. He knew it because his skin prickled and his chest swelled with hope. And because a moment later Justin's radio started to go ballistic.

Will turned in time to see a little reddish figure emerging through the snow, jogging towards the terminal on the slick runway apron. Behind her, the lights in the fog stayed put.

'I am so dead,' Justin muttered.

Kitty slowed her jog fifty feet or so away from Will, but just as he thought he'd catch her eye her left leg went out from under her on the ice and she hit the tarmac with a bone-cracking thud. Without waiting for permission— without even asking for it—he bolted away from Justin and negotiated the slippery asphalt, skidding to a halt next to where Kitty writhed. He scooped down to her and slid his arms under hers and pulled.

She turned her face up to his and said the words he'd been waiting five years for.

'Son-of-a—'

Okay, so it wasn't the words themselves. It was the ones between the lines. Her presence spoke volumes.

He hauled her up.

'Why are you smiling?' she grumped in lieu of thanks. 'I think I just broke my hip.'

Lord, if she cursed at him every day for the rest of his life he'd be absolutely thrilled. 'You're too stubborn to break anything.'

He got her stabilised on her feet but he was in no mood to let her go.

'So that was pretty dramatic,' he said, trying to keep the raw hope from his voice. Trying to keep her close.

She peered up at him. 'I changed my mind.'

'And everyone else's.'

'I'm sure the rest of the flight will be woefully uneventful by comparison to the show we just put on, but they can take off without me.'

'Not with your luggage on board, they can't. Whole plane will have to be unloaded and re-checked.'

She turned back to those irritated tail lights still sitting out in the snow waiting for instructions from…somewhere.

'Oh.'

He couldn't shake the smile still plastered to his face.

'You broke the law, Kitty.' She didn't deny it. In fact, she looked pretty pleased with herself. 'That's two of us in one day.'

'I wanted to explain something to you… Besides,' she brushed off, 'technically I disembarked on staff orders. Kind of.'

That part of the story could wait.

Will steered Kitty back towards the ice-free safety of the terminal as Justin jogged past them towards the grounded flight. They let the gathering snow give them sanctuary as it swilled around them.

'Let's go,' Will said. 'Before they throw us out.'

CHAPTER THIRTEEN

'ARISE THERE BEARS out there?' Kitty asked as Will helped her limp towards a loading door, bypassing the terminal entrance completely.

Déjà vu.

'Bears don't really like the airport.'

'Someone might have mentioned that a week ago.'

It felt like a lifetime ago. Actually, it felt like someone else's lifetime ago. Could a person change that much in six days?

'Through here...'

Will opened a side door, which let them inside the terminal just a few metres from the exit. In moments, they were through and back out into the grey of the car park.

'My bag...'

'Leave it, we'll pick it up later.'

'Can we just cut and run like this? After causing an international incident?'

'You want to go back and explain yourself?'

Good point. How could she, when she barely understood herself?

'Where's your truck?' she puffed, instead.

She thought he'd take her back to his cabin, but they were closer to his land on the edge of Hudson Bay, so Will turned right out of the airport drive and not left. With half the journey already made, it only took ten minutes on quiet white roads to get there. Even the snow lifted a little the closer they got to the bay.

'You want heating or you want to see out?'

If Will put the heater on then the windows were going to mist over within minutes. There was a risk of that anyway, the way her chest was heaving.

'I want to see.'

He killed the engine and tucked his collar higher. Before them, the deep grey silence of Hudson Bay stretched as far as they could see. Stoic, steady, non-demanding. As if it accepted any and all who came to sit there. As if neither of them had to justify today's behaviour to anyone.

'No bears?' Kitty noticed after a moment.

'Maybe there's a dozen of them over in the willow,' he said, glancing at the place the sun would be if it weren't socked in again by cloud. 'Who knows?'

On instinct, she wanted to lock her door—even if bears didn't have prehensile thumbs. This close to the water a little fog hung wispy and pretty against the backdrop of the bay.

'It's so beautiful here. Marcella would have loved to paint it.'

Will stared out at the water. 'She would have.'

'I'm not her,' Kitty said after a moment.

He turned to her. 'I know.'

'But my life *is* hollow,' she acknowledged, her head bowed. That was a more palatable word than 'empty'. 'And that's not a good reason to be with someone.'

His throat lurched. 'Yet, you're here.'

She stared at him and finally—finally—whispered from that place deep down inside where she kept all her secrets. 'What if that's what this is?'

'Is that all you think we are?'

This thing zinging between them. Even now.

'I don't know. I've carried a torch for you for so long. Maybe I just didn't want to feel alone, all this time.'

'Or...' he pressed a kiss to each of her eyes in turn, so gentle and so full of hope it physically hurt '...maybe you were alone all this time simply waiting for me? You just didn't know it.'

Deep inside, something unfurled and reached for the

shaft of light his words created. Something that had lain dormant for a very, very long time.

'You don't think I'm using you?'

Will curled his warm fingers around her cold ones.

'Marcella was desperate for a life of her own, a life of beauty, and I thought that would be enough between us, that we could grow a solid marriage on that. But it was as unsteady a foundation as the rock under our hill turned out to be.' Those beautiful blue mirrors creased. 'I didn't want that to happen with us. I was afraid of that.'

There was something about such a strong man admitting his fear... It made it possible for her to say anything.

'I was so jealous of the life you had in Nepal with Marcella,' she said. 'I thought it was perfect. So easy and equal. I would have traded spots with her in a heartbeat. Because she had Nepal and she had the life. And she had you.'

His smile slipped and she knew she'd hurt him a little. Because his life with his wife had not been at all enviable. And he would always carry that on his shoulders.

'Why did you kiss me, Will? Why not just let me fly off in the morning? If that's what you wanted.'

His head dropped. 'I'd been wanting to kiss you since you bought this damned coat.' He ran his fingers up its cherry padding. 'But things were just too...prickly before the dog run.'

'If I was defensive it was only because I was scared.'

'Of what?'

'That I was intruding—again! That I was no more welcome this time than last. And that you might be constantly searching my face for signs of rekindling infatuation. You were the last one I was going to show that to.'

Understanding dawned in his eyes. He pressed back and brushed her hair with both hands, then pressed his palms either side of her face and he just looked at her—for eternity—wanting her to see him. Really see him.

'Infatuation like this, you mean?'

'I don't want to leave,' she blurted. 'I know I should, I know it would be the grown up and responsible thing to do, but I can't leave you behind. Not twice.' She dropped her head to his shoulder.

He tucked her in close. 'You can stay as long as you want, love.'

Love.

'You're like a dog with a new toy with that word.' Making light of it bought Kitty time to grow used to it. It brought it into the realm of everyday.

When it was anything but.

'It's the novelty.' He smiled. 'My uncle was fantastic but he wasn't *parents*, you know? I spent my childhood feeling sure there must be more to love. Thank God for my uncle's dogs...'

Suddenly his career choice came into sharp focus. All that hairy, unconditional love.

'And then Marcella.'

'She was so beautiful and fragile, like some kind of ethereal creature. I was completely smitten. I married her determined that I could *make* her love me back through sheer determination. If I tried hard enough. If I worked hard enough. But then I met you.' He smiled. 'And it was immediate. I finally knew what it looked like, what I was striving for and how easy it should be. But, I wasn't free to have it.'

For the first time, Kitty recognised that she might not have been the one doing it toughest when she drove off that mountain five years ago.

'You have a lot to answer for, Will Margrave,' she muttered. 'I blamed my career for every relationship that failed to launch, but really it was just that none of them could live up to the standard you set. I couldn't shake you.'

The thought of living a life without him in her heart was almost inconceivable. That was why she'd scrambled off that plane when the flight attendant had given her the out. Not quite as dramatic as the one a week ago, but close.

His smile, then, rivalled the aurora from the night before. 'I like to think I'm memorable.'

Despite the lack of heating, the truck's windows were getting well and truly fogged up now. Robbing them of view but giving them a safe little igloo instead. Will leaned in and pressed his mouth to hers; gently, giving her plenty of scope to protest.

She didn't. Not at all.

'Tell me about quitting,' he said when the kiss ended.

She leaned back. Found his eyes. Considered her answer. 'I took a wrong turn five years ago and I've been charging off in the wrong direction ever since.'

A direction that didn't include Will.

'When did you discover that?'

There was still a note of caution in his voice. But she didn't resent it. Instead, she understood it.

Huh. There was a novelty. *Understanding* Will. Instead of doubting him, instead of fighting him.

'I think I've known for a while. I just hadn't admitted it to myself,' she said softly. 'The last time I was truly happy was in Nepal.'

'Churchill isn't Pokhara,' he warned.

'That's okay, I'm not the same me. I'm not looking to replicate what we had there.' *We...* 'I just want it in spirit. All the freedom. All the beauty.' She turned to him. 'All the love.'

Will stiffened below her cheek and eased her away from him so that he could peer down into her face, his gaze cautious but no less hot. It fairly turned the cold truck cabin into a sauna.

'Are you talking about the Nepalese?'

Their faith and their love for it had certainly been inspiring but, no. 'I'm talking about you. And me.'

'What are you saying?'

She knew what she was saying, but didn't know how to say it. Except by just finding the courage deep inside her. 'I'm saying that I will find beauty and freedom anywhere you are, Will Margrave. I'm saying that maybe I... love you, too.'

It was imperfect but it was a start.

'Maybe?' Will risked before swallowing heavily. 'Or do?'

Something shifted in the ground beneath them. Clunking into place with the kind of relief a glacier might feel when it finally reached the coast. And she knew exactly what to say.

'I do.'

If the windows weren't already so frosted over he would have steamed them well and truly over with the kiss he delivered then; long and lingering and thoroughly exploratory. And utterly full of joy.

The ground lurched again. It took Kitty a moment to realise that it wasn't the ground. Will leaned over and wiped his arm across the frosted window to peer out. A pair of curious, beady eyes surrounded by cream fur peered back in as the bear gave the truck another curious nudge with its forehead. He swore and lurched back from the window, then scrabbled to start the vehicle. The shock sound of the smooth engine turning over was enough to send the curious bear running and then lumbering and finally wandering off away from the truck to rejoin the friends that had emerged from the willow.

Will turned his shocked gaze to hers. 'Maybe he wanted us to quit melting his nicely forming ice.'

Not a chance. They were officially contributing to global warming right here, right now.

'This is us, Kitty. Predators and complicated transport and insane insects in summer.'

'And bears and beluga whales frolicking in your bay

and some pretty amazing tundra flowers judging by the brochures at the airport.'

'That's just the surface polish,' he said. 'Remote living is not for everyone.'

Kitty knew the caution in his voice wasn't for her. Another woman he'd cared about had withered away, once. Despite his best efforts.

'Given we're both probably on the airport's no-fly list now, I think the government may have decided for me.'

'I don't want the government to decide,' he said, all seriousness. 'This has to be your choice, Kitty. You have to want this—and me—for the right reasons.'

Love was the most right of right reasons, wasn't it?

She turned to him. 'If I wanted to go back to Australia? What would you do?'

'Go with you.' His answer didn't even need thought. 'If that's what it takes to be with you. *Is* that what you want?'

She looked around them, at the snow field, at the frozen-over wetlands, at the nothing as far as the eye could see. At the complete and utter freedom. And all the stories waiting to be told.

'I think Churchill is about as disconnected and insular as I can be,' she said. And if there was a town ready to accept someone like that it had to be this one. 'Maybe I could be persuaded to think about a relationship with it.'

'Persuaded? How?'

Had she honestly expected him to laugh? He looked almost nauseous waiting for her answer.

She leaned in close and breathed against his lips. 'Nothing terribly complicated.'

And then she kissed him. Touching his lips like snowfall at first, then leaning more fully into him, then clinging to him like the life-preserver his love was.

'I've always loved you, Will. Don't you dare send me away ever again.'

Ardent heat blazed down on her. 'Don't you dare leave.'

EPILOGUE

'MORNING, KITTY!' THE DENE couple across the street called to her as she kicked her boots free of dirt before climbing a few steps up into the hotel diner to meet Will.

She'd just sorted the big film crew from Norway and sent them off with their guide out beyond the river mouth and she had an hour to kill before she was due to meet with the tourism marketing types wanting to set up wildlife webcams all over the district. She had no idea how Churchill had functioned without a permanent media liaison before but she suspected that the council praised the day eighteen months ago that she'd dropped from the sky. Not that she'd be able to keep the pace up for ever, but while she *could* still do it she was very happy to. To give back to the district that had given her so much. Plus it kept her contacts up within the communities she needed to get her documentaries sold.

And they were one of the greatest joys in her brand-new life—her stories, her way, her pace.

And pace was about to become really significant.

'Morning, beautiful,' the other greatest joy said, planting a kiss onto her head and dropping into the seat across from her. 'How's the cub?'

She slipped one hand over her rapidly rounding belly. 'Busy, today.'

'Takes after its mother,' Will said as their young server arrived with fresh coffee.

'You know you won't be able to put this one in your pocket, right?' she warned him affectionately, rubbing big circles over her bump and enjoying the sigh she imagined she felt from the little person within. 'Starsky might still tolerate that but I'm going to get prickly if you try.'

'Are you kidding? Take a cub from a mother as fierce as you?'

'How was the release?'

'Went just fine. Marcella's Point is proving popular for good bear releases. Right on the edge of the conservation reserve but the chopper can land easily without disturbing the status quo.'

The repeat offenders still went a long, long way from town. Just to be sure.

'I've got some news,' Will said. 'About the Churchill Port redevelopment.'

Kitty's head came up.

'Seems the environmental authorities are going to take an eleventh-hour look at the ice-breaker proposal. Thanks to some recent media attention…'

That might or might not have been the subject of the first short film she'd shot here, right after pulling the pin at CNTV.

Mei had made that choice even easier for her by stealing Kitty's story slot and convincing the programme director that she had missed her deadline. But, she'd managed to find some compassion for her—Mei was like an aging queen in a land where youth and beauty were prized above all else and even sheer deviousness hadn't got her anywhere particularly great. And now she wasn't beautiful any more—inside or out. And she'd missed all her chances in life.

From where Kitty sat—full to bursting with Will's baby, enriched every day by this place and the work she got to do in it, loving life and all the possibilities in their future—Mei was like a cautionary tale.

'So what's the buzz in town?'

She always knew, and he always asked.

'We have a pop goddess in our midst. Literally. One of

the world's biggest. She's up here with an entourage and a film crew to snorkel with the belugas. You should see their gear—'

Will didn't even flicker an eyelid.

'You don't care, do you?'

'I care that it's good PR for the whales,' he defended. 'And if she gets herself stranded out in the Boreal, I'll care *very* much.' He leaned over the table and kissed her. 'Until then, there's only one goddess in Churchill as far as I'm concerned.'

Kitty kissed him back, pouring all the desire, admiration and respect she had into the man she loved as she breathed against his lips.

'Right answer.'

* * * * *

Girl, get over it!

Another familiar refrain, one she'd repeated daily to herself over the last few weeks, echoed in her head. Getting back to normal—whatever that might be— was harder than she thought.

That morning after Nolan left, she'd cleaned up the room as best she could. She then hurried home, determined to live up to the agreement they made. To make sure everything stayed the same. Between her and Nolan. Her and the Murphys. Her and the job she loved so much.

Easier said than done.

Yes, her actions had been dumb that night. Not just dumb, but careless, too. Hey, it wasn't the first time she'd done something stupid in her never-ending search for—

Nope, don't use the L word.

What happened that night had been a combination of lust, booze and foolishness. She'd been lucky the man she'd fallen into bed with had been someone like Nolan.

To allow herself to think one night of great sex would lead to… to something… was crazy. He'd made his feelings about their night together clear when he said they should go on with their lives as if nothing had happened.

Nothing. Yeah, right.

Welcome to Destiny:
Where fate leads to falling in love

HIS DESTINY BRIDE

BY
CHRISTYNE BUTLER

First Published in Great Britain 2016
By Mills & Boon, an imprint of HarperCollins*Publishers*
1 London Bridge Street, London, SE1 9GF

© 2016 Christyne Butilier

ISBN: 978-0-263-91993-6

23-0616

Our policy is to use papers that are natural, renewable and recyclable products and made from wood grown in sustainable forests. The logging and manufacturing processes conform to the legal environmental regulations of the country of origin.

Printed and bound in Spain
by CPI, Barcelona

Christyne Butler is a *USA TODAY* bestselling author who fell in love with romance novels while serving in the US Navy and started writing her own stories in 2002. She writes contemporary romances that are full of life, love and a hint of laughter. She lives with her family in central Massachusetts and loves to hear from her readers at www.christynebutler.com.

To my sisters Peggy and Jennifer
and the sisters of my heart,
the Gamma Theta Chapter of Beta Sigma Phi.
Thank you for letting me borrow your names
to populate the characters, businesses
and locations in my books...
The yellow roses are always for you!

Chapter One

Friday night before Halloween

It was time.

Katie Ledbetter unscrewed the lid to the almost empty mason jar, offered a quick salute and shot back the last mouthful of tequila, lime, triple sec and crushed ice.

Wow, that burned. Still, the heavy layers of self-inflicted what-was-I-thinking and why-didn't-I-see-this-coming fuzziness she'd suffered through since the end of summer were finally gone.

Now she was ready to trudge back into the eighth layer of hell, otherwise known as the dating world. It'd been two months. A long enough sabbatical to nurse any heart, even one as used and bruised as hers.

What better night than when people dressed in costumes to hide their true selves?

At least here amid the noise and crowd at the Blue Creek Saloon's annual Halloween party the deception was on purpose. Tonight one could pretend to be anyone or anything. From sexy to humorous to superhero—even happy.

Then there was the dashing pirate on the other side of the room.

She'd first seen him not long after she arrived, but that'd been a fleeting glance. Since then, she'd spotted quite a few in that same popular costume...

But there was something different about this one.

Even with the distance between them, she could see his masked profile over the turned-up collar of his coat and the long hair hanging from a tricorn hat. From the way he stared into his beer, she'd say he was a pretty gloomy swashbuckler. In a room full of partygoers he seemed very much alone.

It takes one to know one, matey.

"You totally kill in that outfit." Her friend Peggy Katz had stepped up beside her, drink in hand.

Katie blinked and wobbled on her high heels, surprised to find she'd taken a step toward the guy. Then the crowd shifted and her pirate disappeared. Ignoring her disappointment, she turned and propped a hand on one hip. "Hmm, not exactly what I was going for."

Then again, dressed as she was...

Katie had come up with her own version of the comic book villainess Harley Quinn, going old-school with a black-and-red corset, matching fishnet gloves, and a voluminous tulle skirt. A ponytailed blond wig hid her long naturally red hair. She wore a black mask over the top of her face, and white pancake makeup and deep red lips completed her look.

Either way, she appreciated her friend's words. "The object is to capture, honey, not kill."

"Well, you've accomplished that much." Peggy sucked the last of her drink through the straw. "If one more cop, cowboy or clown hits on you and ignores me, I'm going to take it personally."

"Are you kidding?" Katie dropped the throaty Brooklyn accent that went along with her character. "You're a terrific-looking witch, even beneath that crazy orange wig, black cape and pointy hat. Aren't you hot?"

"Oh, please, my hands are like ice. And not because our typical Wyoming winter is swirling outside even though it's October. Besides, I've got plenty to hide. My hourglass figure is shaped more like these mason jars." Peggy gave her almost empty glass a shake. "You ready for another?"

"Sure, why not?" Unlike her friend, Katie was quite warm but figured it had more to do with the high body count in the bar than the alcohol. Still, the last drink had disappeared fast. "I wonder what time it is."

Peggy pulled out her phone. "Almost midnight. Don't tell me you're ready to pack it in. I only get to let my hair down, so to speak, every other weekend. If Bruce decides to fulfill his fatherly duties."

Something Peggy's ex-husband hadn't done much of in the two years since the divorce, but he'd stepped it up lately, making this a rare girls' night out.

A night that included Katie and Peggy crashing next door at the boardinghouse where Peggy's sister—a traveling nurse on a relief trip in Brazil—had a room.

No worrying about driving home tonight. Let the margaritas flow.

Katie shook her head and handed over her jar. "I'm here until they kick us out. Mix, mingle and meet someone new, right?"

"Hey, I'm just the wingman—not that you need one. My only advice? Stay away from the bad boys."

Katie forced a smile. "Oh, you're no fun."

"Personal experience talking here."

Experience Katie shared. She'd dated enough of those

too-wild-to-be-tamed kind of guys herself over the years. This last time? She'd picked one who'd worn an actual star on his shirt and the white hat.

Wasn't that supposed to mean he was one of the good guys?

"Go on, the bar is back this way." Peggy turned, tossing words over one shoulder. "Mix, mingle and meet your little booty off. I'll find you."

Katie's smile slipped as her friend disappeared in the crowd.

The first two—mixing and mingling—were easy enough, but meeting someone new, considering the population of Destiny, Wyoming, was a challenge. Then again, Laramie and Cheyenne were less than an hour away and this event had become popular over the years.

Surely she could find one interesting man who was looking for something…more.

Despite a dating history that went back to the seventh grade, more often than not Katie had walked away with a broken heart. Still, she never gave up on the dream of loving—and being loved—by one special person.

This last time…a deputy sheriff and single dad. He'd been the one.

Or so she'd thought.

She'd done everything right when it came to her and Jake.

They'd been friends before she'd agreed to a date. Waited three months before getting intimate. Then another few months before she met his sweet little girls. So when he'd convinced her to move into his place back in June, almost at their one-year anniversary, she'd believed she'd found what she'd been looking for.

First cohabitation. Then a ring. One day a wedding and more chil—

"Stop thinking about him." Peggy had returned with two

more margaritas. "Don't bother denying it," she continued. "I can see it in your eyes."

Katie kept her gaze on her drink as she took a long sip. "I wasn't…not really," she said. "Okay, I was, but geesh, when it comes to my lack of success with men…"

"You're successful with men." Peggy spoke when Katie's words trailed off. "Just not at finding one who wants the same things you do."

Katie swallowed. "Ouch."

"I was right where you are now a few years ago. I'd bought into the whole he'll-change fantasy. For far too long," her friend said. "Then dating again. Yuck! Now I've only got one guy in my life."

Katie smiled. With his gap-toothed grin, red curls and love of all things Justice League, Peggy's eight-year-old son was one of her favorite people. "Curtis is just about perfect, but I don't think he counts."

"He's the *only* thing that counts."

Her friend was right. Kids came first. Always.

So much so, Katie had eagerly taken on the care of Jake's girls, ages three and five, after she'd moved in. Due to his work schedule, she'd been the one who cared for the girls at night. Then he would get home after midnight, and after a rare, quick—and, okay, fireworks-free—tumble in bed, he'd be snoring.

Days passed and they'd fallen into a pattern, with Katie convincing herself that life was supposed to be that way when it came to family. So when less than two months later Jake said he was getting back with his not-quite-so-ex-wife, Katie had been stunned.

That had been at the end of August.

If pressed, she'd admit she missed the fun and affection Jake's daughters had brought into her life more than the man who'd moved away as soon as she'd moved back into her old apartment over a vacant storefront in town.

"You know, you should've grabbed one of those Murphy brothers when you had the chance," Peggy said, yanking Katie from her thoughts. "Back when all six were single."

Katie ignored the pang in her heart and gave her standard answer to that familiar refrain. "'Those Murphy brothers' are my bosses."

"Not all of them."

"Yes, each has a share in the family business. Besides, Bryant was seeing Laurie when I went to work for them five years ago. And Ric—geesh, he was barely out of high school."

"Like you were much older. You were right out of college."

That was true. She'd met the Murphys at a university job fair that had netted her a few offers. It took only one visit to the quaint town of Destiny and the headquarters of Murphy Mountain Log Homes in a grand, two-story log home on the Murphy family ranch. That same day she'd signed on as their executive assistant.

The fact that the one brother who'd first interviewed her was six feet of perfection with sad eyes like dark chocolate hadn't factored into her decision—

"Now the guys are dropping like flies," Peggy went on. "Two married in less than two years, both expectant daddies. Two more leaving town to live with their amours in jolly old England. That leaves Ric stationed overseas and Nolan—"

"You don't have to give me a rundown, Peg. I know what's going on in their lives better than most. Even with Destiny's thriving gossip mill."

"A mill still buzzing about how the only single brother still in town isn't making time with the high school vice principal anymore." Peggy's declaration came out in a singsong voice. "Care to dish?"

No, she didn't. Katie didn't like to talk about the Murphys.

Especially about Nolan.

The brothers and their parents, the founders of the company, had been good to her from the moment she started working for them. She'd been alone, on her own for much longer than those four years at college. It'd taken her a while to accept their affection and inclusion in their personal lives as genuine.

They were the closest thing she had to family.

She'd never do anything to mess with that.

"So, what's the scoop on none of the Murphy men— or their wives—being here tonight?" Peggy continued. "Seems a bit strange not to see at least a few of them around."

Katie was glad for the change in the conversation. "Both mommies-to-be haven't been feeling well, so I'm guessing their hubbies stayed home with them. Nolan is traveling for business. Even if he were around, I'd doubt he'd be here."

"Didn't he—" Peggy paused and peeked at her glowing phone again. "Oh, what the…it's my ex. I knew it was too good to be true. Don't move. I'll be right back."

Katie, glad for the interruption, pushed any thought of Nolan out of her head, a habit she'd gotten good at over the years. She scanned the sea of costumes, from the homemade to the store-bought.

Hmm, might she get another glimpse—

Oh, there he was again.

Her pirate.

She had a better view this time, even if it was from the back. He'd taken off his jacket to reveal a white shirt with billowing sleeves and a blackish vest. The hat was gone, too. Flowing hair that had to be a wig hung past his yummy broad shoulders. It was held in place by a silk bandanna wrapped around his head.

Boy, he could've stepped off a tall-sailed, three-masted schooner.

She lowered her gaze, taking in tight breeches, knee-high boots with oversize cuffs and a sword hanging from the wide leather belt on a trim waist.

Hmm, very nice.

Then the Captain Jack wannabe turned around. His mask was much like hers; it covered most of his face, except for a strong jaw and sexy mouth accented by a pirate-type beard.

Their eyes met and held, and darn if she didn't get a little breathless. Then his gaze raked over her and Katie's skin tingled. An urge to go to him filled her, but she'd promised to stay put. Without her cell phone—there was no place to carry it in this outfit—Peggy wouldn't know where she'd gone.

Maybe he'd come to her.

She lifted her hand. Alcohol-fueled bravery had her poised to crook a finger in his direction when a group of revelers got between them. By the time they moved past, he was gone again. Darn.

Once he finished this latest beer, Nolan Murphy was out of here.

Damn, he was tired. Worse, he was hot and pissed off. Okay, hot, pissed off and surprisingly, turned on.

What a way to end a crazy week.

It had to be a hundred-plus degrees in the Blue Creek Saloon. Taking off the costume's heavy coat had helped. So had a few too many icy-cold beers that had gone down fast. Anything to stop thinking about his hard-to-please client.

What should've been an easy project—building a compound of log homes, much like what his family had done on the ranch—had turned into a project from hell. After promising to work on a new list of must-haves from the cli-

ent and his three adult children—all women and as opin-
ionated as their father—Nolan had grabbed a seat on a late
flight out of Spokane.

He'd arrived home after dinner and relieved his mom
from babysitting duty. Square footage calculations, source
materials and window placement had continued to fight for
space in his brain.

Then instead of relaxing at home, he'd let his kids convince him that dressing up in this crazy costume and coming to the party was a good idea. Luckily, his brother's lady
love was a costume designer in the movie business and
she'd sent a group of outfits to choose from for Halloween.

But eyeliner?

When Abby had insisted a pirate wasn't a pirate without
darkened eyes, he'd gone along with her putting the crap
on his face, despite the mask that would cover it.

Mainly because it was the first time he and his sixteen-
year-old daughter had talked in weeks without fighting.

The twins had chimed in and helped shave his beard,
which was now mostly gone except for a strip outlining
his jaw and a bad version of a goatee with beads dangling
beneath his chin from braided whiskers.

Proud of their handiwork, they'd insisted on snapping
selfies with him, good-naturedly threatening to post the
images online. He talked them out of that by agreeing to
go snowmobiling if the weekend's prediction of more snow
came to pass.

Abby had gone quiet, except to remind him she was
grounded—under house arrest, as she put it—until the end
of the month.

Meaning he'd have to leave her behind and ask his folks
to keep an eye on her.

Something else the two of them continued to fight about.
If she was old enough to drive and babysit her brothers, she
was old enough to take care of herself.

Nolan took a long draw on his beer. Even with his parents living next door, he wasn't comfortable leaving Abby home alone.

Not after the crap she'd pulled last month.

Asking for yet another favor from his folks was something he didn't want to do. Not after just getting home. Hell, his mom and dad were supposed to be retired.

Thanks to his brothers' love life, the family business was restructuring. Their dad was back with the company again and Nolan's workload had increased, too. His mom claimed she loved being with her grandchildren while he traveled, but it was a lot to ask of a woman who'd already raised six boys.

So he'd left tonight with the promise to discuss their weekend plans over breakfast. He could hear his kids going at it, the twins blaming their sister for spoiling their fun before he even got to his truck.

The joys of being a single parent. Especially to teenagers.

Sighing, he raised the mug to his lips for the last time and after a long chug set it down empty on the closest table. He checked his phone. After 1:00 a.m. and the party was still going strong, with more out-of-towners than he'd expected. He'd run into a few people he knew when he first arrived, most not realizing who he was until he told them.

Yeah, the costume was that good.

Since then, he'd pretty much been drinking alone while brushing off the interest of more than one female. Oh, he'd been charming, speaking in a fake pirate's accent, which proved he'd seen too many reruns of the Pirates of the Caribbean franchise.

And again, had too much to drink.

Not that he was uninterested in pursuing something with the opposite sex. He hadn't been a monk since his divorce five years ago, but lately it seemed he couldn't get a certain redhead out of his mind.

Another daily struggle, thanks to the fact she worked for him. For them.

For the family business, which meant hands off.

He'd thought he'd gotten a handle on whatever it was he felt for Katie, especially since her last relationship seemed to be the real thing, but now—

Nolan cut off the thought. It didn't make any sense to go down a path that could only lead to trouble.

Not just for him. Or her.

There was a whole group of people who'd be affected if he allowed—

Damn, there I go again!

He curled his fingers into a tight fist and pushed aside one image for another, bringing to mind the one person who'd caught—and held—his attention tonight.

And who explained his surprising state of arousal.

Everyone was here to be looked at. It was the point of a costume party, he guessed. When he felt the hairs stand up on the back of his neck, despite the crazy wig, he turned and found her staring.

His first thought had been she was a pretty sexy-looking clown, until the pieces of her outfit came together as a Batman villainess, a cool throwback to his youthful preference for the bad girl.

Temptation to lessen the distance between them had filled him.

Surprised him.

So much so that when she got lost in the crowd moments later, he decided he would finish his beer and end the evening before he did something stupid.

He needed to call one of his brothers. Driving home was out of the question.

He slapped the pirate hat back on and started walking

along the edge of the dance floor, holding tight to the costume's overcoat. There was no way he'd let anything happen to it, considering this wasn't a run-of-the-mill rental getup.

"There you are, lover!"

Luscious curves, warm and radiating a sexy scent of spicy vanilla and lime, slammed into his chest. Nolan instinctively wrapped his free arm around the woman's svelte waistline, mostly to keep the both of them from toppling to the ground.

His first thought was that she must have mistaken him for someone else, but then her lips brushed at his ear. "Play along, please."

Her whispered words, a fiery blast on his skin, surprised him. Her voice almost sounded familiar. "Hey, do I know—"

"But no booze. Whaz up with that?" The blonde switched to a nasally accent, her voice loud again as she gave him a quick squeeze and whirled back around, grabbing at his waist as she stumbled. "Ya see? Not for nuttin', but I told yuz I had a fellow here. Now, amscray."

Nolan had no idea what was going on.

The costumed guy standing in front of him resembled a deranged clown with his red hair and yellow jumpsuit. He was eyeing the beauty hanging on to Nolan with a nasty glare.

He pulled her closer and looked down, surprised to find he was holding the lady he'd caught checking him out earlier. A sexy Harley Quinn, right down to the character's Brooklyn accent and attitude.

An attitude with a hint of fear.

"Me and my captain's gotz plans. So yuz can move on," she slurred, waving an empty glass jar in the air. "No interest here."

"You were interested a few minutes ago," the clown said.

"N-not really." She dismissed him as she handed off the jar to a waitress. "Jusz passing time."

"Just a tease," the guy growled and took a step forward. "Typical of a drunken girl on the prowl—"

"That's enough, matey." Nolan slipped back into full pirate mode with the fake British tenor, his voice low as he angled himself between the clown and the lady. "The lass is taken. So you take a walk."

"Or what? You'll challenge me to a duel, Captain Kangaroo?"

The sword hanging from Nolan's waist was a prop, but it'd do some damage. Still, he didn't plan to be goaded into a fight.

He had no idea who this guy was, but he figured the jerk wasn't a local. Hell, she probably wasn't, either, but she obviously didn't want anything to do with this clown.

"Oh, get lost." Miss Quinn grabbed at Nolan's vest, pressing those curves against him once more. "Come on, Cap'n Jack. Let'z dance."

Dancing was the last thing Nolan wanted to do. Okay, last after fighting.

He was too old, too tired to deal with either tonight.

Yet he shuffled backward, watching the pissed-off clown stomping off into the crowd. Nolan could've escaped then from the slightly tipsy and very sexy bad girl in his arms and been on his way, too.

Instead he tossed common sense to the wind, cursed the booze floating in his veins and pulled her in close.

Chapter Two

"It'z not Sinatra, but it'z slow." Katie enjoyed the solid feel of the sexy pirate. She hoped she still sounded like the Brooklyn villainess she was pretending to be. This guy was as much of a stranger to her as that jerk from a moment ago. Her instincts told her she could trust him, but still... "Hang on, sailor. Thingz might get bumpy."

"Don't you think—"

Lost in the warmth of his embrace as a slow country song played, she reached up and found his mouth with her fingertips on the first try. Light pressure cut him off. "Naw, no thinking. No talking, no names. Jusz dancing."

He went still for a moment, but then his lips creased into a smile and his arms tightened around her. Happy with his submission, she withdrew her hand, moving it downward over the softness of his goatee, the beads woven into his whiskers tapping against her fingers.

Slowly, she traced over his Adam's apple, past his collarbone until her palm rested on his chest. His heart pounded fast beneath her touch in a cadence that matched hers.

Flying into a strange man's arms probably wasn't the best idea, but that clown-costumed jerk wouldn't take no for an answer. And she hadn't been flirting. With Peggy gone for the last hour thanks to her ex bailing on their sick son, Katie had partied on with more margaritas. She'd been heading for the exit when that joker got in her way and wouldn't leave her alone.

Who knew the one guy who'd caught her eye tonight would show up right when she needed him?

Boy, he was tall. Even in her heels, she only came up to his shoulder. She pressed her cheek to the leathery softness of his vest and held tight to a muscular bicep beneath the long strands of a pretty impressive dreadlock wig. A deep inhale brought in a fresh, clean, outdoorsy aroma with a hint of pine from his aftershave.

Hmm, she would've guessed his scent would be more like the ocean.

This fragrance was almost…familiar? No, that couldn't be right.

Then he shifted his hands against her lower back, pulling her even closer, and all rational thought fled. Her skin got all tingly when he laid a hand flat on her tulle skirt just above her backside, causing his costumed jacket to brush against her legs.

They moved in a slow circle, the couples surrounding them doing the same. She was already a bit dizzy and tired, so it was easy to let her eyelids drift closed and get lost in the moment.

Lost in the strength of a pirate's embrace.

The song ended too soon, but the band started another. Her pirate didn't make any move to break his hold. Staying right there was fine with her. More songs came and went; she didn't bother to count how many.

Dreamland was only inches away when another couple bumped into them. She held on as her feet tangled with the pirate's. They stumbled but remained upright. Before she could come up with something witty, she caught sight of that clown loser again on the edge of the dance floor, peering into the crowd.

And he wasn't alone.

The last thing she wanted was to cause another scene or, worse, an all-out brawl that would bring the cops. A given, considering the bar's owner was married to the town sheriff.

She pushed against the wide chest of her pirate. He released her. A gentleman's move she could appreciate, but she missed his strength as he stepped back.

"Oh, bugger, the clown's returned." She jerked her head in the guy's direction, the bangs of her blond wig falling over her eyes. She shoved the fake hair back into place and grabbed her pirate's hand. "With hiz rat pack in tow. Come on, let'z blow this pop stand."

She headed for the other side of the dance floor, glad her new friend followed without hesitation. Weaving through the crowd, she peeked back past the other couples and caught the moment they'd been spotted.

Oh, this wasn't good.

She glanced over her shoulder at her rescuer. "Lose the hat, Captain. It sticks out like a sore thumb."

He grinned, as if he was enjoying this little adventure. "Why are we running, lass?"

"I don't want blood on my outfit." Returning his smile was easy. "Especially yours. Fight or flight? I pick flight."

He let go of her long enough to do as she asked, then handed off his hat to her before glancing over his shoulder. Moving in close, he placed a hand on her lower back and guided her through the crowd.

"Move it, me buxom beauty." He leaned in, his breath

stirring the hair at her temple. "They be creepin' up our starboard."

Katie did as she was told, liking how his pirate swagger sounded even as the quick pace made her woozier. She looked for one of the bouncers when they reached the large double doors, but none were around.

What now? Did they go their separate ways? Did the pirate have a way home? Was he able to drive?

He had seemed to enjoy himself, even after this game of cat and mouse started, and she wasn't going to leave him stranded in the parking lot. Not with that jerk and his friends around, spoiling for a fight.

"Be honest, girlfriend," she muttered. "You don't want this night to end yet. Or for him to go anywhere."

"Did you say—"

"Nothin'. Never mind." Katie cut him off and glanced back again.

Yep, they were still being followed.

She pushed out the doors, shivering in the night air as they stepped onto the wood plank sidewalk that ran the length of the building.

Yeah, insisting she wouldn't need a jacket for the short walk back to the boardinghouse had been dumb. The chill made her shiver, but then the wind and icy temperature disappeared, cut off by the warmth of scratchy wool enveloping her shoulders, not to mention the rest of her.

He'd given her his jacket. How sweet! No one had ever done that for her before.

She shot him a quick smile. "Thanks, pal."

"You're welcome, Miss Quinn."

He recognized whom she was dressed as! A crazy thrill raced through Katie over that fact, but then angry shouts from behind had her slapping his hat against his chest.

He took it and she grabbed his hand again, the solution

to their problem coming at her as bright as a lightbulb. "Follow me."

She hurried across the parking lot, weaving through the now leafless cottonwoods that separated the bar from the boardinghouse. It was snowing lightly, enough that their footprints would be visible, but that couldn't be helped.

Her breaths came out in wispy puffs as she raced up the porch steps to the outside entrance, thankful they didn't have to go through the main lobby to get to the room.

She stopped at the door, her pirate right behind her blocking the wind. She couldn't see their assailants, but their voices carried as they found the two sets of footprints leading this way.

"I'm guessing you've got a bloody key..."

His husky voice faded when she dug into the left side of her push-up bra, having tucked the keys Peggy had given her earlier there. Her heart slammed inside her chest as her first attempt at unlocking the door failed. An unladylike but very Harley Quinn–like curse fell from her lips.

"Here, let me." He grabbed the keys, working one into the lock. Nothing. The shouts of their pursuers were louder now. "Which one is it?"

"Darn if I know." Katie stomped her feet, her toes now frozen. "Those guys are crazy! And getting closer! Hurry!"

They should've stayed at the bar. Should've found security and had those jerks kicked out. Here, they were alone, short of waking up the other tenants. She hated the idea of anyone ending up in a fight because of her—

Just then her pirate's strong arm slid beneath the jacket and grabbed her around her waist as the door opened and they stumbled inside. The warmth of the room slapped against her cheeks and the cold disappeared.

Seconds later she heard their pursuers on the porch, right outside. Had they see them come in here? Would they—

Fists pounded on the door as angry voices called out.

Katie jumped, grabbing at his shirt.

The click of the dead bolt sliding into place echoed in the air. "Be still, lass. The blasted fools will give up soon." Her pirate's voice was calm as he whispered at her ear. He tightened his hold. "It'll be all right."

Moments later, the voices faded and the footsteps continued on until there was nothing but silence. Well, except for her punching out breaths in an attempt to slow the adrenaline racing through her. He was right there, too, his chest rising and falling in a tempo that betrayed his soothing words.

She looked up, wanting desperately to see him, but they were in almost total darkness. The only light came from a night-light on the far side of the room, but his wide shoulders cut out most of it. With his wig and mask she could barely make out his features.

She lifted her hand and traced the edge of his beard, from his ear down to his chin, the sharp intake of breath his only reaction to the contact.

"Thanks, Cap'n," she whispered, "for saving my butt..."

Her words faded as a light thud sounded—his pirate hat hitting the floor.

His fingers brushed aside the bangs of the wig that hung to her eyes. His touch was hot, radiating through her mask as he traced the material down her temple until he reached her cheek and then her mouth.

Her breathing grew short and choppy again as he slowly rubbed at her bottom lip with his thumb, the friction igniting a burst of need inside her. Of its own volition, her tongue darted out, licking the tip of his finger.

A low groan filled the air. His groan. He pulled her up hard against his chest.

Grabbing at wide shoulders, she stretched onto her tiptoes, bringing their mouths to within inches of each other as his hand moved to the nape of her neck.

Anticipation crackled between them and then his mouth crashed down on hers.

Her lips parted, giving permission to the hunger in his kiss, and he took it, deepening the connection in a searing and demanding way. She welcomed his desire and returned it, having never felt like this before.

This alive, this connected.

His jacket fell from her shoulders, the loss of the warmth causing another shiver to race through her, but he tightened his hold as the kisses went on and on. Finally, needing to breathe, they broke apart, his mouth moving to her neck. He made his way to her ear as his hands dropped to cup her backside, tucking her tightly to him.

"Should I go?" he whispered. "Tell me now."

A flicker of awareness at his soft words stole through her.

Did she—was he someone she—

He pressed her even closer, the heat of his mouth on her skin incinerating her thoughts, replacing them with half-hearted mental protests. This was crazy. All of it. The whole night. She didn't do this kind of thing anymore. The careless girl she'd been all those years ago was gone.

To be this way, with him…now…tonight wasn't what she'd been looking for.

But was it what she needed? What she wanted?

The arguments rattled her brain. Yes, she should tell him to go. Ignore everything in her that screamed how much she wanted the exact opposite.

The last hour or so with this man had been the most fun, most wild, most perfect in a long time. This was reckless and wrong and she'd be anguished over her actions come morning, but would she regret more not taking this moment?

She didn't know, didn't care.

She wanted this. Wanted him.

"Stay," she breathed as he sought out her lips again. "Stay with me tonight."

As soon as she spoke, he leaned back. She could almost feel his gaze on her. Fear that he'd changed his mind lanced through her like a sharp stick.

She tightened her grip on his shirt and then his mouth was on hers again. Frantic touches, pushing aside pieces of clothing, shuffling to the large bed against the far wall. His sword, vest and shirt disappeared. He bumbled through removing his boots but took pleasure in the slow rasp of the zippers on hers.

Still on his knees, he tugged at the elastic waist of her skirt, skimming it over her hips and down her legs before getting to his feet again. Loosening the stays of her corset had him whispering a piratey "bloody hell" hotly against her skin when the cords tangled. They finally gave way and he left kisses in their wake.

She reached for her wig, but then he was kissing her again, capturing her hands in his. They collapsed back into the softness of the blankets, and she thought of nothing more than finding solace and pleasure with his every touch, rapture with every kiss and escape in his arms.

Something was...not wrong, exactly, but Nolan still felt as if he were suffocating beneath whatever was strangling him. He turned his head so breathing came easier and brushed at his face and neck, pushing the silky smoothness away, thinking it felt a lot like a cat.

If he owned one, which he didn't.

What the hell was that?

It took a moment, but it all came back.

The pirate costume, the wig, the party, the drinking.

The girl.

Transfixed by her boldness in the bar, he'd been content to hold onto those sweet curves as they danced, enjoying the way she burrowed into his chest. Then their escape, him following her lead into the cold and to a dark room, her in his arms once more and then...

Yeah, and then.

He squeezed his eyes shut and raked his hand higher. His fingers tangled with the wig and he fisted the strands, faintly remembering taking it, and the mask, off sometime in the middle of the night.

He tossed it in the direction of the floor, the jerky movement causing the jackhammer ramming inside his head to go into overdrive. Then he went still; only his eyelids moved as he blinked and tried to focus on his surroundings in the dark room.

He remembered the room. Sort of. Stretching one leg, he felt the cool sheet against his bare skin. And he wasn't lying in bed alone.

Forcing himself to sit up, he heard a soft feminine moan come from his companion as she rolled away, taking the majority of the sheets with her. He swung away as well, planting his feet on the floor, and waited for his head to stop spinning.

And to see if she woke up.

Nope, not another sound except for the gentle breathing of Miss Harley Quinn, alias...who knew?

This was not good.

He never got her real name. Never shared his.

Damn, what made him do such a thing?

Was it the booze? The rush of playing out a fantasy of being someone else for the night? The fact he hadn't been with a woman in over a year?

Hell if he knew, but at least he remembered being sober enough to make sure she'd wanted him to stay.

Oh, yeah, she'd wanted him as much as he'd wanted her.

After a quick search of the floor for most of his clothing, he found the bathroom. He took care of business, ignoring the glass-walled shower that beckoned, settling instead for washing the remains of the makeup from his face with a flowery-scented soap.

Dressing quickly, he checked for his wallet, keys and cell phone, all still in his pockets. It was almost 5:00 a.m. He had to get home. If the kids woke up and found he wasn't there, they would call out the troops.

Namely, his brothers. A Murphy search party? No, thanks.

But first things first.

He reached for the door, realizing he hadn't had to deal with morning-after awkwardness since his freshman year in college. At least back then he'd been gentleman enough to get the girl's name first.

Oh, how times had changed.

He opened the door, allowing a shaft of light to fall across the bed, highlighting the lady's curves and stopping him in his tracks.

The bedsheet only came up to her hips, leaving the rest of her bare for his viewing pleasure, including a tiny waist and the smooth expanse of her back. He noticed for the first time a script tattoo running vertically the length of her spine. It ended—or began—with a grouping of yellow flowers at the dip just above her luscious backside, but he was too far away to make out the words.

A part of him felt like a voyeur for even looking at her, despite the intimacy they'd shared last night, but he couldn't help it.

Or his body's reaction as the memories of the two of them flooded his head.

His gaze continued upward to a mass of red wavy hair, most of it pulled forward and disappearing over one shoulder except for a lone piece that curled—

Wait, red hair? Last night she'd been a blonde.

It had been a wig, part of her comic book character costume. She'd removed it during the night as well.

His gut clenched as he remembered the feel of her real hair trailing over his chest and stomach, but to see it now, the rich, vibrant chestnut color lying against her skin...

It was a very familiar color.

Nolan's gaze ran the length of her once more before recognition slammed into him. Closing his eyes, he slumped against the doorjamb.

No, it couldn't be. There was no way he had—they had...

It couldn't be her.

It couldn't be Katie.

He forced himself into the room and around the end of the bed. Tripping over his boots, he swore softly beneath his breath, grabbed the footwear and kept moving until he could see her.

Even in the dimly lit room, her long red hair stood out against the smoothness of her skin and the white sheet she held against her body. Her wig was long gone and so too her mask.

Yes, the woman he'd spent some pretty memorable hours with was indeed Katie.

His Katie.

Their Katie.

Nolan dropped to a chair across from the bed and stared at her for a long moment before he shut his eyes. Memories of holding her, touching and kissing her and her doing the same to him came rushing back.

His chin to his chest, he opened his eyes again, his gaze on the boots held tightly in his hand.

Put them on. Get the hell out of here.

His gut clenched. Running away wasn't going to fix this. Nothing was. How could he have not known—

She mumbled something, and his head jerked up.

He ignored the intense pain the action created and waited. She remained silent, eyes closed. The air rushed past his lips in a low whoosh as he sat there, taking in the beauty that was Katie.

He'd never seen her like this.

At the office she was always poised and polished, from the top of her perfectly styled hair to her feet, usually encased in high heels, even in the middle of a Wyoming winter. And then there were the times they saw each other on the weekends, somewhere in town or at a family gathering. She was always so pulled together, even casually dressed in jeans.

Now, her curls were a mess and even with traces of the white makeup that had covered the lower half of her face still on her cheeks, she looked...

Hell, younger than her age, which was a full ten years junior to his. Another reason, besides the fact she was his employee, that kept him from acting on—

Dammit, from crawling right back in that bed.

He had to get out of here.

For both their sakes.

He didn't want to do anything to jeopardize her working for his family. Okay, anything *more*. He had to forget this night ever happened, and if Katie woke up thinking the guy she'd hooked up with was a louse who'd walked out on her, all the better.

Especially because it'd be true.

Yanking on his boots, he hunted around for the belt, sword, hat, wig and jacket. He turned for the door, his hand almost on the knob when her soft words stopped him.

"Hmm, I hope you're heading out to grab some morning java."

Nolan closed his eyes.

"I'd like a large," she went on. "Decaf. Minimum four sugars to make it tolerable."

All information he was well aware of.

He took a deep breath and turned back. "Yeah, I know how you like your coffee, but no, I—"

"Wait...what?" She shot up in bed, those red waves bouncing around her shoulders as she clutched the sheet to her chest. "How do you—why are you—oh my god, Nolan! What are you doing here?"

He stayed silent, watching as she processed the night's events. Her gaze went to the rumpled sheets and empty spot beside her, to him, and back to the bed again. "Oh, no, that was *you*? That was *us*? But how—did we—"

We did. Three times. Something else he hadn't done since his college days.

He offered a silent prayer of thanks for the trio of condoms he'd had in his wallet. "Yeah, evidence seems to indicate that was us."

"But you...you were on a business trip."

"I got back early."

"And decided to go to the party? Alone?" She covered her face with her hand. "Please, tell me you weren't there with—"

"No." He cut her off, clearing up that assumption right away. His time with the high school vice principal had ended after a few weeks and, yeah, he could blame Katie for that, too, but there was no way he was telling her that.

Not now. Not ever.

"I was at the Blue Creek alone...until I ran into you."

Her hand fell away. "You mean until I ran into you. Literally."

He nodded again, the stupid beads in his whiskers knocking against his chin. What he'd give for a razor. "Yeah. I had no idea who you were."

"I had no idea who *you* were," she cried. "How could we not know? We've worked together nearly every day for the last five years. I've been to your house. Your family's home. Family events. Geesh, we're practically—"

"I can't explain." Nolan cut her off before she said the *F* word one more time. "Great costumes on both our parts—impressive accent, by the way—and what I can assure you on my end was a lot of booze."

"Mine, too, but that's no excuse. Oh, this is all my fault." Katie shook her head in disbelief. Her fingers churned, gathering the sheets and exposing those long legs of hers. "I thought I was ready. I thought I needed—I should've… I can't believe—"

"This is not your fault." Nolan started toward her but halted when her wide eyes latched onto him again. "I was there—here—too. I could've walked away at any time last night."

"When? When I pushed you onto the dance floor?" She grabbed a pillow and crushed it to her chest. "Or dragged you out of the bar? Across the parking lot until I had you alone in this room?"

"We were trying to get away from those goons."

"That was my fault, too."

"Hey, I kissed you first."

And he wanted to do it again.

Right here. Right now.

In fact, the need to go to her, to pull her into his arms, was so strong he had to take a step back or else he might do just that.

Her beautiful green eyes sought out his, and silence stretched between them again.

He wondered what was going on in that pretty head of hers, especially when her gaze traveled the length of him, taking in his wrinkled clothes.

Was she remembering last night?

How she'd easily rid him of the belt and sword before moving on to the buttons of his shirt. How he'd fumbled with the strings on her top while laying kisses against the sweetest-smelling skin—

"Do you want me to turn in my resignation?"

Her question shocked him. How could she think he'd want that? "What? No, of course not."

"If you don't want me to quit, what do you suggest we do about last night?"

"Nothing." The answer came so fast, despite the enticing images racing through his head, it had to be the right one. The only one. "We keep this—to ourselves. Tell no one and just go back…to, well, back to normal."

"Normal? As in we pretend—" she waved a hand at the empty spot in the bed where he'd lain next to her "—this never happened?"

Her question burned, an acid-filled sting that raced across his chest, but he nodded anyway. "Exactly. The fewer people who know the better."

"Half of Destiny was at the bar last night." She sighed and rested her chin on the edge of the pillow. "Didn't you run into people you know? I did. Quite a few."

"None when we were together. And we left in such a hurry I doubt anyone paid attention. Besides, I wasn't the only guy dressed like this last night."

Meaning if someone remembered her in her unique Harley Quinn costume getting up close and personal with a pirate, it could've been any number of men.

And didn't that thought sit like a rock in his gut.

"What about your brothers?" she asked, her voice soft now. "Do any of them know you went to the party last night?"

"No, but that'll change soon enough."

"Why?"

"My kids were the ones who insisted I needed to get out. Have some fun. And you know my fam—ah, they'll find out."

"Well, everyone knew I was going. I talked about my costume all week."

Nolan dragged his hand through his hair. Damn, this was too complicated to think about, especially when he was hungover and in desperate need of the coffee Katie had mentioned earlier. "We don't have to pretend like we never saw each other."

"Just that we never ended up...you know."

Yeah, he knew.

He also knew that unless they put a screeching halt to whatever this was, or could be, they'd only be asking for trouble.

A lot of trouble.

There was enough upheaval at the headquarters as it was. Add the fact that he and his daughter were barely speaking. And Katie's breakup with that jerk at the end of the summer still had to be hurting—

Whoa, wait a minute. Is that what last night was about? Looking for someone

Nolan pushed away that thought before it could fully form, chalking up the vile taste in the back of his throat to the amount of booze still in his system. "We don't want to screw things up—to change anything. It wouldn't do any good if we—"

Damn, this was coming out all wrong. His frustration spilled out in a growl. "I'm trying to do what's best for both of us. Keeping what happened last night just between us is the right thing to do. Agreed?"

She opened her mouth, the tip of her tongue darting out to lick at her lips. The simple action had the blood rushing from his pounding head southward.

He shifted the heavy overcoat in front of him. He needed to get out of here soon or he was going to forget all the crap he'd just said and—

"Agreed."

Her quiet acceptance should've made him happy, but her soft tone, and the fact she kept her gaze lowered and centered on the bed, bothered him.

More than he was going to admit, which made no sense at all because he'd gotten what he wanted. Which meant he should get out of here. Now.

"So, I'll see you…ah, at the office. On Monday."

"Right. Monday."

"Katie, I'm—"

"Don't." Her green eyes blazed. "Apologizing is the worst thing you could do right now. Worse than sneaking out on me."

He should've known she'd figured out that had been his first idea.

And he wasn't going to say he was sorry. How could he when everything in him wanted to go right back to that bed and be with her again?

"I didn't plan on this—" Nolan backed up to the door. He reached behind him and twisted the knob. "I don't want you to think—I'm not—I just wasn't expecting it to be you."

Katie turned away, biting hard at her bottom lip. She remained silent for so long he wondered if he should just get out of here.

Then she raised her head, and tossed those beautiful red curls back over one bare shoulder. "That's okay. I wasn't expecting it to be you, either."

Chapter Three

A shot of rum didn't go with today's festivities. Nolan didn't care. He needed something stronger than punch or champagne mimosas.

The Murphy family log home was teeming on this chilly yet sunny November afternoon with what he guessed was most of the female population of Destiny. Katie included.

His vantage point at the bar on the far side of the large living room allowed him to keep an eye on her while watching the time-honored rituals associated with a new baby on the way. Or two babies, as was the case today.

The dual baby shower for Fay and Laurie, his sisters-in-law, was in full swing despite the half foot of fresh snow outside. Katie had stepped in to help complete plans for the event after his mother fell on a patch of ice last week and broke her arm. But Katie would've been here anyway.

She was friends with Fay and Laurie. Friends with everyone in his family.

Friends with him.

At least they had been.

But since they'd accidentally slept together two weeks ago, she rarely looked at him.

Hell, she hardly spoke to him unless it was work related. Even then, she used the fewest number of syllables possible.

Something he wasn't used to, because Katie talked. A lot.

She liked to repeat herself, rearranging her words while saying the same thing, all to get her point across. Usually because it took him and his brothers a few pseudosmacks to the back of the head to acknowledge she was right.

So her silence, especially today when she hadn't yet uttered a sound in his direction, bugged the crap out of him. He debated if he should corner her.

Demand to know how long she planned to treat him like a polite stranger.

It seemed like a good idea.

Then again, his last good idea was to spend the night with a bewitching creature who turned out to be—

"A beer. My kingdom for a beer." Adam's words cut into Nolan's thoughts as he joined him, setting a glass of punch on the bar's smooth surface. "Ah, I see the captain is enjoying a bit of the Captain." He grinned. "You going to do that straight or add some soda for taste?"

Nolan stashed the booze away and grabbed a can of diet yuck and a cold beer for his brother from the minifridge below the counter. "Add some soda. And stop calling me the captain."

"Hey, you pulled off that pirate guise better than Johnny what's-his-name. After seeing the pictures, you got to expect the nickname's going to stick for a while."

Yeah, it would. His brothers would make sure of it.

"So, you never did share any details of the bash at the Blue Creek. How was it?"

Nolan added enough soda to his glass to be respectable. "I told you. I told everyone. It was—"

"Fine. So, I heard," Adam cut him off. He leaned in close, dropping his voice. "Who'd you hook up with that night?"

He took a quick swallow, keeping his poker face—thankfully he was the king among his brothers at cards—firmly in place. "What makes you think I did?"

"You didn't?"

"Did I say that?"

"You haven't said anything...yet."

Setting his glass back on the bar top, Nolan returned Adam's stare.

There was less than two years' difference between them, but the man took his role as the eldest brother seriously. Always the protector, ready to knock heads together or defend any of the family if needed.

He'd also been away for most of his adult life, serving in the military.

Now retired, Adam had planned to center his life on his ranch, which butted up against the family's land, until he found out Fay had become pregnant with his child after a one-night stand. He had rejoined the family business, and after a bumpy start, he and Fay were happily married with a son, A.J., not quite a year old, and another baby on the way.

"Well?" Adam offered a raised eyebrow.

Nolan thought about the agreement he and Katie had made that morning, but that was before she refused to look him in the eye. To talk to him. Before they started skidding around each other like a pair of new foals sharing the same barn stall.

Maybe he could get a little brotherly advice and still keep their secret.

"Yeah," he admitted, still not sure he should be doing this. "I met someone."

Adam nodded. "I figured as much."

"How's that?"

"Fay sent me on a late-night run for mint ice cream and corn chips." He held up a hand. "Don't ask. I spotted your truck in the Blue Creek parking lot."

"So?"

"So, four in the morning and yours was one of only a half dozen vehicles still there. You're not dumb enough to bring a date back to your place. Not with your kids around. You end up at hers?"

Nolan nodded, remembering how Katie explained the room at the boardinghouse. Had she dragged him back to her apartment, he would've figured out fast who Harley Quinn was.

Would that have stopped him from being with her?

Her bright yellow floral-print dress caught his eye from across the room. Katie walked among the guests, chatting while balancing a tray of goodies, pretty as a sunny spring day. Her hair was pulled back in a high ponytail that bounced when she moved, and matching yellow heels made her legs look fabulous.

Yeah, she loved her high heels.

He once asked her not long after she started working for them how she managed to keep her balance in those things. She'd said she took a special class in college. Squeezed it between Global Business Ethics and Corporate Law for Entrepreneurs her senior year.

He'd felt like a louse, but she'd laughed and waved off his apology.

She'd then proceeded to point out a missed loophole in one of their biggest contracts, saving them a sizable amount of cash.

"Hello?" Adam rapped a knuckle on the wood counter. "Earth to Nolan."

"Yeah, I'm here." He watched her offer the tray to a

group of ladies. The move allowed that waterfall of red hair
to slide over her shoulder. Just as it had that night. After
the wig came off.

Only he hadn't known the color of his companion's hair
then.

"And yeah, we ended up at her…place."

"You going to see her again?"

"See who?" Bryant joined them. "Don't tell me Nolan's
got himself a new girl."

Nolan groaned. "Tell me why my dating life is so interesting to you guys?"

"Hey, you're the only one left," Bryant said. "Who
knows when Ric will get home again and Liam and Dev
are happily solvent on the other side of the ocean."

"Stop talking like a finance guy." Adam took a sip of
his beer.

"I am a finance guy. What's wrong with being solvent?"
Bryant gestured his desire for a beer, too. "It's important
for a couple to be financially secure, especially once they
decide to start a family."

"You score points with the missus with all that money
talk?" Nolan asked, getting his brother a cold one.

"Thanks to doctor's orders, I'm not scoring much of anything these days." Bryant grinned. "I'm okay with that."

Nolan knew that to be true. Laurie had suffered through
a rough miscarriage a year ago. She and Bryant were over
the moon about this pregnancy and were taking every pre-
caution the doctors handed down. He and Adam were the
celebrating dads-to-be today even though their wives got
all the attention.

"No worries," Adam said. "Nolan's getting the job done."

"Halloween party, right?" Bryant asked, lifting the bottle to his lips.

Adam answered before Nolan could open his mouth. "I
was about to find out if he plans to see her again."

"See who?"

"Who is the question. He never told me her name."

"Well, don't let me interrupt your girl talk. Go on. Spill."

Nolan stared at his brothers' grinning faces. This conversation was getting away from him. Fast. He needed to come up with a diversion, but his mind was a blank.

Except for Katie.

Story of his life for the last two weeks.

He had projects up to his eyeballs. The kids were at each other's throats. Mom's accident threatened to derail her complex holiday plans for both Thanksgiving and Christmas. Still, he couldn't concentrate on anything but what had happened between him and Katie.

This had to stop. He had to find a way to fix things. Now.

Only once he let his brothers in on the truth, they would either kill him for dipping into the company office pool or bust his chops based on nothing but sibling code.

He was so screwed. "Forget about it."

"No can do. Come on, who was she?" Adam pushed.

"No one."

"No one important?" Bryant asked.

Nolan's fingers tightened on his glass. "I didn't say that."

"So she is important. Or could be. Maybe we can help."

Now he was confused. "Help with what?"

"You've been an SOB for the last week and if you can't get help from your bros—" Bryant shrugged "—who can you turn to?"

"I haven't been an SOB."

"Yeah, you have," Adam and Bryant said in unison.

"Hell, even Dad thinks you've gone off the deep end," Adam continued. "You're either snapping our heads off or shutting down completely. With everyone. Even—"

"Fine." Nolan tossed back his drink, the rum burning his throat. "It's Katie."

As soon as the words left his mouth, he wished for them

back. Especially when the blank expressions on his brothers' faces said they had no idea whom he was talking about.

"Forget I said—"

"Katie?" Bryant asked. "Katie who?"

At that moment the object of their discussion turned, her gaze catching and holding Nolan's.

She stood on the other side of the room, near the dining room table covered with gifts. Too far away to hear, but something made her glance his way, her facial expression the same as it'd been since that night. Cool. Professional.

No matter, the stiff set of her shoulders said plenty. Someone called out to her and she turned away.

"Yeah, who's Kat—" Adam started, then stopped. His head whipped to the crowd of ladies then back. "Wait a minute. You mean…" He leaned forward, lowering his voice. "*That* Katie? *Our* Katie?"

Bryant's brows were dipped in confusion for a moment longer before understanding dawned. "Whoa, Katie? Are you nuts?"

Yeah, he was. Especially for opening his big mouth.

"Jeez, she's practically family."

He turned to Adam. "Don't say that."

"She's been like a sis—"

"I really wish you wouldn't say *that*." Nolan cut him off, pushing aside his desire for another shot. He instead went for a beer and got two more for his brothers. They looked as if they needed them.

"What in the world made you pick her?" Bryant asked, matching his tone to Adam's. "Of all people?"

"I didn't exactly pick—we sort of ran into—hell, she was in costume," Nolan growled. "So was I. She was drinking. I was drinking. It was late. It was dark—"

"Spare us the details."

"I didn't know—she didn't know. It wasn't until the next morning we realized what happened."

"How could you not know?" Adam demanded.

Before Nolan could explain anything else, there was commotion at the entryway. Devlin and Tanya came into the room, loaded down with suitcases and presents, surprising everyone.

Thankful for the interruption, Nolan swallowed half his beer as his folks welcomed home another of their wayward sons. Soon, Tanya joined Fay and Laurie just as they were about to start opening the gifts.

Devlin spotted his brothers and headed their way, but stopped to give Katie a big hug.

A flash of something hot filled Nolan's gut. *Don't be stupid!*

Still, the burn didn't fade, especially when his brother left a lingering kiss on Katie's cheek.

"Hey, guys, surprised to see me?" Devlin asked with a big smile when he joined them.

"Believe it or not, you showing up isn't the biggest surprise today." Adam shot Nolan a hard glare. "It's good to have you home."

"You back to stay?" Nolan asked. He got his brother a cold root beer, as close as Dev got to the real thing since getting sober over a decade ago. "For good?"

"Sure are. Tanya finished up her schooling early and we wanted to be here for Thanksgiving." Devlin nodded his thanks for the drink. "When we heard about today, we hoped to make it back in time." He held out his hand to Adam. "Congrats again, Daddy."

Adam returned his handshake.

Devlin repeated the gesture with Bryant. "You, too, Pops. Geesh, two more rug rats to add to the family. So, what else is new around here?"

Nolan stared at Adam, knowing what he'd told him and Bryant was about to be shared with another brother.

Needing more privacy, he gestured to the leather couches

in a nearby alcove. His brothers followed and got comfortable. The laughter and feminine chatter were muted now even with the sliding pocket doors remaining open.

"What's going on?" Devlin asked. "Did someone die?"

"Not yet."

Nolan sighed and ignored Adam's veiled threat. He laid out what had happened two weeks ago between him and Katie, keeping the details light for both her sake and his.

"Dude…" Devlin flopped back against the cushions. "Even I didn't go there. Not that the thought didn't cross my mind, but still. She's practically family."

Nolan braced his elbows on his knees, his eyes locked on the beer bottle hanging from his clenched fingers. "Would you guys *please* stop saying that?"

"I guess this explains why every time we called from London you were working out of your home office instead of here," Dev continued, jerking his head toward the rooms connected with the family business farther down the hall.

"And why our office manager's been quieter than usual," Bryant added. "Laurie said she thought Katie might still be hurting from her breakup with the deputy."

"That was months ago." Nolan hated the idea she might still be hung up on Jake. "She's over him."

He waited for his brothers to argue that fact, but silence filled the air for a long moment. Nolan let it go on, knowing he'd given everyone a shock.

Hell, if any of them had made this same announcement he'd be pissed, too. More so. Not that he had a right to be.

"So, what's next?"

He looked up when Bryant spoke and found three sets of eyes all mirroring that same question. "Nothing. We… decided things would go on the same. Like before."

"Good."

Nolan turned to Adam, not liking the steely glint in his eyes. "Good?"

"She's been through enough in the last few months."

"I know that. What happened was a—" *Mistake.* Nolan held back the word, the taste of it sour in his mouth. "A surprise. To both of us. And yeah, things are a little awkward, but it'll go back to normal. Eventually."

Because that's what they'd agreed upon. What they wanted.

"It's the right…answer," Nolan said.

"Is it?" Devlin asked. "If she's interested and you're interested—"

"I'm not. Never have been." Nolan cut him off, ignoring the way his heart pounded in his chest. *Li-ar. Li-ar.* It didn't matter. The last thing any of them needed was for his stupidity to wreak havoc with the family and the family business.

He cringed at the *F* word again. "Katie's always been… just Katie."

"Until now." Adam set his beer on the table with a thud. "You changed that. Changed everything."

"Not on purpose," Nolan replied. He could see his brother wasn't going to let this go.

"Well, you better *purposely* find a way to fix things with her. Fast. Before we lose—" Adam stopped, his gaze intense. "What?"

Nolan pulled in a deep breath. "She offered to quit. That morning." His brothers started to protest, and he made a slashing motion, cutting them off. "I told her to forget it. She's too valuable to the company."

"Damn straight."

"Look, neither one of us wants to make anything of this. She'd be mad as hell if she finds out I said anything. Keep your mouths shut. Okay?"

His brothers nodded in agreement, Adam going last.

Nolan set his beer on the table, not interested in it anymore. "It's going to take time. To get beyond…whatever this is. Sorry if I cast a gloom on the baby-making pride you guys got going on."

"Not all of us," Devlin pointed out, reaching into his jacket for a small velvet box. "I'm not at the baby stage yet. I'm still trying to wrap my brain around this."

"What—what the hell is that—are you serious?"

Nolan's words overlapped Adam's and Bryant's when Devlin shared the diamond ring he'd found in a store in London and his plan to surprise Tanya with a Thanksgiving Day proposal.

"And don't tell the folks," Devlin warned, stowing the box away. "About this, or that Liam is planning to bring Missy and Casey back for Christmas. He tagged along on the ring shopping, so Missy should be sporting a sparkler on her finger when they arrive."

"Well, it seems Mom's going be surrounded by babies and weddings next year," Bryant said. "She'll be over the moon."

"And pestering you and Liam for more grandchildren not long after the *I do*s," Adam added before glancing back at Nolan. "Guess this makes you and Ric the last single Murphy brothers."

"That's fine with me." Nolan leaned back, more relaxed now than he'd been all day, glad the topic of conversation had moved away from him and Katie. "Don't forget, I did my part already by providing the first round of grandchildren."

Besides, he'd decided a long time ago he and marriage weren't a good fit. Not after those unhappy years with his ex-wife in Boston.

Now there was a union that never should've happened. And probably wouldn't have if there hadn't been a need for a hasty wedding.

He didn't regret his marriage entirely because of Abby,

Luke and Logan, but fatherhood was a far better fit than being a husband.

"So, three and out?" Devlin asked.

"That's right. Messy diapers and 3:00 a.m. feedings are in my rearview mirror." Nolan grinned. "I'm busy enough with work, and while I'm not happy with the arguing, at least my kids can feed themselves. I'll leave the happily-ever-afters and babies to you guys."

Katie bit hard on her bottom lip and hurried back to the party on tiptoes.

She'd slipped out to her office to hunt up a couple of notepads and pens to keep track of who gave what gift to the mommies-to-be.

Overhearing Devlin sharing with his brothers his plans to propose to Tanya stopped her in her tracks.

She was genuinely happy for the two of them. If anyone deserved to find true love and happiness, it was Devlin. He'd gone through a tough time recently. A helicopter he'd been piloting had crashed, stranding him and Adam in the forest with Devlin badly hurt. It'd taken him a long time to get better, and Tanya had been a big part of his recovery.

And hearing Nolan's familiar I'm-happy-the-way-I-am mantra wasn't surprising.

Not really.

Listening to him say aloud what he'd often said in the past, in one way or another, reaffirmed what she'd always known.

He considered his life complete.

Lead architect in his family's successful business. With five brothers he loved and who were his best friends. Single dad to three great kids.

A happy bachelor.

Her long-held, silent crush on the guy wasn't heading anywhere. No matter how attracted she might be to him—

and had been from the moment they met—there would never be anything between them.

Well, nothing more than one stolen night of passion.

Girl, get over it!

Another familiar refrain, one she'd repeated daily to herself over the last few weeks. Getting back to normal—whatever that might be—was harder than she'd thought it'd be.

That morning after Nolan left, she'd cleaned up the room and hurried home, determined to live up to the agreement they made. To make sure everything stayed the same. Between her and Nolan. Her and the Murphys. Her and the job she loved so much.

Easier said than done.

Yes, her actions had been dumb that night. Not just dumb, but careless, too.

Hey, it wasn't the first time she'd been stupid in her never-ending search for—

Nope, don't use the L word.

What happened that night had been a combination of lust, booze and foolishness. She'd been lucky the man she'd fallen into bed with had been someone like Nolan.

To think one night of amazing sex would lead to something was crazy. He'd made his feelings clear. They should go on with their lives as if nothing happened.

So being in the same room with him today—even with fifty-plus other people—should be easy. Easy to continue with her pleasant but business-is-business demeanor. It'd worked at the office. Mainly because he'd holed up in his place next door, working from there most of the time, instead of at the main house.

Like that wasn't a big enough hint he meant what he'd said.

Katie handed off the writing implements and took a load of opened gifts to display on the dining room table. Peggy joined her, holding up an infant's one-piece pajama covered with puppies in green and yellow.

"Boy, it's getting hard to remember Curtis ever being this small."

Katie smiled. "I thought you said Curtis was never that small."

"True." Peggy refolded the outfit. "That boy arrived at almost eleven pounds and went straight into the three-to-six-month size. He's been a handful ever since."

"And you love it."

"I do. Even if it meant us sharing a nasty flu bug for the last couple of weeks. Thank goodness that's over. This is the first time either of us has been out of the house since Halloween."

"I'm glad you're feeling better."

"Me, too. I appreciate the Crock-Pot meals you left for us on the front porch." Peggy moved closer. "We haven't had the chance to chat lately, and this isn't the time or place for any girl talk, but are you okay?"

Katie tightened her grip on the fluffy teddy bears she'd saved from toppling to the floor. "I'm fine." She returned the animals to the table. "Why do you ask?"

"You seem a bit—"

"Frazzled? Well, work's been crazy, despite the upcoming holidays." She hoped her smile didn't appear forced. "Poor Elise, breaking her arm. I was glad to step in and help pull today together for the...for everyone."

"I know they appreciate your efforts. Fay gushed about you when she stopped in the flower shop last week to go over some business stuff." Peggy laid a hand on her arm. "No, what I was going to say is you seem a bit sad."

"Sad?" Katie kept her gaze lowered. "Really?"

"You said all the right things at the Halloween party about starting over, finding someone new."

"But?" Katie heard the question in her friend's voice.

"You've been through a lot in the last couple of months." Her friend gave a quick squeeze and let go. "Maybe you're not as done with Jake as you think."

Oh, she was done. Over and out with an ease that didn't surprise her.

No, it was another man who was haunting her every waking hour now.

Keeping her feelings for Nolan under control used to be easy. Dating often and a variety of men helped. When things got serious with Jake, she'd believed her infatuation with a certain Murphy brother was in the past.

Then...yeah, and then.

This time around, it was going to take her a bit longer to bury her desire for someone she could never have, but she would do it.

She had to.

Goodness knows she had enough practice at it.

She needed to think about the future. Her future. It was time to look ahead, not behind.

"I'm okay." Her smile relaxed now. "Better than okay when it comes to the past."

"What do you mean?"

Katie shook her head, not sure how to answer her friend. Or where the soft warm glow now blooming deep inside her came from. "I don't know, exactly, but it's time."

"Time for what? You're talking in riddles."

Glad when Peggy got asked to help with something in the kitchen, Katie stayed behind, arranging more gifts.

Precious booties that fit in the palm of her hand. Practical burp cloths. Beautiful handmade quilts and blankets. Onesies in all colors and styles, bottles, baby bath gear.

Everything a new life needed.

Not to mention the unconditional love between a parent and a child.

Fay, already a wonderful mother to A.J., was so excited

about having another baby. And Laurie had had tears in her eyes while struggling to find the words to describe the first time she felt the baby inside her move.

Neither woman had met their child yet, but they were forever connected with another human being. Someone to love, cherish and protect with every fiber of a mother's soul.

Had her own mother ever felt that way about her?

It was a question Katie asked herself often over the years.

If she had, how could she have left a three-year-old in an empty church on a snowy winter day and walked away?

Something Katie would never have done.

She would have found a way to keep her child with her, to keep her family together. Beg, borrow or steal, but she would never separate herself from a life she created.

Being abandoned had created a void deep inside her that remained to this day.

It was time to change that.

Time to change everything.

Laying a hand over her belly, she tried to imagine what it would feel like to know a life was growing inside her. A life that would forever be connected with hers. A family of her own.

Right then and there, Katie made a decision.

She was going to get pregnant. She was going to have a baby.

Chapter Four

Boy, when the dream of having a baby in an unconventional way collided with the medical requirements, it was a hard smack to the wallet—and the heart.

Katie sat at her desk, eating lunch while studying the website for a well-known fertility clinic in Denver.

She'd fantasized about what it would be like to be pregnant for a few days after the baby shower. When she caught herself coming up with names and picturing the second bedroom in her apartment as a nursery, she'd started her research.

Now she was sorting through the details of sperm donation, ovarian schedules, intrauterine insemination vs. in vitro fertilization, treatment costs and single mother support groups.

It was all so fascinating. And a bit scary. Scratch that. It was a whole lot of scary.

After she'd started reading, the times she'd had pregnancy scares in the past came to mind. Once in high school, again in college and after dating a seasonal cowboy from one of the local ranches a few years ago.

Was that a lot? She'd been dating since she was thirteen and had been reckless in her youth.

Each time her cycle had been late, pure panic set in. She hadn't been ready for a baby. Emotionally, physically or financially.

That was then—this was now.

She was good. Fine. Better than fine.

Flipping through her calendar, she worked to create a history of her monthly cycles for the previous year. Boy, the crazy turns in her life over the last six months had thrown off her system. She'd never started on the same day twice.

Still, considering her need for chocolate and her less than pleasant mood, that day was fast approaching.

She clicked on the link to the sperm donor database, amazed at the details. Boxes to choose things like height, weight, hair, eye color and ethnicity didn't surprise her. The ability to search for favorite music, hobbies, family traits, religion and even astrological sign did.

Goodness, she'd know more about the baby's father than she did about herself.

So much of her own personal history was a blank page.

She had no idea what her life had been like before the age of three.

Her red hair and fair skin spoke of an Irish heritage, but she hadn't any clue if that was correct. If so, did those traits come from her mother or father or both? What about siblings? Did she have any?

There were fleeting memories of being with other children before she'd been in the foster care system. Boys. Brothers, maybe? But the recall was so vague, she'd eventually decided it was only wishful thinking.

What bothered her the most was she didn't have a way to find the answers.

Being abandoned wasn't the same as being put up for adoption.

There was no paperwork. Only a scrawled note, most of the words unreadable except for her first name, birthday and the last line begging for the little girl to be taken care of.

Katie blinked away the sting in her eyes, her fingers reflexively curling around the necklace she often wore.

A piece of costume jewelry, a silver cross with multi-colored stones, on a long chain reaching to the center of her chest. She hadn't even known it existed until she asked about her file when she was eighteen.

The necklace was the only physical item, along with the note, that connected her to her past. A line in the folder stated she'd been wearing it when she was found asleep in a church pew in Boise.

Had it been her mother's? A family heirloom, perhaps?

She'd taken it to a jeweler in college, but his snobbish attitude about the inexpensive stones had hurt. She'd then tossed the thing in an old box for the longest time, but when she found it a few years ago, she embraced the connection to her past.

As little as it was.

Shaking off her pensive mood before she dissolved into a puddle of tears, she focused on the list on the website. So, what qualities did she want from her child's father?

Tall. At least six feet. She liked tall men. Big shoulders, an athletic body. Brown hair, brown eyes. Intelligence was a given. A strong sense of family—

"Katie, I hate to bother you during your break, but I need—" The scent of Nolan's cologne drifted past her as he bent closer. "What the hell is that?"

His incredulous tone came at her from behind. She quickly minimized the internet browser window with a click.

She swung her chair around, putting her back to the monitor, but Nolan was so close her knees brushed his pant legs. He was standing up straight, his six-pack abs at eye level.

Not that she could see through the hunter green sweater he wore, but she remembered. Oh, yes, the feel and taste of his smooth, taut skin and defined muscles—

She blinked hard, tore her gaze from his stomach and looked up. "Wh-what are you doing here?"

Oh, boy, did that sound as breathless as she thought?

"I work here."

Not for the last two days. He'd been holed up in his home office. Again. This was the closest she'd been to him since…well, since that night. "So do I. I'm on my lunch break."

"So I gathered." His arm brushed her shoulder as he leaned forward again, grabbed the computer mouse and clicked. "And checking off boxes for…what is this? What you want in a man? Is this a dating website?"

Katie spun again. Ignoring the familiar pine and woodsy scent of his cologne and the heat of his skin, she took the mouse from his grasp and closed the program completely. "Not exactly."

"Then exactly what was…" Nolan's voice trailed off as he walked to the front of her desk, shock spreading across his features. "Wait, the banner read…sperm bank? You're looking to—to have a— *Really?*"

She squared her shoulders, pushed back her chair and stood, thankful for her four-inch heels that had her eye to eye with him. "Yes, really. And the word is a *baby*. Now, you needed something?"

"What—when did you decide this?"

"That's none of your business." That wasn't entirely true. The man was her boss. One of them. A pregnancy would affect her work at some point. "Not at the moment, anyway," she amended. "It's something I've been thinking about...for a while."

"Since when? Before Halloween?"

"Yes, I've always wanted—well, no, maybe not—" Katie broke away from his sharp gaze.

She glanced at the open double glass doors separating her office from the rest. Thankfully no one else seemed to be around.

Still, she grabbed files from her desk and headed for the cabinet in the far corner. "Why are you asking?"

"Is that what you were doing? That night? At the Blue Creek?"

"What?" She clutched the paperwork to her chest and spun back around, the pain of his assumption choking her. "You think I was trolling for a baby daddy?"

Nolan had followed and stood inches away, his brown eyes filled with confusion.

And more questions.

He opened his mouth, but nothing came out. His lips then pressed together hard, the muscle along his jaw tightening.

"That was a stupid thing to say," he finally conceded.

"Oh, no. Unprotected sex with a stranger is a genius move. Not to mention knowing absolutely nothing about the man and worrying he might want someday to have a say in raising the child. An excellent plan, Nolan. Why didn't I think of it?"

"Katie, I'm sorry—"

"My plans have nothing to do with what happened... between us." She cut him off, her anger splintering, fueling a slow burn deep inside her. "Besides, we were careful. Every time. Or don't you remember?"

The heat in his gaze told her he did. Just as she did. In vivid detail most nights in her dreams.

She also remembered their agreement not to talk about that night.

She scooted past him and headed for the supply closet. "You've got nothing to worry about. Everything's fine."

"I'm not...worried." He stayed with her. "And I am sorry. That was the dumbest thing I've ever said."

"Amazingly, I agree with you."

"But you need to think about what you're doing. Being a parent is the hardest job there is, and to do it alone? Voluntarily? That's crazy."

Pushing open the door, she turned on the lights, making a mental note to get brighter bulbs in the walk-in closet, now lined with shelves on three sides for everything from printer paper to cleaning supplies.

She set the files on a nearby shelf, forgetting she'd had them in her hands. "As a lifelong maker of crazy decisions, I can tell you this is the sanest one I've made in a long time."

"Katie, you don't have any idea what you are getting into."

"Neither do most when they decide to become parents. And a lot of women—people—are having children this way."

She turned around in the tight space and there he was again. His tall frame blocked the faint glow from the overhead light. The memory of him standing this way, but dressed in costume, flashed in her mind. That same tilt of his head. The same intense scrutiny in his eyes.

How could she have not known it was him?

"You..." Her voice caught, but she pushed on. "You seem to be doing fine as a single parent."

"Because I've had to. Even when I was married, we had a nanny and a maid and Carrie couldn't manage. Hell, Abby was just a little girl and she still ended up—" Nolan cut off his words, letting loose a frustrated breath. "We're not talking about me."

"And there's no reason to be talking about me, either."

"This isn't like you."

She tried to take a step back, but her backside was against the shelves already. "What's that supposed to mean?"

"Well, for starters…you're twenty-seven."

"What? Too young or too old?"

"That's not—"

"I'm healthy, reasonably intelligent and I've got a great job with medical benefits," she rattled off. "Not to mention a tidy nest egg to pay for everything. There are many out there starting with a whole lot less."

"Having a baby involves so much more—"

"You think I don't know that?" She cut him off again, poking at the solid muscle of his bicep. "Do you think I haven't thought about the love, joy and commitment involved in having a baby? Raising a child? Being part of a family?"

"Katie?" A voice called from the outer office. "You in here?"

She gasped, her gaze locking with Nolan's as she recognized his brother Adam's voice. So much for her plans staying private. Never mind that the two of them were in here. Alone.

"Ah, here you…both are." Adam leaned against the doorjamb, a frown on his face. "Sorry. Am I interrupting?"

"Of course not." She grabbed two boxes of the fine-line pens Nolan preferred to work with. "These are what you were looking for."

He took them, his fingers tangling with hers before she pulled away.

"Now, what can I do for you, Adam?" she asked.

"I need to talk to the two of you, actually." Adam straightened and stepped backward, his eyes narrowing on Nolan as they moved into the office. "Liam and I just got off a three-way call with Ellsworth."

Nolan stopped. "Why wasn't I included?"

"Because no one could reach you." Adam's gaze shot from his brother to Katie and back again. "Where have you been?"

"In my home office. With my phone off while I worked on *his* project. You couldn't walk across the yard?"

"It was a quick call. He wants you back in Spokane. Tonight."

"What? Why?"

"He's closed on five hundred acres an hour northwest of the city and is moving the new compound from his vacation spread in Montana to there, seeing as that's where his business is located."

"Great. Everything's going to change. Again." Nolan tunneled one hand through his hair. "Just when I thought I had a handle on things."

"Yeah, it's amazing how quickly *things* can change."

"I was talking about the drawings."

"Me, too." Adam crossed his arms and looked at her. "Katie, he'll need travel arrangements. Probably at least through the weekend."

"Of course." She went back to her desk, surprised at the tension between the two men. Then again, the Ellsworth project was a big one. As in big bucks. Nolan had been working on the designs for a few months.

"Cheyenne isn't good for a flight tonight." Her fingers flew over the keyboard. "He'll have to fly out of Denver."

"Denver's a two-hour drive from here."

"Bryant can take you in the helo. You'll be there in less than an hour," Adam said.

"I can put you in a parlor suite in the Historical Davenport," Katie continued. "You can use the separate living room for meetings and videoconferences if needed."

"I can't go."

Katie's fingers paused on the keyboard, and Adam turned fully to Nolan. "Why not?" they asked in unison.

"Who's going to keep an eye on my kids?" Nolan held up a hand when Adam opened his mouth. "Mom's arm is causing her more pain than she's admitting. Dad's doing all he can to keep her idle. You and Bryant are tied up with your own families. Dev and Tanya left yesterday for Colorado to visit hers."

"They can move into the main house—oh, wait. The auditors. They'll be in the guest rooms the rest of the week."

"I don't want to pull them out of the house. Upset their daily schedules." Nolan shook his head. "Besides, I've had…issues with Abby lately. I'm not talking about what she pulled this past summer with Casey. New stuff." He sighed. "Boy stuff."

"Boy stuff?" Adam repeated.

"She's got herself…involved with a cowboy at the Triple G."

"She's sixteen."

"You don't have to remind me. I've laid down the law. That hasn't stopped her from…pursuing things."

"I'll do it." The words popped out of Katie's mouth, surprising her and her bosses. Nolan started to protest, but she hurried on. "I know the kids. They know me. I'll pack a bag and move in while you're gone."

Adam and Nolan shared another look Katie couldn't decipher as silence filled the office.

"I don't have a guest room," Nolan finally said.

"You have a couch in your home office. Oh, wait—the pullout sleeper in the living room. It'll be fine."

Katie warmed to the idea. What better way to prove she had what it took to be a mom? She could do this. It would be fun.

"I'll get them up in the morning and off to school. Then

walk to the office. At night it's dinner, make sure they do their homework and get them to bed. How hard can it be?"

"There's three of them."

She rolled her eyes. "I know that, Nolan."

He took a step closer to her desk. "Three teenagers."

"I was once one myself. And not too long ago, as someone recently pointed out."

"You have no idea what you're in for—"

"Katie, we appreciate the offer, but are you sure?" Adam cut Nolan off, stepping between them. "This is going a bit above your job description."

"I'd like to help. If I run into any trouble, you all will be close by." She shrugged, trying to appear casual, despite the excitement flowing through her. "Besides, I think I can handle being a single parent for a week or so."

Adam glanced back over his shoulder at his brother.

Katie leaned to one side, peering around him to do the same.

Her gaze caught with Nolan's and held. His stare said he didn't think she could do it. Didn't trust her to take care of his children.

A sharp stab of pain cut across her middle. She laid a hand at her stomach, the yogurt she'd eaten at lunch souring as the seconds ticked by.

"Fine," Nolan said, the word coming with a deep sigh. "We'll...give it a try."

Katie smiled brightly, until she caught Adam once again giving her and then Nolan a strange glare. Before she could ask him about it, his cell phone rang. He left to take the call, promising to catch Nolan before he headed out.

Silence filled the air again.

Feeling as if she needed to reassure Nolan, she said, "Don't worry, it'll be fine—"

"We should go over a few things—"

His words overlapped hers and both stopped short.

Katie motioned to him. "Go ahead."

"The twins are on the freshman basketball team. Practice started this week, every afternoon until four." He pulled out his phone and swiped the screen. "The schedule's on the fridge. Abby picks them up, unless she has to work at the bakery. Her schedule is supposed to be on the calendar, too, but that doesn't always happen. If she's working, the boys either hitch a ride with one of the other players or call me."

"I'll make sure they have my cell phone number."

"They're each responsible for their own laundry. The television and their gaming consoles are off-limits until after dinner. Oh, and don't let them get away with saying they don't have a set bedtime. They do. Abby included."

Katie's head started to spin, but she chalked it up to missing most of her lunch and her excitement. "Why don't you pack? I'll make the travel arrangements, scoot out to grab my things and meet you at your house. Then we'll talk."

Nolan stopped and checked his watch. "I need to tell the kids what's going on."

"Of course. The last flight out of Denver is at eight o'clock." She took a peek at the computer again. "You will have time before you head out."

He looked at her. She could see the hesitation in his gaze. "Nolan, don't worry. I know what I'm doing, and like I said, your family is right here. Everything is going to be..." She paused, hunting for another word, but what else could she say? "...fine."

"How was your meal, Mr. Murphy?"

Nolan stepped back as the room service attendant cleared his half-finished dinner. "It was...fine."

Fine.

That seemed to be the word for the day.

Katie had kept assuring him everything—from her plan

to have a baby to taking care of his kids—was going to be fine.

Hell, even the kids had said as much, except Logan's and Luke's versions came out as "cool" and "awesome" when they were told. Abby? She'd tried to convince him his secretary wasn't needed, but her ranting subsided when Katie arrived with a suitcase, a warm Crock-Pot and an armful of clothes still on hangers.

Having accepted she wasn't going to change his mind, Abby had stomped up the stairs with a whispered "fine" and "I don't care" thrown in for good measure.

Yeah, everything was just…fine.

Except a nasty weather system had blown in, forcing Nolan and Bryant to head out earlier than planned. He hadn't gotten a chance to talk to Katie as much as he'd wanted. Or to get the kids to pick up the house. It was as if a cyclone had gone through, but he could only kiss them goodbye, promise to check in daily and then leave.

Once he was alone again in his hotel room, Nolan ignored the work on the desk and stood at the window looking out at the Spokane skyline.

Because Katie was on his mind.

And not just because he'd left his kids in her care. No, it was her shocking plan to have a child of her own that continued to swirl in his head much like the snow outside.

Throw in his thoughtless assumption about their night together…

He'd been an ass to say that aloud to her.

There was no reason for it, except for the fact he'd experienced a similar moment before in his life. His ex-wife had never come right out and said she'd gotten pregnant on purpose all those years ago, but it'd been implied enough times during their marriage.

Was that why he was so surprised at Katie's plan?

She had no idea what she was getting herself into. How

her life would change once she became a parent. He should know. He'd been all of twenty-one and still a newlywed when Abby had been born.

He thought about Fay and Laurie, both due in February, both with gently rounded bellies and seeming to glow from the inside.

His ex-wife had been like that, too. With Abby, at least. They'd been so young, so sure of themselves. So unprepared. Especially when the twins came three years later—

Nolan shut down the old memories and tried to concentrate on the paperwork but grabbed his phone instead.

No messages.

He'd texted everyone when he arrived at the Spokane airport. Got the usual one-word replies from the boys, nothing from Katie and the capital *K*—text-speak for okay—from his daughter.

When he'd said goodbye, he'd gotten a more subdued Abby to agree to explain how things worked around the house to Katie.

Had she done that? What hadn't he had time to tell her?

The daily chores and important phone numbers were also listed on the refrigerator. But there was something he was forgetting—damn! The security system. Or more precisely, the code for the system, which he'd changed recently.

He got his phone. Almost eleven o'clock. Close to midnight back home. He hoped she would still be awake. This couldn't wait until morning.

"Hello?"

One word, soft and breathless, and his head filled with the image of her curled up in bed.

His body reacted. This was not good.

He crossed the room, sat on the bed and started to lean back. No, he couldn't talk to her while stretched out. It would be too much like phone—

"Nolan? Are you there?"

He jumped to his feet and paced instead. Yeah, he was here. Standing tall in more ways than one. "Ah, sorry. Hope I'm not calling too late. Did I wake you?"

"Not really. I'm nodding off a bit in the living room, doing some…reading."

About sperm donors? That thought cooled him off, but he wasn't going to ask. "I'm sorry, too, if the sofa mattress is lumpy. I meant to switch it out but never got around to it."

"Oh, well, I'm not on the bed. Just wrapped in some blankets on the couch."

He stopped. "What? Why?"

"I couldn't get the pullout to…well, pull out. Not enough upper-body strength, I guess."

"Why didn't the boys help?"

"I didn't think about it before they headed upstairs. Which was a few hours ago. They're asleep now. It's not a big deal."

"Yeah, it is. I'm already asking a lot from you. The last thing I want is for you to be uncomfortable."

"I'm not. I'm—"

"Fine." He spoke the word the same time she did. "I've heard that more than a few times today."

"Speaking of today…" She paused, then said, "What we talked about before Adam came into the office…"

Nolan tensed as Katie's voice trailed off. Was she having second thoughts about single motherhood? Already? "Yes?"

"I would prefer if we kept my plans just between us. For now. I'm not ready to—well, to make anything public yet."

"That's not something you can keep hidden for too long."

"I'm aware of that. I still have some decisions to make before I move forward."

Like when, how and who.

Why this was bugging him so much, Nolan had no idea. The pacing started again. "Sure. No problem."

"Thanks."

Now she sounded relieved. Did she think he'd share her crazy plan with his family? Not likely. Then again, he hadn't kept his word when it came to their agreement about that night...

The king-size bed in his room drew his gaze. The memories sprang to life again in vivid color. "Ah, I'm calling because I forgot to tell you about the house's security system."

"I saw it. One of Devlin's designs. The twins told me the password and how the doors and windows are wired, but movement is allowed throughout the house."

"I updated the code last weekend." He rattled it off, then said, "I didn't tell the kids. I prefer to keep it from them. For the time being."

Katie was quiet for a moment, then said, "Does this have anything to do with Abby's 'boy stuff'?"

It did, but Nolan didn't want to get into that now.

"Maybe I can help," she continued. "I've got some experience in that department. You know, being a girl myself."

She probably could, but he figured she had enough on her plate at the moment. "It's okay, but thanks. So, is everything else *fine* there?"

"Yes, and I'm sorry I didn't reply to your earlier text. I was busy and I thought the kids would be blowing up your phone."

"Hardly. They replied, short and sweet as usual." He didn't get what she was talking about. "Why would they—"

"Ah, no reason." She cut him off. "I thought they would've—but they didn't—so...we're good. We're fine."

Something was off. "What aren't you telling me?"

"Nothing. I mean, it's no big deal."

He dropped his head and closed his eyes. "Katie? Tell me."

"Well..." She sighed. And yeah, that soft sound got his engine revving again. "It started off with my creamy chicken–quinoa–broccoli casserole."

"Your—what? What's quinoa?"

"It's a grain, sort of. It's heart healthy—lots of nutrients. I'd planned to bring the dish into the office, but then I figured the kids and I could have it for dinner."

Nolan hoped she hadn't told them what the casserole was called. The word *quinoa* wouldn't go over very well. "So?"

"I canned the idea when Abby told me the twins don't like broccoli, so I—"

"The boys eat broccoli."

More silence, and he could picture her biting on her bottom lip, a habit of hers. "They do?" she finally said.

Now, it made sense. Abby. "Yeah, they do."

"Anyway, I asked them what they wanted for dinner instead. They said breakfast. Eggs, bacon, pancakes, hash browns, etc. I guess you guys do that a lot?"

They did, at least once a week. "It's a family favorite. It also makes for quite a mess with the number of pans and the griddle."

"Not as much as the soap suds covering the kitchen floor."

"Soap—from the dishwasher that's broken?"

"I didn't know it was broken when I used it."

"And you were cleaning up because…" He tried to picture the chores list, but the image wouldn't come.

"Well, the boys pointed out tonight was Abby's turn for dishes. She didn't eat with us, so—"

"She didn't?"

"No, she took a plate up to her room. Said she was in the middle of homework. Anyway, when an hour went by and she didn't come back down, I went up, knocked and told her we had finished eating."

"And she told you to use the dishwasher?"

"No, that was my idea. All mine. I mean, she mumbled something about doing them later or loading them later." Katie's words came out in a rush. "I couldn't hear her. She had her nose buried in a book. So, when later didn't come, I wanted…to be helpful. On the plus side, your kitchen floor sparkles now."

He bet it did. Thanks to Katie, who he guessed had cleaned up the mess herself.

It seemed that he would be finding time for a phone call with his daughter tomorrow.

Being upset about this arrangement was one thing. Sabotaging Katie was another. She was clearly out of her element, but he'd be damned if one of his kids was going to make this harder than it needed to be.

For all of them.

"I know what you're thinking. I screwed up, but hey, it's my first day. Don't worry, Nolan. I'll get better."

"No, actually I was thinking you should be in my bed."

A long pause filled the air.

"Ah, that didn't come out right," he said. "Sleep. I meant you should sleep. In my bed. In my bedroom."

Silence again stretched between them. Was she as surprised as he at his babbling?

"Why?" she asked, her voice a whisper.

Hell if he knew. The words had just popped out of his mouth. "So…you'll have some privacy while you're there."

"For what? I did bring pajamas with me."

Meaning she normally didn't wear any?

His mind raced back to waking up next to her and those naked curves. Okay, he was heading for a cold shower. "You can't get the sleeper sofa to open, not to mention the twins are known for sneaking downstairs for a late-night snack," he said. "I just thought—I want you to be comfortable."

"Are you sure?"

"Of course." The more he thought about it, the more it made sense. That was all. "This way you'll have plenty of room for your things. The closet in the office is jammed with stuff. There's only a stand-up shower in that bathroom and it doesn't drain well. Mine has multiple showerheads and the tub has whirlpool jets if you want—"

Damn, there went his active imagination again. "I should've thought of it before now," he concluded.

"Okay, thanks."

He heard a rustling noise that could only mean Katie was getting up from the couch, blankets and all. He listened, picturing her walking through his house.

The memory of the two of them earlier today in the supply closet filled his head. Her spicy vanilla scent invading his nose as soon as he got within a foot of her. The warmth of her breath as she lectured him and the heat of her touch after she'd shoved the boxes of pens in his direction and he'd grabbed her hands.

Then he heard the soft click as she opened the door to his room through the phone, yanking him from his thoughts.

"Wow, Nolan...this is nice."

His furniture was oversize and made from hand-peeled cedar logs. The king-size bed, dresser and nightstands were rustic and handcrafted. She was the first woman, outside of his family members, who'd seen the decor.

Five years he'd been living back in Destiny. He'd dated a few different women, but he'd never invited one of them to his bedroom.

Until now.

And he was nine hundred miles away.

Probably a blessing.

"Thanks," he said, wondering if he was going to be able to get any sleep tonight. And every night for the next week. "I like it."

"Mmm, I can see why. I'm practically asleep already." She must've crawled up onto the mattress, her long red hair spread out over his pillows. "Is there something more you wanted to talk about?"

Yeah, there probably was, but for the life of him Nolan couldn't think what it might be.

Katie was in his bed, warm and soft and sleepy.

Right now he wanted nothing more than to be there right next to her. But unless he wanted to explain to everyone why he'd caught a late-night flight back home, that wasn't an option.

So, it was dream time for him.

He could only hope and pray this whole damned trip didn't turn into one big nightmare.

Chapter Five

"You're staying in his house? Sleeping in his bed?"

"Shh!" Katie waved a potato chip in Peggy's direction. "There's no need to tell everyone."

Thankfully, being a mom herself, Peggy was well versed in the art of whispering. Still, the back room at Fay's Flower Shop, where her friend worked as the assistant manager, might not be the best place for Katie to share her news.

"No one is here but us." Peggy looked around the space, teeming with silk mums in rich fall colors, autumn leaves, harvest grasses and artificial pumpkins. "Besides, you've been there since Tuesday. Everyone who doesn't know you're shacking up at Nolan's will find out soon. How come it took you this long to tell me?"

"I'm not 'shacking up,' and this is the first time we've seen each other."

"We talked Wednes—or was it Thursday? I can't remember."

"It was Friday. Which was yesterday."

Peggy nudged her with her soda can. "And you didn't tell me."

"I was up to my elbows in cookie dough. The twins needed a donation for the basketball team's fund-raising booth at the craft fair."

"So you baked."

Katie nodded, taking another bite from her sandwich. She wasn't hungry, but it kept her from yawning. "I like baking, even though I was up until three this morning pulling it all together."

"What? How many did you make?"

"Ten dozen. Five per twin." With enough left over to fill the cookie jar in Nolan's kitchen. "Split into half dozen batches, individually wrapped in cellophane and tied with a pretty bow."

"Isn't that carrying babysitting duties a bit far?"

Probably.

She hadn't had any clue about the cookies until Nolan mentioned it when they talked late Thursday night. He'd told her to find out how many were needed and put in an order at Doucette's Bakery. But after they hung up she'd figured she could make them herself.

Then the next morning the boys shared the number of edibles they'd promised.

"I like to bake," Katie said. "Just never made so many in one sitting before. Luke and Logan helped. It was messy, but fun. By the time Abby got home—" two minutes shy of her midnight curfew "—the last batch was cooling on the counter."

"Hmm, how does she feel about having you around?"

Katie's grip tightened on her bottled water. "She's okay."

"Then why the evil glare from her at the bakery when we got lunch?"

Katie thought back. "Did she? I didn't notice."

"Maybe she doesn't like the idea of you and her dad—"

"There is no me and her dad," Katie insisted, her gaze on her food. "It makes more sense for me to sleep in the only available bedroom than in the middle of the living room. That's all."

Peggy was quiet and stayed that way for so long Katie finally asked, "What?"

"That's my question." Her friend leaned in close, concern in her pretty green eyes. "What aren't you telling me?"

Katie bit down on her bottom lip. She wanted so much to confide in her friend. To talk to someone about the craziness over the last few weeks. But which secret did she share?

Nolan and her.

She needed to get her head, and her heart, on straight when it came to him.

He'd obviously moved on from their one-night stand. Been okay with the distance she put between them at the office. He hadn't pushed. Hadn't tried to make things better.

So she'd been shocked when he seemed upset by her plan to have a baby, even going so far as to suggest she'd placed said plan into motion that night.

Yeah, she was still hurt over his comment, but what bothered her more was him thinking her dream of having a family, having someone to love, was crazy.

Did he think she wasn't smart enough or strong enough to handle—

"Wow, whatever you've got running around inside your head, it must really be something," Peggy said. "I can see it in your eyes."

Katie pulled in a deep breath, then released it. "Okay, there isn't a me and Nolan. Not now." Her words came out in a whisper. "Not anymore."

"But at one time?" Peggy matched her tone. "You never said anything. This must be recent. When?"

"Halloween. The weekend before, actually. The party at the Blue Creek...your sister's room at the boardinghouse."

Peggy's eyes went wide. She then twisted around on her stool to the open doorway. "Jennifer," she called out, "you can take your lunch now."

A few minutes later the teenager who worked part time at the shop popped in. "You sure? You two just sat down."

"Don't worry. I'll listen for the bell."

"Cool. I'm heading to Sherry's Diner to meet up with Thor."

Peggy waved at her. "Go ahead. Take your time."

The girl disappeared and then the jingle of the shop's door being opened and closed filled the air.

Peggy spun back around. "Okay, we're alone. Dish."

"Who's Thor?"

"Jennifer's boyfriend. Plays center on the football team. Huge guy, big shoulders and wavy blond hair to his biceps. Believe me, he's earned the nickname. Don't change the subject. Tell me about you and Nolan. How did you hook up? Was he in costume? He had to be. Wait, I thought you said he was traveling."

Katie spilled the details—from the moment she'd first seen the sexy pirate to waking up the next morning, shocked at whom she'd spent an amazing night with.

"Wow...that's just..." Peggy finally said. "Wow."

"That's one way to put it, and no, I didn't know it was him. He honestly didn't know it was me. Until the next morning."

"But to be so wild and rash, that's not you. I mean, in your past, sure. You've told me some stories, but not now. Was this a payback to Jake?"

Katie shook her head, not surprised her friend had come up with the same thought as Nolan. "No, that mess is behind me. Yes, I'd hoped to meet someone new. Falling into bed with a total stranger who turned out to be not such a stranger? Not planned at all."

"So you agreed to pretend it never happened? Is that what you wanted—oh, I can see that's the last thing you wanted."

"I do, but for a moment—" The sudden sting of tears surprised Katie. She brushed at her cheek as soon as one escaped. "I woke up that morning when I felt him leave the bed. Still in a hazy, dreamy and yes, a bit hungover state of mind. I lay there remembering all that happened between us in the previous hours and how amazing—"

"Amazing?" Peggy interrupted with a grin. "Really?"

"Yes, really. For being considered the safe and stodgy brother of the pack, Nolan was…" Katie paused, the memories still so real. "Passionate. Tender. Creative…amazing. Anyway, I thought me and this stranger could take all that and see where it might go. Exchange names, phone numbers. Get together for a date."

"And then you really woke up."

"Yes…as he was about to walk out on me."

Peggy's jaw dropped. "What?"

"I tried to play it off, asking if he was going for coffee, but it was clear he was trying to make a clean getaway."

"Ouch."

Katie sighed. "Yeah, especially because he'd already figured out who I was. Then, of course, I was stunned to find out who *he* was. Things went downhill from there."

"Except for the split second when you thought something could still come of that *amazing* night."

Katie dropped her chin and shook her head. She couldn't admit to that.

Not to her friend. Not to herself.

"No, Nolan's right. He and I…it would cause too much disruption. To our professional relationship, my job. Not to mention his family, his kids…"

"Okay, so you both agreed to go on as before. Which sounds great in theory, but reality is something different. Boy, this explains your behavior at the baby shower. How's the agreement working?"

"It's been tough. On my end, anyway. Things aren't the same—yet—at the office. The other guys are smart enough to pick up on it, but we're crazy busy with work, especially this latest project, and the babies and the holidays coming up. No one's said anything. At least, not to me."

"And now you're sleeping in his bed."

Katie rewrapped her sandwich, her appetite gone. "I'm watching his kids. It's for the business."

"Hmm, not quite sure I believe you."

"You should. I've got something to prove."

The bell over the front entrance rang out and Peggy stood. "Wait here. I'll be right back. And what do you have to prove? That you're okay with your one night being just one night?"

No, that she had the skills to be a mother.

Watching three teenagers wasn't the same as dealing with a newborn, but babies grew up. One day she'd be faced with crazy schedules, last-minute emergencies and adolescent angst.

It meant a lot to her for Nolan to see she could handle this.

Not that she needed his approval for her life plan, but he was her boss. Keeping her job was a necessity in order to make having a child in her life work.

And being a parent was work.

She had learned that over the last few days. Dealing with teenagers in the morning was like herding cats, especially with one as grumpy as Abby.

Katie was a morning person. Woke up happy, and after a turn with those multiple massaging showerheads in Nolan's bathroom, she was all sunshine and roses.

But her first morning in the Murphy household—

Well, she'd pulled together something easy for breakfast. Fresh-baked blueberry muffins, cereal boxes and a nicely set table with milk and orange juice.

The result? The boys tore through the food while their sister grabbed a muffin as she stomped out the door, yelling for the twins to follow if they wanted a ride. They'd scampered off with "see yas" thrown her way, leaving a mess in their wake.

So she'd cleaned up and gone to work.

Homemade pizzas for dinner had seemed to go over better, even with Abby, who'd been a bit more pleasant, even though she'd made it clear it was due to a phone call from her father.

Katie reached for a bright orange silk mum from the pile and stuck the flower into the half-finished arrangement her friend had been working on earlier.

Hmm, not bad.

She chose another and then another, lost in thought about the best part of the last four days.

The nights.

She'd slip into Nolan's bed and his voice would be the last thing she heard before falling asleep. They'd chat about the kids and how things were going.

She'd first thought he'd called because he'd been worried she couldn't handle things, but it was clear how much he loved his children and missed them when he was gone.

Oh, they'd talk during office hours, too, and sometimes work issues would become part of their nighttime discussions.

But mostly she'd share what happened that day, glossing over some of the misadventures, not sure how often he talked to the kids or what they told him.

It was what she guessed most families did when one parent traveled—

"Oh, no, don't go there," Katie muttered, shoving in a red leaf with an extra push. "You are not a family. You are doing your job."

She checked the time, grabbed the arrangement and marched into the front room as Peggy finished up with a customer who was heading for the door.

Her friend turned to her. "Hey, that's pretty good."

"Thanks. I'm going to take it. The colors match Nol—" Katie glanced over her shoulder. The shop was empty again. "Nolan's bedroom. It could use a bit of softening."

"I see. So, you never told me what it's like sleeping in his bed."

No, she hadn't. She also hadn't told her friend about the erotic dream she'd had the first night or how the sheets still smelled like him the next morning.

"It's comfortable, king-size, with very firm pillows." Katie paid for the flowers, looking up when Peggy held tight to her change. She tugged the bills free, not liking the smirk on her friend's face. "Don't go there. We have an agreement. Onc he's okay with and so am I."

Peggy's grin softened. "Scout's honor?"

"Of course." Katie hated how easily the lie slid past her lips. "I have to be. I don't have any other choice."

"The land is spectacular. Construction will be much easier." Nolan stared at the flat-screen television allowing him and the Ellsworths to videoconference with his brothers in Wyoming and London on a snowy Monday morning. "We're in a good place."

He looked around the table in his hotel suite, the old man and his three daughters all smiling and nodding in agreement. Would wonders never cease?

"But you need another week?" This came from Liam, who was in London. "For land survey results?"

Nolan's gaze went from his brother to the side of the

screen showing the offices in Destiny. Adam, Dev and Bryant were there. Katie, too, sitting on Adam's left, focused on her laptop as she took notes.

"Yes. I stayed at one of the log cabins currently on the land this past weekend—"

"Oh, talk about roughing it." Belle Ellsworth, who sat next to Nolan, broke in with a laugh. "No running water or electricity. Good thing we had lanterns and a case of bottled water."

"You stayed, too?" Adam asked.

"Oh, we couldn't let Nolan stay out there by himself." She reached over and gave his hand a squeeze. "What if something happened to him?"

Nolan extracted his fingers as Katie's head shot up.

"It was only the first night," he said, scraping his hand across the stubble on his chin. "I stayed again last night. Alone. Now, I want to be here when the utility people work out what's needed to support the number of buildings planned."

"Makes sense," Liam said.

Dev and Bryant nodded in agreement while Adam remained silent.

Nolan didn't need their approval. As lead architect, it was his call as to how much time to spend here. Frankly, there was only one person who needed to be okay with this.

"Katie," he asked. "Does that work for you?"

She peered up at him then. Her hair was back up in the same ponytail style as the day of the baby shower.

It was the first time he'd seen her in a week.

They hadn't talked since Friday night. Not wanting to drain the battery on his phone while he was away from the hotel, he'd sent a quick text with his weekend plans, asking her to explain to the kids why he'd be out of touch.

He'd missed their nighttime calls.

It surprised him, as he rarely checked in with his mother

while traveling, doing most of his communicating with the kids. Which he still did, when he managed to catch them. Still, the chats with Katie gave him the details of their day and made him feel like he wasn't as far away.

"Yes." Her words were short. "Of course I'll stay with the kids."

"I'll be back in a week," he promised, trying to read the tone of her voice. "Thanksgiving at the latest."

"You better be here for Thanksgiving," Devlin warned, tapping the ring finger on his left hand against the table. "Mom will have your head if you aren't."

"Oh, we have him for another ten days. How fun." This came from another daughter, who tossed her long blond hair back over her shoulder. "Don't worry. We won't work him too hard. There's plenty of social activities in the city—"

"I'm here to work hard." Nolan focused again on the room in Destiny. On one certain person in particular. "Thanks, Katie. I owe you big-time."

She only offered him a small smile and a quick nod, her gaze not meeting his.

"Well, I think we'll head back to our offices."

Ellsworth stood, said his goodbyes and left, taking his family with him.

Nolan was glad.

Ellsworth was a smart man who'd built a million-dollar trucking company. His equally smart daughters worked with him, but there was too much—Nolan didn't know the right word, drama, maybe—surrounding the three of them.

"Is this worth it?" Adam finally spoke. "We're billing him for the prep work, but is he going to get antsy again before we get the final contract signed?"

"No, he isn't." Nolan would make sure of it. "You saw how much they like what we've come up with, which thankfully doesn't include too many changes to what I'd already designed. We should have the paperwork to his lawyers by the holiday. Signed by the end of the month."

"This is a big win for us," Liam said. "Nolan, I know you've been yanked around for the last few months, but I agree with you. We're on the right path. Even the Disney princesses seem to be happy."

"Disney what?" Adam asked.

"His daughters. Ariel, Belle and Jasmine." Nolan pointed out the obvious. "Dude, wait until you have a girl of your own."

"Don't get distracted by the sparkle," Liam went on with a smile. "I think one or more of those ladies is interested in you, big brother."

"I should head back to my desk." Katie shot up from her chair, closing the top of her computer with a snap. "Get these notes organized."

"Katie—"

"I know you've probably already heard this, Katie," Liam cut Nolan off. "At least I hope my brothers have said it. We appreciate you stepping in. And not only with Nolan's kids. Mom says you're helping with her Thanksgiving plans, too. With a family our size, and the relatives coming in, it's got to be a lot to handle."

This time Katie's smile was genuine as she looked at Nolan's brother. "It's my pleasure, Liam. Your mom is a sweet lady, as you already know."

"And these cookies you made are awesome." Dev grabbed a couple from the plate in the middle of the table. "Better than Mom's. Don't tell her I said that."

Katie's attention switched to another brother, but the smile remained. "I won't."

"Neat packaging, too, on the ones for the boys. Too bad you aren't here to taste these, Nolan. The twins lucked out."

Twins? Cookies? Packaging? What the hell was Dev talking about?

"They were the hit of the team's booth," Bryant added. "First to sell out."

What his brothers were saying finally registered. The cookies his sons had needed for school. Last minute, of course.

"You cooked instead of calling the bakery?" Nolan asked, directing his question at Katie.

She shrugged, her attention on gathering her things. "It was no big deal."

"How many?"

"Nolan, it was no—"

"How many?" he pushed.

This time she paused and stared at him. "Ten dozen."

A hundred and twenty cookies?

"Separated into half dozen plastic bags, tied off with blue and white ribbons decorated with basketballs and—what?" Dev must have seen the expression on Nolan's face. "You didn't know? The boys didn't tell you?"

"I haven't talked to my kids since last Thursday."

"They didn't send you pictures? That's how I saw them."

He'd checked his phone when he got in the rental car this morning and plugged it in. No texts, no missed calls. He'd figured everything back home was...fine.

"No, they didn't."

"I'm sure they'll tell you tonight," Katie said. "You need to call and let them know your plans. Abby, too."

"I'll try. I've got meetings—"

She cut him off. "Not try, do. The twins' first basketball game is Thursday."

Nolan grabbed his phone and checked the calendar. Damn! He hated that he wasn't going to be there. Yes, there'd be more games, but Luke and Logan were excited about being on the team and he'd wanted—

"Don't worry," Katie said. "I plan to take some personal time and go."

"Screw that." This came from Liam. "Just go. Maybe a couple of uncles can be there, too?"

"I'll be at a job site on the other side of Chapman Falls," Adam said. "I doubt I'll be back in time."

"We've got it covered," Dev added.

"Ditto," Bryant chimed in.

Nolan nodded, his appreciation for his brothers stepping in when it came to his kids—the way they'd always done—forming a lump in his throat, making it hard to speak.

"Oh, before I forget, the Sparkle Ball at the high school is next month." Katie stood, her items in her arms. "Abby asked if she could go shopping with her girlfriends. In Denver on Friday. School's out for a teacher conference."

"No way." Finding his voice again was easy. "Denver is two hours away."

"I thought that'd be your response. I've come up with an idea."

Nolan's brothers' attention shifted from Katie to him, back and forth, almost as if they were watching a tennis match. He'd rather have this talk tonight, when it was the two of them, but he didn't know how to say that.

"What is it?" he asked instead.

"I have to be in the city myself on Friday." She paused, her gaze darting around the room before she turned to him again. "For an appointment. I can take Abby and her friends, drop them at the mall, and meet up with them afterward."

An appointment.

He thought about the sperm bank website he'd caught her looking at last week. Was it located in Denver? Was she planning to do a bit of shopping herself?

His gut churned at the thought.

He blamed it on his only breakfast this morning being coffee, not on Katie's baby plans.

Their nightly phone calls had been about the kids, his

family or office stuff. She'd never brought up the subject. Hell, he had no clue how one went about—

"Nolan?" Her voice cut into his thoughts. "Is that okay?"

He nodded. "Take my truck. It's better in bad weather. Just in case. You can fit more people in it, too, depending on how many go."

"Okay, thanks."

"The keys are hanging—"

"I know where your keys are. I should get back to my desk now."

"Katie—"

"Nolan, don't go anywhere." Adam cut him off this time. Pushing back his chair, he kept talking as he stood, coffee mug in hand. "Nothing that needs note taking, but Katie, can you keep the Conference in Session sign on the door, please?"

She nodded and turned away.

"I'll call the kids. And you. Tonight."

She paused when Nolan spoke, her gaze back on the screen.

He wanted to say more, to thank her again for uprooting her life for him and his kids—for everything—but he stayed silent as she acknowledged his words, then left. He watched until she was out of the camera's range. A soft click told him the door had been closed.

It was only a matter of time.

Nolan started a mental count. *One-two-three-four-five-six-seven—*

"Boy, how domesticated." Dev went first.

"Chatting about the kids," Bryant said with a grin. "Comparing calendars."

Dev leaned toward his brother, matching his smile. "She knows where he keeps his keys. That's one step short of—"

"What in the hell are you doing?"

That came from Adam, who was still offscreen. Nolan

wasn't surprised. He sighed. "You want to talk about this now?"

"No, I wanted to talk about it last week when I caught you two getting busy in the supply closet." Adam sat again. "But you hightailed it out of town too fast."

Devlin let loose with a low whistle.

"Getting busy?" Bryant asked. "Whoa, what'd I miss?"

"You didn't miss anything." Nolan said before anyone could chime in. "The only thing we were getting in the closet was office supplies."

"Yeah, right."

"Okay, somebody fill me in," Liam said. "I'm half a world away and totally lost."

"It's nothing—"

"Nolan and Katie hooked up." Adam said. "The Halloween party. One night only. Everything's back to normal. According to him."

Nolan shut his eyes.

The idea of knocking his head against the table came to mind, especially because he wasn't home to do the same to his brothers. The sibling affection from a moment ago was now gone. At least Dad wasn't around to hear any of this, as he'd taken their mom to a doctor's appointment.

"Doesn't seem that way from where I sit. Across the pond. Missing out on the action. *Are* things back to normal?" Liam asked.

"Other than the fact she's staying at his place, watching his kids and sleeping in his bed?" Bryant said with a shrug. "Sure."

"How do you know she's in my bed?" Nolan demanded, then realized how that sounded. "Sleeping in the master bedroom?"

"Hello? You've got kids. Kids with big mouths," Devlin said. "And I think Liam's comment about the princesses hit a sore spot."

"What the hell makes you say that?" Nolan said.

"Hey, I've been around women enough to know when one feels slighted—"

"You said you were going to fix this," Adam interrupted. "Was what happened between you two that night the topic of your huddle in the supply closet?"

"No."

The last thing Nolan would do was share Katie's baby idea with his brothers. He'd learned his lesson the hard way. Besides, the news wasn't his to tell.

If she decided to go through with it. Which, according to her plans for Friday, she probably was. At least the first steps.

"We were talking about work," he finally said.

"I don't believe you."

Still pissed about the broken confidence, even if it was to another brother, Nolan turned his focus to Adam. "There's nothing going on between me and Katie. Other than her helping me—all of us—by keeping an eye on my kids. Got it? I don't want to hear another word about it."

He pressed a button and killed the video feed.

The audio stayed live for a moment longer. Long enough for him to overhear his brothers talking.

"The poor bastard. He has no idea what's about to hit him."

"And there's not a single thing we can do about it."

Chapter Six

With the boys at a sleepover and Abby out with friends, Katie was set for some alone time in front of the television on a snowy Friday night. Mug of hot chocolate. Large bowl of popcorn. Season three of *Gilmore Girls* cued up and ready to go.

She'd loved this show when she was a teenager. Always wished for a cool mom like the single mother portrayed on the still-popular series.

Wrapping her necklace in her hand, she caressed the stones, warming them with her touch. Now, she guessed she could think of it as research for her future plans, even though the daughter on the show was a teenager.

Who knew—maybe Katie would find some answers for dealing with Nolan's daughter.

Or just console herself.

Today had been a total bust in every possible way. First, the fertility clinic canceled her consultation. She didn't get the message until she, Abby and her friends were halfway to Denver.

Not that she would've changed their plans.

Abby hadn't been happy when Nolan laid down the law about her shopping with Katie or not at all. She hadn't said another word about it, so when she announced at dinner last night she and her friends would be ready to go at eight the next morning, Katie had been surprised.

With her appointment canceled, she'd stayed at the mall, telling the girls they'd meet up in a couple of hours for lunch. Only when she'd tried to find them, they were never at the stores Abby listed in her texts. Katie had hit three locations before figuring out the girl had sent her on a wild goose chase.

She'd finally spotted them outside a dressing area, oohing and aahing as Abby preened in front of a three-way mirror, in a dress much too mature for a sixteen-year-old—especially for a small town like Destiny and a father like Nolan—with its low back and thigh-skimming hemline.

The surprise on the teen's face when she'd shown up had been some vindication. Katie then tried to find a polite way to say the cocktail dress was a bit too much, resulting in a hostile stare. Her reaction? She'd suggested Abby send a picture to her dad for his approval.

That had caused the girl to storm back into the dressing room, announcing she hated the dress anyway. After that, lunch and the ride home had been tense.

Then Nolan had called while they'd been on the way back—the Ellsworths were having a party and the old man wouldn't take no as an answer to his invitation. Since Nolan didn't know when he'd be back to his hotel, he'd checked in early.

With Abby in the car, Katie had been unable to talk freely with Nolan. Not that she was sure what she would've shared from the day's events. Once Abby had realized her dad was on the phone, she'd taken it right out of Katie's hand and chatted away.

While Katie drove fuming. For many reasons.

All of which were kind of sad.

She hated that her journey to motherhood had started off canceled, hated that she was jealous of Nolan attending a fancy party with those beautiful Ellsworth women and hated how things were between her and Abby.

It was so different from back in September, when the girl had come to her about her rocky relationship with Casey, an unknown cousin who'd arrived from London weeks earlier searching for her dad, Liam.

The two girls had clashed from the beginning.

Abby had shown up at Katie's apartment, confessing the rotten things she'd done to Casey. Katie had tried to convince the teen the situation might improve if she owned up to her actions with a heartfelt apology. Abby had refused, but then stopped by Katie's desk a few days after that and confided she'd done exactly that.

Katie had earned a surprised hug from the girl that day.

Shaking her head at the memory, she reached for the remote. "Where's that sweet girl now?"

A few hours and three episodes later, Katie was happily lost in the fictional town of Stars Hollow, feeling a kinship with the single mother's rocky road to romance, when her cell phone rang.

Nolan?

"Argh, you're pathetic," Katie chastised herself. "It's not even eleven o'clock. Even earlier in Spokane. He's still partying with the princesses."

She hit the pause button and reached for her phone, surprised to see Peggy's number listed. "Hey, girl. Why are you calling so late?"

"I'm heading home after an exciting night at my folks'. Curtis loves to hang with his grandpa, while my mom dragged me to another Destiny Betterment Committee meeting."

"Ugh. What cause are they fighting against this time?"

The committee, which had accomplished some good things for the town, had also earned Katie's disdain when they tried to shut down the Blue Creek Saloon a few years ago. They hadn't approved of the choreographed dancing done by Racy's waitresses.

Yes, they performed on the top of the bars, but more power to them. If she had the confidence—

"Hey, where'd you go?"

Katie blinked. "Sorry, got lost there for a moment."

Peggy laughed. "Did I wake you up? You sound tired."

"No, just enjoying the wonders of *Gilmore* land. So, what's going on?"

"I was saying how some of the committee are upset about a tattoo shop that's coming to town." Peggy paused for a moment. "Right beneath your apartment."

That got her attention. "Really?"

"There's a big black Harley parked in the middle of the space. So far the motorcycle is the only thing in the store. Haven't you noticed?"

"Except for when I used my lunch hour Monday to pick up more clothes, and today, I haven't been away from the Murphy compound."

"Oh, that's right. The shopping trip. How did that go?"

"It was…fine."

Peggy laughed. "Which means it wasn't. So, is week two of being a single mom harder or easier than you expected?"

Both, but Katie wasn't going to admit anything. "Everything is…okay. The twins weren't happy their dad missed their first game, but the Murphys showed up in force. The boys are with friends overnight. Abby is out until her curfew."

"Ah, you're enjoying some alone time," Peggy said.

"Boy, I can't wait for those days. So, you didn't know about your new neighbor?"

"Nope. My landlord said someone might be taking the place over mine and the storefront, but that was when I first moved back."

"Not if the DBC gets petitions and whatnot against the owner. Which is nuts. Destiny could use some new businesses in town."

"I agree. We had to go to your old stomping grounds in Laramie for my tattoo." Katie loved her artwork, especially the quote she now carried along her spine, but it wasn't something she could see on a daily basis. "Maybe it's time for another."

Peggy sighed. "I've created a monster."

Katie grinned, picturing the three small yet strategically placed black designs on her friend's body. "You need something with a bit of color this time."

"What I need is my head examined—hey, didn't you say you haven't been home all week?"

"Not since Monday."

"I think you left a few lights on."

She frowned. "No, I was there during the day. Oh, it must be the timers."

"These seem brighter than night-lights. Hold on, I'll swing around the back and…" Peggy's voice trailed off. "It's pretty bright up there. In the upstairs apartment, too."

"Wow, that's strange." Katie swung her legs off the couch, shut off the television and took her dishes to the kitchen. "Okay, I'll check it out."

Tugging on her boots, she grabbed her keys from where they hung next to Nolan's and fumbled through them to find the remote starter for her car.

She peeked out the window. The snow had stopped, leaving plenty of white stuff to clean off—

Wait a minute.

Katie looked down.

Her house key was gone.

Office key, office key, office desk key. Nolan's house keys, ignition key. All on the monogrammed ring Elise Murphy had given her last Christmas.

All her keys but one.

What the heck? Had she lost it today—

The answer came to Katie so fast she had to lock her knees to stay upright.

"You want me to wait for you?" Peggy asked. "Just in case?"

"No, you get Curtis to bed," she said, grabbing her coat. "I'm sure it's nothing."

She'd bet ten to one a certain teenager had swiped her key.

Not too original, Abbs. Katie had done the same thing in her crazy youth to a foster family who had a place on a lake. A private party that got way out of control and cost her a night behind bars.

Fifteen minutes later, Katie pulled into the lot behind the row of buildings that housed a number of businesses, some with apartments above, like hers.

She got out of her car and marched toward the back outside stairway. Music blared from her place as she reached the landing.

That girl had guts—she'd give her that much.

Katie headed for her door, not noticing someone else already there until she almost bumped into him. Dressed from head to toe in black—shirt, jeans, boots—the man swung around, his hands braced in front of him in a fighting stance.

"Oh, sorry." Katie jumped back. "I didn't see you. The outside light should've popped—" The yellow glow came to life, causing Katie to blink and shield her eyes. "Whoa, that's bright."

"Yeah, it is."

She dropped her hand when he spoke and found he'd done the same.

Boy, he was tall. And freaking gorgeous.

Dark wavy hair in need of a trim, dark eyes and a few days' growth on his face highlighted killer cheekbones. Strong shoulders led to muscular arms, one covered in colorful tattoos that reached all the way to his wrist. The other arm was marked as well, both visible because he was out in the cold in a short-sleeved T-shirt. The freezing temperatures didn't seem to bother him.

She looked at his face again and found him staring as well, his gaze roaming over her, but not—well, not in a bad or scary way. Or even sexual. He wasn't setting off any carnal bells and whistles for her, either.

In fact, he was looking at her much the same way the Murphy brothers did. Well, except for one brother. Then again, that had been when she was a total stranger to Nolan.

But this man…he was curious about her. That didn't make any sense. She'd never seen him before…

Then it became clear. "Ah, you must be him."

"Excuse me?"

His voice was deep but soft. He tilted his head, the scrutiny continuing, his gaze pausing a moment on her chest. Okay, that could be creepy. She tried to zip her jacket, but her necklace got tangled in the process.

"Your jewelry—" He pointed at her.

"Yes, I—I got it." She shoved the cross inside and yanked the zipper to her chin. "I meant you must be my new neighbor." Or maybe he wasn't. She took another step back. "Right?"

"Yes, that's me. Garland Ledstrom, but people call me Gar." He grinned, his mouth rising deep into one dimple. "From upstairs."

"Down, too?" she asked. "You own the motorcycle? And the soon-to-be tattoo parlor on the first floor?"

"Studio, and boy, this is a small town."

"You have no idea."

He nodded, his smile deepening, and held out his hand. "What I also don't know is your name."

"Katie Ledbetter." His grip was warm and secure. "Nice to meet you."

He studied her again for a long moment, then gave his head a quick shake as if realizing he hadn't let go and released his hold.

"Sorry, it's just that you...remind me of someone." He smiled again, but it was softer, sadder even. "Must be the red hair."

"Ah, is there something I can help you with?" she asked, pointing at her door. As interesting as it was to talk to him, she needed to find out what was going on inside her apartment.

"The music. I was coming to ask you to either turn it up so I can hear it better or lower it a bit." He glanced at her door as well. "But it seems you're not the heavy metal fan. Roommate?"

"No, but don't worry." Katie's smile tightened. "I'm going to take care of this. Right now."

"You need any backup?"

"Thanks, but no." She appreciated the offer, which was strange as she'd only just met the man. "I've got this."

"Okay. I'm heading downstairs." He started past her, stopped and glanced back. "Yell if you need...anything."

She nodded as he turned and headed for the stairs, making a mental note to call Peggy first thing in the morning.

If she made it through the night.

Pulling in a deep breath, Katie went to her door and grabbed the knob. It turned easily in her hand and she stepped inside her apartment.

Lights were on in the kitchen, where two pizza boxes sat on the counter, one still containing a few half-eaten pieces. There were also two six-pack cardboard carriers, but not a beer in sight.

Her anger spiked and she headed for the dimly lit living room, shocked when she saw candles scattered around, along with empty bottles and used paper plates. She caught a whiff of what better be nothing more than herbal cigarettes.

Abby sat curled up on the couch in the arms of a boy. Another girl and her date were squished together on the chair. Everyone was so into their make-out sessions no one heard her enter the apartment.

Time to change that.

She hit the button on her stereo, ending the music. The couples sprang apart.

"Party's over," she said.

Abby whirled around. Surprise then guilt crossed her features. Her skin was pasty and her smile too bright. "Well, look who's here! It's my babysiss-sitter."

Slurred words, too. Terrific.

"I suggest you three leave." Katie glared at Abby's friends. "Now."

The couple on the chair hurried to their feet, gathered their jackets and headed past her, into the kitchen and for the door.

"Hey," she called out, stopping them in their tracks. "Who's driving?"

The teens looked at each other, then back to her.

"I am, ma'am," the boy said.

Twenty-seven years old and she was a ma'am? Wait, the girl was familiar. The one from the flower shop and the guy had long blond hair... "You okay to be behind the wheel, Thor?"

The kid's eyes grew wide as he gave a quick nod.

"I don't need to call someone's parents to come get you?"

Now two sets of eyes were round as saucers. "Ah, no. No way. I wasn't—I mean, we—we weren't drinking."

"Let 'em go." Katie turned back as the kid who'd been tongue wrestling with Abby spoke up. He stood by the couch, taking his sweet time pulling on a battered jean jacket. "The booze is mine."

"Mine, too!" Abby jumped up, unsteady on her feet, grabbing at him. "Don't forget me."

He smiled down at her. "As if I could, babe."

"Abby," the girl at the door called out. "Are you…is it okay if we leave?"

Abby giggled. "Jenn, you sound like my mother. Don't worry. I'm fine."

"You sure are, girl." The guy gripped a battered Stetson and put it on. "Hey, you two. Wait for me. You can give me a ride."

The teens at the door looked at one another again, nodded, then scampered away.

Katie turned back to Abby and her guest. "And you are?" she asked.

"On my way out. Just like you said."

He stepped into the light coming from the kitchen. He was older than the others. Older than Abby. The wandering cowboy Nolan had mentioned?

She grabbed his arm, stopping him. "How old are you?"

He yanked from her grasp. "Old enough."

And a smart-ass to boot. "Too old. She's sixteen."

He peered at Katie through bloodshot eyes before turning to Abby, giving a quick jerk of his head. The teen offered Katie an uneasy look and shuffled to the guy, who locked an arm around her when she reached him. "She's old enough, too."

"You're wrong."

The kid moved a step forward. "I don't know who you think—"

"One more inch, buddy, and you'll be sorry." The low command came from the open door. Katie's new neighbor stood there. "The lady asked you to leave. You should. Now."

The cowboy made a show of tilting Abby's face up and planting a hard kiss on her mouth before he stepped back. "Later, babe." He headed to the door, waiting until her neighbor moved to one side before walking out.

Her neighbor followed, standing with his back to Katie and Abby. Not that she thought she needed him, but Katie was glad he'd shown up when he did.

She turned her attention back to Abby.

"Are you nuts? What were you thinking?"

The girl stepped back, tripping over her feet until she bumped into the back of the sofa. "You know—" she pointed a finger at Katie "—you sounded just like Dad right then. Just like a parent. Good for you."

"Abby—"

"Oh, wait…you're not a parent. Not my parent and I'm not your daughter."

"No, but you are my responsibility, and this is *my* apartment…" Katie's voice trailed off as she noticed the girl's outfit. "Those are *my* silk pajamas. Why are you wearing those?"

"Calm down. We were messing around. Outside. In the snow. I got wet and thought I'd dry my clothes."

"I don't have a dryer. Or a washing machine."

"So I've learned. That sucks." Abby pouted, then went on. "I laid them out and put these on instead. Then my friends showed up. The guys got food and Joe stopped at White's Liquors, but I got cold after they left. So I thought I'd warm up…but they came back, so we ate and drank and…stuff."

And stuff. Katie didn't want to think about what the girl wasn't telling her. "How much have you had to drink?"

"Three beers." Abby's eyebrows dipped in concentration. "No, four. I'm much warmer now."

"Excuse me, I hate to interrupt..."

Katie turned. She'd forgotten about her neighbor—what was his name again? Gar. He had stepped back inside the apartment, but the door remained open behind him.

"The reason I came up," he continued, "is because I've got water in the storage room downstairs. It's coming from behind the wall and through the ceiling. I wondered if you were having issues—"

"Oh, water! The shower!" Abby cried out, slapping a hand over her mouth.

Katie whirled around and hurried into the hall off the kitchen that led to the bathroom and the two bedrooms. Her boots landed with a splat on the thick throw rug.

My God! How had she not heard the sound of running water before now?

"What the—dammit!"

She shoved open the bathroom door, her eyes going to the tub. Water lapped over the edge while the showerhead spewed streams of water. There were more squishes and splats from the rug in here as she crossed the room, twisted the controls and flipped the lever from its up position.

"I'm sorry! I forgot! I mean, I totally f-forgot I was warming up the shower! And I don't know how it filled up like th-that," Abby sputtered, following Katie's lead and grabbing bath towels from a nearby shelf and tossing them to the floor to soak up the water. "We turned on the music, started chowing...oh, Katie, I'm so sorry!"

"Yes, Abby, I heard you." She turned back to find Gar standing in the archway of the hall. "What a mess. I'm sorry about this."

"Can I do anything to help?"

"It's draining." Katie grabbed the bathroom rug and held the dripping mess over the tub. "Oh, wait! Will the water cause more trouble downstairs? Should I flip the lever again?"

"Don't worry, I've got that covered," he said. "Now, what can I do?"

Her gaze darted around the room. "Ah, toss the rug in front of you out on the landing?"

"Got a mop and bucket handy?"

"Closet in the kitchen."

He nodded, and held out his hand. "That should go outside, too." Taking the sodden material from her, he grabbed the rug at his feet and left.

Katie turned to Abby. "You. Put your own clothes back on. Now. Dry or not."

The girl's eyes filled with tears. "I didn't intend for this to happen."

"But you did intend to steal my key and use my apartment without asking."

Abby bit hard on her bottom lip and nodded. "We wanted a place where we could be alone. Joe lives in the ranch bunkhouse and Dad would never—" She stopped, her wet eyes large and round. "Oh, Katie, you can't tell my dad. Please!"

"You're kidding, right?"

"Please, I'll do anything."

"Oh, I think you've done enough." Katie scrutinized her bathroom, still not believing this was happening. "Do you have any idea of the mess you've caused? Not just up here, but downstairs, too? That man is trying to open a business and now—"

"I made a mistake," Abby cried, kneeling on the floor, working a towel behind the toilet. "Haven't you ever made a mistake?"

Okay, that hit close to home. At least this night wasn't

going to end up with Abby waiting at the local jail—all night—for someone to come and get her. "Plenty. I paid for them, too, believe me."

"Then you should understand!"

"No, you need to understand how irresponsible your actions were tonight."

"I do! I get it! I didn't mean—" She stopped, sat back on her heels and placed at hand to her stomach. "Oh, God, I feel sick."

Katie did, too. That was the last thing they needed. Although the two of them were in the right spot. "Sick as in you're going to throw up?"

Abby shook her head. "No, I don't think so. I…I can't believe how fast things got out of hand. I thought I had everything under control…"

"It's amazing how quickly plans can change, huh?"

"Katie, I am sorry— "

Abby's latest apology was interrupted by Katie's ringtone.

They both froze.

Katie reached for her phone in her jacket pocket. Nolan. He was supposed to be at the Ellsworths' and they'd already talked once today. Why was he calling?

"Is that my dad?" Abby whispered.

Katie nodded.

"Don't answer it."

Typical teen reaction. "I have to."

"Don't tell him. Please. We can—you can handle this," Abby pleaded. "He left you in charge, right? I'll do whatever you want. Whatever it takes…"

Katie sighed. Yes, she was in charge, and except for a few minor emergencies and the teenage attitude, she hadn't had anything major to deal with when it came to his kids.

Until tonight.

One more ring and it would go to voice mail. She pressed

the button, having no idea what she was going to do or say. "Hey, Nolan."

"Hey, there." Now here was a soft masculine voice that made her bones melt. Unlike her good-looking neighbor. Dammit.

"Ah, am I calling too late?" he continued. "It's almost midnight there."

Katie glanced at the wall clock. Twenty minutes before the witching hour. "No, it's fine. You back from *your* party already?"

Abby cringed.

"No, the festivities are still going strong. I stepped outside for some fresh air and thought I'd check in."

"Well, there are some festivities going on here, too."

"Meaning what? You're out on a date?"

His question—and the strained tenor of his voice—surprised her. "What makes you say that?"

"Well, it's Friday night. You always did have a busy social life. I doubt that's changed because…you're watching the kids."

But it had. The last time she'd been social had been with him.

Not that she hadn't had the chance to go out with friends. And one of their suppliers had called about having dinner when he was in town last week, but she'd turned him down. A nice guy, but he wasn't—

"I should've guessed this arrangement would get in your way." Nolan cut into her thoughts. "Sorry. Didn't mean to take you away from your…date?"

Boy, she was getting apologies from Murphys all around tonight. "No, it's fine."

More silence as Gar returned with the mop and bucket and went to work on the hall floor, which was only slightly damp thanks to what used to be a beautifully plush, hand-woven shag rug.

"So, where are the kids?"

Katie leaned against the sink. "Chained up in the basement."

"Katie—"

"Hey, if I'm gallivanting around town—"

"That's not what I meant…" Nolan's voice trailed off. In the background Katie heard music and a female voice calling out to him.

"I'm on my way," he said, then directed his words to Katie. "Again, sorry. That was—"

"Work, yes, I know."

He had a job to do, and she did, too. And she was doing damn good at taking care of his kids. She could handle this. Wasn't that what she'd promised?

"The twins are staying at friends', remember? And Abby…" She paused, closing her eyes for a moment. "… is out, too. So am I."

The teen sagged with relief.

Katie shot her a look that hopefully conveyed she wasn't off the hook. "I'm on my way home, in fact," she continued. "Abby's curfew is midnight and she won't want to screw with that."

"Okay. I'll let you go, then. Good night, Katie."

"Good night."

She ended the call, only 80 percent sure she was doing the right thing.

Yes, tonight could have been so much worse, but it wasn't. She needed to know she could handle situations like this. Being in charge, being a parent, meant doing just that.

Abby opened her mouth, but Katie held up a hand. "Go change. Hand out my laundry basket so I can put these wet towels somewhere."

Abby looked at her, then at her neighbor, and disappeared into Katie's bedroom. Seconds later, the plastic tub

Katie lugged her clothes to the Sudz Bucket in sat outside the closed door.

"Not the best way to spend a Friday night, huh?"

Katie glanced up from plopping the soaked towels into the tub with a splat. "I've had better."

"I'll bet. Just so you're aware, I think there was a problem with the pipes before tonight," Gar said. "My shower's been slow since I moved in last week."

"Maybe, but this didn't help."

"True. I turned off the main line for the building. My shop vacuum is sucking up the water." He took the laundry tub from the bathroom and handed the mop to her. "I'll give Mr. Bergeron a call first thing in the morning."

Their landlord. Of course he had to be told about this, but did he have to know everything?

"I appreciate that. Ah, as you probably figured out I've been keeping an eye on a friend's kids. Not doing such a bang-up job tonight, but still—"

"Hey, we were all teenagers once. I'm sure both of us have some stories we could tell," he said quietly. "And ones we'd rather keep to ourselves. Don't worry. Your secret is safe with me."

Chapter Seven

Nolan stood outside in the cold, hands stuffed into his pockets, his breath forming white puffs in the wintry air.

Damn, he was tired. It'd been a long trip, but the drawings were done, ready to be finalized, and then on to the next step in the approval process. The customer was happy and so was he.

Mainly because he was home.

He loved it here. This little speck of land in the great state of Wyoming. No matter where he traveled. Paris. Boston. Spokane. This town and this ranch were his favorite places in the world.

The Murphy family compound was quiet, with a fresh layer of snow covering everything except the stone pathways—thanks to the heated cable system beneath the pavers, which had been his idea.

The main house and his brothers' log homes were dark, just a soft glow of light here and there. The elaborate outdoor lighting was off as well, until he started up the path, kicking off the motion sensors.

Not that the lights were needed.

A star-filled sky and a full moon shone overhead. The snow sparkled as if someone had tossed handfuls of crystals—

Crap, he *was* tired if thoughts like that were creeping into his head.

The taillights of the car service that brought him from the airport disappeared down the drive.

It was almost two in the morning.

He should've waited until after daybreak to fly home, but he'd found a last-minute seat on a flight to Denver and taken it. Now he figured to sneak inside, crash on the couch for a few hours and surprise everyone with a pancake breakfast.

After that the kids would head off to school, Katie to the office, and he could get some sleep in his own bed.

The same bed Katie had been in for the last thirteen nights.

He pushed the thought from his head, grabbed his suitcase and headed for his front porch slowly, the lights coming on as he passed. Hopefully a few more minutes out in below-freezing temperatures would cool the craziness about Katie that'd descended into his brain over the last week.

There was nothing going on between them and there wouldn't be.

As planned. As agreed. Lather, rinse, repeat.

Outside the front door, he pulled out his cell phone and typed in the security code. Slipping inside, he reset the alarm and waited. The house stayed quiet. Leaving his suitcase by the stairs, he took off his jacket as he stepped into the living room, tossing it onto one of the leather chairs.

Huh. There was some kind of pillow tucked in one corner. Two more on either end of the sofa. Not regular-size pillows that one could nap with, but those embellished square and rectangular things his mother liked so much.

His eyes got used to the darkened interior, helped by the glow from a small lamp on one of the end tables. That was new as well, as was the blanket thrown over the back of the leather sofa. A flower arrangement sat on the coffee table where he propped up his feet while watching the television. Where were his remotes? He peered into a woven basket next to the flowers and found them.

What was going on here?

He walked into the dining room and kitchen area. There were more flowers in the middle of the table. Potted plants stood sentry on either side of the glass doors that led to the back deck. The sideboard, usually a chaos of schoolbooks, paperwork and junk mail, was spotless except for framed pictures of his kids at one end and a trio of candles at the other. Another lamp glowed from across the kitchen. Tucked in the corner, it provided enough light to see while rummaging for a late-night snack.

His home looked different.

The same, but different. Better, he admitted. Thanks to Katie.

As he walked back into the living room he wondered if she'd done anything to his bedroom. The door to his personal haven off the front foyer was closed.

Two steps in that direction was too many. He backtracked and sat on the couch.

You are not going there.

He'd love to untangle the mess of burning knots in his shoulder muscles with a hot shower, but that wasn't going to happen, either.

Better to stretch out and close his eyes.

Toeing off his shoes, he leaned back against the end of the sofa deepest in the shadows, using one of those silly pillows beneath his head.

He grabbed the blanket and tossed it over his body. The heavy weight surprised him. So did how good it felt against his chilled body and the slight feminine scent that clung to it.

Well, this would have to do until the morning…

The creak from his bedroom door opening caused him to go still.

Katie was awake.

Had he made any noise? Should he say something to her? Let her know he was here?

He should've at least texted her once he'd landed in Denver. That way, if she did wake up and checked her phone, she'd know he was on his way.

She padded out in bare feet, crossed in front of him and headed into the kitchen, never looking his way.

He sat up when a light came on, then went off again. The refrigerator. He waited, debating his options, when she came back into the room, water bottle in hand, and started for his bedroom.

Again, she never glanced his way.

Still, this wasn't fair. If she came out when he was asleep and thought—what? A total stranger broke in to take a nap?

That was nuts, but she needed to know he was home.

"Katie," he said in a whisper.

She paused, frozen in place. Had she heard him?

"Katie," he repeated, a bit louder. "It's me."

In one continuous move, she spun and hurled the bottle, hitting him smack on the forehead. The force popped the top and icy water showered everywhere.

"Ow, fu—fudge!" He jumped to his feet, the kid-friendly swear spilling out by habit. With one hand at his head, he grabbed his shirt with the other and yanked the drenched material from his chest. "That's cold!"

"Don't move."

Nolan looked up and found his houseguest standing at

the fireplace. She clenched the wrought-iron log poker in one delicate fist and aimed it at him. She was reaching for the panic button on the alarm panel with her other hand.

"Katie, don't. It's me. Nolan." He kept his voice down, not wanting to wake the kids. He moved into the lamp's glow. "It's me."

She stared at him for a moment before her arms sagged in relief. "Nolan? Oh my god, what are you doing here?"

"I live here."

"That's not funny. You scared the crap out of me!"

"Yeah, I figured." He rubbed at the low throb over his eye. "Nice aim, by the way."

"Oh, darn. More water." She shook her head and let loose a snort of laughter. "Sorry about that."

"Don't be. I deserved it." He picked up the now damp throw. "But this didn't. Hope the water won't ruin your blanket."

"It's yours. Wait, you need...hold on."

She returned the poker to its proper place and raced into the half bath. Returning with a couple of hand towels, she handed him one and wiped at the coffee table and sofa with the other. "Geesh, déjà vu much?"

What did that mean? "What?"

"Nothing." She straightened, eyes wide, the towel at her chest. "It was...nothing."

It registered then that she was standing before him wearing nothing but a black-and-white-checked flannel shirt. The sleeves were rolled back to her elbows and the hem hit her midthigh, showing plenty of leg.

The shirt was vaguely familiar. "Is that...my shirt?"

"What?" She glanced down. "Oh, yeah. Hope that's okay. I need to do laundry. Spilled a late-night snack down the front of me earlier."

"Ah, that's fine." He yanked on his wet shirt. "I know the feeling."

"You scared the bejesus out of me when you said my name. When did you get home?" she asked. "And why didn't you call and tell us you were coming?"

"I wasn't sure if I would make it home. Three planes and two delays, but I'm here. Figured I'd crash on the couch and surprise everyone when you all woke up. I should've let you know." He rubbed at his chest with the towel, but it wasn't helping. "Hell, I was just thinking how good a shower would feel."

"I can bet after a long..." Katie paused, then her face lit up. "Oh! Yes, of course." She shuffled backward. "Let me grab a few things and get out of your way."

"Katie, no." Nolan followed her. "That's not what I meant. I'm not going to kick you out of my—the bedroom."

"No, it's okay. It's your bed." She pushed back a mass of red curls from her face. "Your bedroom."

"I'll be fine out here," Nolan countered, refusing to allow himself to be distracted by the sexy tousle of hair.

Which he was only noticing now.

He must be more tired than he thought, because damn, she looked good. "Let me grab something dry to sleep in," he said. "A couple of real pillows and blanket. I'll be—"

"But you said—and well, that's an amazing shower you've got. All those massaging heads that you can position any way you want? I love it!"

Don't go there. Don't go there. Don't go there.

He was losing the battle. The one in his head and the one with the woman in front of him. "Katie...fine. Yes, a shower would be great. Especially now."

Especially a cold one.

He headed for his bedroom. "I'll only be a few minutes, then we can get to bed. To *sleep*. We can each get to sleep."

"Okay, I'll...wait right here."

Nolan glanced back over his shoulder, but she'd turned away and was laying the blanket over a chair to dry. When her shirt rode up on those sexy legs—not to mention how nicely it hugged the curve of her backside—he jerked his head around and almost walked into the door.

Punching out a breath, he backtracked long enough to grab his toiletries bag from his suitcase. He kept his gaze off the rumpled blankets of his bed when he entered his room, grabbed something to sleep in and headed to the bathroom.

He flipped on the light, closed the door and paused to lean against it.

Not the homecoming he'd planned.

Shaking his head, he stripped and got into a pulsating, hot shower. Standing beneath the spray with his eyes closed, his body thanked him for not arguing too much over the need for this.

He tipped his head back, the water flowing over his face, and blindly reached for the soap. He came up empty. Brushing the wetness from his eyes, he found instead a row of bottles all in the same style of dark blue.

"'A warm and stimulating blend of striking spice oils and a sweet, sultry vanilla.'" He read the description aloud, popped the top on the shampoo and sniffed. "Yep, that's Katie. From her hair down to her..."

A hard twist to the cold water valve lowered the shower's temperature. He found his bar of soap on a lower shelf and washed quickly, turning to face the massaging heads so they'd pound some sense into his body and his mind.

It'd been one night. A chance meeting of two people looking to escape their regular lives for a few hours.

What had happened between him and Katie didn't mean anything.

That's what they'd agreed on.

"You work together. She works for you. Getting involved would only screw things up. For the business, for everyone." Nolan repeated the reasons he'd come up with over the last few weeks—hell, the last few years—as to why nothing like that could happen again between them.

Because he didn't want what Katie wanted.

Bryant and Laurie had managed to turn their office romance into a happy marriage, even if it did take his brother five years to put a ring on her finger.

"They were looking for a relationship. Ready for marriage. You're not," he reminded himself, his vow of "never again" ringing in his ears. "She is. She must be. Considering the number of men she's dated over the years."

Two different people wanting different things.

Like babies.

He still thought her plan to have a child alone was crazy.

She was only twenty-seven years old. What was the rush? He thought back to the times he'd seen her with her ex's little girls. Happy, having fun. Buying them ice cream at the diner. At the park playing on the swings.

Then again, there was so much more to being a parent than that.

It was the day-to-day emotional, physical and financial investment in the lives of your children. It was filled with pitfalls. With always wondering if you were doing the right thing. Making the right decisions.

But it was her choice.

Who was he to tell her whether it was the right one or not?

He closed his eyes again and stood there, allowing the pounding spray to hit his body. He had no idea how long he stayed, but finally he turned off the water and dried off. He brushed his teeth, figured a shave could wait until tomorrow and dressed, realizing he should've grabbed a T-shirt as well.

His hand hovered over the light switch, wondering if Katie was already back in bed. A strange sense of what she said earlier, *déjà vu*, came over him as he reached for the doorknob.

Another bathroom, another bed.

Let it go, man. Find a shirt and get your butt back on that couch.

He turned off the lights, just in case, and opened the door.

The first thing he saw was the flickering glow from the gas fireplace. It gave off enough light to see that his suitcase was near the closet and the bed was empty and remade. Fresh sheets. Pillows propped against the headboard, the heavy comforter folded at the end of the bed. The light-weight blanket and top sheet creased back at an angle.

Someone had been busy.

Shaking his head, Nolan headed for the living room, stopping when he found the couch empty.

What the—had she gone home? No, Katie wouldn't leave. Then where—

He marched through the kitchen, passed the laundry room. The door to his office was shut. He hesitated for a moment, rapped hard once and opened it.

"Katie?"

Silence. He walked in and found her lying on her back, eyes closed, huddled beneath a blanket. "I know you're not asleep."

She didn't move an inch.

He leaned over, bracing one hand on the arm of the love seat, his fingers tangling in the silky lengths of her hair. A quick intake of breath filled his nostrils with her signature scent. It swirled around for a moment then headed straight for his gut.

And lower.

"Katie, go back to bed."

"Hmm, I am in bed," she mumbled, snuggling deeper. "Good...night."

Nolan was exhausted and could barely keep his eyes open, but he smiled. He couldn't help it. "I appreciate this, but you're crazy if you think—"

She mumbled again, words he didn't understand, because she rolled away from him as she spoke.

His breath caught, then vanished.

Her shirt—*his shirt*—rode up when she moved, offering an enticing view of her lace-covered backside.

Black lace.

He stared for a moment, feeling a spike of familiar heat that didn't surprise him. Not when he was this close to her. He enjoyed the sight more than he had a right to. Longer than he should.

The debate over what he was about to do next raged for a moment, but this was the only way. He reached for her, blanket, too, and lifted her into his arms.

"Nolan!"

He straightened, pulling her close to his chest, the warmth of her heating his cooled skin. "Let's go."

"What are you doing? Put me down!"

Ignoring her protests, he left the room, and instead of going back to the kitchen, he took the short hallway that led to the front foyer.

"This is crazy!" She grabbed at his neck. "Put me down."

"Shh, you'll wake the kids." Probably not, but it shut her up for the moment. "And I will put you down. When I get back to my room."

She wiggled and squirmed, but he held on tighter, one arm beneath her shoulders, the other her legs. "Stop moving or you're going to hit your feet on the doorway."

"I told you—"

"And I told you this is how it's going to be." He angled into his room, walked to the bed and thankfully stopped short of tossing her onto the blankets. Although the idea of doing so, and following her into the softness, was damn tempting.

"Nolan—"

"Stop." He lowered his face to hers, his voice a whisper, their noses almost touching. "Katie, please…get into the bed."

She went still, her gaze locked with his and a powerful thread of something hot arced between them. Attraction, need, desire. It was all there with no costumes, no masks and no excuses to hide behind.

How simple it would be to take this moment…

Instead, he inched back, hearing her breath catch as he eased her to the carpet, trying to keep her soft curves from brushing against his body. But she held tight as her feet touched the ground, the blanket falling to a heap between them.

"Ah, Katie…"

His lips lost in the red waves of her hair, he couldn't hold back a low groan. Torture. Having her this close was pure torture. He didn't want to cross any line he—they—would regret.

"We can't do this." The reasons he'd recited in the shower echoed in his head, spinning on an endless shuffle. He squeezed her hips. "We agreed the last time was—"

"A mistake," she whispered. "Yes, I know."

He drew back, but her focus remained centered on his chest. She was right, but his stomach churned at that word, much as it had weeks ago when he'd almost said it aloud.

Did she really feel that way?

She might, but the pulse throbbing at the base of her throat told him she didn't care. The way her fingers dug into his arms, the sweet pull of desire between them, made him want to get lost in her heat, taste her skin—

"Katie, tell me to go."

She lifted her gaze to meet his. Confusion filled her beautiful features. "What?"

"Tell me to drop my hands—" his voice was low "—and walk away."

"Nolan…"

"Tell me it would be the best thing for the both of us."

"I…I can't."

He dipped his head again, pausing to give *her* a chance to back away. If she did, he'd let her go. He'd head out of this room—

Instead, her chin lifted. Her lips opened, eyelids fluttering closed. He swallowed hard, and then took her unspoken offer, as wrong as it might be, and kissed her.

Memories from a month ago flooded his senses, quenching a thirst he hadn't realized was there. The first swipe of her tongue over his, teasing him to follow, had him doing just that. He slid one hand from her waist, up over her curves until his fingers tunneled into her hair to circle the nape of her neck.

Minutes passed as he held her, the kisses they shared demanding, mindless and burning close to the edge of control. She leaned into him, pressing her hips and then—*damn*—rotating against the hardness she'd found.

There was so little between them. Scraps of fabric. It would only take a moment to rid them of any physical barrier…

But that wasn't all that stood between them.

Reality came rushing back like the splash of cold water he'd gotten earlier.

They couldn't do this. Shouldn't do this.

How could he have started something that would only make things worse?

Worse for everyone. Worse for her.

He needed to end this madness.

Defuse the passion. Soothe the need—hers, at least.

He released his hold on her neck and banded his arm around her waist. He swept his free hand down her thigh until he met bare skin. Skimming his fingertips beneath her nightshirt, he found the damp heat of her behind her lace panties. She rocked her hips again, gasped when he stroked her there.

Wrenching her mouth from his, she grabbed at his wrist. "Nolan."

"Let me," he murmured against her lips, taking her mouth again. He slipped the silky material aside and caressed her sensitive flesh. Her grip tightened, but she didn't push him away.

Slow and rhythmic, he dipped one finger, two, deep inside her. He ignored his own need and concentrated on her rising pleasure. The way she arched into his hand, the tremors that silently spoke of her coming climax until she dug her nails into his skin, the throaty moan he took with his mouth.

He withdrew his hand and held her close after, softening their kisses until he tucked her head to his neck when she collapsed against him.

Moving forward, he backed her to the bed, easing her to the pillows, surprised when she clung to him.

"Nolan...you don't have to leave."

How easy it would be to forget about everything. To stay with her tonight the way he wanted. The way she wanted. The only problem was tomorrow morning, they'd be right back where they were now.

Another mistake, another regret she didn't need.

He released her, stepped back and slid her legs beneath the blankets. "Get some sleep. I'll be out in the living room."

He retained enough brain cells to grab the blanket and a shirt before he left, closing the door behind him.

Stretching out on the sofa again, he stared up at the ceil-

ing, knowing he did the right thing. Tomorrow she'd move
out and things will be back to normal.

Whatever that might be.

Chapter Eight

"Dad!"

"You're home!"

The sound of the twins discovering their father asleep in the living room the next morning made Katie freeze for a moment. Then she went back to ladling scrambled eggs onto four plates.

Up for over an hour, she'd dressed and tiptoed into the kitchen via the front foyer, wondering if he would call out to her anyway.

As he'd done last night.

When he didn't, she tucked away her disappointment and got on with her morning. Still, she took a peek at him, dead asleep, looking uncomfortable on a sofa that was far too small for his large frame.

A part of her wondered if everything that happened a few hours ago had been a dream.

A dream *or* a delusion.

No, he was there—she was here—and for a few magical, heart-stopping moments in the dead of night, they'd been together.

"Girl, let it go," she whispered, holding back the urge to break into song.

She caught her reflection in one of the glass cabinets. Were her cheeks that pink? "Blame it on the heat from the stove. No one will know you and he—"

"Katie! Dad's home!"

She set the skillet back on the cooling burner with a clang. Pasting on what she hoped was a genuine smile, she grabbed two plates and spun around. "Yes, I see that. Good morning."

The twins returned her greeting, took their breakfast with thanks and headed for the dining table, just as Nolan made his way toward the kitchen.

She reached for an oversize coffee mug and filled it with the steaming liquid, surprised at how her stomach twisted at the strong aroma.

What was wrong with her? She was a coffee girl from way back, but lately...

Hold it together. Get through this meal, get to the office and back to your regular life.

"Here." She pushed the mug at Nolan, who stood at the counter, looking better than he should in flannel pajama pants, a wrinkled T-shirt and bed-head hair, eyebrows in a deep furrow as he stared at her.

"You've got your morning grumpy face on," she continued. "I think you need this."

"You cooked breakfast," he said.

"She's been doing it since you left," Logan said. "Totally cool."

"Sometimes just cereal and muffins. Or sometimes hot stuff like this," Luke added before shoving a piece of bacon into his mouth.

"And sometimes nothing at all when you guys don't get

down in time," Katie said, embarrassed at their praise. "One of you tell your sister her food is getting cold."

"Ab—" The twins started to yell in unison but stopped when Katie shot them a look.

"I'll go," Luke said, grabbing a slice of toast and waving it at his brother. "Don't eat all the bacon or you're dead."

Her smile came easy this time as she turned for the remaining plates then glanced at Nolan again. "Why don't you sit and eat?"

He eyed her over the rim of his mug with an expression she couldn't decipher, but took the plate she handed him and moved to the head of the table.

Katie set the other down next to him, then went to the toaster when her bread popped up. A quick swipe of butter and she took a bite, pausing when she caught Nolan staring again. "What?"

He put the mug down and grabbed a fork. "Is that all you're eating?"

"My stomach is a bit flippy this morning. I hope I'm not coming down with something."

"You should—"

"Daddy!" Abby sailed into the room, a big smile on her face as she hugged her father. "I'm so glad you're home."

Oh, I bet you are.

Katie resisted the urge to roll her eyes; the girl's enthusiasm seemed genuine.

Nolan wrapped his arms around his daughter, placing a quick kiss at her temple. Abby sat next to her father and Luke went back to devouring his breakfast. All three kids ate and talked at the same time, sharing what had happened in their lives as if they hadn't spoken or texted with their father once while he'd been gone.

Not every event, of course.

Her decision not to tell Nolan what his daughter had done last Friday seemed easier when he was far away. Now that he was back, Katie wondered again if that had been the right move.

Abby thought so.

The girl had been a saint since that night. And not just to Katie. Yesterday she'd helped Luke with a school project and offered to take Logan's turn doing the dishes.

Taking a sip of orange juice, Katie watched the scene before her, feeling like an outsider. Then Abby caught her staring and the teen's blue eyes widened as if she was surprised to see her there.

"Ah, Katie, this is good. Thank you," she said, pointing at her food. "Why don't you come sit with us?"

"That's okay. I'm done." Katie tossed her half-eaten toast into the trash, rinsed her plate and stuck it into the dishwasher.

"I'd planned to make my famous pancakes this morning," Nolan said. "Think you all might be interested in breakfast for dinner, too?"

"You can't, Dad," Logan said. "See the Crock-Pot? Katie's already got something cooking. Is it that cheesy broccoli thing again?"

"Yes," Katie said, then turned to Nolan. "I thought you'd like something simple your first night back."

"Oh, and make your biscuits, please," Luke pleaded. "I think I ate six last time."

"I finished off eight," Logan boasted.

"Liar. She only made a dozen."

She blushed again at the boys' compliments. Or was it the way their father's gaze ran the length of her as she stood at the kitchen island? There was nothing sensual in his stare, but darn if her toes didn't curl inside her fuzzy slippers.

Boy, her imagination was on overload today.

"And she doesn't burn the bottoms, Dad," Logan added. "Wait until you taste them."

"That sounds great, guys." Nolan tore his gaze from her. "But I'm sure Katie is anxious to head back to the peace and quiet of her own place."

Silence filled the room as an unspoken communication went on between the twins and Abby before all three went back to eating with a singular focus.

Katie wasn't sure what their shared looks meant, but it stung a little to have Nolan talk about her leaving as if it were no big deal—something to celebrate, even.

Now she had to tell him about her living arrangements and why she was currently homeless.

But the details?

No second-guessing allowed now. There'd been an issue and she'd dealt with it. The way she was supposed to, as the adult in charge. Besides, Abby did seem remorseful for the mess she'd caused.

"Truth be told, I don't have a place to go to," Katie finally said, wrapping her fingers around her necklace. Looking for strength, maybe? "Not for a while, at least."

"What does that mean?" Nolan asked.

"There was an incident at my apartment…over the weekend—"

Abby pushed back her chair and stood. She grabbed her dishes and scooted into the kitchen, giving Katie a pleading stare as she walked past her.

"What kind of incident?"

"The water pipes burst. Well, not burst, but there are… issues. In the entire building. Some of the pipes need repair, some replacing, so it's uninhabitable for the next few weeks." *Geesh, babble much?* "At least."

"Was there any major damage to your apartment?" Nolan asked.

"Hey, Daddy." Abby walked back to the table, coffee-pot in hand. "Refill?"

"Sure, honey, thanks." He lifted his mug, his attention still on Katie. "You were saying?"

"The bathroom, mostly. Not sure of how much work there's to be done. The floor, I think."

"You never mentioned anything last...the last time we talked."

Meaning last night? "Well, I didn't know until yesterday, when I spoke with my landlord and neighbor how much work was needed."

"Neighbor?"

She nodded. "Someone moved into the apartment upstairs. Nice guy. Anyway, now that you're home, my first priority this morning is to find a place to live."

"Stay here!" This came from the twins, in unison.

Abby remained quiet as she returned the pot to the coffeemaker, then walked to the sideboard and grabbed her purse and schoolbooks.

"I think that's a good idea. You should stay here."

Katie blinked at Nolan's words, surprised, especially after last night. Abby, too, seemed shocked—and not altogether happy—with her father's suggestion.

"I'm sure there's room in the main house," he went on. "There's plenty—"

"No, Dad, we meant here. With us." Luke and Logan again spoke simultaneously, saying the exact same words. Something Katie noticed they did a lot.

"Here?" Nolan's coffee mug hit the table with a loud clunk. Now his gaze was a bit shell-shocked. "That's not what—I'm not sure—"

"But Grandma said we've got housefuls of people coming. Aunts and uncles. Cousins and their kids." Luke got up from the table and joined his sister in clearing his dishes, rinsing them and putting them in the dishwasher. "Thanksgiving is Thursday."

"Uncle Liam's place is going to be full up—the boathouse, too," Logan added, grabbing the last piece of bacon on his way to the sink. "Even the guest rooms. Besides, we've got room. Abby's got twin beds."

"No." Katie quickly put a stop to that idea. "Abby doesn't want me for a roommate."

"We'll move a bed to Dad's office. That used to be a guest room," Logan continued. "It's even got its own bathroom."

"He'll give up his office for you." Luke grinned. "Won't you, Dad?"

"You guys, this is Katie's decision." Abby spoke before Nolan could. "She might be tired of cooking and cleaning for you. For us."

The twins grabbed their backpacks. "She'll still be close to work," they said, again in unison. "Come on, Abbs, even *you've* liked having her here, right?"

The girl's gaze shot from her brothers, to Katie, to her dad. "Yeah, I mean...yes, I've liked her being here. It's late. We better head to school."

"But what about—"

"Hey." Nolan held up a hand. "We'll figure something out. Time for you three to go."

The kids said goodbye to their father, waved at Katie and headed for the front door. Nolan got up from the table, coffee mug in hand, and followed.

Katie stood back watching him in the open doorway. Cold air blew into the house and she shivered, realizing the two of them were seconds away from being alone.

Really alone this time.

And after what he'd done last night...

She headed for the bedroom. Grabbing her tote bag, she tossed her purse and pair of heels inside and traded her slippers for black ankle boots. A quick brush of her teeth, a makeup check and she was ready.

Ready to leave.

Except for her clothes in the closet and the few things that needed washing, her suitcase was packed. She had no idea where she would go from here.

She and Gar had had lunch with their landlord yesterday and the man had offered to put her up in a local motel, but guilt over her part in creating the mess, no matter how bad the pipes were, had Katie refusing.

Peggy's place wasn't much bigger, and her sister was due back this week. Katie had other friends, but no one she considered close enough to ask for help.

She sighed. A motel room or the boardinghouse. Those were her two best options.

She hiked her bag to one shoulder and headed out, planning the calls she'd make when she got to her desk—

"Okay, who are you and what have you done to my children?"

She halted, almost running into Nolan, who stood right outside the bedroom door. She stopped herself with a hand to his chest. Oh, she could feel his heart beating right through the soft material.

She snatched her hand back and stepped to one side, heading toward the front door. "Excuse me?"

"*Please, thank you*, eating at the table instead of standing at the island." He followed her. "The boys not yelling full throttle for their sister. Abby willingly taking them to school. Hell, all three rinsed and put their dishes in the dishwasher. Unasked. They haven't done that in ages. You've turned them into…into…"

Katie turned to face him. "Human beings?" she offered when Nolan's voice trailed off.

"They're teenagers. Teenagers aren't human."

She smiled at that. "You've got terrific kids, Nolan. Even if they are teenagers." Even if they screwed up sometimes.

"You've changed my place, too. Flowers, pillows, candles. The lamps. The blanket."

Was any of that a bad thing? "I'll take some credit, but your mom's responsible for the rest," Katie said. "We went to the craft fair a couple of Saturdays ago and before I knew it—"

"She steamrolled her way in and did a Martha Stewart makeover." Nolan studied the room. "I should've known. It's neater, too. How'd you manage that?"

"Well, I'm a bit anal-retentive. You know my motto—"

"A place for everything and everything in its place." He rattled off her familiar saying, then smiled. "I work with you, remember?"

"And work is where I should be. I'm guessing you want more shut-eye." Despite the amount of coffee he'd drunk this morning, he still appeared tired. "Did you get any sleep at all?"

He nodded, his attention on his mug. "I crashed about an hour before the twins came down."

Katie wanted to ask why it took him so long to fall asleep after leaving her, sated but desperate to have him stay. She couldn't. It'd taken her a while, too, after he'd walked out before she closed her eyes.

She'd almost called him back. Almost gone to him in the living room.

Except she hadn't planned on any of what happened last night to…well, happen.

Remaking the bed and vacating his room had been the right thing to do. She should've known he'd come after her. But carrying her in his arms back to his bedroom? Kissing her breathless? Taking her to a delicious climax until she became putty in his hands?

All had been beautiful, wonderful…amazing.

But after all that he didn't want her. Heck, he'd pretty much said sleeping with her again would be a terrible thing.

Not in those exact words, of course.

She'd been the one to call what happened a month ago a mistake. She had to. To hear him use that word to describe—

No, she didn't think she could take that.

Okay, the eyes were getting a bit misty. Time for a good dose of bracing winter air to bring her back from the edge of crazy town.

"I'm going to go." She grabbed her jacket. "I'll tell everyone you got in late and are catching up on your beauty sleep."

Nolan nodded again. At least he was looking at her this time.

"There's a conference call with McDowell and Lantry about the Ellsworth project at two," she went on, juggling with her bag now. "Liam and Bryant are going to want you there."

"The lawyers. Right. I sent you stuff that needs printing—"

"I saw your email." She turned to the door and yanked it open. "I guess partying with the princesses helped, huh?"

"What?"

Okay, that shot wasn't necessary. "I should've said congratulations on getting the final approval on the plans last night. But hey, I was—well, I should say we were a bit preoccupied—"

"Katie, wait. About—"

"I'd rather not talk about last night. If that's okay with you."

He reached for her, his fingers tightening on her arm for a moment before he let her go. "I wasn't.... What I was going to do was apologize for assuming you could stay on the compound. I forgot about the family we've got coming in."

"Oh." God, how stupid was she!

"I'd ask you to stay here at the house, but I wouldn't want you to be uncomfortable after…well, all that's happened."

"That's okay." She turned away and yanked open the door. "I understand. I'm sure I'll find a place. Someplace where I belong."

Nolan looked around the large open living room of his family's home.

His parents had started their log home–building business twenty years ago right here. Renovations had turned most of the oversize house into professional offices and guest suites for Murphy Mountain Log Homes, but this place was still the heart of their family.

He watched his folks happily ensconced in the center of extended family. Coffee and other evening drinks flowed as the desserts on the dining table disappeared. Only Liam and Ric had been missing, but video chats earlier had helped bridge the gap.

Another Thanksgiving moved into its final hours.

The day had started with six-plus inches of snow followed by bright sunshine for the rest of the day. It was a good thing none of the aunts, uncles, cousins and their offspring had to travel, as most were safely entrenched in varying places on the compound.

Katie included.

Nolan spotted her on the other side of the room, chatting with a cousin whose name escaped him. All he remembered was the guy was single. A lawyer from Denver. Or was it Colorado Springs? He didn't know. And didn't care, because when the dude placed a hand against the wall and leaned in close, Katie laughed.

Nolan saw red. Red like the mass of waves that stood out like a beacon against her white sweater as she casually gathered the long strands in one hand and pushed them back from her shoulder.

"You going to let that go on much longer?"

He tore his gaze from the couple. Devlin stood there, his familiar smirk in place. "I don't know what you're talking about."

"Yeah, keep saying that. You might start to believe it." Dev raised the drinks in his hands. "Need to deliver one of these to my betrothed, but if you decide to make a move and need backup—"

"I think you've helped enough already," Nolan said, cutting him off.

Dev's grin returned. "Hey, Katie's family, right? Not officially, of course, but who knows? That could always change."

His brother walked away and Nolan had to admit, Dev had a point. Katie was the only non-Murphy—either by blood or marriage—here today.

Not that anyone said anything.

She'd started coming to family celebrations after the first year she began working for them. His parents had insisted when they found out she was an only child with no family. This year her getting to the compound had entailed walking from his home to the main house.

Thanks to his kids and their uncle Devlin.

While Nolan and Katie had been tied up with the teleconference Monday afternoon, the group had moved one of the beds from Abby's room and a dresser from the main house to his office. Abby had made up the bed with linens from her grandmother and even gave up her television for the cause.

He hadn't been sure Katie was going to be happy with just a twin-size bed, but there was no way Nolan could say no to the arrangement. Especially after she went teary-eyed when she'd seen what they'd done for her.

He decided it was ridiculous for her to stay somewhere

else, and he joined in by moving the leather club chair from his bedroom to hers.

Making the last three days both heaven and hell.

The kids were used to her being around, but it startled him whenever he walked into a room and found her there. Usually up before everyone else, she'd made breakfast the last two mornings and then helped in dinner preparation, finding ways to include the kids, even Abby.

Something he'd rarely been able to accomplish before.

He'd fixed the shower in the guest bath the first night. There was no way he'd survive sharing a bathroom. But even his own glass-enclosed oasis didn't provide the solace it once had, as he often found himself picturing her there with him.

The two of them. Together.

Nolan thought back on when Devlin had stood up right in the middle of dinner and gotten down on one knee to present Tanya with the diamond ring. The place had erupted with cheers and tears. Tears, too, from Katie who'd sat beside him throughout the meal, the table so crowded their legs had been pressed together—from hip to knee—the entire time.

Yeah, that'd put his perpetual state of arousal into overdrive.

Then came the annual snowball fight.

A tradition since they were kids, this year there'd been quite a crowd involved. Toddlers to teens, and adults of all ages.

They'd made up teams, but soon it turned into a manic free-for-all. He and Katie had picked the same tree for a defensive position but had immediately come under attack from a barrage of icy projectiles, resulting in a tangle of arms, legs and laughter.

He'd gone down first, turning to land on his back and cushion her fall. That put her smack on top of him. She'd braced her hands on his shoulders and the way her mouth fell open in surprise, the rush of her warm breath against his chilled skin—

"Yeah, you're not helping your cause," he muttered, re-filling his coffee mug before adding a shot of whiskey. "Not. One. Bit."

"Did you know talking to yourself is one of the first signs of lack of sex?"

"Don't encourage him."

Two different voices. One teasing. One serious. Bryant and Adam. Nolan knew who'd said what before he even turned around.

"Let me guess. Dev sent you to give me a hard time." He took a sip of his coffee. "Forget it. I'm not biting."

"Hmm, too bad. I've heard ladies like—"

"Lay off, Bryant." Adam hefted his sleeping son higher to his shoulder, his gaze not moving from Nolan's face. "How are things going?"

"Fine."

Adam nodded once, then turned away when Fay called his name.

"Don't mind him. He's in full eldest-brother, I-protect-the-clan mode these days," Bryant said. "Must be impending fatherhood."

"He's already a father."

"So are you. You've got that protective streak as strong as the rest of us." His brother reached for the coffee carafe. "Which explains why you've backed off completely—"

"I'm not talking about this." Nolan cut him off. "Not now. Not ever."

"Don't, then. Listen. You're putting up roadblocks where there shouldn't be any. She's single. So are you," Bryant persisted. "You like her. She likes you. You work great as a team in the office, and from what I've heard, things at home are downright…well, homey."

Nolan sighed. He glanced over the crowd again, his internal radar taking him right to Katie in the corner of the room.

His breath caught.

The flirting guy was gone, but in his place...in her arms...was a baby. He had no idea whose. There'd been at least a half dozen high chairs at the dining table today, but this little one wasn't happy.

Katie rocked, bounced and tried a mixture of back rubs and patting motions, but nothing seemed to soothe the infant. Or Katie, as she offered a bottle and the baby refused that, too.

Still, seeing her like that, knowing her plans and his long-ago decision not to get anywhere close to that life again...

Damn, there was much more than just the size of the room between them.

"There's more to it than that," he finally said.

"Than what?" Bryant pushed. "Fix whatever it is—"

The baby's fussing grew. So did the anxiety on Katie's face. One tiny chubby hand reached out and grabbed a fistful of that beautiful red hair.

"Be right back."

Nolan handed off his mug to his brother and was across the room in time to see the tears in both sets of eyes.

"Hey, there," he said, stopping the little one's tugging motion and easily freeing Katie's hair from her grasp. "Someone's a bit frazzled."

"No, I'm fine."

He smiled. "I was talking about the baby."

"Oh. She's fine, too. Just missing her mom. Your cousin asked me to keep an eye on her while she and her husband put their older ones down for the night." Katie blew out a breath that sent the curls on her forehead and the baby's flying. "Four kids under the age of six. How do they do it?"

"Very carefully. Can I help?"

Katie took a step back but didn't go far. Nolan still held onto the baby's hand. "I said I'm fine. Babies are fussy all the time and I need to learn, right?"

"Katie—"

"I mean…" She blinked hard. "She was sweet at first, but when she started fussing I moved back here where it's quieter. She finished the bottle. Mostly. Won't take the pacifier. This is her favorite blanket, but she's still… I can't…this is what I want, so I…can't let one crying infant bother me…"

Nolan reached for the baby and blanket, not surprised when Katie held on tight. "It's okay. Let me help."

"But I'm—"

"You've been up since 3:00 a.m. cooking and baking and being my mom's right-hand man—er, woman—all day. Not to mention taking care of my crew for the last two weeks and working full-time. It's okay to let someone else help."

Katie frowned but released her hold.

Making quick work with the blanket, Nolan wrapped the baby snug, remembering how his kids used to like this when they were upset. He'd even showed Adam when A.J. had been—

"Wow, would you look at that."

Nolan smiled at the wonder in Katie's voice.

The eyelids of the baby girl in his arms drifted closed, dark lashes against pink cheeks. The sight took him back to when Abby had been this size. The nanny Carrie's parents had insisted on had shown him this trick.

"You have a special touch," Katie said.

"Not really."

"No, you do." She shook her head, her eyes filling with tears again. Nolan took a step toward her, but she scooted away. "You probably did when your kids were babies. And you have it now with them. Whereas I just…"

"Katie—"

"Maybe I was wrong." She stared down at her empty hands. "Maybe I'm not cut out for motherhood. Maybe I should just forget the whole thing."

"Hey, what I'm doing isn't magic. It can be taught."

He hated to see her upset, but if a fussy baby was going to bother her...

"Then again, being a single parent means there won't always be someone there to tag in when you get...frustrated. Believe me, I know."

Chapter Nine

Nolan and the kids were due back any time now. Katie wondered again if she should make herself scarce as she stared at the pages of her book.

Shopping in town would be fun with all the stores decorated for the holidays. Then again, she'd finished her list, even stocking stuffers for the kids, a few days ago. She could drive to Laramie, get lost in a bookstore and grab something to eat. That would keep her away until late.

Not that she wanted to be gone.

The kids were planning a holiday movie night and homemade pizza for dinner. A first-Saturday-in-December tradition that included putting up the Christmas tree.

Something Katie thought they should be doing alone... as a family.

She'd helped bring boxes of ornaments and decorations from the attic but had begged off joining the trek into the woods for the tree after learning all the brothers and their dad were going, too.

Which made sense, as they needed four trees—one each for Bryant, Adam and Nolan, and of course, the biggest one to reach high up to the twenty-foot ceiling at the main house.

She'd joined the ladies for lunch, returned home in time to sign for a special-delivery package and then planned to cozy up with a new book.

After reading the same passage five times, she'd tossed the historical romance about dukes and balls and highwaymen aside and looked around her room, still finding it hard to believe she'd been living here for almost a month now.

According to Gar, whom she'd run into while grocery shopping yesterday, work was progressing on their building. The landlord had told him they might be able to move back in before Christmas, which was only a couple of weeks away.

Was that a good thing or not?

As much as she missed her bed and being surrounded by her own things, she loved what the kids and Nolan had done for her.

He'd even suggested she bring whatever she wanted from her apartment, too. She'd gathered more clothes, a set of Egyptian cotton bath towels that she hadn't used to clean up Abby's mess and bakeware, because Nolan didn't have much more than cookie sheets and a single muffin tin—

Darn, where was her brain? She'd promised a special dessert tonight.

Her getaway plan thawed, she headed for the kitchen and started pulling together cheesecake brownies. An hour later she was putting the pan back in the oven for the second layer when she heard stomping and voices on the back deck.

Her insides did a happy dance at the sound.

"Wow, it's cold out!" announced Logan, the first one to come in through the glass doors, yanking off his ski cap and toeing off his boots.

"How cold?" Katie asked, amused by his ruddy cheeks and static-induced hairdo.

"Colder than a hair on a polar bear's butt—"

"Logan." Nolan cut off his son's colorful description as he walked in behind him and offered a gentle slap to the back of his head. "Not cool."

Logan grinned. "Hey, she asked."

Nolan shook his head and unzipped his jacket as Luke and Abby slipped inside, too. Soon the four of them had removed their snowy outerwear, leaving traces of their day-long adventure on the carpet.

Also not cool.

Katie was about to say something when Abby surprised her by noticing the mess, too.

"Wow, we should've come in the other way." She gathered up the assorted hats, gloves, scarves and jackets. "Luke, grab your boots. Dad's, too, and follow me. Logan, can you get mine and yours?"

The teens hurried through the kitchen, disappearing into the laundry room.

"Is it a bad thing I'm still surprised at how—" Nolan paused, his voice low as he walked toward Katie, wiping at the melting snow with his stocking feet "—cooperative she's been lately?"

Katie shook her head at his version of cleaning and double-checked the timer for her dessert. "What do they say about teenagers and their mood changes?"

"True, but for someone who was bitterly against you being here, she's downright pleasant now. To everyone. I mean, I told the kids to be on their best behavior while you were here, but still."

"You did?"

"Of course. You're a guest in our home."

That last statement shouldn't bother her, but she still felt a jab low in her belly. Yes, she was a *guest*. A fact she had difficulty remembering at times. "Well, I've seen them at their worst."

"Hell, I hope not." Nolan let out a bark of laughter as he grabbed a beer from the fridge. "Unless you didn't tell me everything that happened while I was gone."

Katie's heart skipped a beat as she fumbled with the timer.

"Did I tell you I caught Abby doing the boys' laundry last week?" he continued, tossing the bottle cap in the trash. "I was shocked."

Wow, that was news. When Nolan had been gone the girl spent quite a bit of time yelling at her brothers to get their stuff out of the machines so she could do her own.

Maybe getting caught red-handed and worrying Katie might change her mind had reformed Abby's attitude.

Or it was something else.

Had the twins learned of their sister's misadventure?

A long-ago memory came back, of being blackmailed by a kid in one of the foster homes Katie had stayed at as a teen. After catching her sneaking in after curfew, the jerk had held her misdeed over her head for a month, getting her to do everything from his homework to his chores.

Were the boys exacting the same payback?

"Katie?" Nolan leaned against the counter. "Did you hear me?"

"Sorry. Yes, I heard you." She put the timer down. "Perhaps Abby's found the holiday spirit."

"So I should enjoy it while it lasts, huh?"

Which most likely would be as long as Katie stuck around. Before she could say anything more, the kids returned.

"Hey, when are we eating?" Luke asked.

"Yeah, we're starving," Logan added, heading for the stove while Abby went to the refrigerator. "Something smells awesome. What's in here?"

"Dinner is still an hour away. I've got more work to do on the dessert," Katie said, observing the twins with new eyes. "Think I could bribe you two into helping later?"

"Sure," they said together with matching grins, then raced from the kitchen.

"Hey, get out of your wet things." Nolan followed, yelling after them. "Better yet, grab showers. And don't leave your stuff piled on the floor. That's what laundry baskets are for." He glanced back over one shoulder. "I'm going to do the same."

Katie watched him walk away. She turned back when Abby closed the fridge, noticing the flash of surprise in the girl's eyes before it vanished.

"I better go, too," she said. "My jeans are soaked and I've got homework. Can you yell when dinner's ready—"

"Abby, wait."

Katie hadn't found a moment alone with the teen since Nolan's return. Something she was sure the girl was doing on purpose. Should she call her on that? Find out if the twins knew anything?

Abby stopped, squared her shoulders and glared at Katie with a mix of adolescent bravado and fear. A look so familiar it was as if Katie was seeing a reflection of herself at sixteen.

Would she have admitted to anyone what that kid had done to her? No, she'd caused her own mess and paid the price until she'd been transferred out of that house not long afterward.

"Was there something you wanted?" Abby asked.

Katie shook her head. "No, don't worry about it. About anything."

The teen's eyebrows rose, but she hurried out of the room as if afraid Katie might change her mind.

Had she done the right thing?

Boy, this second-guessing her every decision was becoming a habit nowadays.

Katie wasn't sure she liked it.

Six months ago, her life had been heading toward what she'd always dreamed of.

A home, family. When that imploded, she'd been hurt, but she'd worked hard to accept it. To move on. Then six weeks ago, she'd accidentally slept with her boss.

Again, accepted it. Moved on.

Made a new plan for a new life.

Only, she hadn't followed through with any of it.

Instead of moving forward with her baby plan, she'd moved in with said man, taken care of his children, and was now fitting into his daily life with alarming ease…except for them heading to separate bedrooms at night.

Oh, don't go there.

She turned on the radio for holiday music and was filling the sink with hot soapy water when Nolan's voice surprised her.

"We have a dishwasher that works, you know." He'd walked up behind her, setting his beer on the counter.

"I don't mind. It's my mess—" Strong hands cupped her shoulders and gently set her to the side. "Hey!"

Nolan grinned, rolling up his shirtsleeves. "We get to enjoy your tasty mess later. I'll wash. Fair is fair."

"You're the one who spent the day stomping around in the woods," she pointed out but backed away. Who was she to argue with a man who wanted to do dishes? She noticed he'd changed his clothes and the hair around his face was damp. "I thought you were going to take a shower."

"Naw, I just washed up. The boys will probably use up all the hot water anyway."

"Oh, I forgot. You got a package today. I had to sign for it."

Nolan groaned. "Please don't tell me it was from Ellsworth."

"No, it was delivered here to the house. I'm assuming it's personal?"

"Is there a return address?"

Katie walked to the sideboard where she'd left the flat envelope. "Louisburg Square, Boston—"

"Yeah, okay." He cut her off. "I know who it's from."

She did too now. "Your ex-wife."

"More like my former in-laws. Airline tickets for the kids' trip to Boston."

Katie returned the package to its spot so Nolan would know where it was.

"Where's Abby?" he asked.

"She went to her room to change. She also mentioned homework."

"Could you put that in the top drawer for me?"

"Sure." Katie did as he asked, then walked back across the kitchen. Grabbing a towel, she started drying the items he'd placed in the dish rack.

"I don't want the kids to see it yet," he continued. "They know they're going, but I haven't talked to Carrie to confirm she'll be there when they arrive."

"What makes you think she won't?"

Nolan lifted a shoulder in a casual shrug. "It's happened—more than once. My ex tends to get lost in her own world. Her parents are good people and their staff has been with them for years, so they know the kids. I wouldn't let them go if their mother was their sole guardian during their stay."

Katie remembered previous trips the kids had made. "They seem to have a good time when they're with her."

"Yeah, but one- or two-week-long visits, a few times a year, means their mom is more a friend than a parent. She spends a lot of money and does all kinds of neat things…" His voice trailed off for a moment.

"Then she ships them back to the reality of school, chores and rules," he continued. "The joys of single parenting. Or should I say joint parenting? Shared? What's it called when one person has all the fun and the other all the responsibility?"

"Frustrating?"

He laughed. "Yeah, it is that."

Leaning against the counter, Katie tried to appear casual despite the knot in her stomach. "Is this going to turn into another lecture?"

His brows dipped in confusion for a moment. "No. What I went through—am still going through—is totally different than what you're…planning."

Katie tilted her head. He had a point. "You thought you'd have a partner, for life, to help you raise your children."

"That's the idea when you marry and have kids, right? Then again, neither of us planned…anything." Nolan's gaze was on the window now. "I was in Paris as part of a college work-study program when I met Carrie. She was so different from the girls back here. Wild, free. An artist. We burned hot and fast—"

He stopped, and glanced Katie's way. "Sorry, didn't mean to run off at the mouth."

"It's okay. I don't mind listening."

"You want to hear this?" he asked.

She wanted to know everything about him. "Sure. If you'd like to talk."

He went back to washing and rinsing. Quiet settled between them. Not surprising. Why should he want to share?

"Like I said, we were together, then we weren't." Nolan started talking again. "I'd chalked it up to a fling when she showed up one day. Pregnant. Before I knew it, we were back in the States, married and living in Boston with her wealthy family. I transferred schools, went to work for her dad's architectural firm, and we had Abby."

Katie concentrated on putting the silverware away. "You were happy."

"For a while, but looking back…it was like playing house. Playing at being adults. We didn't have it rough, considering how young we were. There were servants and a nanny. Carrie continued to paint. I busted my ass at school and for my father-in-law. Hate to admit it, but I wasn't around much during Abby's first couple of years. After I got my degree, I moved up in the firm. We got our own place, complete with maid and nanny."

It sounded wonderful, but there had to be more to the story. Otherwise, they'd still be together. "And then the twins?"

"Carrie wanted another baby, a sibling for Abby. I thought we should wait awhile, but as usual Carrie went ahead and—the second pregnancy was different. Harder. The boys were good sized at birth for twins, but they weren't happy babies. I was working a lot and didn't pick up on how much Carrie had withdrawn from them. From Abby."

"Oh, that's sad."

He turned off the water, grabbed another dish towel and dried his hands. His fingers twisted the material as he continued, his voice low now. "I'm not proud of how I gave in to the pressure of a lifestyle that wasn't me. Wasn't what I wanted. As the years went on, it was the nanny raising the kids. I'd come home late and find Carrie had dismissed her for the night, but then she'd gone off and gotten involved with her art. That left Abby to keep an eye on her brothers, and she was still a little girl herself."

Katie turned away again. His story was breaking her heart.

She hoped he couldn't see her brushing away the tears

with the towel as she walked to the far cabinet. "That must've been rough."

"I cut back on my office hours, made sure the nanny only took orders from me. It seemed to work for a while." He followed, his footsteps soft behind her. She turned around, surprised to find him standing so close. The two of them were almost in the alcove that led to the laundry room.

"One day Carrie announced we should go back to Paris. Back to where it all started. Recapture what we used to be," he whispered, his voice miserable, his gaze off in the distance. "I was confused. Abby was almost ten, the boys were six. It wasn't until she mentioned boarding schools that I got it. She wanted to leave the kids. I refused, of course. She said she was going anyway. With me. Or without."

Shocked, Katie's mouth dropped open but no sound emerged.

How could a mother walk away from her children?

It was a question she'd been living with her entire life. To find out Nolan had asked that same question since his marriage ended...

She blinked back more tears. "I'm so sorry, Nolan. I don't even know how to respond to that."

"Believe me, neither did I. I stayed in Boston for almost a year after she left. Tried to keep up with that world until I accepted it wasn't what I wanted. I didn't fit in. Me or my kids."

He pulled in a deep breath and released it. His shoulders relaxed, his tone lighter now as he looked at her. "I filed for divorce, got full custody and moved back to Destiny. Went to work for the family business. Got on with my life."

"And found me." Oh, that hadn't come out right. "I mean you found—you hired a secretary."

"Yeah." He reached out, tipping her chin with his fingertips. "I found you."

* * *

Nolan sat back, watching his kids arrange the ornaments on the brightly lit tree. They rehashed old stories and memories as the branches of the Douglas fir filled with decorations. Expensive glass and porcelain trinkets from his ex-wife and her family. Handcrafted beauties his mother either found locally or made herself every year. His favorites were the ones the kids made in grade school.

There would be another tree-trimming party next weekend at the main house that would include the personalized hand-lettered glass ornaments his mother had created over the years for each member of the family. He'd bet she already had ones for Liam's soon-to-be fiancée, Missy, their daughter, Casey, and Tanya ready for this year's tree.

But tonight was about him, his kids…and Katie.

It should feel strange to have someone else involved with their holiday ritual, but Katie—who'd made a kick-ass taco pizza for dinner and a brownie dessert that was nothing but crumbs now, and gotten weepy for him after he'd blabbed his life story—fit right in.

How in the hell did that happen?

Not just because he'd somehow been doing the dishes one minute and the next was telling her about his failed marriage and sorry attempts at early fatherhood as naturally as if they'd been discussing the weather.

She hadn't said much, but when he'd finally been smart enough to shut up he'd spotted the tears. An ache had filled him at the idea of her crying for him. For his kids.

It was so powerful he couldn't stop from touching her.

If Logan hadn't picked that moment to come barreling down the stairs, Nolan would've hauled her into his arms.

He looked at her again, sitting curled up near the fireplace, a part of all that was going on, but separate, too. The kids tried to involve her in hanging an ornament or two, but she'd begged off, having stayed a long time in the kitchen after dinner, cleaning up.

Now, she appeared lost in thought, her gaze on the dancing flames and crackling logs. What was she thinking? Was she missing her own tree?

Nolan figured she must put one up at her place.

Would she be back in her apartment before the holidays?

She'd mentioned the work was ongoing and she hadn't yet gotten a firm completion date. He'd meant to ask Norm Bergeron, her landlord, about that when he'd seen him at the hardware store, but the man had been preoccupied and the thought had slipped from Nolan's addled mind.

The Ellsworth project was in full swing, and without a place to work at home, Nolan had been spending lot of time—day and night—in his office at the main house.

And yeah, part of that was to keep his houseguest at arm's length. Instead of where he wanted her. In his arms, in his bed—

Nolan cut off that thought before it could get any more... detailed.

A feat he was getting pretty good at lately.

Despite sly remarks and innuendos from his brothers about the two of them, he was working overtime—pun intended—to make sure nothing happened between him and Katie again.

That moment in the kitchen wasn't helping, because something *was* happening.

Katie was becoming part of his life. Both in and out of the office.

And part of his kids' lives.

He thought back to earlier today. How eager he'd been to get home the moment he'd spotted the glow from the windows when their all-terrain vehicles rolled into the yard. He'd tried to convince himself it'd been his stomach growl-

ing or the fact he was freezing his ass off that fueled his
impatience, but had it been something else?

Because she was here? Waiting for him?

He was getting used to having her around.

And for the life of him, he didn't know if that was a
good thing or not.

For him. For his kids.

They'd always gotten along with Katie, but it was different this time. Now she was having an influence on them.
He'd seen it the first morning he'd returned from his trip,
and the changes were more evident with each passing day.

What would things be like once she was gone again?

Not to mention how all of this togetherness had to be
affecting her life.

What about that night he'd called from Spokane and
caught her on a date? His blood had gotten hot at that.
The way it had on Thanksgiving when his cousin put the
moves on her.

She had every right to do what she wanted with her life,
from dating to babies, but when he'd pictured her kissing
some guy good-night before coming home to crawl into
his bed—

Nolan stood, determined to rid his brain of this crazy
back-and-forth mental argument he had going on. He
grabbed the empty platter and was about to head into the
kitchen when the kids' huddled conversation on the far side
of the tree stopped him.

"I think we should do it," Logan said.

"No, they're for Christmas," Abby shot back in a hushed
whisper. "Not before."

"So? You didn't even want to do this in the first place."

"I changed my mind."

"Yeah, big surprise there." Luke added, "Besides, she
doesn't—"

"Hey," Nolan interrupted. "What's going on?"

Three sets of eyes turned his way. Then his children looked at each other in that familiar silent sibling communication thing.

They'd been doing it all their lives, just like Nolan and his brothers. Hell, he and the guys still did it at times. It was sort of cool knowing what your siblings were thinking without saying a word.

Not so much when it came to his own kids. "Well?" he asked.

"We got presents for Katie. We think she should get them tonight," Luke said.

Nolan peeked at Katie through the tree's branches and found her still transfixed by the fire. "I'd say it's up to you all, but—"

"Good. It's two against one. We win." Logan grinned.

Abby narrowed her gaze at her brothers, spun away and headed up the stairs. Nolan went into the kitchen, put the dish in the sink and wondered if he should go after her.

A few minutes later she returned, gift bag in hand.

"Katie?" Abby stood by the chair and waited until she got her attention. "My brothers...and I each got you a little something. A thank-you for staying with us while our dad was gone."

Surprise lit up Katie's features. "Really?"

Abby nodded. "After...that thing happened, you know, at your place and you had to stay on, we were going to wait. Give these to you at Christmas, but—"

"But we decided you should have them now," Luke finished, taking the bag from his sister and handing it off to Katie. "Here."

"Yeah, go ahead," Logan said. "Open them."

Katie stared at Nolan over his kids' heads. He could only shrug, arms crossed over his chest. He had no idea what was going on, other than the fact that he was pretty proud of his crew right now.

"Okay, well, thank you."

She reached inside and took out the first gift. A big smile came to her face when she unwrapped an ornament. A miniature cookie sheet topped with a red bow. "Oh, how sweet. It has tiny Christmas cookies on it, even ones that spell out the year. Let me guess…this one is from Logan."

The kid grinned. "How'd ya know?"

"Because you've got a sweet tooth like your father. Thank you. I love it."

Everyone laughed as she laid the ornament in her lap and reached back into the bag. With the next gift many layers of tissue paper had to be pulled back to reveal a little cloth rag doll. Dressed in blue and white with bright red yarn for hair, it fit in the palm of her hand.

"Oh!" Katie pressed her fingertips to her lips, then whispered, "Oh, my."

"Do you like it?" Luke asked. "Remember that day we tore apart the main house looking for A.J.'s lost monkey? I told you about the bear I used to carry everywhere when I was little. You said you'd always wanted a Raggedy Ann doll when you were a kid, but never got one. I know this one is just to hang on the tree—"

"Of course I remember."

She blinked hard, dropping her gaze to the doll ornament. Not before Nolan caught sight of the bright sheen in her eyes.

His chest got tight. There was that urge again, to have her in his arms. He fisted his hands where they couldn't be seen.

Why hadn't she ever gotten the toy? Surely her folks had—

"This is…perfect." She looked up again, her smile back in place. "Thank you, Luke."

His son returned her grin and elbowed his brother. Both were pleased with themselves. There was one gift left, and

Nolan was curious what type of ornament Abby had chosen, guessing she'd gone along with the theme.

Katie pulled out a small box from the bottom of the bag. She removed the wrapping paper carefully, lifted the lid to reveal a purple beaded dragonfly, the double set of wings made from a shiny ribbon that shimmered in the firelight.

"Abby, it's stunning. Did...did you make this?"

Nolan shifted so he could see his daughter's face, surprised when she shrugged and gave a quick nod. "It's no big deal."

"But it is. This is beautiful and so well done. Thank you."

A silent moment stretched between Katie and his daughter before the teen stepped away and went to the storage boxes for the family ornaments.

She returned with three hooks and held them out to Katie. "Here. You can put them on our tree. If you want."

The boys thought it was a good idea, but Katie hesitated, her gaze moving back and forth between the kids and the tree. She captured her bottom lip with her teeth.

Nolan cleared his suddenly dry throat. He hadn't meant to, but she now looked at him.

Questioning if he was okay with this.

He answered with a slight tilt of his head toward the tree.

Katie stood. "Yes, it would be nice to see them on a tree. Here, give me a hand."

The kids attached the hangers but insisted Katie be the one to add the ornaments anywhere she liked to the already crowded tree.

She mimicked the kids, moving the ornaments to different spots until she'd decided exactly where each fit. Finally, she took a step back, eyes bright and a smile on her face, hands clenched to her chest as she stood there and studied the tree.

Nolan did, too, as he leaned down to grab his luke-
warm beer.

It took him a few minutes to find the cookie sheet, rag
doll and dragonfly. He was amazed at how perfectly they
blended in with the rest.

The dryness in his throat returned, and he downed a
couple of slugs of beer to moisten it. But it didn't help, because the dryness was followed by a lump that wouldn't go
away no matter how much he tried to drown it.

Chapter Ten

Katie's stomach rumbled for the third time.

She rolled over and peered at the bedside clock. Three thirty a.m. Who got hungry at this time of night?

Someone who'd been awakened when her boss returned from another late night at his office, it seemed.

She sighed, staring at the ceiling.

That was now a habit of Nolan's. Disappearing to the main house under the pretense of work, usually within a half hour of the kids heading off to bed or out of the house for whatever reason.

Yes, he was busy, but they were deep into week three of sharing his home. Which meant cooking and eating together, helping the kids with homework, putting up holiday decorations and watching each other's television shows even if zombies gave her the creeps and she hadn't yet lured him to the wonders of public television's *Masterpiece*.

Oh, and having meaningful one-sided conversations about their pasts.

Despite all that, did he think she didn't get the hint?

He was being kind letting her stay, and no, he didn't want a repeat of what happened the first night he'd returned home.

Certainly nothing as messy as what had transpired between them the weekend before Halloween.

She got it. Message received. Loud and clear.

Sort of.

Katie crawled out of bed, wrapped her hair into an untidy knot on top of her head and reached for the robe that matched her blue silk nightgown. No flannel pajamas tonight. Sometimes a girl wanted something decadent against her skin.

And something indulgent in her stomach.

She headed into the living room, her fingertips grazing over an ornament as she walked by the tree. In her wildest dreams she'd never expected the kids to give her such wonderful gifts.

And so personal! She loved how each had touched her heart. Not to mention how at home they seemed nestled among the fragrant branches.

In the soft glow of the kitchen, she opened the freezer and moved things around until she found the pint of triple chocolate fudge she'd started on last night.

With the container wrapped in a dish towel and spoon in hand, she ignored the nearby dining table, hopped up on the counter—ooh, a little chilly on the backside—popped the lid and dug in.

She closed her eyes and let the cold spoon rest on her tongue. The heat of her mouth melted the scrumptious treat until it slid off in a burst of chocolaty perfection. She might've moaned a little after the third spoonful, but no one was around—

"Maybe you should start eating ice cream for breakfast."

Katie let out a yelp of surprise. She jerked her head up,

spotting him leaning against the doorway. "Nolan! You scared me half to death!"

His arms were crossed at his chest, his feet at the ankles. He was a picture of casual sexiness in those damn flannel pants and a simple T-shirt.

He put a finger to his lips, warning her to be quiet.

"It's after three," she whispered fiercely, embarrassed at being caught while…well, enjoying herself. With ice cream. "What are you doing here?"

"I live here."

The memory of him using that line before came flooding back. "Yeah, I know."

She scooted to the edge of the counter, ready to jump. But Nolan crossed the room and now stood in front of her, hands braced on either side of her.

"Don't go anywhere. You look comfortable." He smiled but kept his voice low. "And don't stop…eating on my account."

"I had a craving."

"So I heard."

Katie narrowed her eyes, hoping the shadows hid the hot blush washing over her face. "That's not funny."

He took a step back, opened the silverware drawer and pulled out a spoon. "Mind if I join you?"

"You prefer coffee flavor. Or vanilla." *Go figure.* "This is chocolate. Times three. With brownies. Powerful stuff."

"I like living dangerously."

That wasn't true. Nolan was as safe and steady as they came. The Murphy brother everyone counted on to do the right thing.

Including her.

Except for one night back in October. And again when he returned from Spokane. What about that stolen moment right here in this kitchen when he surprised her by sharing a personal part of his life, bringing her to tears and leaving her positive he'd been about to kiss her…

Not to mention right now.

She liked this. Liked those other times, too. Liked what was going on between the two of them. The darkened room, the late hour. The intimacy, the flirting. He'd been so distant recently, the change was a surprise.

Maybe she was dreaming. If so, she didn't want to wake up.

Looking down, she studied the inside of her pint, pretending to decide if there was enough for two. What she was actually deciding was how far she'd let this go. After all, they had agreed—

"Please?"

One softly spoken word and she caved. Katie tipped the container in his direction.

Nolan dug in, filled his spoon and popped it into his mouth. "Hmm, tastes funny."

"It's the brownie pieces, and you're eating too fast," she said when he went back for seconds. "You'll end up with a—" The second bite brought forth the wince he did his best to hide. "Brain freeze."

Nolan nodded and easily jumped up to join her on the counter. Side by side, almost touching.

Not as close as Thanksgiving dinner, but he'd been directed by others to sit next to her then. This time the decision had been his, and despite the space between them, heat emanated from his body, passing through the silkiness of her nightgown and robe.

She took a swipe at her dry lips, tasting the sugar-laced sweetness there, and offered him access to the ice cream again. "Want more?"

His gaze dropped to her mouth for a moment. Then back to her eyes. "I'll wait. You go ahead."

Her spoonful was smaller, and she ate it slowly, without

sound effects this time. It was a bit disconcerting to have someone watching her. Which explained why she took her time drawing the spoon back between her lips.

Did he just groan? It was soft, barely distinguishable, but she was sure she'd heard—

"You missed some." His voice was rough as he brushed at the corner of her mouth. "Right...here."

She reacted without thought and caught the edge of his thumb with her tongue.

He went still.

She did, too, except for her heart racing so fast in her chest he had to be able to see it pulsing beneath her skin. Only his gaze was locked with hers as a hot spark of awareness crackled between them before he pulled away.

"Did I..." Spoon in hand, Katie brushed at her mouth. "Did I get it?"

"Yeah, you got it."

He went back for another scoop the same moment she did. Their spoons clanked. They wrestled back and forth until she emerged victorious, sending him a smug grin before she put the spoon in her mouth.

"You know, I never thanked you. For what you did for Abby while I was gone," he said. "Getting her out of a sticky situation."

The lump of ice cream lodged in her throat, a visceral reaction that had her choking and slapping a hand to her chest.

"Hey, you okay?" He reached for her, but she waved him off. "What happened? Go down the wrong pipe?"

Interesting choice of words.

Katie didn't know what to believe. How had this romantic and intimate moment between the two of them switched gears so fast? Had Abby talked to her father about what she'd done?

Or did he find out some other way? "Yes...and I'm okay. How do you know about that?"

"She showed me." Nolan took another spoonful of the frozen treat. "The dress she's wearing to the dance next week? She says it's vintage '80s, with big shoulders and lots of beading. All I care is it covers her from her neck to her knees, so I'm happy."

Katie had no idea what he was talking about.

Abby had found a dress? How did that tie in with the mess she caused at her apartment? "What's the sticky situation again?"

"The day you took her and her friends shopping in Denver. She'd tried on a designer dress, but it was too expensive. Her posse was pressuring her to buy it anyway. You played the dad card telling her to ask me first. Got her off the hook." He laid the events of the day out in his matter-of-fact way. "She appreciated that."

Stunned, Katie had had no idea Abby saw what had happened that day in that light. Or that she'd unknowingly given the girl a way out.

"All that fuss and she's going to the dance dateless. Go figure. Thankfully, the loser cowboy is long gone."

Wow, the surprises kept coming. "He is?"

Nolan nodded. "I ran into the guy who runs the Triple G last week. I mentioned the kid's name—Joe something—and Mick said he'd let him go."

Another reason the teen had been such a homebody lately? "Because of Abby?"

"No, he was seasonal. Mick had thought about keeping him on, but something didn't sit right about the kid," Nolan said. "Thank God. Out of sight, out of mind."

Foolish man. Did he think Abby—with her cell phone virtually attached to her hand—was out of touch with the cowboy? Unless he *was* a loser and the teen was nursing a broken heart.

"It's none of my business—" Nolan waved his spoon back and forth "—but I never asked how your appointment went. In Denver. I'm guessing it had something to do with your baby plan?"

Katie put her attention back on getting another scoop of the dessert. "Yes, it did, but I didn't go. The consultation was canceled."

"By you?"

She peeked at him sideways under her lashes. "He asks hopefully?"

"I didn't mean it that way."

No, he didn't. She could see the sincerity on his face. "The clinic canceled. I...I haven't set up another appointment yet. Between work and the kids and the holidays..."

Her voice trailed off and silence stretched between them.

The feelings and fears she'd been battling for weeks over her decision to have a child filled her head. Her heart. The frozen treat that moments before tasted so good now sat like an icy lump in her chest. She was hit with a wave of nausea and the room tilted. Wow, a visit to her own doctor first sounded like a good idea—

"Hey, let me take that." Nolan gently pried the container and spoon from her grip. He set them to one side but didn't let go of her hand. "You sure you're okay?"

She nodded, not trusting her voice yet.

"You don't owe me any explanations. Your life is your own. I don't understand why you think this is right for you. Still, if you'd like to talk to someone, I'll listen."

Katie wanted to tell him about her dreams and plans for the future. Why having a family of her own was so important. After what he'd shared with her about his kids—

But her stomach rebelled.

She yanked her hand from his, slapped it across her mouth. Scrambling off the counter, Katie raced out of the kitchen. She barely made it back to her bathroom.

Oh, yeah. Definitely romantic.

* * *

Nolan took another picture of Abby with his cell phone.

Damn, she was so grown-up. Fancy dress, fancy shoes. Her hair was a riot of curls that bordered on the chaotic even though he was well aware of the work that had gone into getting ready for tonight's event.

A black stretch Hummer sat in the parking lot. Rented by the father of one of Abby's friends for tonight, it could hold up to a dozen teens. The Murphy compound was the last stop before the dance.

They'd come by to pick up Abby and her cousin Casey, who'd arrived from London on Wednesday with her parents. The trio had returned to Destiny the week before Christmas so Casey could attend this event.

She and Missy had first come to town a few months back. Casey had attended the high school, making friends during her stay. Including the star quarterback. The boy's grin tonight said he was happy to have Casey back in town.

A boy Abby had been interested in, too, at one time.

That bit of teen drama had been the beginning of a rocky road between the girls, but thankfully they'd worked things out.

It was good to see them smiling and standing side by side for the pictures.

Wasn't it just yesterday his little girl had balanced on top of his feet as they danced together?

"Wow, that's a big sigh, Dad."

The words caught Nolan by surprise. He glanced over his shoulder. Katie stood there, cradling a mug in her hands, as if she needed its heat despite the mild December night. "Did I do that?"

She nodded. "Tonight bringing back some old memories?"

"Just a few."

"I bet you and your brothers went to this dance every year."

He hadn't even thought about that yet. "Yep, and thankfully all it called for back then was your best jeans, boots and a button-down shirt. The tuxedos, even Western style, are a bit too much for me."

She smiled, but the action didn't have its usual brightness. "Getting all dressed up must make them feel…grownup. Even when they're not."

"I suppose." Nolan backed up until he stood with her. "I bet you got all decked out for your high school formals."

The smile disappeared and Katie became interested in the patch of snow at her feet. "I never went to any."

"Really?"

"Yeah, it…" She paused and then glanced at him. "It just never worked out."

Her answer didn't mesh with the flash of hurt in her eyes, but he let it go. "Did I thank you for helping Abby?" he asked. "You two were upstairs all afternoon."

"It was only a couple of hours, and Tanya was there, too. She saved the day."

"Yeah, who knew a curl thingamajig would be so important."

"It's called a curling iron. It was important when Abby's died in the middle of doing her hair."

"And you didn't own one."

Katie smiled and tipped her head back and forth, sending her ponytail flying. "Curls aren't anything I have to worry about creating, and yes, you did thank me already. So did Abby." Her expression changed, her voice quieter now. "I think she's missing her mom on a night like tonight."

Nolan looked at his daughter again, whose blond hair and blue eyes reminded him more of his ex-wife every day. "Yeah, I'm sure she is."

"They're lucky to have you. Your kids." Katie's gaze

shifted between his parents and his brothers and the women in their lives, who stood around chatting or taking pictures. "To have all of you. They might not realize it or appreciate it now, but someday they'll come to know how important their family is."

The wistfulness in her voice tugged at him.

Nolan wanted to pull her into his arms and hold her, comfort her.

Crazy as the thought might be, it was becoming a regular occurrence.

Thanksgiving. The night he'd spilled his guts to her about his past. Last week when he'd found her practically making love to a pint of ice cream on his kitchen counter.

She'd blamed the ice cream for a sudden illness that lasted a couple of days, and they hadn't had the chance since then to be alone again.

Until tonight.

The twins were already with friends for an overnight stay and Abby had plans to do the same with a girlfriend after the dance. Meaning it would be just the two of them.

"I think your daughter wants you."

Katie's words jerked Nolan out of his thoughts. He saw Abby waving at him. "I should go, then."

"I'm heading back inside. Please tell her again I hope she has a good time."

Katie walked back toward his house. Nolan turned the other way toward his daughter and her friends. Moments later, the limo departed and most of his family drifted away as well. It was only him and his folks still outside.

"Is Katie feeling any better?"

"She's fine." Nolan turned to his mom. "Why? Did she say something?"

"Well, that bad ice cream hit her pretty hard. She was still deathly pale the night of our tree-trimming party. Even now, she seems a little peaked."

"Peaked?" Nolan asked. "Who says that anymore?"

"Your mother," Alistair Murphy said with a smile. "I shouldn't have to state the obvious, but Katie has been working hard for the last few months. Between the office, taking care of your kids and helping your mom."

"Thank goodness the cast is gone." Elise flexed her arm, displaying an impressive bicep. "I'm back to being me again. In time for Christmas, which is five days away!"

"You have plenty of physical therapy ahead," Nolan reminded her and returned to what his parents said. "And yes, Katie's had a lot on her plate—" and on her mind "—lately, and being sick didn't help."

"Perhaps she misses her apartment. She mentioned earlier it's likely going to be after the new year before she can move back," his mother mused. "Then again, the five of you seem to be getting along just fine—"

"It's time for you to get back inside." Nolan's dad cut Elise off and steered her toward the main house. "We've got a pile of presents waiting to be wrapped."

"Oh, right. Would you and Katie like to join us?" Elise asked.

"No, thanks, Mom." Boy, that answer came out fast. "I think we're going to...well, we might—"

"Hey, don't invite interlopers on our date." Alistair pulled his wife close, placing a kiss at her temple. "Tonight's about us. Us and presents. Good night, son."

Nolan watched his parents walk away, taking a moment to frame them in the camera lens and snap a quick photo.

They'd met and fallen in love in college, tied the knot within six months of their first date and welcomed their first child a year later. Married over forty years, with six kids and a successful business, they were still crazy about each other.

All of that set a high bar for happiness.

He headed across the yard to his place, thinking how

he'd once believed that kind of joy was attainable. Even though he, Adam and Liam had screwed it up once already. Hell, Liam had failed twice at marriage, but that didn't stop him from giving it another go.

Adam was happy with Fay and their growing family, and Liam had proposed to Missy, his high school sweetheart, the morning they flew home. Now there would be two weddings in the next year, though Liam and Missy had said they planned to have their ceremony soon, since they were working to make Destiny their permanent home.

That's what he'd do, if he ever took the plunge again.

Something intimate, family only. Like Bryant and Laurie, who'd married in the beautiful log chapel located right here on the compound. One of the original buildings when this had been a working ranch, his parents had refurbished it years ago—

Whoa!

Nolan halted, shocked at the thought running through his head.

Where in the world had *that* come from?

He was firmly in the never-again camp. Had been for years. Yeah, he was glad his brothers had found someone special to share their lives with, but that didn't mean...

He was happy.

He and the kids were happy. Just the way things were. He wasn't interested—

The door opened. Katie stood with her mug still in hand. "Hey, I saw you walk up and thought you'd like—are you okay?"

Nolan gave his head a quick shake, stepped inside and got out of his boots. "Yeah, I'm fine. What's that?"

"Hot chocolate." She closed the door. "Want some?"

He walked past her, heading for the dining room. "Thanks, but I need something a bit stronger." Then he caught the scent of... "What are you drinking, again?"

"It's called bittersweet hot chocolate with red wine. I'm naming it minty cocoa heaven." She stirred the blend with a candy cane before taking a long sip and sighing with contentment. "I stole some of your California pinot noir earlier. Simmered it with melted chocolate, milk and a pinch of kosher salt."

Had he not noticed her obsession with all things chocolate or was this a recent development? "When did you make that?"

"When you ran the boys to their friends' house. Before Abby's ride…arrived. You sure you don't want a sip of a slice of heaven?"

"No, thanks." Whiskey neat. Right now. "How many of those have you had?"

"Two. So far. This is number three."

Nolan digested that information while taking the first shot. Then he added ice cubes to his glass before filling it halfway. The next mouthful was smaller, went down more slowly.

He stared at the amber liquid, still shocked at what'd been circling in his head a moment ago.

Weddings? *His* wedding? And to whom—

"Nolan?"

He looked up and found Katie standing near the couch in front of the fireplace. The television was off and soft holiday music filled the air. The only light in the room came from the Christmas tree and the crackling flames behind her.

"You sure you're okay?" she asked again.

"Yeah." He locked away those crazy thoughts, took another swallow and joined her. "You?"

She smiled. "I'm feeling fine."

He'd bet she was. Maybe wrapping presents with his folks wasn't such a bad idea.

"You seemed a bit preoccupied over there."

"I was just thinking…how much Abby reminded me of my ex. Tonight. All dressed up."

"I've seen pictures of her in the kids' rooms. She's beautiful." Katie sat on the floor between the couch and the fireplace, cradling her mug in her hands. "The boys are all Murphy, from their looks to their personalities, but Abby…"

"Yeah, she's a lot like Carrie. In many ways." Nolan purposely took a seat on the couch. "She inherited her mother's artistic talents and temperament, I'm afraid."

Katie glanced over her shoulder and smiled. "I think she's got some of her dad's creativity, too."

Nolan thought back to the intricately beaded snowflake and angel ornaments his daughter had surprised everyone with at the tree-trimming party.

"I'd like to think so." He leaned back, took another sip from his glass and relaxed. This was nice. The soft glow from the tree, the fire. The company. As long as they kept their conversations about the kids or family or creative talents…

"So, how about you?" he asked, determined to keep things on the right track. "You take after your mother or father most?"

His question stunned Katie.

It shouldn't have. It was something people had often asked over the years, but as always, she had no way of knowing the answer.

"I don't know."

His brows dipped in confusion. "What does that mean?"

Wow, had that nugget from her personal history just popped out of her mouth? And why now?

She dropped her gaze. She could blame the wine, but it was greatly diluted by the hot chocolate.

Maybe it was time for the truth.

She'd managed to keep her past from everyone in town,

even the Murphys, for the last five years. She wasn't ashamed of how she grew up, but it was the pity she'd gotten over the years—from teachers, friends, previous employers—she hated.

Except this felt right.

After what Nolan had shared with her about all he'd been through with his ex-wife, he'd understand.

As much as she tried, she couldn't grasp how in the world his ex or her mother had walked away from her children. Love faded. Marriages ended. She got that. But the love between a parent and a child...

"Katie?"

"I... I don't remember my parents." Oh, this was harder than she'd thought it would be.

Even after all these years.

She tucked her legs to the side and turned to face the fireplace. "I was abandoned when I was three. Left in a church in Boise, Idaho. Just me, a blanket, a note mostly unreadable except for a few facts and a necklace I assume was once my mother's."

She reached for the jewelry, but came up empty. She hadn't put it on today but found she missed it desperately right now.

"What? You never told us...any of us...that before." Nolan's tone was incredulous. "My mom asked—you said you were an only child. Your parents were gone."

"All true. As much as I know it to be. I once believed I might've had brothers, but—anyway, as an adult, it became easier to give a standard answer when asked about my..."

Her throat tightened and the words disappeared.

She closed her eyes and bit her bottom lip. It hurt, but she succeeded in holding back a threatening sob. When his leg brushed against hers as he settled beside her on the carpet, she clamped down harder.

Should she move back? Give him room?

Then he touched her hand and she opened her eyes when he took the mug from her, watching as he placed it with his glass on the stone hearth.

"Do you know why you were left?" he asked, his voice gentle as he settled back against the couch, one elbow propped on the cushions. "Have you ever tried to find out? To learn anything?"

Katie shook her head. "The note found with me gave a birth date and my name. Sort of. Years later, I discovered the authorities had to piece it together because only the first three letters, L-E-D, of my surname were readable. It was noted in my file the 'better' part of Ledbetter was added because the note asked I be given a better life."

"And you kept the name? I mean, you were never adopted—"

"Nope, I'm a foster care kid." She cut him off, the familiar words triggering a long-practiced physical reaction. Squared shoulders, lifted chin. She smoothed her hair back before giving a tug on her ponytail, then pulling the length of hair forward over one shoulder. A delay tactic, but if she saw pity in his eyes, she'd lose it for sure.

Still, she made herself face him, digging deep for a bravado she didn't feel. "I lived in a variety of foster homes until I was eighteen. After that I was on my own."

His gaze held a mixture of compassion and interest. "There was never a chance to stay with one of those families?"

"Oh, a couple of times…one of the first places I remember, they seemed to like having me around." She shrugged. "Then the woman got pregnant and they thought—well, decided a toddler would take away their attention from the newborn."

His eyes went soft. "Katie…"

"A few years later I was in another home. They already had kids, and the parents wanted to make me part of the family. Even told me so," she pushed on. If he wanted to know the whole story, she was going to tell him despite the ache in her chest. "Then the father lost his job. Things got tight, so...you know, something had to go."

He cupped the back of her head, his hand warm and tender. His fingers threaded through her hair, gently massaging. "What a crappy thing to do to a kid."

"Oh, I got used to it." She dropped her hands to her lap, playing with the buttons at the bottom edge of the shirt she wore beneath a thick sweater. Whew, it was warm sitting this close to the fire. "There were other places and group homes over the years. The older I got...well, let's say I wasn't the easiest person to get along with. Abby's got nothing on some of the stunts I pulled."

"I can't believe you were that bad."

"She's never spent a night in jail."

His hand stilled. "Jail?"

"Yeah, my foster mother at the time was upset at my behavior and thought a night in juvie lockup would straighten me out. It did, too. Barely fifteen and couldn't care less about anything or anyone, even myself. After that I decided it was time to think about what I wanted, where I was going...to end up."

"You must've been scared out of your mind."

"Oh, I was." She tried to laugh it off, but the memories lingered, even after all these years. "The experience got me on the right path. I studied hard and found out I was pretty smart. Made honor roll every semester. Graduated with the second-highest GPA. Went off to U of W in Cheyenne on a full ride. After graduation I met you...all of you...and, well, you know the rest."

His hand dropped away, his arm resting behind her now. "Wow, that's incredible."

"Not everyone is as lucky as you and your brothers," she said, missing his touch. "To grow up with great parents, in this amazing place. To know the love and commitment that goes along with being part of a family. No matter what you might do wrong or how much they drive you crazy, your family is yours. Something you're a part of. Somewhere… where you belong. Where you're wanted."

Nolan cupped his hand around her shoulder and pulled her to his chest. She should've resisted but didn't have the strength. She leaned into him, loving the warmth and solidness of him as she tucked her head into his neck.

"You amaze me," he said, his lips moving against her forehead. "After all you've been through and…now I get it."

Chapter Eleven

Nolan was working to process everything she'd told him when Katie stiffened in his arms, then pushed herself away, one hand on his chest.

"Now you get...what?" she asked.

"The whole baby thing is about wanting a family."

"Yes." She gave a quick and decisive nod. "Ready or not, that's what I want. That kind of love in my life."

Trying to picture smart, confident and caring Katie as a scared and lonely kid, desperate for a family—for a home—was hard. And heartbreaking.

"I can understand that. What's the saying? If you wait until you're ready you'll be waiting the rest of your life?" He kept his words soft and soothing, remembering how he'd stuck his foot in his mouth the last time they'd talked about this. "But like I said before...parenting isn't easy."

"I know that."

"I don't think anyone truly knows what parenting entails until it happens to them." He shook his head, the memories unearthed by another conversation between them still fresh in his mind. "God knows I was clueless in the beginning. Stayed that way, too. Took some hard knocks before I was even somewhat equipped to do the job. Then my marriage fell apart. Right back to square one. On a totally different square."

"Are you happy?"

Her question surprised him. "Huh?"

She pulled farther away and sat back on her heels. "Answer me." She aimed for her hips with her fists. Missed the first try, but succeeded on the second. "Are you happy? With your life? Your children?"

"Of course."

"I want that, too. I want that happy."

"Katie—"

"Let me show you." She pushed up straight to her knees, grabbed the bottom hem of her sweater and yanked the soft material over her head.

"Katie, what are you doing?"

She started attacking the buttons of her shirt. "Showing you."

"Showing me what…"

His breath disappeared as inch after inch of her milky-white skin came into view with each button's release. She fumbled a bit, but then she reached the last one, grabbed the open edges and spun around, giving him her back. She yanked the shirt off her shoulders and downward; the sleeves pooled, the material low on her waist.

She twisted, craning her head around to look at him. "You see that?"

All he saw was the delicate curve of her neck, the way the glow from the fire danced over her smooth skin and the black lace and sheer straps of her bra.

"Nolan?"

"Sorry." He jerked his gaze back to hers. "See what... exactly?"

"My tattoo."

Now that she pointed it out, he clearly saw the scripted font he'd first noticed that morning in the boardinghouse. Coming out of the bathroom. Finding her naked in bed.

"Yes, I see it."

"Can you read it?"

He tilted his head. The words ran in a vertical line that disappeared below the edge of her stretchy black pants. Pants she often wore around the house, having no idea what they did to her curves. Or his sanity. "Not all of... let's see...'too old to—'"

She arched her back, her thumbs grabbing at the low-slung waistband and inching the material down even farther. The full text, along with the cluster of yellow roses just above the sexy curve of her backside, was visible now.

"'You're...you're never too old to live happily-ever-after.'" He read the words aloud.

"Damn straight." She snapped the waistband back to her hips. "Happily-ever-after. That's what I want. What I've always wanted."

He heard strength and conviction in her tone, but when he met her gaze again, the loneliness she'd lived with all her life shadowed her eyes.

The truth hit him square in the chest.

She was going to do this, and no one—especially him— would change her mind. "You deserve it. All of it."

"We don't always get what we deserve, but this kind of happy is possible." She turned away, shimmied her shirt back up her arms and tugged it back over her shoulders. "Attainable. For me."

He missed being able to see all of that skin, but tried to stick with the subject at hand and ignore the other stuff now running through his head. "You know, some people put more thought into choosing a home to build or their next vehicle than they do having a child."

He remembered how he'd become a father, both times. Still, he loved his kids more than his own life, no matter how they came to be.

"It's a life-altering decision," he continued. "There are probably as many ways to describe what parenting means as there are parents in the world, but I finally learned it meant going from selfish to selfless in a heartbeat. Until you're ready for that shift in priorities... It took me a long time to realize that."

She scooted back around to face him, one hand holding her shirt together. "Are you saying I won't be able to do that?"

"No, I—"

"Because I can. I know I can. I've proved that over the last month." She blew out a breath. "I mean, yeah, the crying baby on Thanksgiving got to me, but like you said, I can learn what I don't know. I'll read, take classes—"

"Katie, I completely agree with you. You should do this."

That stopped her. Her beautiful green eyes widened in surprise. "I should? Really?"

He shifted, stretching out one leg along the front of the couch and bending the knee of the other. He leaned back on one arm to keep himself from doing what he wanted to most—touch her. "Yes, really. You're amazing. The transformation the kids have gone through since you moved in... that's nothing short of remarkable."

Frowning, she dropped her butt back to rest against her heels. "But you don't know—"

"I do know." He leaned forward again, cutting her off. "I know it's not them angling for better presents. And it's not a we've-got-company-so-be-on-your-best-behavior kind of thing. You've changed them. Changed me."

This was important. She had to know how much he believed in her. "You've brought…something to my home that I can't describe. Something I never realized was missing. You're you, Katie…and that's enough. More than enough."

She stared for two full seconds before she cried out and launched herself at him. Nolan caught her, anchoring her against his chest as she wrapped her arms around him.

"Thank you! Thank you! Thank you!"

Her words were hot against his skin as she clung to him. He gave in and tightened his hold, tucking his face to her neck, breathing in her signature scent. Every line, every curve of her body matched his perfectly…as if she were meant to be in his arms.

He didn't know who moved first, if she pushed him backward or he took her with him as he slowly descended to the floor. Maybe it was gravity, but it didn't matter.

They were now stretched out together. Her on top. His hands skimming the length of her back to her hips, holding her in place. He groaned under his breath as they turned to each other, and he settled his mouth on hers.

She tasted minty and chocolaty and perfect.

A perfection he remembered from twice before and wanted again and again.

A perfection he had no right to take, to explore…to enjoy.

Because she was looking for happily-ever-after and he wasn't the man to give it to her. Not in the way she wanted.

Even though it was wrong, he stayed in the moment a bit longer, feeding the hunger that had been building for days. The way she kissed him back, thoroughly, possessively and with a growing desire, told him she wanted this—wanted him—as much as he wanted to be with her.

That couldn't happen. Not now.

He turned her gently until she lay on the carpet, her low moan of protest kicking him in the gut as he eased away.

She held on tight, trying to bring him back down on top of her.

Soft kisses on her lips, cheek and forehead slowed the passion before he propped up on one arm and stared down at her. "Katie...wait."

"'Wait,' he said." Katie paced back and forth in her friend's kitchen the next morning, a hand to her queasy stomach. "So I waited. Then he started in on what I wanted versus what he...didn't. I thought he was talking in riddles. Then my head cleared and his words made sense. I bolted to my room."

Peggy sat at her table, still dressed in her pajamas consisting of a T-shirt and running shorts despite the freezing temperatures and snow falling outside.

She placed her coffee next to Katie's untouched tea. "Hmm, so much for my advice on not letting him tell you no. You've got to give the man credit for not taking advantage of you. Of the situation."

She did, but that didn't lessen Katie's embarrassment. Or the hurt of being rejected. Again. "Did I mention I had a couple of spiked hot chocolates before all this? I guess that made it easier for me to practically force him to agree that I know what I'm doing when it comes to this crazy baby plan of mine."

"It's not crazy. I told you that two weeks ago when you finally shared your plans with me, but about that..."

Katie halted, then turned. "What?"

Her friend's gaze narrowed. "Have you eaten breakfast today?"

Her stomach flipped at Peggy's question. "I was showered and out of there before he stirred. There's no way I could face him over a plate of eggs. Not that I find that type of breakfast appealing. Right now I'd kill for a bowl of Cocoa Puffs cereal, but what does that—"

"How about pregnancy? Is that appealing to you?"

"What?"

Peggy stood and held up a finger signaling Katie should stay put as she left the room.

Katie obeyed. Sort of.

She started to pace again because the movement seemed to settle her crazy stomach.

She'd been thankful when Peggy answered her early call, even more so to find out Curtis was already with his grandparents. Girl talk was the first thing on Katie's agenda, even if her friend didn't know the whole story.

She didn't know Katie's personal story.

Keeping her past from Peggy wasn't something she was proud of right now, but she figured she'd spilled enough secrets between the events of the last two months and her baby plan.

Besides, it still didn't feel right to tell anyone...except Nolan.

Peggy returned, a box in her hand. "Here. I think you should do this."

"What is—" Katie looked down, stunned. "Are you kidding me? You just happened to have a home pregnancy test in your bathroom drawer?"

"Dresser drawer, and yes, I did something stupid a while back that thankfully didn't—it's an extra," Peggy said. "Are you telling me the thought never crossed your mind? As sick as you've been lately?"

"I'm not...no, I can't be. I was drinking last night."

"A few sips of wine aren't going to hurt the baby."

"No, there isn't—we haven't—except for once..." Her voice trailed off, the possibility too overwhelming to comprehend. "It's stress. The last few months have been downright maddening. The night with Nolan, me making this baby decision, watching his kids, losing my apartment, falling in love—"

Katie slapped her hand over her mouth.

Did she just say that?

Three words casually tossed into a list that made up the craziness of her life. As if being in love with Nolan was the simplest and easiest thing in the world.

Now she felt even sicker.

She dropped her hand, pressing it gently over the other and holding both protectively over her stomach as she stared at her friend.

"Oh, sweetie…"

She backed away from Peggy's outstretched hand. "No, I did not just say that. I don't—I can't be in love with him. I can't be preg—oh, God…"

Collapsing into the nearest chair, she closed her eyes, the move making her feel even dizzier. She took a deep breath, followed by a slow exhale. She had to do that twice before she could face her friend. "What if I am?"

"What if you are…what? In love or pregnant?"

"Either." Would she wish more for one than the other? How could she when the two were so intertwined with the same man? "Both?"

"Only you can truly answer the first part." Peggy crouched in front of her and pressed the box into her hand. "The second? That's going to take a little bit of help."

Katie pulled her car to a stop in the Murphys' parking lot, shut off the engine and sat there.

The clock on her dashboard displayed the time: 11:11.

She'd read once that when a person noticed this, it meant that moment held special meaning. Someone else had told her she should make a wish. She didn't know what she believed. She wished…

Closing her eyes, Katie wished she knew if this was the right thing to do.

Still reeling from saying the words *love* and *Nolan* in

the same sentence, she'd done the test in a blur, waiting double the recommended time before checking the results.

She should've been dumbfounded by the positive outcome.

They'd been careful. Taken precautions.

Still, somehow it all made sense now.

Everything—the nausea, fatigue, mood swings, food cravings—fell into place.

Including her first thought, which had been to tell Nolan.

Peggy tried to convince her to wait. Get confirmation from her doctor first. Take some time to be comfortable with this life-changing news. There was no rush. Let the excitement of the holidays go by.

Wait until she was back in her own place.

Yeah, that last bit of advice had stung. Her friend was being realistic. Katie understood that, but…she'd gotten what she wanted. A dream come true. How many people could say that?

A baby.

She was going to have a baby, but with a man who'd made it clear he wasn't interested in happily-ever-after. At least, not with her. And certainly not one that included any more children.

Still, Nolan was a good man and a great father. He was going to want to be involved with this child's life. But what about her? Would he insist on doing the right thing by her and the baby?

Of course he would. He'd done it once before. The last thing she wanted was a husband and a family because she'd trapped the man into living up to an obligation.

That's why telling him couldn't wait.

This was too important. Life altering. He had a right to know about the baby.

What about how much she loved him?

Could she tell him how everything they'd shared over the

last several weeks had only made her realize she'd fallen for him the moment they met five years ago? How she'd managed not to see it until just before she'd taken a test that was going to change their lives forever?

Having no answers didn't deter her. She left her car and headed for the covered porch, almost stopping to knock at the front door. How silly was that?

Stepping inside, she removed her jacket and hung it up, along with her purse. The living room was empty, so she walked toward the kitchen.

What if he wasn't here? His car was outside, but had he gone to the main house to work?

She should have called and made sure he'd be here. Alone. The twins had gone skiing for the day, but had Abby come home yet?

She hoped not. She needed to talk to Nolan first, to tell him everything, even though this would affect the kids as well.

Not to mention the rest of the Murphys. Another niece or nephew. Another grandchild. Oh, how were Nolan's parents going to take the news?

Her mind reeled with questions she hadn't even thought of before. Maybe Peggy had been right. Maybe she should wait until—

"You're back."

Katie glanced up and found Nolan standing by the kitchen island.

She grabbed for the back of the closest dining chair, thankful for something solid to hold onto. "Yes," she said, pausing to swallow past the sudden lump in her throat. "Are the—um, is Abby home yet?"

He stared at her for a long moment. "No, not yet."

"Ah, that's…good. We need to—we should talk."

"I agree." He folded his arms over his chest, staring at her in a way that made her uneasy. "I'll go first."

She blinked. "I don't understand."

"Really?"

"Yes, really."

She picked up on the tightness of his jaw. The hardness in his eyes. His feet apart in a shoulder-width stance. All signs that he was angry, but about what she had no idea.

"I…" She paused, licking her dry lips, then went on. "I…need to tell you something."

"Well, it's about time. Did you think I wouldn't find out?"

Find out? How was that possible? She'd only just learned about the baby a couple of hours ago. The Destiny gossip mill was good, but there was no way he'd learned—

Abby. He'd found out what Abby had done.

"I see a metaphorical lightbulb is now shining bright over your head," Nolan said. "You know exactly what I'm talking about."

"Nolan, I can explain —"

"No need. I ran into Jennifer's father this morning." He waved a hand in the air, dismissing Katie's words. "He apologized profusely for his daughter's part in Abby's grand plan. Insisted Jennifer was going to do the same to both you and me. That he'd only found out late last night when he and his wife overheard the girls chatting about their private party. In your apartment. A month ago."

"Nolan, please—"

"Of course, I stood there looking like a fool, as I had no idea what he was talking about. How could you not tell me about that?"

"I was wrong not to. I can see that now."

"Can you? And did this realization just happen?" His sarcasm stung. "Or was it after you grasped how Abby got one over on you?" He leaned forward, his gaze piercing. "Until now, that is."

Feeling weak, Katie pulled out one of the chairs and

sat. "I handled it, Nolan. As soon as I found out what was going on, I went to my apartment. I got rid of her friends and cleaned up the place as best I could."

"She caused hundreds of thousands of dollars in damage—"

"No, she didn't." Katie cut him off. "The pipes were bad in that building for years. It was only a matter of time before something like this happened."

"And that makes it okay?"

"Of course not. Believe me, I wasn't happy about what she'd done. I made that clear to her."

"Then you let her off the hook." He leaned up against the counter, shaking his head. "You were too concerned with being my daughter's friend instead of being the one in charge. Of doing the right thing."

"I did do the right thing," she retorted. "You left me to handle things. I handled the situation."

"Was she punished for stealing your keys?" he asked. "Grounded? Told she'd be putting part of her savings toward the damage she caused?"

Katie opened her mouth, but having no answers, snapped it shut again.

"You know, there is more to bringing up kids than baking cookies and movie nights. How is Abby going to learn from her mistakes, learn there are consequences to her actions, if she gets away with doing something like this?"

"She didn't get away with it. She was caught."

"Yeah, luckily you figured out what was going on that night. What might've happened between her and that son-of-a—that loser who thought a sixteen-year-old girl was okay to hang around with? I told you last week I was glad he was out of her life."

"You might be glad, but I doubt Abby is."

The warning tone of his voice was low. "What the hell does that mean?"

"Have you talked to her about this guy? She's not a little girl anymore. Just because she's sixteen doesn't mean her feelings aren't true and deep—"

"Have you talked to her?"

Katie shook her head. "I...I didn't think it was my place."

"You know, it's no wonder she's been so sweet to you all this time. To me. To all of us." One eyebrow rose. "Do the twins know about this?"

"I don't..." What did it matter now if she shared her suspicions? He was going to believe what he wanted. "I don't know."

"Of course they do. That's why she's been letting them run roughshod over her all this time." Nolan let out a bark of laughter, but there was nothing humorous in his tone. "You know, I might've been too quick in my judgment last night."

Last night? "What are you saying?"

"I'm not sure now you do have what it takes to be a parent." He started to clap, a slow measured applause that mocked her and all she'd done here. "Congratulations. My kids have been playing you for a fool for weeks. Yeah, that's admirable parenting. About as good as my ex."

His words—and the cold, casual way he spoke—cut deeply. She couldn't stop from laying a protective hand over her belly. "You don't mean that."

He pressed his lips into a hard line and a muscle along his jaw jumped. It appeared for a moment as if he was going to say something, but he remained silent.

Unable to take him or his hurtful attitude any longer, Katie bolted.

She grabbed her stuff and ran to her car. Tears blinded her as she got behind the wheel. Not waiting for the defroster to kick in, she used the wipers to clear the heavy snow from her windshield as she sped away.

She had no idea where she was going, but anywhere was better than here.

How could Nolan say those things to her? Yes, she'd been wrong not to tell him about Abby. She knew that now, but she'd done what she'd thought—

Her car's audio system rang with an incoming call. She pressed the end call button. There was no one she wanted to talk to right now.

A few seconds later a call came in again.

For a brief moment she'd thought it might be—no, Nolan had made his feelings quite clear.

She hit the answer button before the caller ID spoke. "Hello?"

"Katie! Thank God you picked up." Abby's hushed voice filled the car's interior. "Are you alone? Are you at the house?"

"Yes, I'm alone, and no, I'm not at your house. I'm in my car and I don't—"

"Please!" Abby cut her off. "I need your help. Please come get me."

Oh, this was the last thing she needed. Exhausted from the day's events, she just wanted to find some place private to crawl up into a ball and…and…

"Katie? Did you hear me?"

"Abby, I…you need to call your father."

"No! I can't do that!"

"Abby, he knows…" Katie stopped. Now wasn't the time and it wasn't her place. Not anymore. "He knows you're at Jennifer's. If you need a ride—"

"But I'm not!" The girl cut her off, the alarm in her voice rising. "I snuck out hours ago, before sunrise. I had to! I had to meet Joe. He was leaving town. Leaving me."

"What? Where are you now?" Katie demanded. "Are you with him?"

"No! I'm out past Razor Hill Road. There's a bunch of old cabins up there. He took me to one and tried to convince me to run away with him. He said he loved me. He wanted us to be together. So I—I agreed and we headed out, but then I couldn't do it." Abby started to cry. "He wouldn't take me back to town, so I made him pull over on the highway. Now I'm walking…"

Katie turned her car around at the next road, not an easy feat in the accumulating snow. "Are you okay? Did he hurt you?"

"N-no. He just…he broke my heart."

A familiar feeling, but still… "Abby, call your father," she repeated. "He'll understand. He loves you. He'll pick you up in a heartbeat."

"No! He'd never understand! He hated the idea of me with Joe. He'd kill me if he found out what I've done."

There was no reasoning with the girl. Not that it mattered. Katie was already on Highway 287, which led out of town. "Okay, I'm heading your way. Is there any place you can stop and wait for me?"

"No, I'll just keep walking. Darn all this snow! My feet are freezing!"

"What are you wearing—" Katie rounded a corner, the back wheels of her car skidding across the icy pavement. "Damn! Abby, the roads are getting bad. You need to get as far onto the shoulder as you can."

"I'm trying but the snow… I've got on my pink ski jacket and jeans—oh, I see you! I see you!"

Katie spotted the girl, too, waving frantically about a hundred yards away. Minutes later, Abby was belted into the front seat next to her and cranking up the heat. Something Katie's delicate stomach—or was it the tiny life growing inside her—protested, but the poor girl was shivering.

"Th-thank you so m-much, Katie. Y-you have no idea how m-much I appreciate this." Abby checked her cell phone for what had to be the twentieth time. "Wow, it's after twelve. If you'll drop me off on the street behind

Jenn's once we're back in town, I can cut through the side yard and be back inside—"

"I'm taking you home, Abby."

"What?" The teen's eyes grew wide. "No!"

"Yes."

"But you can't."

Katie turned her car around again, her grip tight on the steering wheel. The roads were getting bad and the Murphy compound was the last place she wanted to be, but she had to do what was best for Abby.

Because Nolan had been right.

As much as it pained her to think that way, she hadn't done right by him or Abby by keeping her mouth shut.

Deep down, she'd second-guessed her decision from the beginning, but she was too busy enjoying the pretend family life she had with Nolan and the kids over the last weeks to do anything to upset that perfect little world.

A world that never existed. And never would.

"You need to tell your father everything," Katie said. "About today and what happened last month at my apartment. Or I will."

"How can you say that?" Abby cried. "You agreed to keep it secret—"

"I was wrong. We both were to keep that from him."

Abby pouted, crossing her arms over her chest. "You just want to get me in trouble. You think it'll get you in good with my dad. I know you like him!"

She loved Nolan, loved the kids, but that wasn't the issue here.

"If you want to be treated like an adult, Abby, you need to start acting like one." Katie brushed away new tears and glanced at the teen. "That means being accountable for your actions. You did something wrong and got caught. Now you need to pay the price."

"Yeah, like you know what you're talking about! You can do whatever you want, whenever you want."

"That's not true—"

"Yes, it is! You come and go as you please. You don't answer to anyone but yourself. You have money and make your own rules. God, you are so lucky!" Abby banged her fist against the door. "You don't have someone who wants to know your every move. Where you're going. Who you're going with. You know what that makes you?"

Lonely…with no chance for the happily-ever-after she truly wanted.

The happily-ever-after that sprang to life the moment she woke up after that amazing night with Nolan. The happily-ever-after that had continued to build over the last two months and felt complete now that she knew Nolan's child was growing inside her.

Her tears came faster, making it almost impossible to see out the snow-covered windshield. Then a strong wind rattled her car, pushing them into the other lane.

She yanked on the wheel, desperate to stay where she belonged, but then her wheels hit a patch of ice. Her control over the vehicle vanished and they started to spin.

Abby cried out and Katie instinctively shot out her arm to protect the girl as they continued to twist and turn before coming to a screeching halt in a snowbank.

Chapter Twelve

"Your daughter will be fine, Mr. Murphy," the emergency room doctor said, offering what must be a much-used smile for anxious parents. "She has a grade-two sprain of her right wrist that we're bandaging now. Bumps and bruises as well, but that's to be expected. She'll be released soon."

Nolan nodded, the pounding in his chest proof that his heart still worked. For the last hour or so he hadn't been sure it did. Not since he'd gotten a phone call from the sheriff, with the news of a car accident involving—

"What about Katie?" he asked "Is she okay?"

The doctor's smile faded. The pounding in Nolan's chest went deathly quiet.

There was no sound, no movement, nothing.

It was as if the world—his world—had up and disappeared.

After concentrating on the paperwork attached to his clipboard for a moment, the doctor finally spoke. "How is Ms. Ledbetter related to you?"

"She's my..." Nolan's mind went blank. He struggled, unable to find the words.

What was Katie's connection to him?

Say it. Just say it.

He cleared his throat, hoping the action would release what his head and heart already knew. "She's..."

"She's family."

Two words, spoken in unison by his brothers—Adam, Liam, Devlin and Bryant—all of whom stood right behind him. Their strength, solidarity and concern for Abby and Katie rolled over him in a comforting wave, as it had from the moment they, and the rest of his family, took over one corner of the hospital's waiting room.

Nolan had run into Dev as he raced to his car. He'd quickly told him about the accident, adding he knew nothing more than an ambulance was taking Abby and Katie to Laramie.

A fact that had him fearing the worst.

He'd been the first to reach the hospital parking lot thirty minutes later, thanks to the continuing snowstorm. The caravan of Murphy vehicles wasn't far behind, bad weather be damned.

"She is?" The doctor's eyebrows rose in surprise. "I hadn't realized—"

"Katie has worked for the company for the last five years, Kent." Alistair Murphy came up to stand next to Nolan, addressing the doctor by his first name.

His father knew this man. Would that work in their favor? Nolan hoped so, because he wasn't going anywhere until he found out what was going on.

"She doesn't have any family," Alistair continued. "We consider her one of us."

"That's all well and good, Al, but I'm afraid I can't release any information—"

"Can't?" Nolan cut him off. "Or won't? Is she seriously hurt? What aren't you telling us?"

His father placed a hand on Nolan's arm, then reached into his suit jacket. "We have a health care directive signed by Katie. For situations such as this."

Nolan released a deep breath, thankful his father had had the presence of mind to grab that form from the office. The doctor took it. Finally, he looked at Nolan, his father and his brothers as well as the people gathered in the seating area behind them.

"All right, I'll add this to her file. We're a bit concerned about Ms. Ledbetter's condition," he went on, keeping his voice low. "She was awake when the EMTs arrived, but complaining of head pain. She slipped into unconsciousness when they were en route. She's stable and we're running tests, but she still hasn't awakened."

"Tests?" Nolan asked, his brothers joining in at the same time.

"We're proceeding with caution, gentlemen, again, based on her...condition. She's breathing on her own and doesn't have any external injuries. As soon as we have the initial results back, we'll know more and we can figure out what the next step will be. Someone will come and talk to you then."

Nolan failed to find solace in the man's words. "Can I see them?" he asked.

"Your daughter, yes. I'll have a nurse take you back. Ms. Ledbetter? Not until we know more."

Not the answer Nolan wanted, but one he had to accept as the doctor left.

"Come on, guys." Alistair spoke to all of them, but it was Nolan he nudged. "Let's sit and tell the ladies what's going on. Your mom's going to want to call Ric, but I think we'll wait for a while."

He stepped away and shook his head. "I can't...sit."

"You go, Dad," Adam said. "We'll stay here and watch Nolan pace."

Their father nodded and walked back to the group in the seating area.

Nolan gave his brother a sharp look, but there was only worry in Adam's gaze. "Maybe you should go to your wife," Nolan said, turning to include Bryant. "You, too."

"Fay and Laurie are fine. Believe me, both of us tried to get them to stay home." Bryant jerked his chin toward the group in the far corner. "You see how successful we were."

True to his brother's word, Nolan started to pace. He couldn't help it. He'd never felt so helpless in his entire life. So in the dark.

How had this happened? How did any of today happen?

One minute he'd been contemplating picking up flowers and pastries for Katie—an apology for once again taking things farther between them than he had a right to the previous night—and the next he was being apologized to by the father of one of Abby's friends.

Finding out what his daughter had done, and Katie's part in covering it up, had sent him into a blinding rage. He'd been trying to decide which of them to deal with first when Katie had returned to the house, wanting to talk.

Yeah, he'd talked all right. He'd damn near blasted her— no, wait, he had blasted—

"The sheriff was gone when most of us arrived," Dev said. "What did he say?"

Nolan gave a quick shrug and kept walking back and forth in the center aisle of the waiting area. "Only that it was a single-car accident. From what they could tell, Katie lost control, probably due to the bad roads and lousy weather."

But that didn't explain why Abby was with Katie in the first place. She should've been at her friend's house. Had Katie gone to get her after their argument? She'd been upset when she stormed out of the house, but he had no idea why the two of them were out on the highway.

"Did you get ahold of the boys?" Liam asked.

This time he nodded. "The family they went skiing with is bringing them here."

"Good." Adam took a few steps backward. "But we're already taking up a lot of space and you're in the way. Let's sit."

"I already said I don't want to sit with –"

"Then park your butt here." Dev moved to a corner couch opposite the rest of the family. "With us. You're going back to Abby soon. She's got to be upset and worried about Katie, too."

"Yeah, the last thing she needs to see is her father about to lose it," Bryant added, plopping down next to Devlin.

"I'm not going to lose it," Nolan snapped, then realizing how harsh he sounded, he lowered his voice. "I'm...fine."

"No, what you are is seconds away from exploding." Liam sat down, too.

Adam joined him, leaving a spot empty between them. "I agree. You want to share why?"

"Are you freaking kidding me?" He stared at his brothers, jabbing one hand in the air at the double doors that separated him from two of the most important women in his life. "My daughter and my—and Katie are back there. Hurt and alone. Katie's unconscious. They don't know why or how bad off she is. Do I really have to explain why?"

Bryant sighed and sat forward, bracing his elbows on his knees. "I wish you would just say it."

"Yeah, put yourself, and us—" Dev shook his head and crossed his arms over his chest "—geesh, put everyone out of their misery and admit it."

"I've been back three days, man." Liam leaned back and stretched out his legs. "And it's clear to me."

"What in the hell are you all talking about?" Nolan's

gaze shot between his brothers before he turned on Adam. "Do you know what they're talking about?"

"Dammit, if anyone has been against this from the start, it was me, but even I can see it now," Adam said, his words coming out low between gritted teeth. "Do we have to spell it out for you?"

"Yeah, I guess you do."

"It took me being lost in the forest. Both Dev and Liam had their ladies leave the damn country. Bryant almost cost us one of the best accountants we've ever had before he wised up, which isn't too far off from the mess you've got yourself in. Trust me—trust us—things will be a whole lot better once you finally say it out loud."

Nolan tried to follow what his brother was saying, to put the pieces together, but his brain seemed to have reached its limit and had shut down. "I don't—"

"Just say it." All four men spoke in unison.

"Then say a fervent prayer that you get the chance to say it again...to her," Adam added. "I don't know how many times out in that godforsaken backwoods I prayed for another chance...to make things right. You'll regret it the rest of your life if you don't—"

"I love her."

The words fell from Nolan's mouth.

Simply stated. Not in the heat of anger or because his muddled brain had finally grasped what his eldest brother was trying to say.

It was purely the truth.

A truth that had been deep inside his heart for much longer than he realized.

Longer than her living in his home, longer than the night they'd shared after the Halloween party. What he felt for her might've started out as an attraction, being impressed with her smarts and her beauty. But now it was so much more than that, more than he could even put into words.

"I love her," he repeated to the men he was closest to in the world. "I love Katie."

Silence stretched between his brothers as they looked at each other, visibly relaxing as they smiled.

"It's about damn time," Bryant said.

"You all owe me a Benjamin," Dev said, his grin wider than the rest as he pointed to each of them. "I won the pool."

Liam offered Dev a swift kick and they all laughed.

"You sure you don't want to sit down now?" Adam asked. "That's the first time you've admitted that. Even to yourself."

Yeah, it was, but no, Nolan didn't want to sit.

He wanted to see Katie.

Now.

Wanted to know she was going to be okay, to beg her to forgive him for being such a jerk—and not just today, but all the way back to the morning they woke up together in bed—and to tell her how much he loved her.

He could only pray he would have the chance.

An hour later, having commandeered the wheelchair from the orderly, Nolan pushed Abby into the waiting room.

His head spun from the stories she'd told him. The moment he'd pulled back the curtain and found her curled up on the hospital bed, she'd broken out in tears. A sight that had him blinking back some moisture as well.

Learning the details of the night at Katie's apartment was nothing compared to his shock at what had happened earlier today between Abby and that cowboy.

His daughter had almost run away from home.

Because she'd fallen in love. Or what she thought was love.

Katie was right. He and Abby were long overdue for a heart-to-heart talk, about a lot of things.

"Hey, sis, cool wheels." Logan raced to his sister, Luke

right behind him. "You okay? Granddad said you were, but you were back there with Dad when we got here—"

"Yeah, we wanted to make sure you were...ya know, okay," Luke finished for his twin.

"She's fine, guys." Nolan was quick to reassure his sons. "Some bumps, bruises and a sore wrist. Which means she's off kitchen and laundry detail." He leaned forward over Abby's shoulder, his hands braced on the wheelchair handles, making sure he had the twins' full attention. "For. Quite. A. While."

The realization that their blackmailing plan had been found out, and their own chore load had increased, dawned in their matching brown eyes simultaneously.

Nolan walked onward, joining his family, then stepping back as Abby was enveloped in gentle hugs and well wishes. He made eye contact with his dad, who shook his head. That meant still no word on—

"Dad, how's Katie?" Luke asked. "Is she going to be okay?"

"Yeah, what's going on?" Logan added. "Granddad said she was unconscious—"

Abby gasped, twisting around in the wheelchair. "You didn't tell me that! Why didn't you say anything? You let me run on about my problems—"

Nolan gave a swift cut with his hand through the air, effectively shutting down his kids' questions. "Hold up, all of you. Give me a minute and I'll share with you what we know about Katie."

"I'd be interested in hearing that myself."

Nolan turned around.

There stood a man in a snow-dampened leather jacket, dark jeans and combat boots. His cropped hair was a mess, probably from the motorcycle helmet he held against his leg as it dripped onto the tile floor.

"And you are?" Nolan asked, wondering who this guy was and why he wanted information about Katie.

"Garland Ledstrom." He stretched out his hand. "People call me Gar."

Nolan returned his quick handshake. "Nolan Murphy."

"Yes, I know who you are." He nodded, his gaze moving over the group of them. "All of you. I haven't been in Destiny that long, but the Murphys are pretty well-known."

"But we still don't know who you are," Adam said, getting to his feet, his sleeping infant son in his arms.

"I'm a tattooist. I plan to open a studio in town as soon as I can get it set up." He gave a small smile, his gaze back on Nolan. "There was a slight issue with the storefront I'm renting, but it's being worked out."

Abby let out an audible gasp from behind Nolan's back, and it came together. "Katie's new neighbor, right?" he asked.

The man nodded, his expression serious again. "That… and more. I'm also her brother."

A collective hush fell over the group for a moment. Then chaos ensued.

Everyone started talking at once, questions flying with no answers, until they were instructed to keep their voices down by one of the nurses.

Leaving the kids with his mother and the ladies with promises to find out exactly what was going on, Nolan, his brothers and their father moved to one side of the room with this stranger to continue their discussion with more privacy.

"I can see I've dropped a bomb with my announcement," he said, meeting each of them with a steady gaze. "My plan was to wait until after the holidays before I approached Katie. But I heard about the accident and had to come. How is she?"

"She's been unconscious since she arrived." Nolan spoke

before his brothers or father could, giving only the basics. "They're running tests, but that's all we know."

"I'm not surprised you all are rallying around her. Talk has it you're a good company to work for."

"Katie is more than an employee," Alistair Murphy said, having already made that statement a few times. "She's like family to us. Besides, she told us she doesn't have any of her own."

"I understand why she believes that. I was seven years old when my baby sister…disappeared," Gar explained. "It wasn't until eighteen months later I found out what our mother had done. Left her in a church in Boise. Katie was only three at the time. My brothers and I—"

"Brothers?" Liam asked. "She has more family than just you? Parents, too?"

"No, our parents…are dead. My siblings and I—we all ended up in the foster care system over that period of eighteen months. None of us were over the age of ten at the time."

"You said your name was Ledstrom," Devlin pointed out. "Hers is Ledbetter. Were you adopted?"

"Dev, that's not any of our business," their father said.

"Are you kidding me? With what he just told us?"

"No, I was never adopted. I lived in a series of foster homes until I was an adult. I can't explain why her last name is different. Believe me, it didn't help with my search."

"Maybe Katie was adopted," Bryant said.

"Then why tell us she had no family?" Dev shot back.

His brothers started to protest against the man's claims again, but Ledstrom's words—when Nolan compared them to what Katie had shared only last night—rang true. Even down to the difference in their last names, except for the first three letters.

"Why was she left?" Nolan asked. "Why didn't your par-

ents seek assistance? From local authorities? A nonprofit?
Or at least surrender her—all of you—legally?"

The man held their gaze, but Nolan watched as he put
up an internal barrier. "That's a long story," he said. "One
I'm still putting the pieces together to. I prefer to share it
privately with Katie. It will be her decision what she tells
others."

"Why are you looking for her now?" Bryant asked.
"After all this time?"

"Because we're family," Gar said, then paused, his jaw
tight for a moment. "I couldn't until... I joined the army at
eighteen. Served for over a decade, the last half with Special Forces, before I got out a few years back and started
the search for my siblings. Katie is the first one I've found."

"Do you have any proof of your story?" Liam asked.
"Birth certificates? Paperwork of any kind?"

"I don't have anything official. Our family situation
was...unique." He set his helmet on a nearby table, then
reached inside his jacket for a battered envelope. "My notes
are back at my motel room, but I have a few photographs."

He pulled the pictures out and handed them to Nolan.

They were a couple decades old. The once brilliant colors were faded and muted now. The first snapshot was of
a young boy sitting in a chair with a big smile on his face,
holding a toddler in his arms.

Nolan looked up. "This is supposed to be you and
Katie?"

Annoyance flashed in the man's eyes. "It is."

A quick glance at his brothers and his father, all of whom
crowded around him to see the photo, told Nolan they had
their doubts, too.

He flipped to the next photograph. It was a more for-
mal portrait of a woman, posing with four children, three
young boys and a little girl she held on her lap. A quick
comparison told him the two from the first photo were in

this one as well, but it was the woman who captured Nolan's attention.

And took his breath away.

Katie.

Well, not really, but the likeness was uncanny. From the red hair to the way she tilted her head to the tentative smile.

"Damn…"

The whispered expletive from Devlin said what all of them were thinking.

"This is your mother," Nolan said softly. "Katie's mother."

"That was taken a few months before Katie…left us," Gar said. "One of those free coupon family portrait places in a mall. It was the last time I remember seeing my mother smile. Believe me, I was stunned the first time I saw Katie. How much she resembles her. And there's the necklace—"

"What necklace?"

Gar gestured and Nolan brought the last picture to the front. It was a cropped image from the previous one, a close-up of the jewelry worn by the woman.

"It's hard to make out, but she's wearing a silver cross with—"

"Multicolored stones," Adam interjected. "Hangs from a silver chain. Katie has one just like it."

"Your mother asked her about it once," their father added. "It's got a Southwest, '70s style to it your mom loved. Katie said it used to belong to someone in her family."

"Her mother," Nolan said. "Katie wears it quite often."

"She had it on the night we met," Gar said. "Outside her apartment."

"It was left with her when she was abandoned." Nolan's fingers gently rubbed at the photo. "Katie got it from her file when she aged out of the foster care system."

Silence reigned until Nolan looked up and found his family staring at him.

"I guess you know all that, son, because Katie told you?" his father asked.

He nodded. Had he said all of that aloud? Hell, it wasn't his story to share.

Another reason for Katie to wake up and yell at him. The list was getting longer and longer.

"Excuse me, Mr. Murphy?"

Nolan turned, along with everyone else in his family, to find a nurse there.

"Oh, I'm guessing you're all Murphys. Dr. Greenwood asked me to let you know that Ms. Ledbetter is awake. She's a bit agitated and confused, but they are getting her calm and making her comfortable."

"How is she?" Nolan asked. "Can we see her?"

"I was told that two may come back at a time and only for a quick visit. The doctor will speak with you there." Her gaze moved over the group. "Who's coming with me?"

He stepped forward, then turned back to his family. To Katie's…brother. "If you all don't mind, I'd like to go first."

"Of course," Alastair said, his smile wide and relaxed now. "Go ahead, son. I'll pass along the good news to everyone else."

Nolan waited until his father walked away before he turned to Gar. "Do you…would you like to join me?"

The man surprised him when he shook his head. "I appreciate the offer, but I think I'll wait out here. It would probably be best if she and I met—officially—after we're certain she's going to be okay."

Still reeling from the man's announcement himself, Nolan accepted his decision. He looked back to his brothers. "So, who's my wingman?"

"Age before beauty." Devlin gave Adam a light jab to the shoulder. "You're the oldest. Go ahead."

Adam grinned and shot back with a punch of his own.

He turned, anxious to get to Katie. Adam was by his side

as they walked through the hallways, the nurse explaining that Katie had been moved out of the ER to a regular hospital room.

When they arrived at a closed door, the doctor was waiting.

"How is she?" Nolan asked again.

"She's going to be fine. We're still not sure what brought on the unconsciousness. There are a few contributing factors beyond the accident's impact, including dehydration, and her blood pressure was extremely low when she arrived," the doctor said. "She has a few cuts and bruises, but she's stable now and aware of what happened. We assured her your daughter is okay. She was concerned."

Relief at the doctor's words caused Nolan's knees to go weak. He wasn't surprised to find out Katie's first thoughts had been for Abby.

Boy, he had so much to make up for.

The awful things he'd said to her earlier…how stupid! Thank God he was going to have the chance to make things right with her.

The doctor pushed the door open. "Please, keep your visit brief. She's probably sleeping—on her own—and needs her rest. Do not wake her. We plan to keep her at least overnight for observation."

Nolan glanced at Adam, answering his brother's nod of understanding with his own. He stepped inside the dimly lit room, ignoring the sharp twist to his gut at the sight of Katie lying so still in the hospital bed.

He walked to her bedside, noticing how pale she was, how bright her red hair was against the white sheets. There was a bandage on her forehead and a few on her arms.

And her eyes were closed.

He reached for her hand, wrapping his fingers gently around hers. Her warmth had him dropping his chin and closing his eyes as his breath came out in a rushed release.

"Nolan…"

Adam whispered a warning over his shoulder, but he shook it off. "I thought…I thought I'd lost her. She's been right in front of my eyes for so long…but I couldn't see that. Wouldn't see that all I wanted or needed was right there the whole time."

He opened his eyes, wishing Katie would do the same. It was a battle to hold back from asking her to do so, to show him she was truly all right.

"She's fine," Adam said. "You've got a second chance. Both of you."

His brother was right. There was time. They had all the time in the world to make things right—

Katie's hand twitched in his and a low moan had him focusing again on her face.

She turned away from him, pressing her head against the pillow, but the pain in her wrinkled brow and the way she squeezed her eyes tight put him on alert.

"Baby…"

The word slipped past her lips, but Nolan wasn't sure he heard her right. "Katie? Did you say something?"

"Nolan…"

That had him leaning over, bending closer to her. "Katie, I'm right here."

"Ba…by," she repeated, her free hand moving to rest low on her stomach. "Nolan…"

"Katie, I'm here." He couldn't stop from laying a hand gently to her hair, his lips inches from her cheek. "I'm right here."

"Should I go get someone?" Adam asked.

Nolan pulled back, trying to figure out if she was awake or not. "I don't know—"

"Please…don't hurt the baby…" Her faltering words were choppy but stronger as she withdrew from his grasp, both hands protectively over her middle now. "Please save…my baby…"

Nolan bolted upright, the breath whooshing out of his lungs.

Baby?

His brother yanked on his arm, pulling him back toward the open door. Two nurses rushed in and hovered over Katie, checking the machines and talking in soft soothing tones.

The doctor brushed past them. "You two should leave."

"Forget it," Nolan stated. "I'm not going anywhere."

"Then wait outside. Now."

Nolan let his brother lead him from the room and the door closed behind them.

Baby?

"Is Katie pregnant?" Adam asked.

"I don't know." He turned and stared at his brother. "From what she said in there… I didn't know."

"Yeah, I kind of figured that from your response."

"If she is, it had to be…the party. The night of the Halloween party. But when—why didn't she say anything—"

Today. When Katie returned to the house and said they needed to talk.

That she had something to tell him.

Pain, like shards of glass slicing at his insides, dropped Nolan into the nearest chair.

Katie had needed him and he'd slammed her with angry words, never letting her say what she'd wanted to. Worse, he'd basically told her she'd be a terrible mother, when in reality she'd done an amazing job with his kids, despite hiding what Abby had done.

And now…

Now she was in there and he had no idea what the hell was going on. And for the first time, he wondered if he even had a right to. Or if Katie would forgive him for how he'd treated her.

If it was true that she was pregnant, then his baby…

His baby.

A baby he might never get the chance to meet. For the first time in ages, Nolan bowed his head and prayed.

Chapter Thirteen

"Would you spell your last name again?"

"L-e-d-s-t-r-o-m."

"And you're my brother?" Katie searched for any simi
larities between her and the man she'd thought was just her
new neighbor, wanting desperately to believe Gar's story
and the photographs in her lap. "And I have two more?"

He grimaced. "Are you sure this isn't too much for you?"

Was he kidding? This was the most amazing thing to
happen to her in...forever.

Well, after waking and finding out she, Abby and her
unborn child had survived a scary car crash.

Now this...

When she'd been told she had a visitor this morning, her
first thought had been Elise Murphy or one of the guys.
Not Nolan. No, he'd be home with Abby, as he should be.
Thankfully, the teen hadn't needed to stay at the hospital.

What happened yesterday was something else for him
to be angry with Katie for—

"This *is* too much. I shouldn't have said anything." Gar frowned.

"No, I'm sorry." Katie stopped him. "I was... My mind wandered. I'm glad you told me."

"But you were expecting someone else," Gar said. "They were here yesterday, you know. Took over most of the waiting room."

She tamped down the fluttering that raced through her. "Well, of course they were. Abby was in the car with me."

"True, but they stuck around after the girl was released. No one left until one of them—Adam, I think—gave us the good news. Even then, your guard dog boyfriend stayed the night."

"Boyfriend?" Now she was confused. "I don't have a boy—"

"Nolan Murphy?"

Darn, that flutter was back and stronger now. Why in the world would Gar think that? "Oh, no, he's not—wait, did you say guard dog?"

"Yep. Right outside your room." He jerked his thumb toward the door. "Camped out in one of those uncomfortable hospital chairs."

Shock filled her. "You must be mistaken."

"He was here when I arrived this morning. Trust me, he looked like a guy who'd slept sitting up," Gar said. "He told me the doctors were releasing you. Then he took off."

Katie could understand the Murphys waiting until they were sure she was out of the woods. They were good people like that, but to have one of them be here all night. And for it to be Nolan ...

Had he come into her room? Sat at her bedside?

She didn't remember seeing him. People had come and gone, but they'd been hospital staff. She'd tried to take their advice and get some rest, but it was almost impossible with the thoughts running through her head.

Thoughts about the past several weeks and the future, for her and her unborn child.

Grateful for the chance to plan such a future, she'd faced some hard truths about her situation.

Nolan wasn't going to feel the way she did. About them or about another unplanned baby.

Yes, he'd want to do the honorable thing, but what if they tried to be a family and it didn't work? She couldn't put him or his kids through that again.

Not to mention she'd once more be abandoned when things fell apart.

Even with learning she had siblings, she still felt she only had herself to count on. That was okay. It was what she had planned from the beginning. To be a single mother.

Without the complication of the baby's father. She and Nolan would work out some sort of arrangement when it came to visitation.

And she'd have to learn to live with a broken heart.

"Hey, did I lose you again?"

Katie blinked, turning to the window, hoping the sunshine streaming in hid her tears. "I'm sorry...it's just hard to believe Nolan was here all night."

"Believe it."

The words carried from the opposite side of the room in a low but powerful voice.

Nolan's.

She closed her eyes, cursed the reflex that had her brushing at the wetness on her cheeks.

What was he doing here? Hadn't Gar said he'd left?

"Well, I think that's my cue."

Katie turned back and found Gar on his feet.

"You can keep the pictures, if you like," he said. "I've got copies."

She nodded, glancing at Nolan in the open doorway. He

had a duffel bag in one hand. "Yes, I'd like that. When...
will I see you again?"

"Christmas Day, if not sooner," Gar said, shooting a
quick glance over his shoulder at Nolan. "I wrangled an
invitation to the Murphys'."

"Oh." The holiday was only three days away and Katie
had no idea where she'd go once she got out of here.

He turned back to her. "I only did so because I assumed
you'd be there, too."

"She will be."

Katie opened her mouth to protest, but what other option
did she have until her apartment was finished?

"I'm not going anywhere, Katie," Gar said. "And whenever you want to take that test, I'll be ready."

She smiled, wanting to hug him. Was it too soon? She
settled for reaching out her hand, content when he grasped
her fingers with his. "Thank you. For everything. I'm so
happy you found me."

The fact she'd been important enough to search for made
her want to cling to him, afraid if she let go, he'd disappear.
She forced herself to release his grip.

"Me, too." His words were rough-edged and he stopped
to clear his throat before he said, "We're not done. I'll find
them. I promise."

Gar turned and headed for the door, nodding once before continuing on his way.

Now it was the two of them.

Her gaze flickered to the clock on the wall. The hands
were angled so it read a little after eleven—11:11, possibly?
Was it only twenty-four hours ago she'd gone to Nolan's
place to tell him about her wholly unexpected but amazing news?

She closed her eyes, determined to find a way to handle all this, knowing she had a lifetime of such moments
ahead with this man. Pulling in a deep breath to calm her

nerves only resulted in her head being awash with Nolan's clean, woodsy scent.

"Katie, are you okay?"

Her eyes flew open. He now stood right next to her bed. Hair damp around the edges. Freshly shaven. Dark smudges beneath eyes that were concerned and guarded at the same time.

"Katie?"

"I'm…" She paused, not sure she could sum up all she was feeling. Overwhelmed? Excited? Nervous? She placed a hand over her belly. Grateful.

Yes, she was all those things and more.

Meeting his gaze, she said, "I'm—"

"Fine." He finished her sentence, shaking his head as he continued, "Of course you are."

An uncomfortable silence stretched between them.

"Do you want—"

"Do you mind—"

They spoke at the same time, both stopping as their words overlapped. Then there was more strained quietness that seemed to go on forever until Katie couldn't take it anymore. "Go ahead."

"I was going to ask if you mind if I sit for a minute."

"No, of course not." She waved at the chair. "Please."

He sat, putting the duffel bag down. "I brought you some things. They said you were going to be released today."

"Oh, okay. Thanks." She fiddled with the photographs Gar had left behind. She looked at the one of her sitting on her mother's lap and pictured herself posing that way with her own child—

"It's pretty amazing, huh?"

Katie's gaze flew to Nolan, her heart skipping a beat. Did he know? Had he somehow found out? "What? What is?"

"About your brother."

Oh, that. She nodded, trying to ignore the rush of—

whatever—that filled her. "Yes, it was hard to take in at first, but the information he has, and these pictures…well, who knew I had brothers. A family of my own."

A muscle jumped along Nolan's jaw. "You believe him, then?"

"You don't? How much did he tell you?"

"Nothing specific. Just that he'd been looking for you—and his brothers—since he got out of the army. He knew about the church in Boise, and those photographs seem pretty convincing."

"Yes, they do." Katie thought back to what Gar had told her about those harrowing months with their mother and brothers all those years ago. The desperation, the fear. Her heart ached for what all of them had gone through. Gar had only been seven years old at the time and his memories were strong. "He agreed to a DNA test."

"Good." Nolan nodded. "Liam's already checking him out. Making sure his story is legit."

"That's not necessary—"

"Yes, it is."

More silence. More discomfort.

Should she say something? Yes, of course she should. He had to know she was carrying his child. But how did you announce an unplanned pregnancy? Just blurt it out?

"Everyone is glad you're okay," he finally said. "We were worried until the doctors gave you the all clear."

"How's Abby?" Katie asked, skirting the subject.

"She's…fine." Nolan's lips rose almost in a grin, then it disappeared. "Physically. A sore wrist, muscles that ache from her head to her toes this morning and will for a while, but she's okay."

Had the girl talked to him? Katie had tried hard to convince her she needed to tell her father everything. "And emotionally?"

"I think that will take a bit longer." Nolan's gaze was

softer now. "She told me about the party. Being with that... that Joe in the old cabin. How he convinced her to go off with him. How I almost—" He stopped, looked away and swallowed hard. "Almost lost her."

The waver in his voice had Katie wanting to reach out, to comfort him, but it wasn't her place.

Still, she couldn't hold back his name as it slipped past her lips. "Nolan..."

"You were right, Katie." He leaned forward, his eyes on her. "About everything. We still have things to work on— she and I—and we got a good start on it. She's talking, finally. I'm listening. We're going to be okay."

"Oh, that's wonderful, Nolan."

"Please, let me finish." He held up a hand. "I was wrong. Stupidly, horribly wrong in how I spoke to you yesterday."

"You were upset."

He gave a halfhearted laugh. "Upset? I was pissed and... hurt that you decided to keep something like that from me, but that's no excuse for the things I said. I'm sorry. So damn sorry."

"Apology accepted." It was that easy. His remorse was deep. There wasn't any reason for her to do anything else but apologize herself. "I'm sorry, too."

"For what?"

"For not telling you when I should have. And for the accident. For putting your daughter in danger—"

"Are you kidding? You saved her. After what I said... accusing you of being unfit to parent...you could've hung up the phone. Let her find her own way back to town."

The idea of doing any of those things stunned her. "I never would've done that."

"You're right. Again. You wouldn't have. Even when you had no reason to, you put my child's safety ahead of your own. And from what Abby said, you convinced her to tell me everything."

"I was trying to help."

"You were being a parent. A good one."

A rush of tears filled Katie's eyes. Did he mean that?

"Just like you've been doing from the moment you agreed to watch over my kids. If anyone knows how hard it is to raise children…and how cool it is to give in, give them everything they want, be their friend because it's a hell of a lot easier than being the grown-up, it's me." He sighed. "Instead of being smug in my own sometimes lazy parenting, I should've been thanking you for being…there. Being involved."

His words were like a balm to her soul.

She had to admit what he'd said yesterday had cut her deep, but would she have told Abby something different in the car if he hadn't said those things? Maybe. Maybe not. But with his apology, he'd restored her confidence.

She and her baby were going to be…just fine.

Maybe it was time she started proving that to herself. Standing on her own two feet. The Murphys had always been there for her. A safety net…and maybe even a crutch.

"Thank you, Nolan. You saying that means more than you will ever know."

"Good." He sat up straight, rubbing his hands together and then across the tops of his thighs. "I wanted you to know… I've seen the light, so to speak. I know that now. I know *everything* now."

Not everything. Katie opened her mouth, but then a nurse came into the room.

"I'm sorry to interrupt, but I've got your release paperwork. You need a final exam," she announced, then turned to Nolan. "Which means you, sir, need to leave."

"She didn't tell me. I know how scared she must be, especially with me being so clear I'm done with starting a family again…but I was wrong." Nolan spoke into his cell phone with Adam while pacing the hospital corridor. "So damn wrong."

"Maybe she was going to when the nurse came in. Did you tell her how you feel?"

"It never got that far." Nolan explained their conversation, knowing he only had himself to blame for this mess.

"So, what's plan B?"

Nolan stopped and stared at Katie's closed door. "Hell if I know."

"Wrong answer. Figure out a way to fix this. Fast," Adam shot back. "We're doing what you asked here at the house, although the kids aren't happy about it. The rest is up to you."

"I know that. I'm in love with Katie. I want her and the baby to be in my life and I want the child to grow up knowing his or her sister and brothers."

"Then tell her that, and give her a big-ass diamond," Adam said.

"That's all you've got?"

"Do something crazy and romantic. Women like that stuff."

Okay, he could use that. "Any suggestions?"

"You know this woman better than any of us. In more ways, I might add. What's important to her? What does she want more than anything else in the world?"

In a flash it came to him. He stopped pacing and relaxed. That was it. He'd give her exactly what she'd always wanted.

Katie settled in the corner of one of the leather couches in the Murphys' living room, exiled from kitchen duties after a wonderful Christmas Eve dinner she'd barely tasted.

Finding out she was pregnant played havoc on her taste buds...or was it the fact that she'd been back on the compound for over forty-eight hours and hadn't told Nolan about the baby?

How could she, when he'd banished her from his house?

They'd returned from the hospital after a quiet yet tension-filled ride to discover Nolan had moved her belongings from his place to a first-floor guest suite in the main house.

Abby and the boys had been waiting for them at the front door. Katie took one look at the girl and opened her arms, pulling her into a long hug, quieting her apologies and brushing away her tears. Then the kids gave her a tour of her new room while sharing the news that their Boston trip was postponed until winter break early next year.

Nolan said the change in living accommodations was because of the doctor's orders to rest. She wasn't to cook, clean or pick up after his crew. Elise Murphy said her orders were to spoil her. She was doing a great job. Breakfasts in bed, Katie's favorite movies lining the shelf near the large-screen television. And with the offices closed until after the new year, she'd been shooed away from her desk three times.

A desk she wasn't sure she should have anymore.

Maybe what she needed was a fresh start. If she continued to work with the Murphys, how could she maintain her independence? And facing them daily, knowing the baby she carried belonged to this crazy, wonderful family while she was still an outsider, would be so hard to bear.

But more than that—so much more—was the fact that Nolan wasn't in love with her. Attracted? Yes, that much was clear, considering the last few months, but she now knew she wanted a happily-ever-after that included a deep and abiding love.

For her and her baby—

"Katie? Hello?"

She looked around, realizing most of the family had

joined her and someone must've been talking to her...about something. "Oh, sorry. I guess I was in a turkey fog."

Fay rubbed her pronounced belly. "That's okay. Happens to me all the time. Not an easy feat with A.J. around, but I blame his little brother or sister for making me want to sleep whenever I get a few minutes to just sit."

Katie resisted the urge to mirror her movements, a habit she enjoyed when she was alone even though her waistline was still flat. "Where's the little one now?"

"Adam's feeding him in the kitchen while the guys finish the dishes. With the gift opening about to start, we want him to have a full belly."

Oh, yes, the annual Murphy family Christmas Eve tradition. Each person chose one present from beneath the enormous, beautifully decorated tree to unwrap tonight. The rest would be opened tomorrow when everyone gathered again after their own Christmas morning celebrations. Then the open house Elise and Alistair hosted yearly for anyone who'd like to stop by would begin in the afternoon and go late into the evening.

"Hey, are we ready to go?" Logan asked as the guys came in from the kitchen.

"Yes, we're ready." Nolan pushed the ottoman from a chair where Devlin sat, Tanya perched on his lap, toward the end of the couch where Katie was.

"Okay if I join you?" he asked as he took a seat.

She nodded, having lost the ability to speak. Other than a quick good morning, it was the first time he'd spoken to her today. Dinnertime had found them sitting side by side, but they'd each purposely participated in different conversations going around the table.

"Can I get you anything?" he said. "Something to drink?"

"No, thanks. I'm..." Her voice trailed off when Nolan mouthed the word she'd been about to say next.

Fine.

He smiled, then turned his attention to Adam, who stood in front of the tree.

"All right, y'all, listen up." Adam had handed off his son to his wife and now held a basket. "This year we're going to draw names for the order of opening gifts. Those under the age of twenty-one—and you, Devlin—aren't allowed more than five minutes to decide which gift to open."

Everyone laughed and the fun began.

Katie watched as name after name was drawn and gifts were opened, resulting in much laughter and shouts of joy amid a growing pile of crumpled wrapping paper.

She remembered the first time she'd experienced a Murphy Christmas.

The chaos and noise had been new to her, even with fewer people back then, but the love and happiness were the same. Year after year, as their family grew, those emotions grew as well.

To think that next year it would be her, her baby and hopefully, her own brothers filling a room with this much gladness and delight. The thought made her both happy and sad at the same time.

Then again, Nolan might want to have the baby here with him and his family for the holiday. How was she going to handle that—

"Katie?" Elise placed a hand on her arm, yanking Katie from her thoughts. "It's your turn, sweetie. The clock's about to strike midnight and you're the last one."

She nodded, using the excuse of tucking her hair behind one ear to keep her gaze on her lap.

You can do this. Enjoy this moment...

"Katie?"

This time it was Nolan saying her name. Softly, tenderly. She forced a smile and turned to him, surprised to see a wrapped square box in his hand already.

"Oh, you've got mine." Maybe not the nicest thing to say, but she was grateful to find her voice at all. "I don't get to choose for myself, huh?"

"This is a very special gift." He handed it to her. "For you, from me."

Her smile was natural as she balanced the box on her knees. Like Missy and Laurie had done, Katie took her time untying the silvery ribbon bow. Then she unwrapped each end, peeling back the embossed paper with glittering snowflakes.

When she got to the box, so light in her grasp, she had no idea what it might be. She lifted the lid and pushed back the tissue paper, revealing a white frosted glass ornament, hand-painted in a delicate scroll with her name.

Her breath caught and then disappeared entirely.

"I…I don't understand. These are for…oh, my, it's so beautiful." Her eyes flooded with tears, making it impossible to see. Blinking hard, she brushed them away, unable to look away from this most unexpected gift. "These are for family…"

"That's right."

She looked up when Nolan spoke. He'd moved and was now in front of her on one bended knee.

"This one is for you," he went on, gently lifting the ornament by the matching ribbon laced through the small hole at the top. "Only for you."

Of course it was for her. Her name was on—

Then the ornament slowly turned and the princess-cut diamond ring threaded through the ribbon caught the light and sparkled.

She gasped, a sound that echoed throughout the room as the others realized what was happening.

"Nolan…"

"Five years ago I was sure my life was all planned, but then I met you, Katie. You are everything I never knew I needed." He separated the ring from the ornament and put it back in the box before reaching for her hand. "I want to share all that I have, all that I am, with you. To build a happily-ever-after for both of us. All of us. I love you. Will you marry me?"

This was a dream.

A wonderful, amazing, lovely dream she'd never believed would come true. Here was this man who, for reasons she couldn't fathom, offered her the world—his world—wrapped up in the beauty of an exquisite ring and the words she'd always wanted to hear.

He went to slip the ring on her left hand "Nolan...wait."

Confusion filled his eyes.

"I'm... I'm pregnant," she blurted without thought, needing him to know before the ring was in place.

"I know about the baby, Katie."

She jerked her hand out of his. "You know?"

"You mentioned it in your sleep at the hospital."

Oh, God.

It all made sense now. Heat washed into her face as she realized everyone was staring at her. Had he told them all about the pregnancy?

It didn't matter.

She couldn't accept his proposal. As much as she wanted to believe all he'd just said, to be his wife, help him raise his children, including the one she carried inside her, she couldn't.

Panic made her dizzy as she shot to her feet. She scooted away from the couch, backing up toward the Christmas tree. "I won't be another woman who traps you. I won't."

Nolan got to his feet and started toward her. "You're not trapping me, sweetheart."

She shook her head, her tears making him—the entire room—blurry. Which was a good thing. Was this really happening in front of his whole family?

"No, you've made it clear. You're done with babies. Messy diapers and 3:00 a.m. feedings aren't what you want anymore. You're happy with your life the way it is."

"Yeah, that was me two months ago. But I was also running scared from the most amazing woman I've ever met. These past few weeks have shown me, and hopefully you, we're meant to be together. You, me and the kids. All of them. There is nothing I want more in this world than to marry you and create a family."

She wanted that, too. So very much.

He reached her then and drew both of them in front of the tree.

"Believe me." Taking her hand in his, he placed them both gently over her middle. "I'm happy about the baby. Our baby. And I do love you. I have for a long time, longer than I ever realized. Much longer than just these past couple of days, when it took the all-consuming fear that I might lose you to finally admit it to myself. And that was before I knew about our child."

"I knew I loved you before I found out about the baby, too." A sense of relief filled her that she could say the words out loud.

He smiled, pressing a soft cloth into the palm of her other hand. She looked down. A handkerchief. Of course. It should surprise her that he carried one, but it didn't.

It was so…Nolan.

"You love me?" he asked, his gaze warm as he watched her wipe at her eyes and her cheeks.

"Yes, I love you. You are everything I've ever wanted," Katie said. "You always have been."

"Even though I'm part of a package deal?" He grinned, looking across the room to his kids. "You take me, you take them, too."

Katie laughed through her tears. "I guess I'm saying

the same thing, but are you sure? I mean, what's everyone going to think?"

"Everyone? As in this crazy, wonderful family of mine?" he teased, taking another quick look around. "Or the good people of Destiny? I'll tell you what they'll think. That I got exactly what I wished for this Christmas...a true and lasting love."

He lifted her hand and brought into view the ring again, holding it up in the glow of the tree's lights. "Katie, will you do me the honor of becoming my wife?"

"Yes."

No hesitation, no second-guessing. This was right. Loving Nolan, loving his children and being loved by him in return was exactly what she wanted.

He slipped that beautiful ring on her finger. A perfect fit.

The room exploded in shouts of joy and laughter. There were hugs and kisses and welcomes to the family from everyone—the sweetest ones being from Abby, Luke and Logan, the twins already asking if it was okay to call her Mom.

Then Abby handed her the ornament and Katie placed it on the tree, right next to Nolan's, on the branch above where the kids had hung theirs.

Nolan encircled her from behind, his hands at her belly, his chin resting lightly on her shoulder. "It looks perfect."

"Yes, it does."

"So, you busy December 31?" he whispered.

Katie shook her head, but then understanding dawned. She turned around. "Nolan, we can't—"

"What better day to start a new marriage, a new family, than the one day that symbolizes new beginnings?"

"A wedding? On New Year's Eve? That's a week away."

"Our baby is going to be here by the Fourth of July—"

"You calculated that fast."

He grinned. "I'm an architect. It's a skill."

"Still—"

"Everyone we love is right here. Your family—your brother—and all of mine." He leaned in close and whispered, "Even Ric will be home in a few days. Come on, we'll fill the log chapel with flowers and candles and all the people who are important to us. What do you say, Katie Ledbetter—"

"Katie Ledstrom?"

"Katie Ledstrom-Murphy is fine by me. As long as you'll allow me to make you my Destiny bride?"

She sighed, laying her head on his shoulder, overflowing in the blissful happiness of this magical night and joyous season. "Yes, forever and ever, yes."

* * * * *

'Mistress,' Nikolai slotted in cool as ice.

Shock had welded Ella's tongue to the roof of her mouth because
he was sexually propositioning her and nothing could have prepared
her for that. She wasn't drop-dead gorgeous... *he* was! Male heads
didn't swivel when Ella walked down the street because she had
neither the length of leg nor the curves usually deemed necessary
to attract such attention. Why on earth could he be making *her* such
an offer?

'But we don't even know each other,' she framed dazedly. 'You're
a stranger...'

'If you live with me I won't be a stranger for long,' Nikolai pointed out with monumental calm. And the very sound of that inhuman calm and cool forced her to flip round and settle distraught eyes on his lean darkly handsome face.

'You can't be serious about this!'

'I assure you that I am deadly serious. Move in and I'll forget your family's debts.'

'But it's a *crazy* idea!' she gasped.

'It's not crazy to me,' Nikolai asserted. 'When I want anything, I go after it hard and fast.'

Her lashes dipped. Did he want her like that? Enough to track her down, buy up her father's debts, and try and buy rights to her and her body along with those debts? The very idea of that made her dizzy and plunged her brain into even greater turmoil. 'It's immoral… it's blackmail.'

'It's definitely *not* blackmail. I'm giving you the benefit of a choice you didn't have before I came through that door,' Nikolai Drakos fielded with a glittering cool. 'That choice is yours to make.'

'Like hell it is!' Ella fired back. 'It's a complete cheat of a supposed offer!'

Nikolai sent her a gleaming sideways glance. 'No the real cheat was you kissing me the way you did last year and then saying no and acting as if I had grossly insulted you,' he murmured with lethal quietness.

'You *did* insult me!' Ella flung back, her cheeks hot as fire while she wondered if her refusal that night had started off his whole chain reaction. What else could possibly be driving him?

Nikolai straightened lazily as he opened the door. 'If you take offence that easily, maybe it's just as well that the answer is no.'

Visit **www.millsandboon.co.uk/lynnegraham**
to order yours!

MILLS & BOON®

MILLS & BOON®

Mills & Boon have been at the heart of romance since 1908... and while the fashions may have changed, one thing remains the same: from pulse-pounding passion to the gentlest caress, we're always known how to bring romance alive.

Now, we're delighted to present you with these irresistible illustrations, inspired by the vintage glamour of our covers. So indulge your wildest dreams and unleash your imagination as we present the most iconic Mills & Boon moments of the last century.

Visit **www.millsandboon.co.uk/ArtofRomance** to order yours!